Temptation

BOOK IV OF THE MARTYR SERIES

By MC Hunton

DEDICATION

To all the survivors.

A Warning To Readers

Temptation focuses primarily on Lust as an antagonist, which means some content that is discussed and shown may be unsettling. This novel includes discussion of sexual assault, as well as depicts graphic violence and other difficult topics. If you would like to talk in more detail about the specific triggers you may find in this book, please visit www.MartyrSeries.com.

Your mental health matters. Stay safe, friends!

CONTENTS

ACKNOWLEDGMENTS

To Talia and those endless Wednesdays you dedicated to making this manuscript shine.

To my Temptation Support Text Group, who lived and breathed this book for two straight months.

And to Scott for still being here, four novels in.

CHAPTER ONE

"Thorn, have you ever wondered *how* I've managed to survive six hundred and forty-three years on this revolving hellscape of a planet?"

"By not getting involved in bullshit like this?"

"By not—*precisely.*"

Thorn Rose's thin lips pulled into a smirk as she threw Cain Guttuso a look in the dark. They stepped into the intersection at Broadway and 66th, and headlights from passing cars highlighted the sour look on Cain's face. He adjusted his heavy jacket, and Thorn pulled her hood over her head, tucking her long, black ponytail in at the base of her skull.

"Then stick close," she said. "I'll protect you."

"I'm sure you mean well," Cain grumbled, "but considering how often you find yourself getting stabbed, shot, or otherwise torn to shreds, you'll forgive me if that isn't a particular comfort."

Thorn chuckled as she trudged east, but her humor quickly withered.

Boots crunched through icy dregs left behind from the latest winter storm as her sharp, black eyes took in Lincoln Square. There was no such thing as "comfort" in a city like

New York. Even at 3:00 a.m., eight days into February, she was surrounded by the ice-cold sensation of human energy. The corruption in their souls leaked from their bodies, drawing her attention to the left and right as people hailed cabs outside of closing bars and up above her, where thousands more lay sleeping in towering apartment buildings. She hunted for something familiar.

Nothing. Not yet. Thorn took a deep breath, and her ribcage expanded against the kevlar vest hidden under her wool coat. As she sighed, hot vapor twisted in a pale imitation of cigarette smoke around her face.

"Are we close?" Cain asked. They passed beneath a streetlight, and the white peppering his dark hair glittered like freshly fallen snow.

"Yes," Thorn said. A flame flickered inside the cavern in her core, filling it with the illusion of warmth. She strode forward more urgently, acutely aware of the thigh holster tucked beneath her long jacket—and the heavy pistol nestled inside it. "We need to start getting people out of the area. Have them head out in different directions, and make it look natural."

"Yes, I recall," Cain said, the words coming at the tail end of a dramatic huff. "This is our *third* attempt at taking Hunt's life. I might be old, but I'm not senile."

This time, the joke didn't even turn up the corner of Thorn's mouth.

Third attempt. This was their *third attempt* at infiltrating one of Wrath's hideouts—their *third attempt* at catching her off guard, cornering her, and ending her reign over this godforsaken city. The bitch had escaped both before. Thorn hoped this would be the strike that landed, the final blow to kill Autumn Hunt and destroy Wrath's host for the first time in ninety-two years.

The fire in Thorn's half-empty chest roared at the thought, furling between her lungs with hot, eager passion. Sparkie, the innocent part of her soul that Wrath had ripped out when it claimed Thorn as its vessel over a century ago, flew in frenetic circles above her head. The lizard's red-webbed wings caught an icy draft, and he shot upward, where his blue scales all but disappeared in the darkness. He let out a hungry cry.

"Hush," Cain said. "The entire point of bringing me along is because I can do this with *subtlety*."

Thorn breathed deep and forced the tight muscles in her jaw to relax. The lizard quieted. Cain's hand landed on her shoulder. They exchanged a look, he smiled, and Thorn nodded.

People began to disperse. Not all at once, but one or two at a time. Distinct points of energy suddenly paused, turned, and walked off in different directions… along the sidewalk, across tired intersections, and even from the building. Those still awake at this hour moved from their homes and made their way out. Thorn stopped at the corner of the luxury apartment complex and watched as a woman dressed in pajamas, slippers, and a warm winter jacket strode from the front entrance. The doorman inside the foyer nodded, confused, but didn't ask any questions as he allowed her out. He sat back on the chair behind his podium, and her cold aura disappeared into the winter chill.

"Avoid the front entrance," Thorn murmured, glancing at Cain. He was pressed against the brick wall to her back, his eyes closed as he focused on delicately thinning the herd. "And move the doorman."

"He is proving difficult *to* move," Cain said. "He's dedicated to his post, and pushing harder gives me less energy for the others. Would you rather I focus on him?"

Cain opened his eyes and looked up. Thorn's nails, left exposed from her protective, fingerless gloves, tapped on her bicep as she frowned.

They ran into this occasionally—people difficult to Influence because their focus was so inherently against the suggestions Cain planted in their brains that the commands didn't take. Thorn was sure *she* could sway the doorman. Since her abilities were tied to Wrath, she commanded significantly more strength than Cain did. Having a host nearly a century old made the Sin impossibly powerful, and Thorn had the unique benefit of tapping into it.

But that connection came with a cost. A *hundred* costs. So many that, fuck, Thorn had lost count of them throughout the decades. One was that Wrath felt whenever Thorn used her Influence. She couldn't risk announcing their position. Not now. Not when they were so close.

Thorn sighed and shook her head. "No," she said at last. "You're right. We'll deal with him later. Get rid of as many people as possible."

Cain nodded, and Thorn felt them move again: ice-cold pinpricks of human essence exiting the area like ashes scattering in the wind.

Fewer people meant fewer casualties—and fewer souls Wrath could use against them.

Fewer, but not none. Thorn's eyes narrowed. Influence didn't work on the unconscious, so hundreds of sleeping bodies still littered the building. After several minutes, when the last moving aura finally made its way up to the rooftop—far enough that Thorn could barely sense it—she nodded. That would have to do.

She raised a hand and touched the communications device in her left ear. "We're in position. Where's TAC?"

"Ready and waiting for your signal," Chris Silver said. Her voice rang through the speaker. "I have people at the rear exit and near each fire escape, as well as on the neighboring roof and along the street to cover us in any direction. If Hunt runs, we'll catch her."

"Good."

"Any sign of her yet?"

Thorn shook her head. "No. Cain is still clearing the—"

Her throat tightened around the words, choking them so deep that Thorn felt like she was going to gag. A glistening of familiar, frigid energy made her whole body freeze.

"There she is," Cain murmured to Thorn's left.

There she was.

Every muscle in Thorn's body lit up with a fierce, obsessive fire. Her teeth ground together until her jaw ached.

Autumn Hunt.

Her aura lay still, like she was asleep. Thorn's heart raced, and her tongue darted across the bottom of her teeth. She didn't dare let herself feel hopeful, so she got angry instead. She barked sharp orders into her mic.

"Hunt's on the ground floor." Thorn pushed away from the wall and wrapped the bottom of her face in a deep, red scarf. She couldn't feel Cain, whose soul was just as empty as hers, but she heard his footfalls crushing the ice behind her. "In the southeastern corner unit. Get ready. We're going in the front."

"Roger that," Chris said. "TAC, in position."

All around the perimeter of the complex, energy moved. Sets of two, closely clumped together. More than Thorn was used to—but then again, their TAC department was larger than Thorn had seen in decades. A mechanical percussion rang out in her ears as straps pulled tight on kevlar vests and clips snapped into firearms. The feeling of Hunt's energy, a shield of discarded soul desperately clinging to a body it could never reconnect to, laid as still as the ocean's swell before a storm.

Thorn turned the corner and headed to the entrance. Cain, drawing his scarf to conceal his face as well, rushed to her side.

"Just storming right in, eh?" he rambled through the fabric. The words came out faster than his typical, smooth cadence. "Moments like this make me grateful I was Envy's host. Your methods are… very abrupt."

"Our only chance at killing her—"

"Comes from catching her off guard, yes," Cain interrupted with a sigh. "What do you intend to do about *him?*"

He asked it just as the doorman looked at them through the glass, his thick face furrowed. Up close, Thorn could see the muscle he kept hidden beneath his blue overcoat. His eyes passed over hers, sharp in the dark, and he got to his feet. Then, he abruptly stopped, and his hands moved to his temples as Cain's Influence poured into his brain. In the delay, Thorn opened the door, slipped behind him, and wrapped her arm around his throat. He kicked out as she pulled him down and pushed his head forward with her other hand. Her bicep and forearm pinched into his neck, right against his carotid arteries, as she forced him to his knees in a swift, effortless motion.

Seconds later, in silent protest, his eyes rolled back into his head, and he went limp in Thorn's arms.

Wrath's energy shifted.

Thorn froze as the Sin rose. Her mouth ran dry, panic building inside her throat. Wrath's cold aura moved slowly across her apartment. Thorn looked to Cain. He stared at her, his expression stretched in horror. When Wrath stilled again, Thorn slumped the doorman's body into his chair.

"She's awake," Thorn murmured into her mic. Cain's shoes squeaked on the tile behind her as she rifled through the unconscious man's pockets.

"All units, hold back," Chris said. "Does she know you're there?"

"I don't know," Thorn answered. Wrath couldn't sense her or Cain, but she could have felt the doorman's scuffle with the void around him. Thorn finally found the keycard and paused. Wrath's familiar signature was still up but not hurried. Thorn breathed a low, shallow breath. "It doesn't seem like it. Stand by."

Thorn stepped toward the door to the lobby. Before she opened it, she glanced back at Cain.

"Stay here," she said. "Hunt doesn't know about you. If she sees you, she can target you."

Cain's eyes narrowed, and he indicated the green fabric covering his nose and chin. "Isn't that what this is for? Besides, if I stay behind, who is going to stop *you* from getting yourself stabbed, shot, or otherwise torn to shreds?" He shook his head. The color drained from his face, leaving him looking gray in the dark. "I'm already deep enough in this, what did you call it… *bullshit?* I may as well jump all in."

Despite the gnawing anxiety inching up her spine, Thorn smiled behind her scarf. She opened the door, stepped over the threshold, and said, "We're going in."

Dim light illuminated the lobby, casting Thorn in an eerie glow. Her boots landed silently on a plush, navy rug in the center of the room. Elevators sat on either edge, and beside those were two doors leading to the ground-floor apartments. Thorn unzipped her coat. The sound seemed impossibly loud in this vacant space. Her eyes darted around, noting an intricate wall of mailboxes behind the unmanned desk, expensive artwork set in golden frames, and a black lens in the corner.

"We cut the camera feed?" Thorn whispered as she pulled her gun from its holster.

"Yep," Holly Andrews chimed in her ear. Even all the way back in the Underground, where the security lead was watching this whole ordeal safely from her office, her voice was so crisp she might have been sitting on Thorn's shoulder—a little angel of covert intelligence. Or a devil. Thorn never knew which. "Not that anyone monitors these things anyway, but when they check tomorrow, they'll realize they had an unexpected and catastrophic system failure."

Thorn nodded, but she didn't speak again. The door to the eastern corridor opened with a creak as she slowly made her way through it. The complex stretched out more than a hundred feet ahead. Rich, cherry-stained doors dotted the white paint and geometric wallpaper. Every dozen feet, glass doors opened to a central courtyard on the right, spilling cold city light into the hallway.

Wrath's energy was still upright, pacing in a way that made Thorn's throat tighten. She was suddenly very aware of just how many sleeping bodies still occupied the space around her. Cold energy tucked away in ground floor units and hovered overhead—three, seven, thirteen stories above. When they were ten meters away, Thorn could make out the shape of the Sin's body. The length of limbs, arms held out in front of her as she walked backward. Something flowed from beneath the door, soaking into the hall carpet. She frowned.

The hairs on the back of Thorn's neck stood on end at the exact same moment she sensed something off—not with her supernatural, Sin abilities, but with one of the five she'd been born with.

A smell…

Thorn's nose wrinkled. "What the fuck?"

Cain sucked in a gasp. "Gasoline!"

A spark ignited the hallway. Hot, orange fire poured out from the gap beneath a door toward the end of the corridor. Thorn's eyes widened as the carpet melted, and a gust of heat pushed toward her. A shrill, ear-piercing tone shot into her skull as overhead sprinklers burst to life. Throughout the building, ice-cold energy jumped up.

And Wrath's power surged into them.

The pit of Thorn's soul filled with a sudden, blinding power, the beacon of Wrath's Influence all-encompassing and overwhelming as she Puppetted ten, twenty, thirty people all at once. Thorn gasped for breath and faltered backward. Cain's hands wrapped around her shoulders to steady her.

Doors slammed open down the hall, and a pack of frigid energy barreled toward their backs, trapping them between a wall of bodies and the flames. Thorn pulled Cain behind her as a drove of screaming men and women sprinted down the hallway.

A man wearing nothing but boxers lunged at Thorn, followed by more than a half-dozen other blank-faced, mindless tenants. Thorn stretched out her senses, hunting for the fragile threads of Wrath's Influence tying them to her power.

She found one, thin and taut like a cord of fishing line, and she sliced through it.

The line snapped back as the first Puppet was severed from the Sin, and he collapsed onto the carpet. Wrath's power grew furiously in response, and one of the fleeing women suddenly stopped and spun around, her eyes a hollow canvas of hive-minded purpose.

"There's an alert going out to the fire department," Holly said. "Trying to scramble it… What the hell is going on in there?"

"She set the place on fucking fire," Thorn shouted as she mentally downed another Puppet. More rushed forward. Above, they swarmed like rats in the walls. Sweat dripped down the divot of Thorn's spine as the blaze pushed closer, and the sprinklers soaked her head, her shoulders, her coat in a heavy deluge. The water didn't squelch the flames. If anything, it propelled the gasoline faster in all directions, forcing them to spread. "Keep your distance, but watch for Hunt! She's trying to escape."

Thorn and Cain continued to force the Puppets back, slowly inching away from the inferno now engulfing the hall. With her Influence, Thorn reached into their minds one by one and cut the bonds connecting them to Wrath. Cain used a less delicate approach. He grabbed his firearm and shot people in the legs, disabling them through pain. A bullet smashed into a man's thigh, and he went down screaming. Wrath's control disintegrated as soon as he hit the ground.

It wasn't enough. Every time they cut a body off, another joined it, and Wrath's army of Puppets never shrank. People drew closer, faster, with more urgency. Thorn prepared to fight them off a different way, but suddenly…

Suddenly, they flew *past* her.

The horde ignored Thorn and Cain as they ran by, mindlessly, *helplessly* barreling toward the flames. Thorn's eyes widened in horror as the first woman hurled herself into the fire.

Her howling pierced through the hall, drowning out the crackling sound of flames licking against the walls. One after another, the Puppets pushed through. They climbed on top of each other before succumbing to the pain and going unconscious, face-down, in the blaze.

Thorn's heart pounded in the empty cavern in her chest as she holstered her firearm. She tore off her coat, the wool sodden and heavy. Cain grabbed her wrist.

"We must go!" he shouted.

But Thorn tugged out of his grip. She dragged a body from flames and threw her coat on top of it to smother the fire. Raging heat glared against her face as she pulled out another and another. Then Cain was beside her, swearing under his breath as he helped her haul Wrath's unconscious victims away from danger. Thorn's fingers burned as she patted the flames out, but her fire-retardant gloves protected her palms and arms.

In the room where it all fucking started, Wrath's energy moved.

Thorn's attention snapped up as she sensed the bitch head to the far wall. Above, a flood of cold, human souls gushed through the windows, onto the fire escape, and toward the ground.

Thorn's heart dropped.

"Fuck," she gasped. "She's using the Puppets as a shield. Fire escape, southern wall!"

The entire building was surrounded by a massive, turbulent force of energy as escaped tenants, gawking civilians, and Martyrs hovered outside. Thorn couldn't distinguish her people from the rest, but Chris's orders rang sharp in her earpiece. She ripped the scarf from her face and snatched her jacket off the unconscious Puppet at her feet. Cain stood behind her as Thorn looked into the fire. The flames were beginning to dwindle.

"What the hell are you doing?" Cain asked.

Thorn took a deep breath, smoke burning all the way to the bottom of her lungs, and she raised her coat in front of her. "I'm going to fucking kill her."

Silently, with all the rage of a burning building, Thorn sprinted toward Hunt's apartment. She kicked the door until the wood cracked and splintered beneath her heel. Fire licked at her shins, the heat searing through her boots.

On the third strike, the door flew open. Thorn ran through just as Autumn Hunt swung one leg over her windowsill. She paused in the frame, her gray eyes wild, her long, dark hair a mane of frantic, furious panic around her tawny face. The minute she saw Thorn, her lips twisted into a snarl.

Thorn's stomach twisted with them. She threw her coat to the ground and grabbed her gun. The grip slipped in her bleeding, blistered fingers, and Wrath dove from the apartment. Outside, a massive wave of Puppets rolled off the metal staircase. They obscured her body, and her cold energy merged into theirs, disappearing entirely.

"Shit!" Thorn hissed.

She sprinted to the window as Sparkie bolted toward the earth and drifted above the sea of bobbing heads. People filled 66th and the adjoining streets while sirens wailed in the distance. Thorn leapt from the building as Wrath and her entourage sped away on foot. They headed east, and Thorn's heart plummeted.

"Don't let her get to Central Park!" she screamed.

Martyrs pushed through the crowd—bulky blocks of black kevlar and beige cargo pants—heading north and south on Central Park West as Wrath's swarm tried to cross it. Thorn ran toward them, desperately feeling through the storm of cold energy in the cold air blanketing this cold fucking city. Sparkie spiraled overhead.

The Sin's horde collided with onlookers on the far side of the street. Bodies slammed into one another, and Wrath's Influence spread even further, catching the crowd like fire. She drove a violent wave of terror and loathing into the minds of innocents gathered on the sidewalk. Thorn finally caught a glimpse of her—the flash of that hateful face between dozens of mindless ones—and she raised her weapon…

Without warning, without reason beyond the horrifying ideas Wrath was planting in their heads, the crowd shifted.

Then, they were running. Fear fell into panic, and Thorn's stinging finger didn't even have the chance to tighten on the trigger before people assaulted her on every side. Shoulders slammed into her, rattling her left and right, forward and backward, and it took all of Thorn's finesse to stay standing.

Then Autumn Hunt's Puppets collapsed in a single, fell swoop, like the Sin had gathered all their strings in one hand and sliced through them with a sharp blade. Thirty people landed hard on the icy pavement, and hundreds more screamed around them.

Men and women scattered in every direction, Wrath's Influence driving them into an uproar. Thorn latched onto that Influence and forced her way through, shoving panicked civilians to the side as they trampled over anyone unlucky enough to find themselves lying in the street. But Wrath was faster than Thorn, and she had a lead. The beacon moved quickly, almost a block away now. Just as Thorn burst onto the other end of the crowd—

It disappeared. Thorn squinted into the dark.

Autumn Hunt turned the corner and sprinted west on 65th.

"No!" Thorn roared. The word was devoured by sounds—screaming, sirens, someone shouting her name. It all faded away, obliterated by the rolling noise of her heart thundering in her ears. The fire in Thorn's chest flared, like Wrath had thrown a fresh gallon of gasoline right into it.

Thorn ran as hard as her powerful legs would take her. She darted between people as she turned the corner, and Sparkie swooped overhead, crying into the night, swerving left and right and searching the streets for any sign of the Sin. Chris's voice crackled—something about pulling back—but Thorn hardly registered her.

A fire engine screamed by the corner of Broadway and Columbus, so close to Thorn that it nearly slammed right into her. She stopped in her tracks, her chest heaving, clouds of condensation rising into the air. Sirens came to life around her.

Suddenly, a pair of hands grabbed her shoulders.

Thorn spun, ready to fight, when Cain's face filled her view. He'd lost his scarf, and his mouth pulled into a worried frown. He reached out again. This time, his fingers wrapped around her arms and held tight.

"The police are on their way," he said. His voice sounded distant and muffled. "Thorn, did you hear me? We have injured Martyrs, and the police got through our communication blocks. We have to *go*."

His bright eyes implored her. Thorn's shoulders pulled up in a sigh, and she glanced around, where the few people still insane enough to be awake at this hour gawked at her—her wet hair, bare arms, and bleeding hands. Her fury growled, and Sparkie screeched high in the sky above, but Thorn nodded.

Cain led her back up 65th. Just ahead, past a blinking line of red fire trucks, the darkness of Central Park promised an escape. They hurried across the street and into the cover of barren, skeletal trees. As soon as they did so, Sparkie dove onto Thorn's shoulder. His body was freezing against her skin—his claws little pinpricks as he held on tight.

The more distance they put between themselves and the incident, the quieter the sirens became and the less overwhelming the sense of human coldness was. After a quarter of a mile, they climbed a stone wall, forced their way through a row of bushes, and found themselves at the southern edge of Sheep Meadow.

As soon as Thorn's boots crunched against the snowy grass, Chris's voice chimed in her ear.

"Thorn?" She spoke the name with a practiced calm that almost hid the worry behind it. By the tone, Thorn gathered they were on their private channel. "Where are you?"

Thorn's throat tightened, and she forced a deep breath to loosen it. "Headed to the medical checkpoint," she said. "How many injuries?"

"Three," Chris said. "Trampling damage. Last one's getting treatment now. Everyone else is securing the area and determining the safest routes out of here." A long, telling pause filled the line. Thorn's jaw slammed shut before Chris even asked the question.

"Did you get her?"

Thorn's fists clenched hard. The angry flesh on her exposed fingers screamed.

"No."

Another second of silence, followed by, "Roger that. Let's get out of here."

Thorn didn't respond.

The meadow stretched ahead of her. Their emergency medical vehicle was parked along the eastern edge, disguised as a park ranger unit and tucked into the shadows between two streetlights. Thorn might have missed it entirely if not for the sensation of people around it. She could count three, but she knew there were more. One more.

As they drew nearer, Thorn found Darius Jones.

He stood beneath the open hatch at the back of the SUV. Like the rest of TAC, Darius wore beige cargo pants and a form-fitting, black turtleneck that accentuated the strength across his shoulder blades. His bulletproof vest shifted as he leaned into the vehicle, pulling his shirt up just enough to show the pistol clipped to his belt. A pistol he never used because Darius wasn't here to hurt people: he was here to heal them.

A young TAC officer sat inside the cargo area, clutching one knee to her chest while her other leg dangled over the bumper. Darius pulled the hem of her pant leg up to reveal a swollen ankle. He murmured something, and though Thorn couldn't make out the words, the deep rumble of his voice made its way to her in the dark.

Then he wrapped his hands around the woman's leg, and his healing power poured into her. She let out a soft sigh as her injuries resolved. When he was done, Darius helped her to her feet. She thanked him eagerly, he smiled, and she walked around the car.

As soon as she was gone, Darius looked out to the

meadow.

His striking green eyes, contrasted against deep olive skin, searched the night. His forehead was tight, his strong jaw forced together as he hunted for something. When he spotted Thorn approaching, that tension dissolved, and he lit up.

Then his attention snapped to her hands, and a crease of worry drew between his brows.

"Well," Cain said, so suddenly and so loudly that both Thorn and Darius startled. "That could have been *much* worse."

He came to Darius's side, awkwardly close, the way he always was whenever Darius was around. Thorn couldn't blame him. Part of her ached to know the feeling—to be near enough to the Virtue that could destroy her Sin and set her free that her spirit got a taste of what that freedom would feel like.

If Cain's proximity made Darius uncomfortable, he didn't show it. He laughed and gave a broad smile that looked exceptionally bright at three in the morning.

"Yeah," he said. "No major injuries. Broken collar bones, twisted ankles, that sort of thing." His eyes darted to Thorn's hands again. She crossed her arms, holding them tight. "And according to Skylar," Darius went on, "we haven't attracted any police attention out here. No one's looking for us—Sins or civilians."

Cain drew in a breath. "Thank god for small blessings."

A momentary pause fell. Cain glanced from Darius to Thorn and back again before he cleared his throat.

"I suppose we're preparing to go?" he asked. Darius nodded, and Cain did, too. "Well… I'll see what I can do to help."

His gaze lingered on Darius before he bowed in Thorn's direction and walked around to the front of the vehicle where Chris, Skylar Fulton, and the new TAC officer Darius had just healed had gathered.

When Cain was gone, worry crept across Darius's face

again.

"I'm fine," Thorn said before he could speak.

Darius indicated her crossed arms. "You look like you're trying to crush yourself. Have you tried—"

"I'm *fine*," Thorn repeated. "I'm not that angry."

His eyes moved between hers, narrowed, and he sighed. "You *promised* you'd try this."

A guilty weight grew behind Thorn's armor, and her teeth ground together. Darius lifted his hand between them and tapped his thumb to each fingertip.

"Humor me."

He chanced a smirk as he landed on his pointer finger again, and Thorn's eyes snapped back to his. His smirk stretched into a fully-fledged smile.

"What do you see?" he asked her.

Thorn ran her tongue against the bottom of her teeth. Impatiently, she held a hand level with Darius's and pressed her thumb against a bleeding, aching forefinger.

What did she see?

Darius's face. His bright eyes. The day-old stubble casting a shadow on his jaw and throat. The TAC uniform he wore that clung to him in all the right places. The vise around Thorn's chest began to loosen. She pulled her shoulders back and took a long, slow breath.

"I see Amsterdam Tower," she said as she glanced over his head, where a brightly lit apartment building broke up the dark horizon. Her thumb moved to the middle finger, and she exhaled her fury, allowing it to fade into the world around her. "I hear Cain complaining about the snow." From middle to ring. "I smell the god-awful air freshener in this car."

She jutted her chin toward the SUV, and Darius laughed. Thorn relaxed into a smile, and her thumb tapped against her pinky.

"And I feel…"

Not Darius. Of all the people in this city, his aura was unreadable to her. Where her spirit had been torn and tainted, his was protected by a Virtue full of so much positivity that her Sin senses couldn't even dream of seeing the soul beneath. Thorn considered him for a moment, and her fingers pinched harder together.

"These burns," Thorn said. She looked down at her hands, which were raw and red at the end of her fingerless gloves. She opened her palm, and the wounded flesh on her fingertips stuck together. "Fuck."

The smile on Darius's face flickered. "Come here."

He turned back into the vehicle, and Thorn stepped up beside him. She tugged at the straps on her kevlar vest until they opened. As she tossed it into the cargo area, Darius returned with a burn kit.

Thorn raised a brow. "I don't need that."

"Just because your body heals three hundred times faster than everyone else's doesn't mean you don't need treatment," Darius said as he opened the kit anyway. "Plus, I need to practice my first aid procedures. Sit down."

Thorn rolled her eyes and leaned against the bumper as Darius rifled through a selection of special ointments, sprays, and medical bandages. He read the instructions, his lips moving soundlessly. At last, he glanced at Thorn's hands.

"They look like second-degree burns. Can I take off your gloves?"

She nodded.

He started with the left. Slowly, Darius peeled the wet fabric away from Thorn's skin. He shook his head. "You're soaked. I should get you a blanket, too, to prevent hypothermia."

"I don't get hypothermia."

"You *could.*"

A mangled river of acid scars revealed themselves on the inside of Thorn's forearm, getting thicker and more gnarled the nearer Darius got to her hand. A shiver of intense sensation poured into Thorn's nervous system as the glove grazed against the *Peccostium* sitting below her wrist. The mark of the Sins appeared, its black curves and sharp points crisp on a circular patch of unmarked flesh surrounded by a nest of tight, white skin.

"So," Darius said, his voice low with focus as he gingerly loosened the fabric around her wounds and slid the glove off them. He turned Thorn's bare hand over in his to examine her injuries. "How did that grounding exercise feel?"

"I told you," Thorn said. "I wasn't that angry."

Darius chuckled while he sprayed her burns with medication. They were already beginning to heal. Minutes ago, all five fingers had been covered in weeping blisters from the second knuckle up. Now, the blisters were flat and pink.

"Then it's the perfect time to practice," he said. "Get used to it when you're only *mildly* outraged, so it's easier to do the next time you want to tear your office to shreds." His eyes flashed up to hers. "I can tell it helped. You're more relaxed."

A shiver spread across Thorn's shoulders, and Sparkie hid behind her wet hair as Darius moved to her right hand.

Two distinct points of cool energy came around the car. Chris Silver appeared next to the tail light. As always, the young TAC director was still armored and ready for action. Her kevlar vest was securely wrapped around her chest, her weapon at the ready in a holster at her hip, and her long, yellow hair tied tightly in a low ponytail at the base of her skull.

Thorn stood, quickly pulled her hand out of Darius's, and made a fist. The newer, fresher flesh cracked around her knuckles.

"All our units are safely out of the area," Chris said. Skylar came up behind her. Even at this hour, Chris was alert, but Skylar stifled a yawn behind her hand. "Cain is taking Lewis to grab the car you two took in. Are we ready to go?"

"Yes," Thorn said. "Let's get the fuck out of here."

Darius shoved all his first aid supplies into one of the hidden compartments in the back of the SUV while Thorn and Chris organized the TAC gear in another. Skylar shut off her surveillance equipment, folding the monitors into the ceiling and shoving her computer elements beneath seats. Then, Chris climbed into the driver's side, and Skylar took the seat beside her, leaving Darius and Thorn in the back.

Thorn watched Central Park dart by in the dark as Chris pulled them from 72nd Street onto West Drive. Her stomach twisted into knots as they neared 66th. People filled the streets, and bright emergency lights cut between dead winter trees. The rage in Thorn's gut swirled again, and she pressed her thumb against her forefinger. What did she—

Darius's whole body stiffened. Thorn spun to see him staring past her. His mouth dropped open.

"Holy shit," he breathed, and he twisted around, looking over his shoulder and into the thick of the city as they continued down West Drive.

"What?" Thorn followed his gaze. She saw nothing but buildings looming over them, the steel and glass towers cutting through the foliage.

"I think…" Darius shook his head and looked at her. "Thorn, I just felt a *Virtue.*"

Whatever lingering fury Thorn held onto drowned in a flood of shock.

Wrath had escaped. Again. But there was a Virtue in New York City.

CHAPTER TWO

Upbeat, classical music rang through the room. Warm bodies pressed around Darius as Martyrs swayed and slid in a synchronized circle, following trails of woodwind ensembles and stringed quartets. He concentrated on his footwork without looking at the ground, marveling at how much combat training with Thorn had helped him on the dance floor.

Parker Boseman's hand was tight around his, and her tongue poked out between her teeth. In the muggy air, her ringlets were especially bouncy.

Without warning, Darius stepped back, raised an arm, and led Parker beneath it in a graceful twirl. He used her momentum to whip her around and caught her again before skipping right back into rhythm. The tension in her forehead melted with a laugh.

"That was great!" he said.

Her tawny cheeks, already warm from all the exercise, flushed further.

"Thanks, I just—oh, crap!"

Parker misstepped, and her toes crashed into Darius's, bumping them off tempo. He chuckled, paused, and guided them back into the swing of things. Parker's face was even darker now.

"What did Mackenzie say? The research team is all left feet?" She laughed.

"*Mackenzie* is all left feet," Darius said.

Parker laughed again. "Where is she, anyway?"

The two of them looked around. Fourteen Martyrs danced across the floor. Cain moved among them, adjusting hand positions and commenting on footwork. Darius couldn't help but smile when he pulled Alexis Claytor away from John Waters and took the woman's place to show her how to respond to her partner's lead. John's ocean-blue eyes widened, and Alexis hid a grin behind slender fingers.

"She said she had something important to take care of before our meeting this afternoon," Darius said.

Parker's face lit up. "Oh! The meeting about the Virtue in the city?"

An excited jolt rocked his chest—a familiar shadow of that Virtuous magnet pulling at his soul. It threw off his concentration, and he turned a half-step into a full.

"Damnit! Ah—yeah. Yeah, about that whole mission."

"I can't believe you had to wait two days!"

Darius chuckled. "Well, we got back at four thirty yesterday morning," he said, like that answered anything.

The truth was, he'd been so thrilled at feeling even a blip of Virtue power in New York that he hadn't been tired at all—and he'd hardly slept since.

The song rallied to an end. Darius and Parker stepped away from one another, him bowing and Parker giggling with a curtsy. The Martyrs moved toward the edges of the room, creating a wide circle of bodies. Darius's Virtue power made him sensitive to the warm energy their souls let out. Normally, the sensation was pleasant—a positive reminder of mankind's goodness—but now, he was hot. He tugged at his neckline as he squeezed between John and Alexis.

Cain walked into the center of the dance area and clapped his hands. His Familiar, a large, brown tabby cat named Crescendo, twisted around his ankles.

"Half of you aren't half bad," Cain said. A chorus of laughter encircled him. He smiled. The gesture fell just short of sincerity. "Take a few minutes to get some water, and then, ladies, pick a new partner. We'll be moving on to the tango next… a very *intimate* dance. Public foreplay, if you will. Perfect for weddings."

More laughter rolled through, this time a little awkwardly. Cain lit up at the sound, like it was more pleasant to his ears than the music. Darius caught his eye and smiled as the crowd moved toward water coolers in each back corner. He liked this side of Cain. It was much warmer, much happier, than what Darius had seen when he'd lived alone.

"Whelp," John said as they reached the line. He wiped sweat from his brow with the back of his hand. Strands of black hair stuck to his skin. "I can officially cross 'dancing with Cain' off my list of things I never wanted to do."

"What?" Alexis said, an amused glint in her eye. "Uncomfortable dancing with another man?"

John blew out a mouthful of air and dismissed the comment with a wave. "No, of course not. I'm uncomfortable dancing with *that* man."

"At least it wasn't the tango," Darius offered with a grin. He and Alexis exchanged an amused look as a warm energy pushed up behind them, and Gabe DuPont's deep voice rumbled in a laugh. The humor on John's face tightened.

"He's got a point," Gabe said. He crossed his muscular arms with a shrug. "The tango gets you *real* close…"

He threw John a smile, which John didn't return. The two were approximately the same height, but Gabe looked every ounce like the SWAT officer he'd been a year ago. John pulled his shoulders back, but it hardly helped. Darius suppressed a smirk as he reached the cooler and grabbed water for himself and Alexis.

"Looks like you have a few people hoping to get 'real close' to you, DuPont," she said. "Is this why you signed up for dance classes?"

She tilted her platinum-blonde head over his shoulder,

where four women watched his back with a little more than appreciation. Most of them, Darius noted, were new blood. Six months ago, when Gluttony's host had been destroyed and his Influence began to dissolve, it left the NYPD in shambles. Gabe had led the charge in bringing some of the disenfranchised cops over to the Martyrs, their Tactical department had nearly doubled, and he'd been rewarded with a promotion to Tactical's assistant director to help organize the merge.

"Ever since Cain started running classes, Chris has ordered all of TAC to take on at least one extracurricular," Gabe said. He scratched the back of his neck with a modest chuckle. "She says it's good for our 'mental health.'"

At the mention of Chris's name, John's expression dissolved into a dissociated stare. Darius cleared his throat. "Is she taking her own advice this time?" he asked.

Gabe rolled his amber eyes and raised his hands. "I've been on her case to pick up something for weeks now. All hear is that she's 'just too busy.' You know how she is."

John's whole body tensed. Darius frowned, but before he could speak, a bright energy bounded into their circle.

"John!" Parker said. "You got a tango partner? I… uh. I don't really know anyone else."

She grinned through the nerves, wrapped her arms around herself, and looked across the room. John's face warmed into the charming smile Darius was used to seeing on his face.

"I got you," he said, putting on the air of an older brother as he hooked an elbow. Parker gratefully linked hers through it. They moved toward the dance area, and he glanced over his shoulder. "I'll see you guys after class."

Soft music began to play again as Cain walked back to the center. "Ladies," he said, "if you have not yet selected a partner, I recommend you do so quickly. We start in two minutes…"

Alexis drained her water in a quick gulp and threw her cup into a bin beside the cooler. She looked between Darius and Gabe. "All right, DuPont. Let's see what everyone's so excited about."

The two of them moved off, and the pack of waiting women deflated behind them. Darius was about to follow when he felt someone approach.

"There's no way *you* don't have a partner already," a playful voice said.

Darius turned around as one of their newest recruits, a TAC officer named Madison Lewis, propped one hand on her hip. Her head tilted with feigned shock, and her bright eyes lingered as they took him in.

"Not for this round," Darius said with a smile. A few seconds of silence followed, Madison watching him like she was waiting for something, so he awkwardly gestured toward her left leg. "How's your ankle?"

"It's great," Madison said, the apples of her cheeks turning pink. Long, brunette hair fell in beach waves around her face. She whipped it behind her ears. "Did… I ever thank you?"

Darius chuckled. "You did."

"Oh! Well, thanks again! Does it always feel like that?"

He blinked. "…Like what?"

"So… warm?" Madison pulled her full lower lip between her teeth. "I've heard other people talk about your healing power, but I didn't expect it to feel good… you know? It kind of tingles."

"Oh, uh…" Darius crossed his arms. "Well, this was just a little sprain. I think bigger wounds are more uncomfortable, but I'm not really sure. I'm usually on the other side of the equation."

He laughed, and Madison giggled with him. She looked down at her feet and edged closer.

"Get into position," Cain announced. A rousing tango number pumped robust orchestral tones through the room. Darius glanced at the other Martyrs, who had paired off and begun to dance in a circle. When he turned back, Madison was watching him. He took a deep breath, smiled, and held out a hand. Madison grinned as she dipped her fingers into it.

Darius had been in this class for weeks now. He knew all the styles, the basic steps, and some simple moves that looked flashy enough to be impressive from a distance. Despite that, he hadn't ever realized just how right Gabe was about this particular dance until today.

Madison was pressed so tightly against him that he could feel every tremble in her body—could hear the shallow, nervous breathing that had nothing to do with exertion or exercise. Maybe he was imagining it, but it seemed that every time Darius tried to pull back, Madison drew in, and her hand wandered from its designated spot on his shoulder to wrap around the curve of his neck.

The tango *did* get you real close… and part of Darius wished Cain would cut in just to give him some space.

Darius stepped into the courtyard and took a freeing breath. The temperature in the vast, open space was at least five degrees cooler than the studio. As Martyrs dispersed, their human warmth dissipated, too, giving him some much-needed relief.

It wasn't just that the air was cooler. It was fresher. Darius looked at the greenery adorning the room. Concrete planters, which lined a wide, central aisle stretching from the elevator to the gym, burst with wrought iron terraces covered in dense, leafy vines. Low-profile houseplants sat at the center of every table, and along the walls, new pots had been added, flaunting the kind of bushes that thrived in the artificial light shining down on them from above. Darius knew it was impossible, but he could almost feel a breeze. When the Martyrs Memorial Garden had been reduced to ashes and Cain returned to the Underground, he'd promised to breathe life back into this dying place. Darius hadn't realized he meant it literally.

John stepped beside him, propped his hands on his hips, and spoke like he was reading Darius's mind.

"Things have changed a lot down here, huh?"

Darius chuckled. *That* was an understatement. Cain hadn't stopped with the plants. The courtyard was full of movement. Alcoves around the edge had been repurposed from old, dusty storage rooms to different studios for extra-curricular activities. This one was used for dancing, yoga, meditation, kickboxing, and various fitness classes that didn't require equipment. Others were dedicated to differ-ent arts: pottery, sculpture, painting, photography, and even music. People filtered in and out, practicing at their leisure, but Cain also taught dozens of classes and workshops throughout the week, and he'd scouted (or pressured) many talented Martyrs to join the cause. Darius oversaw medita-tion sessions every Monday and Wednesday, Gabe had of-fered to teach mixed martial arts, and even Thorn had been roped into coaching swim lessons on her free days. Darius suspected Cain had bribed her.

As he took it all in, he couldn't help but smile. The Un-derground was thriving, the Martyrs growing, and three of the seven Sins had been destroyed. Despite all they'd lost, it was starting to feel like they stood a chance.

A gentle hand ran across Darius's back. "Thanks for the dance," Madison said. Her fingers lingered at the cusp of his shoulder blade. "I'll see you soon!"

Her lips lifted into a smile. Darius could only manage an awkward nod as she walked away. John gawked after her.

"What's going on *there?*" He elbowed Darius in the ribs.

Darius laughed. "Nothing's going on."

"Why not? She's gorgeous. You should ask her to be your date for the wedding."

He tilted his head toward Madison as she made her way to the west wing of rooms. John was right—Madison Lewis was a beautiful woman. Darius wasn't oblivious to the way the men and women in the Underground regarded her whenever she walked through the courtyard. She turned heads with that dazzling smile.

"Nah," he said. "I'm not looking for anything."

"Who said it has to turn into anything?" John asked as he followed Darius along the edge of the room. "It's just a date!"

"I don't really *date*."

John scoffed. "Bullshit! You can't convince me you were single until you joined the Martyrs."

The smile on Darius's face tightened, and he took a deep breath to loosen the old, familiar pain of loss that locked between his lungs.

"No," Darius agreed, "but when I lived out in Alphabet City, relationships weren't about… dating."

He let the thought linger, and John finally seemed to get it. His eyes went wide before he had the grace to wince at his insincerity.

"I'm sorry, man. All I'm trying to say is there's more to life than *work*."

John gestured around the dining area as they approached. A couple dozen Martyrs had gathered for an early lunch, and more than half of them were clothed in Tactical colors, pouring over training schedules while they ate. Gabe had beaten them here, and he was already deep in a conversation with Seth Graves about upcoming shifts. John considered them with a dark frown.

"Don't worry about me," Darius said. He slapped a hand on John's shoulder with a smile. "I'm good."

John huffed. "Whatever you say, but I still think you should take a shot on her."

Someone gasped at a nearby table, and a lukewarm aura shot up.

"*What!*" Mackenzie McKay's voice peaked, hitting octaves that made Darius's ears sting. She scurried over, squeezed between him and John, and peered up at them with bright blue eyes. A small, black garbage bag cinched around her hair. "Who is Darius taking a shot on?"

"Nobody," Darius insisted. When Mackenzie did little

more than grin wider, waggling her eyebrows in a way that made the piercing through the left bounce wildly, he rolled his eyes and gestured toward her head. "This is the 'important business' you needed to take care of before our meeting?"

"It was the only time Skylar could fit me in," Mackenzie said as she poked the plastic around her skull. Her voice carried the subtlest note of an old Irish accent. "She's too busy with wedding stuff between now and the big day."

Mackenzie gestured over her shoulder, where Skylar Fulton was picking at her lunch at the table Mackenzie had abandoned. She waved, and the three of them walked over.

"What color did you go with this time?" Darius asked. He pulled at the edge of the bag to sneak a peek, but Mackenzie grabbed it and held tight.

"Navy," Skylar said. She relaxed back in the chair, and her silver hoop earrings swung against her neck. "Like our wedding colors."

"I'm getting in the spirit!"

Skylar raised her hands. "Hey, I'm not complaining."

"You're almost down to single digits," John said. He pulled a seat out beside her, leaned over the table, and grinned. "How freaked out is Raquel?"

"So freaked," Skylar said. She pulled a strand of dark hair behind her ear, revealing the bleached blonde beneath it. "But she's trying to be cool. It's pretty adorable, actually. If you really want to watch her squirm, ask about the lights."

"Yes, brilliant idea." Mackenzie nodded vigorously. "Harass a bride less than two weeks before her wedding. What could go wrong?"

Darius and John laughed as an alarm beeped from Skylar's wrist. She glanced at it. "Time's up. Go wash."

"Excellent!" Mackenzie said, and she turned to Darius. "I'll be back in a flash, and then we can head out."

"Hurry," he called after her as she zig-zagged through tables toward the industrial kitchen. "We've got ten minutes!"

She threw him a thumbs-up and zoomed around the counter. On the other side, Kenia was running a cooking class, looking more frazzled beneath her hair net than she ever did when she single-handedly prepped food for a party of eighty. She glowered at Mackenzie as the Irishwoman peeled the plastic off her scalp, dunked her head in the sink, and used the pull-out faucet to rinse the dye.

Darius sank into the third seat at the table and sighed before he turned to Skylar. "I didn't know you did hair."

"Oh, I don't," she said. "Mackenzie is my one and only client."

"Why?"

"Because she's fun and wants to do cool stuff with it," Skylar said with a shrug. "If I started doing other people's hair, more would ask… It's just easier to cut it off with the one. The security department is always swamped, even when I'm *not* in the middle of planning my wedding. Raquel would hate it if I picked up a second gig."

"Big jump," John said, snagging a few cold french fries off Mackenzie's plate and popping them into his mouth. "From hair to code."

"I was a stylist to pay for college—and subsequently dropped out of college," Skylar said. "Turns out you can learn everything you need to be halfway good with coding for free online. Good thing, too. It's the only reason I'm here."

She glanced down at her plate. Darius frowned and exchanged a look with John. "Holly recruited her after the Sins killed her family," he muttered quickly.

Darius sucked in a breath. Holly was the only Martyr he knew who hadn't come into the Underground dragged behind a hearse.

"They'd stopped talking to me years before that. Turns out, not *everyone* loves their kids unconditionally." Skylar shrugged and picked up a fry, but instead of eating it, she twirled it between her fingers. Her french-tipped nails caught the light. "Dad worked at Wall Street and got into some heat. I don't really know all the details, but there was an 'accident,' and three days later, Alan and Holly showed up at my apartment, worried I might be a target, too."

For a few tense seconds, neither John nor Darius spoke. Skylar glanced up at them, and her eyes crinkled in a smile.

"Jesus, you two, stop looking so sad." She threw the fry at John. It flopped against his chest. "This has been the best thing that's ever happened to me. What I do matters, I've learned a lot, and I met the love of my life. Don't ruin it with… whatever *this mood* is."

She waved her arms in a vague gesture around them, and the two men laughed. Mackenzie's aura moved their way again, and she stopped by the table with her hands on her hips.

"All right," she said. Neat, clean hair ruffled around her face in a fresh pixie cut. It was still damp, and the navy looked darker than it would be when it dried. Mackenzie typically picked bright, loud colors, and the deeper tone highlighted dark circles under her eyes. Darius hadn't noticed them before. She grinned. "Let's go before you make me late."

Then, with a dramatic flourish, Mackenzie spun on her heels and headed to the elevators. Darius rolled his eyes as he got to his feet, said goodbye to John and Skylar, and followed after her. By the time he reached her side, she'd hit the button to go up.

"So," Mackenzie said, running her fingers through her hair. Her nail polish, the color of fresh pumpkins, was chipped at the base and bitten at the tips. It stood out against her blue hair like buoys in the ocean. "Who you taking a shot on?"

She threw him a sly look and bit her tongue in a smile. Her piercing clinked against the back of her teeth. Darius groaned.

"*Nobody,*" he repeated. The elevator dinged, the doors opened, and they walked on. Mackenzie leaned against the wall.

"Fine," she said, wrinkling her nose. "I'll ask John."

"I guess I'll have to find a way to keep John quiet," Darius said cryptically. He threw Mackenzie a coy, sideways glance.

Her pierced brow arched, and the corner of her mouth pulled up. "Seems a little dark for you, *Kindness*." She punctuated the line with a wink. "I'll figure out who she is. Just you wait."

Darius laughed as the elevator reached the top floor and opened to a foyer, looking directly at a set of glass doors to the garage. Through them, he watched a motorcycle glide to a stop across the lot, it and its rider a matte, black silhouette in the dim lights. His smile deepened as the bike's electric engine flicked off.

"Oh, shit!" Mackenzie said. "Thorn's running late, too! C'mon, let's go!"

The Irishwoman hurtled around the corner and down the hallway leading to the formal entrance and hospital waiting room before she turned toward the back offices. Darius arrived by the other set of doors just as he felt Mackenzie's aura tuck into the conference room. Thorn strode in from the garage and pulled her helmet off, revealing a tight jaw and hard, piercing eyes. They snapped to him, and a wave of tension melted off her face.

"Hey." Thorn unzipped her kevlar bike jacket. It opened at her throat, exposing pearly skin behind the black fabric. As she shrugged it off, she nodded toward the hallway. "What's up with McKay?"

"She's going to beat you to the meeting," Darius said.

Thorn scoffed, draped her jacket over the crook of her elbow, and straightened her fingerless gloves. Dark, silky hair was beginning to fall free from its elastic, and stray pieces draped around her slender face. Darius caught a smirk teasing at her lips. "She can have this one."

They made their way down the hallway, past Tactical, to the Research and Discovery headquarters. The door was propped open, and a man without an aura hovered halfway outside while he gave orders back into the room.

"This is a good start," Nicholas Wolfe said, slapping his fingertips on a tablet in his hand, "but I want everything we can find around Lincoln Square. Go as far south as 42nd and north as 96th. This Virtue was in the area at three in the goddamned morning. They've got to live nearby. Daniel, you're in charge til I get back."

"Yes, sir."

Nicholas's face scrunched in a grimace. "Knock that 'sir' shit off," he said. A murmur of laughter replied, and he smirked. "Keep up the great work."

He glanced over his shoulder, spotted Thorn and Darius, and said goodbye to his research team before he closed the door behind him. When Lina Brooks had been killed, Alan offered Darius the position of director of the Research side of R&D, but Darius declined, suggesting Nicholas take the opening instead. At first, no one was sure how the former Virtue would do in this role—he hadn't exactly made a lot of friends inside the Underground—but the department was thriving beneath him.

"Looks like I'm not the only one running late," Nicholas said, gesturing to Thorn's motorcycle gear with a frown. "Were you at the apartment? What did you find out?"

Thorn sighed and stepped around him to open the conference room door. "Nothing good," she said, striding inside.

Nicholas glanced at Darius. His blue eyes narrowed—eyes which had once been full of duty and Diligence and were now as empty as Thorn's had always been. He and Darius followed behind her.

Mackenzie cleared her throat.

"About time you all showed up," she chastised, but a twitch at the corner of her mouth revealed the fragile charade. She sat on the far side, across from Chris, who glanced over her shoulder and passed Darius a wide-eyed look that told him she and Alan were the only two who had arrived on time, and that the tension in the room wasn't in his imagination.

"Thank you for that, Miss McKay," Alan Blaine said. He stood at the head of the table, towering over them all at six foot four. He threw Mackenzie a dark look down his sharp nose, and his lips tightened into a frown behind a trimmed goatee. The man was a streak of ink in the room—long, narrow, and pure black from his shined shoes to the trenchcoat he wore over his slacks and button-up. As he drew a deep breath, his head jerked in their direction just enough that his veil of pin-straight, shoulder-length hair flicked around his pale face.

"I understand that we have a lot going on in the Underground lately," he continued, his deep voice a monotone that barely hinted at his frustration, "but these leadership meetings are important, and I would appreciate punctuality."

His eyes landed on Thorn, cold and half-empty. She watched back, just as unmovable as she always was. After a stony second, she thudded her helmet onto the table with a crack. Her left hand dipped into the satchel cinched to her thigh and drew out a silver box, which she flung onto the wood in front of her uncle. Sparkie poked his head out of Thorn's bag before diving back inside.

Darius's mouth went dry. "Is that a…?"

"Bomb," Thorn finished. "Yes."

A shudder moved through the room, bringing Darius and Nicholas to the chairs on Chris's right as Thorn walked behind Alan's back to join Mackenzie. The smile plunged from the Irishwoman's face as Thorn draped her jacket onto her seat and lowered into it.

"Hunt planned for at least a dozen possible scenarios for her escape," she went on. "The leasing records say she recently moved to the unit closest to the fire escape, her apartment was full of empty canisters of gasoline, and she threaded hosing under the door to soak the hallway and start the fire out there. Explosives like this lined the window, so if we'd tried to enter the room that way, we'd have been blown to hell. We can't even begin to guess what kind of Programming the tenants were under, and the police found an arsenal of firearms under the bed."

Darius frowned. "I thought Wrath didn't like to fight with guns."

"She doesn't," Thorn confirmed, crossing her arms. "This tells me she's willing to do whatever it takes to get out alive."

Alan's dark eyes snapped back to Thorn's face. He pressed his fingers into a tall steeple and rested them against his lips as Nicholas shook his head.

"Jesus Christ," he said. "It's like dealing with Sloth all over again."

"Can't blame her for being paranoid," Mackenzie said, picking at her polish. Orange flakes littered the table. "This is the third time we've tried to kill her since August."

"And the final time," Alan announced, straightening his back. Thorn's focus zeroed in on him, laser-sharp and hot as hell. "Until further notice, all plans to destroy Autumn Hunt are on hold."

"*What?*" Thorn snarled, leaning into the table with her palms flat against it. The elegant curve of her throat tightened. "I've been working on this for seven months!"

"And we have failed for seven months," Alan said. Thorn's eyes narrowed, and the bridge of her nose wrinkled between them. "She is anticipating us. She knows what we are attempting to do. We are losing our upper hand, and I fear the next time we do track her down, we would be *lucky* to only suffer the loss of four civilians."

"No!" Thorn jumped to her feet and walked behind her chair, propping her hands on her hips. A tickle of her anger crackled in the air as the remnants of Wrath in her soul searched for an outlet. "Damn it, Alan, this might be our only chance!"

"You need to consider the possibility that we have missed this chance," Alan said, his tone a steady contrast to Thorn's. She jerked around to watch him. Her grip went so tight that her nail beds pressed white. "She is clearly taking deadly precautions, and I fear the risks of going after her could very well outweigh the reward."

Thorn's jaw ground together, and she took a long, slow breath that dilated her nostrils and made her chest stretch outward. Her lips pursed as she shook her head. "I can get her," she began, but Alan cut her off with a hand.

"You can," he said, "and you will, but not now."

The room quieted. From his peripheral, Darius caught the tension in stolen glances and shifting posture, but he didn't look away from Thorn. She glared at Alan, solid as a statue, the muscles along her bare shoulders and biceps contracted and angry. After a moment, Nicholas cleared his throat, and Thorn's eyes finally flicked his direction. She caught Darius watching her. He chanced a smile, and she turned away, dropping her hands to her sides and exhaling hard.

"We still need to take advantage of the Sins' weakened infrastructure while things are messy," Nicholas said, "and we're running out of time. Cassius LaFleur's disappearance may have slowed him down, but Mayor Bently has finally appointed a permanent commissioner. We're going to have more problems with the NYPD as they get organized, even with the undercover operatives we have on the inside now. On top of that, the media conglomerates that Lust had under his thumb look like they came back under Sin control really fucking quickly after he was killed. Greed and Wrath might be the only two left standing, but they're damned efficient at what they do. We've got to do something."

"Do you have a suggestion, Mr. Wolfe?" Alan asked. Thorn finally took her seat beside Mackenzie again, leaning back in her chair with the edge of one hand pressed against her closed mouth as she watched Nicholas.

"I think we should take out Greed instead," he said, "before Lust and Envy repossess."

More shuffling. More tension. The way it always was in one of these meetings when someone suggested destroying a Sin's host. Mackenzie's feet tapped against the ground while Thorn's eyes were angry slits against her white face.

"It won't be easy," Chris said, crossing her arms around her Tactical turtleneck. "Greed might be higher profile than Wrath, but it doesn't mean he's a sitting target. For one, he hasn't been seen in public since last July. We also don't have a lock on where he lives, and throughout the centuries, Greed has been one of the only Sins known to hire out protective services rather than rely on Puppets or Programming. Rumor has it that Anton Claytor is mixed up with some of the most powerful families in New York, too. Bonanno. Davis. Giuliani."

"He's also *nothing* compared to Wrath," Thorn said, venom lacing the words. She was still reclined back, her hand poised just beyond her lips, almost like she was holding a cigarette. "Claytor has only been a Sin for thirteen years. Hunt is going on ninety-two. As far as we know, she's the longest-lived host in the last five centuries, and she's more powerful than the other six were *combined*. Destroying her changes *everything*."

"It is off the table," Alan snapped. "I won't hear more on the matter."

Thorn's whole body stiffened, and her shoulders raised in a breath. Darius pulled his focus away from her to address the rest of the group. "What will it take to target Greed?" he asked.

Chris clasped her hands and propped her weight onto her elbows. "We'll need to increase our surveillance on him and start narrowing down his patterns, see if we can't anticipate where he'll be."

"I can get a Research team to help with that," Nicholas said, smoothing back his trimmed, blonde hair. He had a little more white at the temples than when Darius met him two years ago. "Claytor is involved in a lot of money-grabbing events that fatten up his accounts. We'll dig up anything we can on them."

"I suspect Anton Claytor will be easier to find than

Autumn Hunt ever was," Alan agreed, drawing all eyes back to him. He focused directly on Thorn, seemingly immune to the violence in her glare. "Mr. Mulligan is working the Greed case now?"

Thorn dipped her head once to confirm. Alan mirrored the gesture.

"Ensure he connects with Mr. Wolfe. Get him all the information he needs to formulate a plan. Now." Alan cleared his throat and shifted, melting from his rigid, authoritative posture to a more relaxed one as he leaned over the table. "We also must address a much more exciting development. Mr. Jones?"

Five pairs of eyes turned toward him, an undercurrent of eager anticipation alight across them—a foreign experience here. Darius smiled.

"There's a Virtue in New York City."

"You are certain?" Alan pressed.

"Absolutely," he said. "It was quick—there and gone as we drove past the incident on 66th—but it was there."

Mackenzie frowned. "Past the incident... they were *at* that complex?"

"I don't know," Darius said. "I didn't get the feeling the Virtue was with all that energy, but it was gone too fast for me to get a good read on exactly where it was."

"A first responder?" Chris offered. "A cop, firefighter, or EMT?"

"Maybe," Darius said.

A nod tilted Nicholas's chin upward, and his brows rose before he pulled out the tablet he'd brought in from R&D and slid it onto the table. "Well, we've started collecting intel about Lincoln Square," he said, indicating the screen. Darius lifted the device and glanced at the spreadsheet of news articles, social posts, local events, and public call logs while Nicholas spoke. "I didn't realize how close you were to the strike zone, so considering the possibility of a first responder might change things, but right now, we're running under the assumption that the Virtue lives there."

"Do we see any patterns in the data?" Darius asked, passing the tablet to Chris, who scrolled through it, too. "Hotspots? Stand out events?"

"*You'll* be the one to tell us if any events stand out," Nicholas said, "since you're the only one with that Virtue sixth sense. But as for patterns or hotspots, no. Not yet, but we just started looking at it yesterday."

"What's the plan, then?" Chris asked as she handed the device to Alan next.

"Well," Mackenzie started, throwing a glance over her shoulder at Thorn before she faced the table again, "we figure it makes the most sense to send Darius out there *himself* to look for this Virtue—since, ya know, he's got that whole Virtue detector thing going on."

She threw a hand out, twirling it in a few graceless swirls in his direction. Thorn's attention, sharp as a blade, landed on Darius, too, and the edges of her expression softened.

"We want to put together a special unit for this mission," Nicholas said. Alan nodded as he considered the new Research director. Nicholas went on. "Mackenzie volunteered to be the primary navigator and driver, and we'd have a dedicated TAC team along for security."

"With lots of guns," Mackenzie chimed in.

"Plus detailed routes and schedules. If we want extra Tactical patrols in the area, we'll know exactly where to send them." Nicholas gestured his head toward the device in Alan's hands again. "Our whole plan is laid out on the second tab."

"How often do we want to go out?" Darius asked as he leaned back in his chair.

"A couple times a week," Mackenzie said. "Changing the days and times just in case anyone paid enough attention to see a pattern. We'll take different cars for each trip, and Holly's nerd team can track our location the entire time."

Alan nodded, impressed. "This is very thorough," he said, raising the tablet. Thorn opened her palm toward him, and Alan handed the device to her as he went on. "Excellent work. I see no reason why we cannot start assembling this unit immediately. Thorn?"

Now, all the attention focused on her. Dark eyes darted left to right, the only part of Thorn's stern face that moved at all as she read through Nicholas and Mackenzie's proposal. Nicholas tensed on Darius's left, crossing his arms around his baby-blue button-up. Darius suspected he was getting ready for a fight.

After several long moments, though, Thorn's head rocked in the slightest nod Darius had ever seen. She passed the tablet back to Nicholas. "Looks good."

Darius's stomach flipped as Nicholas blinked.

"Really?" he said. "You're good with Darius spending this much time in New York?"

Thorn's glare sharpened, but all she said was, "We need to find this Virtue."

Chris reclined in her chair and sighed. "I can't believe we've got a lead on *another*, and it's so close."

"Virtues are known to reincarnate in the same vicinity to where their opposing Sin has power," Alan said. "Teresa Solomon, Mr. Jones, and Mr. Wolfe were all born in or near New York City. Samira Khoury is the only exception we have seen to this rule, and evidence indicates Temperance may have landed in Georgia because Leroy was living there, spreading Gluttony's Influence. There is a good chance the remaining Virtues are in the city."

Mackenzie whistled through her teeth. "I can't believe we only need to find *three*."

Darius nodded. "Charity, Chastity, and Patience," he said. Alan's attention turned to his hands, laced upon the table, while Thorn caught Darius's gaze. She took a slow breath and wrapped her arms around herself, like she was trying to smother the hope before it had the chance to breathe. "I wonder which one we're closing in on now."

CHAPTER THREE

Shelves of medical supplies lined the wall in front of Darius, stocked with containers of gauze and gloves, neatly stacked flats of IV fluids, and plastic lockboxes so full of pharmaceuticals that even Max Douglas, the most prolific drug dealer who ever tried to work on the Williamsburg Bridge Street Market, would have traded his left hand to get ahold of them.

"Okay…" Raquel Hernandez stood at the back of the hospital's inventory closet, neatly packing a stack of abdominal pads into a trauma pack laid open on the table. "What's next?"

Darius scrolled down the list on his tablet. "A bleeding control kit." As Raquel moved to the shelves to grab it, he shook his head. "This is a *lot* of gear for a recon mission."

Raquel laughed and nodded. Strands of wavy, brown hair fell loose from a messy bun at the back of her skull. "That tells you all you need to know about our line of work, doesn't it?" She stood on her tiptoes and reached to the back of the tallest shelf, where the bleeding control kit was just beyond her fingertips. Darius came over and grabbed it for her, handing it off as Raquel sighed a thank you and returned to the table. "It's better to be over-prepared."

She tucked the latest item into its designated spot beside the oral sedatives, liquid skin, and tourniquet while Darius marked "bleeding control kit" off the checklist.

"Looks like that's everything," he said.

"Good." Raquel zipped the bag up. "I don't think we could fit anything else in here."

"Thanks again for helping me."

Raquel flashed a grateful smile as she hauled the pack off the table and passed it to him. "No problem. It's the least I can do after all you've done for us. Are you all set for your Virtue-tracking mission?"

"We're finalizing the details now," Darius said. "After this, I'm meeting with Chris for our gear assignments."

The two of them walked out of the inventory room, and Raquel frowned as she shut the door behind them. She input her access code, and the lock latched with a mechanical click.

"Oh, nice," she said, but the timbre of her voice shifted, and Darius glanced at her. "Hey, do you know if Chris is coming to the wedding?"

She didn't look at him as she asked, clearly trying to seem nonchalant, but the apples of her brown cheeks darkened.

"I don't know," Darius admitted. He heaved the pack over his shoulder as they walked up the center of the hospital ward. All the beds were empty, curtains pulled back to reveal clean cots and white walls all along the narrow room. A handful of warm energies pattered around the space—nurses performing maintenance duties in the calm between chaos. "I haven't talked to her about it. Why?"

Raquel sighed. "She never RSVPed, and I'm a little worried she's not going to. She dropped out of the bridal party after she and John broke up, which I get, but I didn't think she'd avoid the wedding entirely… I guess it's awkward when your ex is there, though."

Her mood faltered, and Darius frowned. Before he could say more, they reached the nursing station near the main doors, and Raquel's smile beamed back to life like it had never left her face in the first place. The head nurse, Colette, sat behind the desk and spoke with one of the new TAC members who was leaning against the counter. She glanced up as they approached.

"Oh, Raquel," she said, "Mr. Garfield is here for his 4:00. Would you mind scanning his prescription out of the medicine locker for me?"

"Of course," Raquel said. She reached out for the man's medical card, which he handed over instantly. "I'll be right back."

As she spun on her heels and headed back the way she'd come, Colette typed a few things into a terminal.

"Good afternoon, Darius," she said, her voice carrying the patience of age and an old accent he could never quite place. "It's always good to see you here under nonemergency circumstances." She smiled, her dark eyes kind and warm. Colette was a couple of years older than her husband, but she didn't look it. Where Dr. Harris was graying at the temples and creased from years of scowling, Colette's calm outlook on life seemed to have kept her solidly sub-fifty. "Did you get everything you need?"

Darius slapped the pack across his shoulder. "Yep, we're good to go."

"Mr. Garfield tells me he's been assigned to join you."

"Oh?" Darius glanced at the TAC officer, embarrassed to realize he was one of the recruits from the NYPD whose name he didn't quite know yet. He was older than most of the others, maybe in his mid-forties, and he moved a little stiffly as he came around to shake Darius's hand. Darius grabbed his palm and said, "I'm sorry…?"

"Kit," he said with a laugh. "The guy with the broken back."

It flooded back to Darius, then. Kit Garfield had been in a shootout with the Martyrs years ago, well before Kit knew what the Sins were or that he was working for one. He'd crawled away with three cracked vertebrae, lucky to be alive, but he'd suffered from chronic pain ever since—an old pain Darius couldn't fix, Virtue or not.

"That's right," Darius said. "You're on the team?"

"Got the orders this morning," Kit said.

Darius nodded just as Raquel returned to the desk with two round, white tablets in a plastic cup. She handed them to Kit along with his medical card.

"Here you go!"

Kit thanked her and slipped the card back into his wallet. His eyes lingered on the pills like they were made of gold, and he dry-swallowed them. When he handed the container back, Raquel blinked and glanced at Darius, who shrugged and adjusted the pack on his shoulder.

"Well, Kit," he said, "are you headed to Tactical, too?"

"Yes, sir, I am. My partner's already there."

"Yeah, I see that," Darius said. Kit frowned, and Darius tilted his head toward the doors. Chris's robust and alluring energy pulled at him from across the top floor alongside another he didn't know yet. It felt familiar, and it itched at Darius's mind to place it. "They're waiting for us. Let's get going."

From the outside, the tactical room seemed unassuming—nothing but a simple door among many in an even simpler hallway—but inside, it rivaled the hospital in size. Eight alcoves lined the right side, home to hundreds of lockers full of TAC gear. The weapons vault tucked into the far left corner, its reinforced steel door ajar. Chris's voice echoed through.

"Where did you say Garfield went?"

"To medical, ma'am," Madison responded.

A groan built up in Darius's mouth, and the smile threatened to drop from his face, but he managed to catch it as he slipped through the door.

"He's here now," Darius said. The words felt extra loud. There was no softness in this room, and the concrete walls took any sound within them and magnified it to at least twice its standard volume. Racks of firearms lined the space, and heavy drawers locked all the ammunition safely away.

Chris and Madison stood on either side of a metal table laid out with a small arsenal. Darius gestured to it as Kit walked in behind him. "How many guns do four people need?"

Madison stifled a laugh behind slender fingers as Chris threw Darius a stern but amused look. "We have to be prepared for anything."

"Yeah," he said, heaving the trauma pack from his shoulder and setting it down by the door. "Raquel and I just put together enough medical supplies to handle a small plane crash."

"Hopefully, you won't run into any plane crashes," Chris said, "*or* Sins, but if you do, I need to make sure you come home in one piece."

She turned back to the table. Darius stepped up to her right as Kit positioned himself at one of the shorter ends, his feet planted shoulder-width apart as he crossed his arms. Madison's spine straightened as she mimicked Kit's posture. Chris indicated them.

"Unit Twenty-Seven has been assigned to this mission," she said. "Kit Garfield and Madison Lewis. Combined, they have over thirty years of experience on the force, and Garfield worked at the 20th precinct in Lincoln Square, so he knows the area well."

Darius looked between the two and dipped his chin. Kit nodded back as Madison's lips pulled into a smile, and she mouthed the word, "Hey." Darius gave a tense smirk.

"Everyone in the vehicle has passed their TAC assessments," Chris went on, "which means you will all check out and carry a handgun." She lifted a pistol and turned it over in her hands. "This is a Glock 26. Designed to be concealed carry, but it will still accept larger magazines. You can tuck it in a back holster under your shirt to avoid detection without sacrificing the power you'd need in a Sin situation."

She set the Glock back down and moved onto a rifle.

"The M4 Carbine. Just two. These stay in the locked compartment under the cargo hold in the back of the vehicle unless you absolutely need them. Hopefully, you won't.

Each will come loaded with one magazine and another two for backup, but the goal isn't to win a fight—it's to get the hell out of there and make your way to safety as soon as possible."

Chris laid the M4 back on the table and drew a deep breath as she looked between Darius and the two TAC officers across from them. "Since this is a recon mission, you're also going in plainclothes. In a standard patrol, you would rarely leave the vehicle, but it's possible you could find yourselves walking around parts of the city on foot. We don't want to draw attention, and four people dressed in uniform would turn some heads."

"What about armor?" Kit asked with a frown.

"You'll have some in the car," Chris said. "Kevlar vests and helmets. But you won't wear them unless you have to. Again, this is a *recon* mission."

Kit shifted right to left, putting more weight onto his left. When he didn't comment further, Chris turned back to the table.

"All this gear, including your armor and communication devices, will be stored in gear closet four. You three, Mackenzie, and I will have access. Before you leave, you will sign each piece out and mark it on your inventory, and when you return, you'll put it all away and sign it back in. Got it?"

"Yes, ma'am," Kit and Madison said in unison. Darius simply nodded.

"Good," Chris said. "Check back tomorrow evening for your final schedule. Mackenzie should have it done by five. Until then, you're dismissed."

While Chris began scanning the weapons' asset tags into a pad on the table, Kit and Madison relaxed and made their exit. Kit left without a word, but Madison paused in the doorway. She looked back at Darius, a coy smile dancing on her face as she eyed him up and down. "You coming?"

"I was thinking I'd help Chris wrap up here," he said.

"Okay," Madison said. "We'll just catch each other later, then?"

Darius nodded awkwardly. "Sure."

She smiled a little wider and lingered a little longer, her manicured nails gripping the door frame before she slipped out and swaggered toward the hallway. Darius let out a low sigh as Chris snickered. He turned to find her giving him a sly look over the top of her device. His eyes widened, and he pointed at her.

"You know!"

Now Chris laughed, the sound resonating around them like an instrument in a music hall.

"I have no idea what you're talking about," Chris lied, badly, her nose wrinkling with the grin she was trying to squash down. "Mackenzie's the one who requested Unit Twenty-Seven for this mission."

"Oh, god," Darius groaned, running a hand down his face. "*Mackenzie.* John's got a big mouth."

Chris turned back to her device. "The official reason logged in her request is that Kit really does know the area well."

"And the *unofficial* reason?"

Her green eyes darted to him, and she pulled a strand of yellow hair behind her ear as she smirked. "Because John's got a big mouth."

Darius groaned again as he crossed his arms and shook his head. "I have no idea what to do about this, Chris."

"Why do you have to do anything?" she asked with a shrug. "Madison's got a crush. That's all. Half the women down here have had a crush on you at one point or another."

She finished logging the weapons, set the tablet aside, and grabbed all four handguns. As she moved toward the door, Darius hauled the medical kit onto his back and snatched the rifles off the table.

"Wait, really?" he asked as he followed her. "How do you know that?"

Chris stopped outside of gear closet four and typed a code into the lock, smiling at Darius while she did it. "For one, I've been in the women's locker room, and you haven't. And for another, it's called transference."

"Transference?"

"Yeah," Chris said. She stocked the Glocks in individual cases and reached for the first rifle. Darius handed it to her. "It's when a patient starts to develop feelings for someone who cares for them. It happens a lot with doctors, therapists, counselors… Elijah had a problem with it for a while. Abraham, too."

Chris's face fell, and Darius's stomach flipped at the mention of Abraham Locke. He knew Holly had kept tabs on their old counselor after he'd asked Alan to wipe his memory and give him a fresh start, but Darius hadn't had the heart to check in on how he was doing. He was afraid of the answer. Erasing twenty years of his life had probably landed Abraham in an institution—a possibility he'd found more appealing than staying with the Martyrs after losing what remained of his family last year.

Darius cleared his throat. "Well, how do I stop this transference thing?"

"I don't know that you can," Chris said as she stored the gun. "Think about it, Darius. You're a literal saint who's healed us back from the brink of death. To make things more complicated, we live in an enclosed, underground compound without much interaction with the outside world. This is bound to happen."

"Great," Darius grumbled.

"I wouldn't sweat it," Chris said. "Madison will get over it once she gets to know you and realizes you're not all that great under the Virtue anyway."

Chris knocked him playfully with her elbow as she grabbed the second M4. Darius slumped the trauma pack off his shoulders with a chuckle.

"Thank you. That helps."

Chris laughed. "Seriously, though, I can talk to her about this behavior, or I could reassign a new team to the task force."

Darius sighed. "No, it's fine. It'll pass… eventually."

Once Chris secured the second rifle, Darius set the pack at the bottom of the locker. She closed the door, typed the code, and the mechanism latched shut.

"So, how's Raquel doing?" Chris asked as they headed out. She paused outside the weapons vault and locked that up, too. The massive metal door shut with a thud. "Panicking about her wedding?"

"A little, I think," Darius said, casting her a quick look. "Have you decided if you're going?"

"I don't know," Chris said. They reached the hallway and turned left toward the elevator. "I wouldn't want to cause any drama with John. It might be better if I sit it out."

Darius frowned. "It's not his wedding, and Raquel loves you. Besides, avoiding John forever won't help him move on."

"Yeah," Chris agreed, but Darius could tell she was saying it to placate him. The elevator reached the top, and they got on.

"What would you do instead?" Darius asked.

Chris shrugged. "Work, probably."

"I thought Alan gave the whole Underground the day off?"

"He did, but I have plenty to do."

What John had said the other day came roaring back to Darius—*"there's more to life than work"*—but he knew mentioning that would only frustrate Chris further. The last thing she needed was her ex complaining about the same old shit through a different mouthpiece.

Instead, he laughed and said, "Man, you need a hobby."

Chris rolled her head back. "Sounds like Gabe has a big mouth, too."

"Well, is he wrong?" Darius asked as they hit the lower level, and the doors opened to the courtyard. He spread his arms around it. "You have a ton of options now. Painting, sculpting…"

"Art isn't my thing."

"What about swimming?" Darius pressed.

"I don't know how."

"Now's the perfect time to learn!"

"No, thanks. I'd rather keep my feet on dry land," Chris said with a laugh, and she touched Darius's shoulder. "I see your concern, and I appreciate it, but I'm fine, okay?"

For as long as Darius had known Chris, the hollow glint of a shell-shocked warrior had lingered under the surface like a chronic illness she couldn't overcome. It was less prominent now, and when she smiled, he almost couldn't see it at all. In the last few years, she'd gone from being part of an organization that was starving to death in the face of a war it couldn't win to watching three Sins burn into nothing and heading the first TAC department of this size in the last six decades.

Even after everything this job exposed her to, Chris was content exactly as she was. It wasn't just her. The entire Underground felt that way.

It was happy here.

***

"Fuck," Thorn murmured.

She walked behind her desk, running her fingertips against her lower lip. The Gray Unit's cold energy filled her office. Thorn rarely held meetings here, evidenced by the fact that she had almost no formal seating. Alexis Claytor had pulled Thorn's office chair around to the front while her brother, Caleb, and Peter Mulligan had taken either end of a worn, crimson couch Thorn used more often to crash between shifts than she ever did to entertain guests. Gabe DuPont had joined them, and he reclined against the wall by her door. Thorn spun to him, and Sparkie's wings shuffled in agitation from where he hid behind her hair.

"Tell me everything you can about this new police commissioner."

DuPont crossed his muscular arms around his black,

tactical turtleneck. "Her name is Adeline Faust. She was one of the top captains in Brooklyn at the time Terrance Moore was killed, and she's been holding out for the commissioner spot since Cassius LaFleur went missing last September. She's known for being cutthroat but fair. Well, as fair as you can get in a corrupt system like the NYPD."

"I don't trust 'fair.'" Thorn glanced over her shoulder at the wall of maps, photographs, and articles behind her, tied together within a tangle of thread. Her eyes tracked the red lines between dozens of crimson tacks marking police stations around the city. "Alexis, how many of your new sympathizers have been transferred?"

"Six so far," Alexis said. She reclined back, kicking one leg up and crossing the heel over her knee. "But I think we'll see more. Faust is putting all her people in place. I wouldn't be surprised if fifty, sixty percent of ours get moved around."

"How much does this fuck up what you've been building?"

"It's going to be a pain in the ass for a while," Alexis said. "Some people aren't in a position to help anymore, so I'll have to come up with a new system for how we get information and who can help scramble police communications."

Thorn shook her head. When Gluttony was killed and his Programming faded, almost every person who worked in the NYPD was affected. Cops had woken up in the middle of the night with nightmares of atrocities they'd committed under the Sin's control, leadership suddenly remembered shadow operations they'd never authorized, and hundreds had been fired or institutionalized to shut them up.

The Martyrs had taken advantage of the chaos.

While DuPont recruited ex-cops into the Underground, Alexis had come up with the idea of tracking down the people who were smart enough not to open their mouths and lose their jobs. Using a sophisticated system Holly put together to hide her location, IP address, and even her goddamned voice, Alexis had slowly built up an anonymous network of low-risk operatives in the city—people who didn't know the Martyrs, didn't know the Underground, didn't even know Alexis—but knew there was a supernatural evil at work and wanted to fight it any way they could, even if it just meant feeding the people on the front lines information. Thorn had never had something like this before, and part of her wondered if the Sins had caught on. Her team had been fucking with police communication for a while now…

"How can we know Wrath didn't plant Faust?" she asked.

"Technically, we can't," DuPont said, shrugging, "but there hasn't been any sign Hunt's involved."

"We know she's trying to grab control of the NYPD," Thorn snapped, throwing a hand out as she twisted back around. "She does this every single time Gluttony loses a host."

"She did try," DuPont agreed. "Right at the beginning, and we saw her everywhere, but she's been on the run for months now. As far as we can tell, she hasn't been anywhere near Adeline Faust."

Mulligan leaned forward, and the sensation of his aura shifting made Thorn turn to him. He watched her with a dark curiosity beneath his mop of strawberry-blonde curls. "Is there something we're missing? Have you felt her using her Influence?"

Thorn considered him for a moment, propped her hands on her hips, and shook her head. "No," she admitted, turning back to the wall. "Not enough for something like this."

She looked right at Autumn Hunt, staring back from a printed photograph in the middle of the web. The thing was a mess—a fucking hodgepodge of guesswork and half-baked conspiracy theories—but for the first time in decades, Thorn felt like she was finally closing in. She could almost taste Wrath's blood in the water. How the fuck was she this close and still so goddamned far away?

Thorn took a deep breath as she tore her focus away and attached it to another face—the only other Sin still standing. White-blonde hair. Pale, hungry eyes. That smug, contemptuous look.

"Maybe it isn't Hunt," she said, angry at the very thought and bitter that her desperate attempts to keep their focus on Wrath were clawing at nothing. "But I won't assume there's no Sin involvement. What about Claytor?"

Alexis and Caleb's energy froze, like they'd looked Medusa dead in the face and turned to stone behind Thorn's back. When she spun around, she found Caleb staring at the ground while Alexis's focus sharpened. Her cold eyes locked with Thorn's and held there.

"What about him?" she asked.

"Has Adeline Faust been seen anywhere near him?" Thorn went on, exasperated. "Has she been in the Financial District? Has she attended any of his events? Is there any link between the two of them at all?"

Alexis broke eye contact at last, exchanging a dark look with Caleb. God, every once in a while, Thorn was struck with just how much they looked like their father. They'd been young when Greed had possessed him and sent Puppets to murder their family, Alexis just past her nineteenth birthday and Caleb a few years younger. Over a decade had gone by since then, and Thorn knew at least part of them still hung onto some fragile hope that the man they thought they knew could be saved.

"I can check with Holly," DuPont said, "but as far as I know, he's still MIA."

"Yeah, I haven't seen anything, either," Mulligan said. He glanced over at the Claytor siblings on his left before he turned to Thorn again. "But I'm still pretty new to the case."

Thorn's jaw tightened as she nodded. She hated losing people. Putting a new body in place was easy enough, but reestablishing the rapport and history her operatives built was impossible. Elena Cortez had worked in Greed's circle for three years, and losing her had cost Thorn both an incredible agent and a ton of hard fucking work in getting close to the Sin.

"I need to know everything you can tell me about him," Thorn said. "There has to be *something*."

Mulligan winced and shook his head. "Not much. I got news yesterday that he's been invited to an event at the end of March, but who knows if he'll actually show up. I can get you a report."

"I need it as soon as possible," Thorn said. Then, she paused. "Alexis, Caleb, you're free to go."

Caleb got to his feet, but Alexis's eyes narrowed. "What? Why?"

Thorn's jaw ground together. "Because I need to talk to DuPont and Mulligan about Anton Claytor, and—"

"And you don't think we're mature enough to handle it?" Alexis cut in. Now she stood, but she didn't move toward the door. Instead, she crossed her arms, glaring.

"I didn't say that," Thorn said, throwing her a hard look, and she gestured between Alexis and Caleb. "You two aren't allowed anywhere near the Greed case."

"So I'm not allowed to have an opinion?"

"Claytor—"

"You're going to try to kill him, aren't you?" Alexis cut in. "Destroy Greed's host?"

Caleb's attention snapped to Thorn, and Mulligan's eyebrows shot up, disappearing behind his hair. DuPont's aura shifted as he stepped away from the wall, but Thorn didn't look at him. Her focus locked on Alexis. "Yes. We are."

Alexis's jaw tightened, but when she spoke, there was a forced professionalism Thorn was all too familiar with. It was like looking in a mirror. "We're swapping targets *now*? Why? Wrath's the bigger threat, and we've *never* been this close."

"I know," Thorn responded, working hard to keep the venom out of her voice. She was never good at this part of the management job. Always wearing her rage on the edges of her gloves, more visible than her scars. "I'm not happy about it, either, but Hunt is onto us. Didn't you read the report I sent you?"

Alexis's cheeks went a violent shade of pink that made her platinum hair seem even whiter. That told Thorn all she needed to know. She propped her hands on her hips. "Maybe you should have," she hissed. "If you won't leave, then at least you can sit the fuck down."

Caleb immediately did, plopping quietly back onto the couch, and Alexis glowered at Thorn for a moment longer before taking her chair again. Once they were settled, Mulligan cleared his throat.

"What's a strike against Greed even going to look like?" he asked.

"I don't know yet," Thorn admitted. "The first step is finding him. I want you at that next event. If he's there, gather as much intel as you can."

Mulligan nodded and sat up straight again, throwing his hands behind his head. He glanced at Alexis before he said, "Or... and hear me out on this... we could try to track him."

Thorn's eyes narrowed as Alexis and Caleb's focus swung to Mulligan. DuPont frowned.

"Track him?" he asked. "Like, plant a bug on him?"

"Well, yeah," Mulligan said. "This would be the first time we've seen him in over six months. He could disappear for that long again, right? If we can get a tracking device on him, we can follow him. At the very least, it could show us where he's hiding out now."

Thorn didn't move, didn't speak, as she considered the thought, chewing on it as Caleb shook his head. "Getting a device on him would mean getting *really* close to him," he said.

Mulligan shrugged. "It's worth trying, isn't it?"

"It will be risky," DuPont countered. "If you get caught—"

"He *will* get caught," Alexis said. "I don't know if you forgot, Mulligan, but the Sins can sense you."

"I would have to be clever," Mulligan said, "but if we want to plan a strike to destroy Greed's host, we can't wait for him to come out of hiding in another six months. We need to be proactive."

Alexis scoffed, but Thorn threw her a sharp look, smothering the complaint in her operative's mouth, before she turned back to Mulligan. "*If* we're going to try this," Thorn said, "we need to put a *lot* more thought into it. I'll want TAC patrols, protective measures, everything. Get me all the information you can about this upcoming event."

"Yes, ma'am," Mulligan said.

Thorn turned to Alexis. The other woman stared at her, face still flushed and angry.

"I need you to sort out your assets in the precincts," Thorn said as she walked around to the front of her desk and leaned back against it. "What you built here is fucking impressive—and important. I want to know if we can rely on it for this operation. It could save a lot of Martyr lives."

Thorn could count on one hand the number of times she'd seen this look on Alexis's face—eyes wide, mouth opened in a humbling shock that stole the sourness from her expression. She didn't seem to know what to do with the compliment, and she nodded awkwardly.

"Thorn?" Caleb asked. His voice surprised her. He wasn't one for drawing any unnecessary attention to himself. "Is there anything I can do to help?"

The muscles in Thorn's face softened, grateful at least one of Anton Claytor's children wasn't constantly trying to fight her on everything.

"We still need to watch for signs Lust has attached to a new host," she said, but then a thought occurred to her. She bit the inside of her cheek. "Though… your apartment is on the Upper West Side, isn't it?"

"Yes, ma'am."

Thorn nodded. "Keep an eye out for the new Virtue, too. That's where Darius and his team are looking, and you're already established there. If you see anything, report it to Mackenzie, got it?" The apples of Caleb's cheeks tinted pink as he nodded. Thorn did, too, and she looked back at the rest of the room. "I think that's it. Get out of here. Except you, DuPont."

As the Gray Unit left, DuPont drew further in. When the door snapped shut, Thorn asked, "Is Darius's team all set to start looking for this new Virtue?"

"Almost. Mackenzie and Nicholas are still arguing over schedules, but everything else is good to go."

Thorn's brows furrowed. "And TAC has additional patrols ready?"

"We will," DuPont said, crossing his arms again. "Once the schedules are sorted. I need to know what days they'll be out so I can organize my people accordingly. With Mackenzie behind the wheel, it's been a challenge. Routine isn't exactly her strong suit."

Thorn rolled her eyes. "McKay would be ten minutes late to her own goddamned funeral if it were up to her."

DuPont laughed. "She's the only recon driver left. The research team has nearly doubled our leads, so the rest of her people are swamped."

Thorn sighed. Nicholas might not have had Diligence etched into his soul anymore, but she was starting to think it was coded into his DNA, too. "Well, do we know *anything* about when they'll head out?"

"Their first day is Saturday," DuPont said, and Thorn made a mental note to make sure *she* was in town that day, too. "But after that, we're holding off a week because of the wedding."

"Ah, that's right," Thorn murmured with a nod. "I forgot about the wedding."

DuPont chuckled, his mouth turning into a charming, crooked smile. "How did you *forget?* Everyone's going to be there."

A knot twisted in Thorn's stomach. She pushed away from the desk again and moved behind it to where huge maps of New York City's boroughs loomed over her like a dark cloud. A bittersweet grip wrapped around her stomach.

"Not me," Thorn answered at last. "I have way too much shit on my plate."

Like finding Patience, destroying Wrath, and breaking free from this immortal curse at last. Then, maybe she *could* care about things like weddings.

Sparkie crawled onto her shoulder as she considered Lincoln Square and homed in on the exact corner where she'd almost killed Autumn Hunt, where Darius had felt that tell-tale pull…

Virtues were born in close proximity to the Sins they were meant to destroy. It didn't get much fucking closer than this.

CHAPTER FOUR

Snowflakes as white and light as scraps of gauze floated from the sky, crashing into Thorn's visor and clouding her vision as she rode through Lower Manhattan. Frigid air tore through the seams in her kevlar bike jacket and added to the icy pressure of human energy around her. Men and women, tucked safely inside their heated sedans and taxi cabs, watched her through the windows, undoubtedly grateful they weren't stuck on a motorcycle in a storm like this.

Broadway narrowed as construction pinched two lanes into one. The sensation of an aura drawing in on Thorn's left caught her attention, and she slammed on her brakes just as a car cut directly in front of her. Thorn's tires spun on the wet asphalt. She jerked to the side, barely managing to slide to a stop and avoid a collision. Behind her, a vehicle laid on its horn. She glanced over her shoulder to see the driver squish a fat middle finger against his windshield. Thorn ran her palm across her visor to clear the water built up there and swore.

God, she hated the snow.

It wasn't because of the cold, or the damp, or the dumbass drivers with bad attitudes and short fuses. Her accelerated healing meant it took longer for extreme weather to affect her—a goddamned blessing in a world where extreme weather had been the new normal for decades now. Slick roads and black ice were nothing compared to the real threats Thorn faced on a daily basis. In fact, it wasn't about what the snow was or what it did at all.

It was because all Thorn could see in the frozen flurries and white skies was Donovan's face—battered, bruised, broken—right before Autumn Hunt buried a blade in his back.

Thorn's heart plunged at the memory. She twisted and merged into traffic, turning as she headed northbound on Trinity Place. A cold fire ignited in her chest, resentful that she wasn't here for Wrath.

The snow fell harder, making its way between skyscrapers as Thorn weaved in and out of slow traffic and parked cars, searching for a sliver of space to squeeze her bike into so she could go the rest of the way on foot. When she pulled between two vehicles on the side of the road, a huddle of people shuffled by, peering at her from the gaps between scarves and beanies. She shut the engine down and drew her helmet off. Brisk air rushed against her face as Thorn looked down the street. A nondescript building jutted thirty stories into the sky.

In just over one month, Anton Claytor would rear his indulgent, blonde head right fucking here.

The fundraising event was for Mayor Richmond Bently. Wolfe and his team had found more of the good mayor's same old bullshit: fancy dinners, wealthy donors, and a promise to clean up the city, which really meant cleansing the impoverished and underserved from Manhattan proper so they couldn't mess up the city's "image." Claytor was at the top of the guest list, and if he actually showed, this would be his first public appearance since Gluttony's destruction last summer. Clearly, Wrath wasn't the only one afraid of the Martyrs right now.

Thorn swung her leg off her bike and locked her helmet to her handlebars, careful to ensure it wouldn't fill with snow. She should've taken one of the new coupes, but they made it so fucking hard to move within the city. Thorn pulled her hood on and tucked her hair into it. The wet strands clung to her throat, and Sparkie shuddered inside her jacket. He pressed his body as close to Thorn's sternum as he could, his scales warm against her bare skin. The two drew in a synchronized breath as Thorn headed down Trinity Place.

The Mezzanine was one of the longest-standing event spaces in the Financial District. It had exchanged ownership several times in the decades since it had opened but always remained predictably the same: expensive, extravagant, and a magnet for people like Bently who wanted to make a big show and look great doing it. The Sins had never used it—not as far as Thorn knew, at least—but it had gained a reputation in the last seventy years as one of the to-go places for celebrities and politicians alike.

Traffic slowed, and Thorn hopped across the street, finding reprieve beneath a network of scaffolding lining the building. On the ground floor, high-end boutiques demanded all the attention, but around the corner, tucked inside a narrow alley, the street-level reception was masterfully masked behind an intricate, wrought-iron door. She tried to open it. Locked.

Thorn frowned, stepped back, and looked up at the building. The Mezzanine commanded over six thousand square feet of the second story, and most of those six thousand feet were empty at eleven in the morning. From where she stood, Thorn could feel a couple of cold auras moving about in back rooms with the busy energy of people at work.

More auras moved on the ground. Pedestrians walked along the sidewalk, drawn to the scaffolding to avoid the snow now sticking to the open street. Thorn strode along the building, scanning storefronts. A jewelry shop. Home goods. High fashion. She paused, considering the sleek dresses on sickly mannequins.

This would work.

An elegant tone chimed in the back of the shop as Thorn entered. A pair of well-dressed, well-groomed, well-raised women glanced up from a cashier's podium at the center of the room. Their flawless faces fell into forced civility as they took in the state of this dark smudge inside their perfectly poised establishment. Eyes traveled up her body, taking in the damp hair, armored bike jacket, and scuffed boots with a professionalism that barely managed to hide the distaste on their faces. Thorn knew she didn't look like the kind of person who could afford something off the sale rack here. She also didn't fucking care. She pulled her hood off, flashed them a smile, and put on her warmest voice.

"Good morning," Thorn said.

"Morning," one of the women responded, her tone a courteous customer-service falsetto that Thorn knew was higher pitched than was normal for her. "How can I help you?"

This was clearly the senior associate, based on the way her partner busied herself with her phone behind the counter. She was also tall. The heels made it even more pronounced. Thorn stood at five foot nine and rarely had to look *up* at other women, but she did now. Her smile widened.

"I'm a speaker at an event in the Mezzanine next month," she said, "and I'm looking for a dress. Most of my fellows work with larger brands, but I prefer supporting smaller businesses like this one." She gestured around the room. "May I see your evening wear selection?"

The tiniest details betrayed the saleswoman's surprise. Heavily shadowed eyelids opened wider. Painted lips twitched downward. A quick blink. When she recovered, all pretense melted from her expression.

"Of course! Right this way, ma'am."

She led Thorn to the back of the shop, which was much larger inside than it looked from its front windows. While they walked, she asked Thorn what style and colors she preferred, what length she had in mind, and if there were any particular details she wanted to see. Thorn answered with a candid casualness as her eyes scanned the room. Beady camera lenses lay hiding behind black, glass orbs, and a subtle door along the far wall bore a sign saying, "no public restrooms." Thorn suspected as much.

"Here are our formal dresses," the associate said, opening her palms to a display larger than Thorn had expected. "Based on your taste, I recommend looking at the Cassidy Yates collection to the left."

"Thank you," Thorn said. "And the dressing rooms are…?"

"In the far corner," the woman said, indicating a direction over Thorn's shoulder. "They are open, so please, help yourself."

"Excellent, thank you."

The saleswoman smiled, flaunting rows of straight teeth that were a little too white. "Of course. Call if you need anything."

She strode off, her heels clicking on the tile. As soon as she was gone, Thorn spun to the display, grabbed a handful of Yates evening dresses without looking at them, and made her way to the dressing rooms.

Like most expensive boutiques, there were only two separate stalls, both large and well-lit. Thorn took the one in the back, locked herself inside, and hung the dresses on a hook. The second she unzipped her jacket, Sparkie scurried out of her shirt and to her shoulder. Then, both of them looked at a ceiling vent in the corner.

It took all of sixty seconds for Thorn to stand on the bench, reach the grate, and pry it open wide enough for Sparkie to dive inside. The part of Thorn's consciousness that she shared with her Familiar was momentarily thrown into darkness. She closed her eyes. As Sparkie's adjusted to the light, she could visualize the ducts—feel hot metal against her stomach, smell the musky odor of recycled air, and hear his claws scratching against aluminum as he headed upward.

Thorn sighed and opened her eyes again. He wouldn't make it to the Mezzanine event space on the second level for a couple of minutes. She glanced through the gowns, calculating how long she could pretend she was trying on clothes before she drew attention. One of them slid off the hanger, and Thorn crouched down to grab it. The black fabric glided between her fingertips, smooth and lightweight. She stood up and held it in front of her body as she looked into the mirror.

It was stunning—a sleek, floor-length piece with a plunging neckline, open back, and slits up each side that would tease at her legs from ankle to thigh. Thorn ran her left hand down it, pressing the dress against her stomach. She could feel the tight edges of her scars pull, and the *Peccostium* tingled at the sensation of pressure. Sparkie found the Mezzanine's main hall, and Thorn slipped the dress back onto its hanger and returned it to the hook.

Her Familiar was on the third floor, peering down from a vaulted ceiling through a two-tiered chandelier to the ground below. Not much for visibility. He pushed against the vent, but it was locked securely in place, so he darted down the shaft to another for a better view.

The reception area entered through a stairway in the center of a vast room, easily large enough for three hundred people. Banquet tables dressed in navy linens surrounded the venue. Thorn had been right. The auras she'd felt belonged to a couple of uniformed staff performing prep duties while they danced along to music blaring from speakers mounted to the walls. The lights were off, but it didn't matter. Massive, floor-to-ceiling windows allowed plenty in. They faced westward, and Thorn imagined she could see the One World Trade Tower if the snow wasn't falling so hard. A full kitchen and bar pressed against the opposite wall, and a hallway that Thorn suspected led to more rooms and the emergency exit. That wasn't ideal. She never liked getting her people stuck in a situation with only a couple of ways to get the fuck out.

Sparkie darted away to check just as Thorn felt an aura approaching from the cashier's podium. The woman who helped her.

"Fuck," she murmured. Sparkie spun a complete one-eighty and started rushing back the way he'd come.

Just then, Thorn's phone rang. It vibrated against her leg, and she dug into the satchel cinched to her thigh to pull it out. Her eyes went wide at the name flashing up at her. Jay Coons. She hadn't seen him in months. Sparkie hit the first drop and leapt into it, plummeting toward the second story as Thorn weighed her options. She needed a little more time.

"Hello?" she answered.

The associate paused, her cold energy hovering just outside the door with an arm outstretched as though she were about to knock.

"Hey, Teagan," Jay said. "Wow, I gotta say, I'm surprised you answered."

Thorn propped a hand on her hip and shook her head, staring at the door where the saleswoman was still waiting, probably eager to tune into a conversation she had no business hearing. That would save Jay from some sharp words. Instead, Thorn said, in the most neutral tone she could muster, "It's been busy. How are you?"

"How am I?" Jay repeated, confused. He'd dealt with Thorn's bullshit long enough, even under the ruse of Teagan Love, that he was starting to see through it. "I don't have time for this. Look, can we meet up? I've got to talk to you."

"How important—"

"Jesus, Tea, can you meet up or not?"

Thorn bit her tongue and wondered if she should have chosen the sales associate. With a sigh, she nodded. "Where do you want to go? Michelangelo's?"

"That works. I'm in the area already, so…"

A heavy quiet fell. The woman still lingered outside the door. Sparkie had made it to the vent, and he could see her over the divider between the waiting room and the rest of the store. Fuck, Thorn had to get her out of here if she was going to open the grate again without getting caught.

"Sounds good," she said. "I can be there in twenty minutes. I just have to check out."

That did the trick. At the mention of money, a grin brightened the saleswoman's face, and she twisted around to return to the register. Thorn rolled her eyes as Jay said, "I'll get us a table." He hung up without a goodbye.

Thorn pulled her phone back and looked down at the screen, black and empty. Then, she helped Sparkie from the vent, grabbed the dress that had fallen from its hanger, and made her way out. When she paid, the senior associate was all smiles, but her cohort watched Thorn curiously, like she was wondering how the hell she was going to get this thing home on the back of a motorcycle in a snowstorm.

———

Half an hour later, Thorn walked into Michelangelo's to find Jay sitting in the back. If it wasn't for the familiar aura that Thorn had grown to know so well, she might not have recognized him. A thick, black beanie covered his auburn hair, and he wore a light blue jacket instead of the dark colors she usually saw him in. He stared at his phone, his knee nervously bouncing under the table. When the door opened with a flurry of wind and snow, Jay's blue eyes moved up. They caught Thorn, and his jaw clenched. He didn't stand up to greet her as she walked across the diner and pulled her hood down.

"Did you order?" she asked.

"No."

Thorn's brows twitched upward as she took her seat and snatched a laminated sheet off the table. She had never understood Jay's attraction to this place. Even the menu reeked of the new age, toxic positivity bullshit Michelangelo's had become known for. Meaningless quotes in

meticulous, hand-drawn calligraphy lined the margins, saying things like, *"no bad vibes,"* *"trust the process,"* or Thorn's
personal favorite, *"you are a gift."* She frowned as a waitress
came to their table.

"What can I get started for you?"

"Just a coffee," Thorn said, handing her the menu.

Jay nodded. "Same."

The waitress wandered away, and for the few minutes it
took her to return with two steaming mugs, Jay and Thorn
sat in a silence so dense Thorn could feel it in her chest. A
couple of years ago, when their arrangement was still fresh
and the sex still fun and exciting, Thorn had looked forward
to time with Jay. It had been easy. Straightforward. A god
damned reprieve from the trauma of the Underground. She
could forget herself for a moment—get lost in a warm body
and trivial conversation about literally anything that didn't
have to do with Thorn or her fucked up life.

Now, though, things were broken. She'd made sure of
that, with the fighting, the disappearing, the holes punched
in walls. He didn't smile when he saw her anymore. Instead,
there was contempt behind his hard expression.

A bite of pain pinched in Thorn's gut. She'd outstayed
her welcome in his life. Lingered too long, tainted his spirit
with the Wrath attached to hers. The damage was done.

Thorn sighed and leaned forward. "Look—"

"No," Jay cut in. He groaned and ran his hands down
his face. Reddish stubble scraped against his fingertips.
"Don't. I've been working myself up for this conversation,
and I've gotta make it fast. I'm technically working right
now, and my boss will fucking kill me if I fall behind."

He indicated a logo embroidered on his jacket. Mercourier Delivery Services in bold text with tiny wings on either side.

Thorn frowned. "What about The Cross?"

"I'm still there," Jay said, "but my rent went up, and bar-
tending wasn't enough, so I picked up a side gig a couple of
months ago. You'd know that if you ever came around." His

face darkened, cheeks going an angry shade of pink before he waved the bitterness away. "Anyway, that's not the point. Tea, I can't do this anymore."

He gestured between them. Thorn's heart skipped, but her eyes narrowed.

"*This* isn't anything."

"It is to me." Jay's voice tightened with emotion, and he cleared his throat to loosen it. "I don't know if you were fucking around with other people, and honestly, I don't wanna know, but I wasn't. I didn't want anyone else. For a long time now, it's only been you."

He paused, like he was waiting for something, *hoping* for something, but Thorn's lips pressed together and didn't open. The hope dissolved, and Jay sighed. "But I can't wait for you anymore 'cause it's pretty obvious you're never gonna feel the same way."

Thorn simply shook her head. Jay nodded, his neck rigid and tight.

"So. That's it," he said. He grabbed the coffee, still untouched on the table, so hard that his fingers went white. "I figured you were ghosting me, but I needed to know it was really over. I can't wait around or have you calling me and fucking up my day. I just can't."

Thorn drew in a slow breath, pulling her shoulders back as she lifted her mug and brought it to her lips. "Okay."

Jay paused, staring at her, before he shook his head. "We've been sleeping together for almost five years, and that's all you've got to say?"

"What else do you *expect* me to say?" Thorn snapped, her breath casting ripples over the surface of her coffee. She watched him with sharp eyes, and the sting of hurt that flashed across his face was enough to make Thorn's chest ache.

"Okay," Jay repeated, mimicking her, mocking her, as he pushed his chair back and got to his feet. He threw a handful of crumpled bills on the table. "Coffee's on me."

Then he left, stomping out the door and disappearing

into the storm outside. Thorn's gaze followed him through the windows until his aura, cold but somehow less so than the rest of this city, faded away. She turned back to her mug with a sigh, surprised at the feeling of loss blossoming in the emptiness between her lungs.

It was better this way, she thought as she finished her coffee, gathered her things, and made her way out. Sparkie pressed against her heart as she walked into the snow. It was better to be alone, to avoid distractions, so she could focus on her work. Romance was a complication. One of the worst. She'd had to remind herself of that a lot lately.

The storm had nearly covered her bike by the time Thorn got back to it. She brushed off the seat and threw a leg over. After she put her helmet on, she pulled out her phone and paused. Snow fell harder than ever, and her eye was drawn to a figure walking toward Michelangelo's on the other side of the street. A man, tall and handsome, wearing a navy peacoat. His blonde hair was covered in white flakes, like they were magnetized to him. He seemed to sense Thorn's gaze, because he suddenly looked her way, catching her in his piercing, blue eyes. He paused, and he smiled. Dimples pinched into his cheeks, perfectly symmetrical.

Thorn didn't smile back. Instead, she turned to her phone, typed a quick message, and hit send. Then, she slipped the device into her satchel without waiting for a response. As she pulled into traffic, tires sliding in the slush building up, the man watched her ride by.

"This new Virtue better like the snow."

Darius smiled as Thorn's text lit up his screen, a welcome break in a morning of frustrations.

"Jesus, doesn't *anyone* in this bloody city know how to drive?" Mackenzie groaned. She slammed her head onto the steering wheel, blasting the horn at a car that had run a red light to cut them off. Madison shifted uncomfortably in the back seat, and Kit sat beside her, clutching the handle above his door like it would save him from being thrown around if Mackenzie decided to hop onto the sidewalk and plow her way past traffic.

Darius typed back, *I hope not. Mackenzie might run them over.*

The Irishwoman swore again, and Darius looked to the dashboard screen, which displayed the map and itinerary she and Nicholas had put together for this first trip into the city. They'd barely made it through a quarter of their planned stops, and it was already noon. At this rate, they wouldn't get home until midnight.

"Please, for the love of whatever gods are running this shit show, tell me you feel something," Mackenzie moaned.

"Just a swarm of energy up ahead," Darius said. "I think there was an accident…"

Sirens blared around the corner, like the universe thought this whole thing was funny. Mackenzie pressed her face against her window and sighed. The heat from her skin created immediate condensation, and a halo of fog circled her head.

"This is supposed to be the storm of the year," Kit commented. "It's gonna get worse."

"Ugh, don't tell me that," Mackenzie said. Kit shrugged, and Madison let out a nervous chuckle. Darius looked back at the map on the dash.

"Seems like we can turn at—"

"I know," Mackenzie snapped. She tapped her fingernails on the wheel, and her tongue piercing clacked against the back of her teeth to the same rhythm. Ten minutes passed by—minutes that felt like hours, punctuated by Mackenzie's percussive noise and the occasional groan or colorful adjective—before the road opened. She jerked out of the gridlock.

"Fuckin' finally," the Irishwoman grumbled. She poked around their navigation terminal, swerving a little in her distraction. "Jesus, we're so behind. Wolfe is gonna lose his shit."

Darius cast a glance back to Madison and Kit. Both re-cruits sat awkwardly still, and Darius tried to pass them a comforting smile. Kit didn't return it—he looked every bit as worked up as Mackenzie—but Madison did, and she raised her brows as though to say she was having a good time despite the setbacks. Darius turned to the front of the car, looked down at his phone, and sighed as he put it away.

The early afternoon passed with the same monotonous disappointment the morning had. Heavy snow, slow traffic, an impatient driver, and zero signs of the Virtuous pull that had drawn them here in the first place. By the time two p.m. came around, Mackenzie was more frustrated than ever, and Darius knew they were getting nowhere.

"I think we should call it," he said.

"Thank fuck," Mackenzie said, but she didn't sound thankful. Her tongue piercing slammed into her teeth as rapidly as ever as she checked the clock for the tenth time in two minutes. "We can try again next week."

"The wedding's next week," Madison said.

Mackenzie groaned and blew out a lungful of air, filling her cheeks. When they deflated, they seemed hollow. "That's right. Two weeks, then. Better than dealing with all of *this.*" She waved her hands in front of the windshield like she was batting away a swarm of gnats.

Darius smirked. "Want me to drive? So we don't have to deal with all of *this?*"

He mimicked Mackenzie's wild flailing, aiming at the Irishwoman herself. For the first time in hours, she cracked a grin and laughed. It opened a valve, releasing the tension in the car so vividly that Darius could feel relief rush in to take its place. In the back seat, both Madison and Kit's auras palpably relaxed as Mackenzie playfully punched Darius in the shoulder.

"I'm fine, ya jerk," she said with a wink. "Guess I need to get out of the Underground more often, huh? I'm out of practice dealing with the masses of morons in this city."

"The snow doesn't help," Darius said.

Mackenzie nodded without acknowledging the out and reached across to the terminal display. "Let's get the hell outta here," she said. "But first, I've had way too much goddamned coffee. Anyone know where the closest public bathroom's at?"

"The pharmacy on Broadway and 72nd," Kit said.

"Ah, I knew there was a good reason I brought you along, Garfield."

Thanks to the storm, street parking was worse than usual, so Mackenzie double parked up 72nd. She threw on a ratty sweatshirt, zipping it up to her throat as Kit grabbed his jacket, too.

"Who else is coming?" she asked.

"I'm good," Darius said.

"Yeah, me too," Madison agreed.

Mackenzie glanced between them, her eyes pinching together in a suppressed grin. "Keep the car nice and hot for us, yeah?" Her expression barely held back her joy at the situation as she and Kit left. The pair rushed up the street, and Darius watched as they disappeared into the snow. He didn't turn toward the back of the car until their auras faded.

"So," he said, "how do you like your first Virtue scouting mission?"

"It's… interesting!" Madison pulled a strand of hair behind her ear and leaned forward. "I didn't really know what to expect."

Darius laughed. "Honestly, neither did I."

Madison's lips pushed out in a delicate frown, and she shook her head. "But I thought you'd found three Virtues already?"

"Just two," Darius said, "and not like this. Every single recon mission I've done in New York has been a bust. Up until last week, I'd never felt a Virtue here."

"Ooh, that's exciting!" Madison said. "I'm glad I get to be a part of it."

She smiled, and he returned the gesture but said nothing.

He glanced over his shoulder, hoping to get a sense of Mackenzie's aura returning through the snow.

"It's a bummer we'll miss next week, though," Madison went on.

"Yeah, Nicholas and I tried to find another day we could come out," Darius said, "but half of the Underground is going to be busy getting ready for the wedding anyway, including him, and he's pretty sure everyone will be hungover the day after."

Madison's smile cracked to a grin. "Oh, it's going to be *that* kind of party."

Darius laughed. "Apparently."

"So, do you have someone special you're bringing along, or are all those dance classes going to go to waste?"

"Nah," Darius said, but he paused when he looked up to see Madison's eyes locked onto him, her cheeks a hopeful blush of pink. Whatever he was going to say got stuck in his throat, and he cleared it as he desperately searched for a way out of this conversation. In the distance, he could finally sense Mackenzie and Kit on their way back. "Uh, no one special, really. Just Chris."

The hope in Madison's expression shifted, and her eyes narrowed. Before she could pry, the driver's side door opened, and Mackenzie dipped back into the vehicle.

"Bollocks, it's cold," she said. Kit climbed in behind her as Mackenzie sniffled and rubbed the underside of her rosy nose against the back of her hand. "Everyone good?"

She glanced into the rearview mirror and then to Darius, pausing on him with her lip pinched sheepishly between her teeth. When everyone confirmed, and Darius rolled his eyes with a smile, she shifted the car into drive, and they were off. Darius grabbed his phone out, halfway hoping for a response from Thorn but not surprised when he didn't have one. Instead, he navigated to Chris's contact and drafted a new text.

"So... I need a HUGE favor..."

He hit send.

CHAPTER FIVE

The overhead lights shut off, and the darkness was disorienting. If not for the glowing warmth of human auras dotted around him, the sounds of quiet whispering from distant corners, and the feeling of the ladder he was holding in his palms, Darius could have easily gotten lost.

"All right," Stevie Arias said from the center of the room, "let's turn them on!"

All at once, an intricate, laced webbing of warm, golden orbs came to life. They draped from the vaulted ceilings, rolling overhead in graceful waves. Darius marveled at the sight. A stunning sea of floating lights filled the courtyard with a romantic ambiance.

"Can we raise them a little?" Raquel asked. She stood to Stevie's right, arms crossed as she looked around. "I want it to feel like we're outside."

"We can," Stevie said, "but the higher we go, the more likely we'll get reflections off the ceiling. Wanna give it a try?"

Raquel bit her cheek. "Yeah. I do. Is that okay?"

"Of course!" Stevie flashed a smile, looked out at the room, and shouted. "Let's pull it up another… twelve inches?" She glanced at Raquel, who nodded. "Twelve inches!"

From above, John groaned. Darius looked up the ladder he was bracing against the wall to see him unraveling a length of rope from a hook bolted to the concrete. All around the courtyard, other pairs of Martyrs with their own ladders did the same, and the network of string lights shimmied upward bit by bit.

"Stop!" Raquel called. "Right there! That's perfect!"

"You're sure?" Stevie asked.

"She's sure!" John called, his voice echoing. "Can we get down now?"

A chorus of laughter erupted around the room. Raquel propped her hands on her hips, tilting her head as she threw John a playful glare.

"Yes," she said. Then she spun, looking at everyone else, too. "Thank you all so much!"

People shuffled, warm energy climbing down from heights just tall enough to be dizzying. Stevie turned on the main lights again, and the room lit up. The ladder shook as John descended, so Darius tightened his grip. Behind them, Raquel's voice murmured in the distance before her aura moved their way. By the time John's feet hit the tile, she was at Darius's side.

"I'm sorry, guys," she said, taking in a deep breath. "Am I being too picky?"

"Nah," Darius said. "You're totally fine."

"Yeah, don't sweat it," John agreed. "You only get married once. Every light bulb better be in the exact right place."

He stuck his tongue out, squinting up at the ceiling while he mimed pinching one of the glass orbs between his fingers. Raquel rolled her eyes with a smile.

"All right!" Stevie's voice drew their attention, and auras all around the space spun to face her. "We're done for the day. Let's pack it up."

The room buzzed as Martyrs began putting the cleaning, maintenance, and work supplies back in boxes. Darius pulled the ladder off the wall and started folding it up. Raquel moved to help him, but John wrapped an arm around her shoulders, pulled her tight to his side, and planted a brotherly kiss on the top of her head.

"You deserve to have the best wedding ever, okay?" he told her. "Now get outta here. We've got this."

She grabbed his hand. "You sure?" John just raised his brows in response, and she laughed. "Okay. Thank you."

"Any time."

Raquel drew away, thanked Stevie again, and headed down the stairwell beside the elevator. John came to Darius's side and helped him secure the ladder. For a moment, they were quiet. Then, John cleared his throat.

"Hey, uh," he began, and his energy shifted awkwardly. Darius looked up to see his face set into a serious expression, blue eyes fixated on the strap he was tightening. "I wanted to say thanks."

Darius frowned. John still didn't look at him. "For what?"

"For convincing Chris to go to the wedding," John answered. His voice was neutral. Too neutral. "Raquel was super worried she wouldn't. It means a lot to her."

Darius paused. John latched the final security clip without glancing in his direction. At last, Darius shook his head. "John, you know it's not—"

"I know," John cut in, facing Darius at last. The neutrality broke. "And honestly, man, even if it was, it's not my business. Just… thanks. For being there. For Raquel. For Chris. For me."

He cracked a smile—a smile that looked way too small on his face—and held out his hand.

Darius took it. John's fingers were strong around his palm, and Darius held tight. "Of course, man."

A second passed, and John cleared his throat again as he nodded and pulled away.

"Anyway, now that *that's* out of the way." John broke the tension with a smooth chuckle and grabbed one end of the ladder. His voice flooded with warmth again. "You wanna help me with this?"

They dragged the ladder across the room and piled it alongside a half dozen others by the elevator. Stevie's maintenance staff had pulled their gear into a perfectly organized pile, but a few stray boxes that belonged in other parts of the Underground lay scattered around the wrought iron tables, full of random tools and supplies. Darius grabbed one of these, read "sculpture and pottery" on the lid, and headed in that direction. He opened the door to a dark, empty room, adjusted the box in his arms, and flipped the switch with his elbow.

Like the rest of the art studios, this one was an organized disaster. Cain had ripped out the old carpeting and left the concrete floor bare, which was already stained in a vibrant, colorful mosaic of spilled glaze. To the left, four pottery wheels sat in a grid beside a tall cabinet full of tightly sealed blocks of clay. A cylindrical kiln took over the entire back corner, standing out like a mechanical monster next to a rack of fired and finished pieces: vases with cracked varnish, mugs painted with blooming red flowers, and decorative plates with names of the dead etched into them. To the right, two sculpting workstations covered the wall. A storage room door had been left ajar behind Cain's desk, and Darius made his way toward it. When he pulled it open, he froze on the spot.

There was a peacock in the closet.

It dominated the space. Carved from black marble, it looked like a shadow. It had been crafted with its tail flared out, making the whole thing five feet tall and wide. Darius gawked as he put the box on the ground for a better look.

It was delicately carved in intricate, immaculate detail. Every vane in every feather stood out distinct from the rest, and even though there was no color, carefully chiseled lines rendered the patterns in stunning monochrome. Darius was struck with the urge to stroke its back to see if it was as soft as it looked. He reached out to do so when someone cleared their throat behind him.

"I see you've found my latest masterpiece," Cain said.

Darius jumped, his heart pounding. He turned to see the old Forgotten Envy standing a healthy distance back. Cain's fingers pressed into narrow pockets in his slacks, and a smile stretched across his face. Darius shook his head, scoffed, and gestured into the closet.

"This is amazing."

"It is, isn't it?" Cain said. "It was certainly the most difficult of the four to construct. I'm very proud of it."

"Four?" Darius asked, and when he looked again, he realized the peacock wasn't the only marble statue tucked away in here. A fox peered up at Darius with blank, black eyes from the floor beside it. Overhead, a macaque clung to a marble branch. And, held aloft by a thin metal bar, a perfectly carved bat hovered just out of Darius's reach.

He shook his head, and Cain answered the question he hadn't voiced aloud.

"The Familiars of the Martyr founders we have lost," he said. "I finished constructing their new home in our memorial chamber and was just about to move them."

"Do you need help?" Darius asked.

Cain's smile widened. "I would love that."

Darius didn't turn out to be much help. Cain was strong enough to move the statues single-handedly, and Darius's most useful skill was guiding a large, flatbed dolly through the studio while Cain pushed it from behind. While most of the alcoves had been converted into places for Martyrs to create and explore, one had been turned into something else entirely.

A place to mourn.

Of all the areas Cain had remodeled, this was his greatest achievement. He'd torn out the entire exterior wall, replacing it with retractable glass panels and black curtains, which were always kept open just enough to walk a funeral procession through. Right now, they were wider, making it easier for them to pull the dolly in.

"Just up the middle," Cain directed from behind the statues.

A central aisle ran the length of the room, with black carpet set against pearly, white tiles. The far wall was paneled in translucent, alabaster slabs that glowed from behind, casting a warm, ethereal light across the podium and upraised dais. Cain had obscured most of the ceiling with black drapes, and two chandeliers lit either half of the room. They hung heavy with obsidian shards and bright crystal, positioned above circular benches adorned with black and white glass flowers.

They reached the dais, and Darius stopped to look around. His focus lingered on the right and left walls. Cain had installed massive, granite plates upon them, and over the last few months, he'd carved the names of every Martyr lost into the stone. There were hundreds. Friends, children, parents—entire family lines, completely wiped out. Darius wondered how many more would be added. He wondered when it would be his.

"I have been planning this display for decades," Cain said as he stepped up to Darius's side, and Darius turned to face him. Cain reached one hand out and tenderly stroked the peacock's head, running his finger along the underside of its beak almost out of habit, like he'd done it hundreds of times before. "It was going to be a fountain at the center of my garden, but I had never gotten around to doing it. It never felt right. Maybe they just wanted to come home."

Cain glanced around the Underground, and Darius didn't miss the bitterness sneaking into his tone.

"What were they like?" Darius asked, indicating the four stone Familiars with a gentle nod. The hardness melted from Cain's jaw.

"Like family," he said. He moved back to the dolly and started with the peacock, heaving the thing around with a remarkable strength that looked wholly unnatural coming from someone of Cain's slender stature. "We argued and we bickered and we didn't always see eye to eye. But we also loved. Fell in love. Defended and fought for one another… until we fought *against* one another in the end."

With a grunt, he hoisted the peacock onto the dais and stepped back to admire it.

"Alexander was the oldest of us," Cain said, holding a palm out to the bird. "He had been alive over eighteen hundred years by the time Envy abandoned me, and I would not have survived that transition without his support and guidance. He was born before the time of Christ, and in fact, he claimed he met the man on more than one occasion." Darius's eyes widened, and Cain laughed. "Though, of course, I could never be sure which of Alex's stories were true and which were not. He was, after all, a product of Pride."

Cain shifted the peacock to the back of the dais and moved onto the macaque.

"Sadik was a gentle soul," he said. "He was under a Sin's control for far longer than the rest of us combined—two hundred years at least. Most of what we understand about how the relationship between Sin and host functions, we learned from him."

"What do you mean?" Darius asked.

Cain shrugged as he positioned the monkey to the left of the peacock, where it looked out at the room with a dark, haunted scowl. "Over time, he became more aware of Gluttony and realized that Sin and host do not share thoughts… When the two are linked, the only thing they can take from each other is emotion. A Sin cannot tap into what you know, but it can feed on what you feel."

Darius nodded, chewing on that thought, as Cain lifted the fox and the bat together.

"Judith and Yin," he said, indicating each animal respectively. "Without these two extraordinary women, the Martyrs would have ceased to exist. Both were at one point possessed by Greed and, in the course of their lives, amassed the fortunes that allowed us to build… *anything*. I never thought they got enough credit for that.

"Judith was an adept businesswoman," he said as he positioned the fox to the right. Then, he set the bat in the center, hovering over them all. "And Yin, a fierce warrior. We lost her first."

He turned Yin's Familiar to face outward. Glistening light from the chandeliers caught the marble, highlighting gold veins in the black stone. The webbing in its wings was shaved so thin it was nearly translucent.

"You said you fought against one another in the end," Darius began, looking from each marble face to the next before he landed on Cain to find his eyes locked onto him. "What happened?"

"Wrath returned."

A hush fell over them, and the memorial chamber seemed darker. Cain took a slow breath and stood back as though to admire his work, but his bright, empty eyes were distant. "The Martyrs were thriving," he said solemnly. "We had finished building the Underground and amassed an army—hundreds of people. The Sins were scattered and disconnected from each other. Their power was… unfocused. For a while, things looked good for us. For fifteen years, we were happy. Then Alan felt Wrath's Influence."

Alan's name came out of Cain's mouth like it was attached to a stone, sinking through the water.

"It was the first time he'd sensed the Sin since his escape seventeen years earlier," he said. "Naturally, we hunted it down. Sins are least powerful in the first year of a new possession, and we wanted to destroy the host early. In hindsight, we should have known. It was easy, as though Wrath *wanted* to be found. The moment Alan recognized her, it was over."

"Thorn," Darius said.

Cain nodded. "Wrath taunted him, so *proud* of the pain it was causing. Alan insisted we save her, insisted that she *could* be saved. A seventeen-year possession was unheard of and indicated that the host and the Sin were not harmonious. He believed we could get through to her, and for years, we tried, but Wrath disappeared again. For the first decade, it focused on bringing the other six together. Their power quickly grew. The next time we saw Wrath, it was ten years into its possession and much stronger. We fought. We lost. Martyrs died. Others were kidnapped and tortured. Alex proposed then that maybe we needed to free Thorn another way—by killing her like we had intended to before we knew who she was. Alan wouldn't hear it.

"It went like that for another year," Cain continued with a sigh. He stepped away from the dais and sat on one of the circular benches. Darius followed as though led on a string and took a spot beside him. "We would attack, lose people, retreat. Then, Yin was killed."

"By Thorn?" Darius asked.

"By Wrath," Cain corrected. "We were all devastated, but Alex was furious. He and Alan fought like I had never seen before, and the Martyrs fractured. Alex left, determined to see Wrath destroyed. Judith went with him, and so did nearly one-third of our number."

"But you didn't?"

"No," Cain said, shaking his head. "Sadik and I believed Thorn could be saved. We wanted to believe it… maybe we *needed* to. We were right, of course, but Sadik never lived to see that. Wrath killed him six months later, and Judith, two years after that. Then, it took Alex. Alan had been given the chance—the choice—to kill Thorn so that Alex may live, and he chose Thorn."

Cain's voice tightened, and he wrapped his hands in his lap. Darius's heart clenched. "I'm sorry," he said.

But Cain shook his head. "Thank you." He glanced at Darius, his eyes drawing him in like he had just remembered how to breathe. "I understand why Alan did what he did, and I would probably have done the exact same thing in his position. So, I forgave him, but Thorn did not. Not for years. Decades. I wouldn't be surprised if part of her still resents him for it."

Darius frowned. "For saving her?"

"He did not save her." Cain's expression sharpened, and a flash of indignation crossed his eyes. "Thorn saved herself. Four years after Alex was killed, she forced Wrath out and hurt it more than anyone had ever hurt it in all its existence. No, she could not forgive Alan for *trying* to save her and, in the course of doing so, allowing so many people to die at her hands."

"It wasn't her," Darius said.

"That's true," Cain agreed with a sad nod. "But knowing that didn't ease anything. Witnessing an evil you are powerless to stop can leave deep wounds, and time is not always enough to heal them."

Cain glanced back up to the dais—at four stone Familiars from four dead Forgotten Sins looming over them like spirits in a shrine. Darius took a slow breath, stared into their marble eyes, and marveled at how unfair it was that he could heal a gunshot wound without a second thought but was powerless to heal the soul.

The second Thorn walked into Alan's office, she knew they were about to fight.

"Sit," he said without looking up from the report in his hands. It was clearly one of hers, handwritten in a tight, delicate style of cursive that they'd stopped teaching when Donovan had been in school decades ago. Alan peered down his long nose, adjusting his reading glasses. Her writing was smaller and more difficult to decipher than typed text, and Alan always took more time with it. Thorn wondered if he was frustrated that Sin healing didn't make up for congenital vision problems.

"What did you want to talk to me about?" Thorn asked, pointedly *not* sitting. Alan sighed and lowered the paper, removing his reading glasses as he did so. His wolf familiar sat to his left, her ears alert.

"We moved toward targeting Greed because it is less

risky than continuing our hunt for Wrath," Alan said. An edge of frustration snapped in his tone. "And now you want to plant a *tracking device* on him?"

Rae's eyes narrowed, and her black tail swept in an annoyed arc. Thorn refused to acknowledge her, but Sparkie's wings flared up from her shoulder.

"We can't move against Greed if we don't know where he is," Thorn said.

"We do know where he is," Alan argued, indicating the report before he laid it on the table. "At least, we know where he is going to be. While I agree that we should monitor him and learn what we can about what he is currently doing, launching an operation to track him? For what purpose?"

Thorn's mouth dropped open. "Isn't it obvious?"

"No," Alan said. "It is not." He sighed and got to his feet, walking around the front of his desk to face Thorn more personally, but he leaned back against it to bring himself down to her level and not stand so intimidatingly tall above her. She crossed her arms to show him she wasn't ready to let this go.

"Anton Claytor is keeping a low profile," Thorn countered. "This is the first sign of him we've seen in months. If he slips back into hiding after this, who knows when we'll find him again?"

"He will come out of the woods sooner or later," Alan said evenly. The furrow to his brow didn't soften. "You have been at this long enough to know that."

Thorn took a deep breath, holding it hard inside her chest. "I don't want to wait anymore, Alan," she said. "For the first time in decades, the Sins are more terrified of us than we are of them. For the first time, we have the goddamned high ground! What use is it if we don't take it?"

She propped her hands on her hips to keep them still. Alan simply considered her, and Rae padded up to his side. Her sleek, black fur looked like a shadow, and she sat back on her haunches and watched Thorn with a piercing, blue gaze. Alan's dark eyes were narrow and unconvinced.

"What use is this 'high ground' if taking it gets our people killed?" Alan asked. "I don't know if you recall, but we have attempted to plant devices on the Sins in the past—"

"I do recall," Thorn snapped.

"—*and* it ended disastrously." Alan crossed his arms. "Your operative was caught, kidnapped, and presumably killed. What makes this attempt any different?"

"For one, we have Cain, and none of the Sins know he's alive," Thorn said. "Plus, we're more prepared. We have better technology, a better team."

"That does not mean—"

"Jesus, Alan, I don't understand what you expect from me."

He blinked, taken aback, and shook his head. "What do you mean?"

"I mean," Thorn said, stepping up to him again, her fingertips pressed so tightly to her hips that she felt her heart pounding in them, "that you cut off the search for Wrath, told me to focus all of my team's energy on hunting down Greed instead, and now you're telling me I need to wait. Wait for what? For Lust and Envy to repossess? For the Sins to get more powerful again? That window is *closing,* Alan, and we might not get a chance like this again."

"I understand that," Alan said. He drew his arms away from his chest to fold his hands in his lap. "But rushing this could be a foolish endeavor. We have time to get it right."

"We could spend the next century planning and still not get it right," Thorn said. She threw a palm out, gesturing to the door behind her. "We're wasting time that the rest of the Martyrs don't have when the perfect opportunity is *right in front of us.* This is the strongest group I have ever fucking seen."

Thorn paused, waiting for a rebuke, but Alan just watched her. His brows drew down in a concern that felt downright condescending. Even after more than a century, sometimes she felt like all he saw when he looked at her was that scared ten-year-old girl who hadn't yet been corrupted by Wrath—who had just been introduced to the violence of the world by watching her father's blood paint the walls after her uncle blew a bullet into his brain.

But Thorn wasn't that little girl anymore, and she wasn't afraid.

"I'm not the only one ready to go on the offensive," she said. *We can do this.*

Alan said nothing for a few more moments, and Thorn stared at him. At last, he sighed.

"I need to see a more concrete plan," he said, "Where will our people be stationed? How are we entering the event? What protections and safeguards will be in place? And, most importantly, are the benefits of success worth the risks of what we will lose if we fail? Get this to me as soon as you can."

A knot in Thorn's chest loosened, but just barely. She nodded. "You got it."

"And," Alan went on, "I need you to be open-minded to other solutions. Being so strictly held to one objective and one means of reaching it can blind you to other opportunities. Don't make that mistake."

His eyes lingered on hers for a moment, far away and distant, like he was lost in thought. Thorn's teeth clenched, and she wondered which one of his own mistakes he was remembering—maybe something that had to do with Wrath and the people it murdered with Thorn as the weapon.

But she doubted it. Alan had never seemed to regret that, and Thorn never understood why.

CHAPTER SIX

A shrill tone pierced into Thorn's skull, louder than she expected through the noise-canceling headset in her tactical helmet. The bridge of her nose wrinkled as she considered the meter in her hand.

"What's it read?" a woman's voice rang through her com system. Thorn glanced up at the window to the control station above the shooting range. Taylor Simmons, their new weapons expert, watched her through the glass with her arms crossed and brown eyes narrow.

"One hundred and forty decibels," Thorn answered. "Enough to put some Puppets down."

A rattling of keyboard strokes filled her ears as Holly took notes. "All right," she said. "Move to the next test distance…"

Thorn stepped back to the designated position up the firing lane, and Chris said, "Test three of our sonic disruptor device. Distance: three meters. Starting decibel rate: one hundred and sixty. Activation in three… two… one."

A clunky, cylindrical item on a table below the sound-proof glass exploded with a high-pitched blast. It shot at Thorn like a bullet, and she tensed as it slammed into her with an almost physical force, but much less of a force than it had the last time. She frowned as she looked down at the meter.

"What's wrong?" Chris asked.

"We're down to one thirty."

"That's still loud enough to hurt like hell," Simmons argued.

Thorn didn't answer right away, frowning as she did the math. It wasn't looking good. "Let's try one more," she said. "Six meters."

Thorn moved again, gave the go-ahead, and Chris activated the device. Thorn closed her eyes, but her headset reduced the sound to something closer to a droning helicopter engine than a gunshot. She glanced down at the meter. "Fuck. One twenty-four. I'm coming up."

She pulled the helmet off and made her way back to the control center. Her boots thudded against naked concrete as she trudged across the empty lane, and her eyes locked onto the prototype of their new weapon. It didn't look like much—a giant tin can tethered to the wall with wires—and so far, Thorn wasn't impressed. She shook her head, climbed the stairs, and opened the door to the booth. Four pairs of eyes instantly turned toward her.

"What the fuck was that?" she asked, stepping up to the metal table in the center of the room. Taylor Simmons stood to her right, Holly across from her, while DuPont and Chris held back by the opposite wall. Thorn gestured out the window to the shooting range below. "Six meters? All this thing can get me is *six* meters?"

Holly and Simmons exchanged a tense look. The pair of them were opposites in nearly every way. Where Holly was short and pale, Simmons was an impressive woman with a full figure, deep brown skin, and a head of natural hair that made her appear even taller than she was—which was already a couple of inches taller than Thorn. DuPont had poached her from the police department four months ago, and ever since, she and Holly had been working on developing a non-lethal form of Puppet control. Thorn had expected them to be further along than this.

"It's more than six meters," Simmons argued, crossing her arms. "The average human being will start experiencing discomfort at one hundred and twenty decibels—"

"And I *told* you," Holly cut in, exasperated, "that wouldn't be enough!" She pushed her fingertips beneath her thick-rimmed glasses to rub her eyes. The lenses disappeared behind boyish, brown bangs,

Simmons clicked her tongue. "This is military standard," she said. "They've been using weapons like this for the last forty years, and *everything* is maxed out at one sixty."

"I don't care what the military is doing," Holly said. "They're not fighting off supernatural baddies, but *we* are! This sonic bomb doesn't have enough range to effectively put down a mob of Sin-controlled Puppets."

"It's not a bomb," Simmons said.

"It's basically a bomb," Holly said. "A noise bomb."

"No," Simmons said. "It's a crowd control device, and it has a lot more range than you're giving it credit for. Anything upward of one hundred and twenty decibels is enough to rattle people's focus and make them exit an area. That gives us more than a twenty-meter radius!"

"Yes," Holly said, crossing her arms around an oversized hoodie that made her seem even tinier than she already was, "which would be great if we were dealing with normal people. Did you not hear that part about 'supernatural baddies' and 'mob of Sin-controlled Puppets?' We need to put them in enough pain to cut them off from the Sins, and the pain threshold is around one hundred and forty!"

Simmons's face scrunched as DuPont sighed and stepped up to the table.

"Well, why don't we just… boost the starting decibel rate?" He threw Chris a look and shrugged. She could only do the same in return.

"It's not that easy," Simmons said. "For one, we'd have to hunt down a device designed to go higher than this. Like I said, one-sixty is military standard. But even if we *do*, this is all about disabling Puppets without killing them, right?"

"Right," DuPont said with a nod.

"Well, then we can't go over one hundred and eighty decibels, and even that's pushing it. Any louder could cause fatal side effects. Pulmonary embolisms, contusions… even burst lungs."

Chris winced. "We can't risk that."

Simmons opened a palm toward her. "My thoughts exactly."

Thorn shook her head, walked to the gear locker, and put the helmet away. "We don't want to kill civilians if we can avoid it, but we won't be able to avoid it at all if they're still tied to the Sins. Six meters isn't cutting it."

"Well," Simmons said, "how about you tell me what kind of range you want, and I'll see what I can do to get us there."

Thorn paused, her brows drawing together as she thought back to every tactical operation she'd ever been in that had gone south. God, there were a lot of them.

"Twenty meters is fine," she said after a moment. "But I need a minimum decibel rate of one forty."

"I'll see what I can do," Simmons said. "That brings up another problem, though."

"Oh?" Thorn shut the gear locker with a snap and turned back around.

"Our hearing protection," Simmons said.

DuPont crossed his arms around his black tactical turtleneck. "Our helmets already have noise-canceling technology."

"Right," Simmons agreed. "The same stuff the NYPD uses. I know the specs on those devices. They take thirty decibels off gunfire, but with a high-frequency sound like this, we'll be lucky to get fifteen to twenty, and it's less effective with this kind of blast compared to consistent sound. If I can increase the starting decibel rate—and that's a *big* if—we're going to run into issues if our people are too close to this thing when it goes off."

"I can handle that," Holly said, waving a hand dismissively. "I'll start working on a program to delay detonation. When we activate the bomb—"

"Not a bomb."

"—the system will be able to hold off until our people are far enough away. Theoretically."

DuPont's cognac eyes narrowed. "Theoretically? We need more than theoretical. This is for *combat*, not crowd control. We'll cut existing Puppets off, but it won't necessarily stop the Sins. They could gather more, and we can't have any Martyrs down."

Holly arched a brow. "I know how important my job is, DuPont."

Chris cleared her throat, glancing from DuPont to Thorn. "So, we need to up the starting decibel rate and ensure our teams are protected from the louder sound."

"And get the device smaller," Thorn said. "I need something I can throw into a crowd."

Chris nodded, considering the weapons specialist. "Is that doable?"

"Should be," Simmons said, but her tone was tight.

"Good," Chris answered. "Then I need you and Holly to work out a timeline for this thing to be fully functional."

"Yes, ma'am," Simmons said. Holly, who had never had the patience for protocol and titles, simply nodded.

"All right," DuPont said, turning to Chris for confirmation. She dipped her head. "Let's get the hell out of here."

The five of them broke. Simmons went down to the shooting range to gather her prototype while Holly snapped her laptop shut.

"Well, that was a mess," she said with a sigh. She glanced up at Thorn and wrinkled her nose. "I did bring you something less… problematic, though."

She dipped her hand into her front pocket and drew out a couple of small, square objects, which she dropped into Thorn's outstretched palm. They landed softly in the center of her glove.

"Tracking devices," Holly said. "These have a big range, and they're pretty accurate. Two biggest limiters are battery life and getting close enough to plant them."

Thorn nodded, lifting one of the trackers between her fingers and turning it around. It was small, under an inch in both directions and as thin as a quarter.

"What do you need tracking devices for?" Chris asked.

"I want to try to get one on Greed," Thorn said. When Chris's eyes widened, she sighed. "If I can."

"That's going to be a challenge," DuPont said.

The door opened as Simmons walked back into the room. She packed the sonic weapon into a case on the table, and Holly tucked her computer under her arm. "It's still not the dumbest thing we've tried to do," she said, "and if we get it, it'll be insanely useful." Then, she turned to Chris. "Speaking of useful, when do you want that timeline on your desk?"

"What's the earliest you think you can get it done?"

"With Skylar's wedding tomorrow and the rest of my team presumably hungover for the following forty-eight hours?" Holly frowned as she thought about it. "Probably Friday." She threw Simmons a look. "Unless that's too hard for *other* involved parties…"

Simmons raised her brows. "I can do Friday."

"Perfect," Holly said, turning to Chris again. "Speaking of the wedding, Skylar says Darius asked you to come?"

Thorn's breath caught in her throat. Beside her, DuPont's aura froze, and the two of them exchanged a quick look.

"Yeah," Chris said with a chuckle. "He talked me into it."

She opened the door and held it for them. Thorn left first. The dark, damp basement air pushed around her in a muggy cloud, but somehow, she felt cold. When everyone else had joined her, Chris locked up.

"Great," Holly said. "I'll see you then. The rest of you probably, too."

Simmons and DuPont agreed, but Thorn's mouth pressed shut. They made their way upstairs to the courtyard, and she paused. It was so different now. A new network of lights hung above them, and the center aisle had been laid with a sleek, black carpet. Across from her, in the back of the room, Cain had constructed a beautiful iron arch draped with glistening silver and navy lace. The maintenance staff was putting up rows of seating to make room for the first Underground wedding most of them had ever seen. People bustled around with a purpose that, for once, had nothing to do with this war they were fighting.

After tomorrow, things would go back to normal. It wouldn't take long for costs and casualties to smother the joy, like they always did. The battle with the Sins demanded center stage.

But for the first time, that battle didn't feel so hopeless.

———

As far as Darius was concerned, Chris Silver was one of the most predictable people in the Underground. She woke up at the same time every morning, ate the same three meals religiously (overnight oats, a protein shake, and baked chicken with fresh veggies), and followed her daily rituals with monk-like discipline that put the rest of the Martyrs to shame. When you needed to find her, she was either in her office, at the gym, or on a duty shift in the city. By now, Darius knew her so well that even the pattern of her movement carried a familiar signature—quick yet steady, calm, and confident.

So when he reached her room and felt her aura darting around with nervous energy, he paused.

"Chris?" he called through the door as he rapped his knuckles against it. She stopped moving. "You okay?"

Her robust warmth rushed toward the door and pulled it open. Chris's face appeared in the crack, her cheeks tinged with red. She clutched something against her chest.

"I can't zip this damned thing up. Can you get it for me?"

She opened the room to him. Clothing was laid out on the unmade bed—a dozen discarded dresses in different colors that had clearly been put on and taken off immediately. He raised his brows as he looked at her. Chris sighed.

"I couldn't figure out what to wear," she said, "and now I'm stuck."

She turned her back to him. Her blonde hair was pulled into an elegant but simple updo, exposing her back and all the scars cutting across it. One stood out more prominently than the rest—a deep, ragged line of fibrous flesh digging from her left shoulder to right hip. The zipper was caught on the cobalt garment right where that scar bridged her spine. He pinched the fabric beneath the slider and tugged until it came free.

"There you go."

Chris let out an exasperated scoff. "Thanks." She stepped away from him, sitting at the edge of her bed to pull on a pair of black heels that looked like they'd never been worn. Her forehead knit into a series of lines. Darius frowned and shoved his hands in his front pockets.

"You okay?" he asked again.

"Yes," she said in a way that sounded distinctly like "no." She drew a deep breath that lifted her shoulders, and they stayed there when she exhaled. As she got to her feet, she looked him over, and a forced smile pressed her lips together. "You look very nice."

Darius glanced down at the suit—charcoal gray slacks against an emerald top. He'd worn the matching jacket but didn't know how to tie the tie, so he'd left it back in his room.

"Thanks," he said. "You do, too." He gestured toward her floor-length gown. It was tight enough to show off her figure but loose enough to look comfortable. She let out a hard laugh and shook her head as she reached for a black shawl draped over one of her open dresser drawers.

"I feel ridiculous." She threw the cover on and spun to

check the back in a mirror hanging from her door. "None of my other dresses fit me anymore, and this one…"

Her voice drifted off as she adjusted her shawl, making sure it hid all the scars across her shoulders, but her arms were still exposed, bearing more marks from past battles. She ran her hands down them, fingertips lingering on the hard, upraised skin.

"I should've bought one with sleeves," Chris murmured at last.

Darius watched her for a moment, his mouth a tight line. He wasn't used to seeing Chris so unsure of herself, and again, he found himself wishing he had the power to heal old wounds.

"For what it's worth," he said, "I think you look beautiful."

"Thank you," she said, and she pinched the bridge of her nose as though she could press the fresh glint of tears back. "I'm sorry. I guess I'm just more comfortable in uniform. Let's get going."

Chris reached for the door, but Darius grabbed her by the shoulder.

"No, I'm sorry," he said. "I shouldn't have put you in this position. If you don't want to go, don't go. I'll be fine, okay? You're more important."

The tension in Chris's back softened, and she smiled. This one felt genuine.

"I appreciate it, but I really am fine."

"You're sure?"

"Positive."

Chris opened the door and walked into the hallway. Darius followed by her side.

"I'll make it up to you," he said.

She waved him away with a scoff. "You've saved my life more times than I can count. If anything, this is me making it up to you."

The Underground glowed with warm energy. As they made their way down the hallway, passing the branch that led to his room before turning left and heading to the court-yard, Darius was struck with how impressive the Martyrs felt gathered so closely together. When they walked out into the open, they met a chorus of murmuring voices dancing off high ceilings. The overhead lights had been turned off, but the network of bulbs Darius had helped hang filled the space with a delicate ambiance. Chris's eyes widened as she looked up.

"Let's find a place to sit," Darius said.

He led the way through tables dressed in white linen, through plants adorned with strings of fairy lights, through smiling people until they hit the end of the aisle. A plush, black carpet ran between silver chairs and stopped just short of an archway on a raised platform. Beyond it, the rest of the room faded into shadow, creating the illusion that they were somewhere more magical than an underground bunker.

Nicholas stood by the back row of chairs and stepped up as they approached. "Hey, Darius." He extended a hand, and Darius took it. "Chris. Glad you could make it!"

Like the rest of the bridal party, Nicholas was dressed in navy, his suit the color of the night sky with a white shirt beneath it. He'd styled his blonde hair back from his face, and he flashed them a smile. Behind him, wearing a match-ing outfit, John guided more Martyrs to their seats. He cast Chris and Darius a glance over his shoulder as he let Mac-kenzie into one of the rows. Chris made a point not to look at him, but Darius nodded in his direction before turning to Nicholas again.

"This looks amazing," he said.

Nicholas nodded. "The girls have great taste. You guys are in the reserved area up front."

"We are?" Chris asked.

"Well, yeah," Nicholas said. "Raquel wouldn't have it any other way. Come on." He turned on his heel to lead the way. There were two spots toward the far end of the very front row. Alan sat alone there, one ankle crossed over his knee and his hands folded precisely in his lap. Of all the Martyrs, Alan looked the most natural. The only difference between his formal wear and what he had on every other day was the black suit jacket and narrow tie over his red button-up shirt. As Darius and Chris approached him, he got to his feet.

"Thank you, Mr. Wolfe," Alan said, waving Nicholas off. Then, he turned to Darius and Chris and shook their hands. "Darius, Christine. Please, sit."

The three of them lowered into their chairs. Darius glanced around the room.

"I've never seen this many people in the courtyard at once before," he said.

Alan nodded. "Yes, Christine's recruitment initiatives have been wildly successful." He tilted his head toward Chris, fixing her with a smile. "At this rate, we may run out of space to accommodate all of them."

Chris laughed and shook her head, thanking Alan for the compliment and explaining how she doubted very much that they would fill the Underground anytime soon. Darius, meanwhile, searched the crowd. There were nearly two hundred people here. The front rows were filled with Skylar and Raquel's closest friends: Dr. Harris and Colette alongside their sons, Julien and Remy; the hospital staff; the security team; and Stevie. Everyone else filled in behind them.

There were no "sides" here, no one who belonged more to Raquel than to Skylar or the other way around. People from all walks of the Underground mingled together. Toward the back, Seth and Gabe sat with Amelia Chan, swapping stories with a group of new TAC officers and recon agents back from assignment. Madison was one of them. She caught Darius's eye and wiggled her fingers in a wave. In front of them, Mackenzie was speaking animatedly with Parker, who looked equal parts amused and concerned at her wild flailing while her father, Marcus, rolled his eyes. Even Conrad Carter, his muscular bulk and buzzed head looking misplaced in a suit, laughed with Alexis as she fixed her dangling, chain earrings. Caleb was one of the only people still up and about. He had his camera out and was taking photographs of the guests as they settled.

"I insisted the entire Underground take the day off," Alan explained. Darius glanced over to find him admiring the empire he'd built, too. A proud, paternal expression settled into Alan's sharp features.

"Looks like everyone made it," Chris observed.

"Almost everyone," Darius said. A flicker of disappointment bloomed between his lungs, and Alan cast him a look. His thin mouth touched on a frown. Then, a soft, instrumental melody began to play, and the entire congregation stilled with a whisper.

Cain stepped onto the platform. His sleek, blue suit shimmered in the lights, and he stared down the aisle. Alan's body stiffened beside Darius. He glanced over, but Alan's face was as hard to read as a stone. Cain's statues betrayed more of their feelings than Alan ever did.

With the Martyrs seated, John and Nicholas quietly disappeared. Their warm energies tucked back into one of the dark studios along the side. Minutes later, the music shifted.

Heads spun to watch Holly walk up the carpet, arm in arm with Nicholas. He held himself tall; Holly barely reached his shoulders, even wearing heels. Her silver dress glowed under the overhead bulbs, and she clutched a handcrafted bouquet of crystal flowers to her chest. When they reached the podium, they moved to Cain's left and stood, Nicholas nearer to the center.

Next came John, accompanied by a nurse Raquel had asked to take Chris's place when she dropped out of the wedding party. Darius glanced back to find Chris's green eyes glistening, but a smile rose to her lips as she watched them. John shook Cain's hand, and the two took their spot on his other side.

The music swirled into a wedding march, and the congregation got to their feet. Raquel and Skylar paused at the end of the aisle, standing hand-in-hand with smiles so wide they brightened the entire room. Both wore sleek, strapless gowns, Raquel's a pearly white that looked stunning against her brown complexion, and Skylar's a deep, elegant navy. When they reached the podium, Skylar hugged Nicholas while Raquel threw her arms around John's shoulders. He brushed a strand of hair from her cheek and murmured something against her ear. She wiped a tear as she and Skylar turned to face each other.

Cain cleared his throat and opened his arms to the room.

"Good evening," he said, his voice booming from speakers around them, "and welcome. Please, take your seats."

The room shuffled, and as one, sat down. Cain waited for the noise to quiet.

"My, what an impressive force we have here," he went on. "After being away from the Underground for so long, it is a welcome sight."

He smiled and clasped his hands, those bright eyes moving across the audience.

"We are here to celebrate Raquel Hernandez, Skylar Fulton, and the love they have nourished." He tilted his head at the women when he said their names. "We are also here to bear witness to the life and future they have embarked on together. To support them as colleagues, as friends, as family."

Cain paused, then, taking a deep breath. The smile on his lips flickered.

"As this is a joyous occasion, I won't speak much on the hardness of our world. We have all seen what lies hiding in the dark, and we know firsthand how it can make us feel… powerless."

A wave moved through the room, full of discomfort and understanding. Darius exhaled a slow sigh.

"But love shows us otherwise," Cain went on. His voice was stronger now. "It allows us to weather the storm. It thaws us when the coldness of all we have endured has made us numb, and it digs deep into our souls to heal wounds we thought would never stop bleeding. It helps us laugh when we want to cry, open up when we start to shut down, and shines a light through our deepest shadows to prove that we can do more than simply survive. We can thrive. When everything in this world works to rob us of what makes us human, love keeps us grounded."

If Darius wasn't mistaken, Cain cast a glance in their direction. Then, he opened his arms again, hovering a palm just behind both the brides' backs.

"Raquel and Skylar's love is more than that," he said. "It's a beacon. A symbol. Their union stands as a testament that love is a force more powerful than hatred, than fear, than even death."

Raquel nodded, tears glistening behind her mascara. One fell, and Skylar brushed her thumb against Raquel's cheek to catch it. Cain looked between them, and his expression warmed.

"Raquel," he said, "Skylar, are you ready to come together and become one, in body and in soul?"

Raquel could only nod while Skylar said, "Yes."

Cain turned to Nicholas. "The rings, please."

Nicholas and John dug into their pockets and drew out small, black boxes. They handed two gold bands to Cain. The Forgotten Sin held them up to the room.

"The ring has always been a symbol of completion," he said. "Of wholeness. Of infinity and eternity. Raquel and Skylar have chosen to exchange rings as a sign that they are bound, not through ownership or possession but through partnership and decision."

He handed one ring to each of them. Raquel grabbed hers with shaking hands as Cain turned to her.

"Raquel, do you take this twoman to be your wife? Do you promise to honor her, to choose her time and time again, and to walk through life's valleys and climb its mountains with her by your side?"

"I do," Raquel said. Her voice was so full of emotion that it made Darius's throat tighten alongside it. She held

Skylar's hand and slipped the band onto her ring finger.

Cain turned to Skylar.

"Skylar, do you take this woman to be your wife? Do you promise to honor her, to choose her time and time again, and to walk through life's valleys and climb its mountains with her by your side?"

Skylar nodded, slipping a ring onto Raquel's finger before she gripped her hands and held them firmly. "I do."

Cain smiled. "The power of this marriage does not lie within me," he said, this time more quietly, like it was meant for Raquel and Skylar alone. "It lies within the two of you, in your hearts, in your souls, in the very atoms of your beings, and my god, I am awed by that power." Then he stood up, and he addressed the room again. "I am honored to be the first to announce you as newly minted, newly married, and eternally bound. You may now kiss and make this union official."

Cain bowed and backed out, shrinking into the darkness behind the arch. Tears streamed down Raquel's cheeks as Skylar wrapped her hands around her face and drew her in for a passionate kiss. They stood there for a moment, frozen in time, linked in love, smiling against each other's mouths as they laughed and cried and whispered sweet secrets the rest of the room couldn't hear.

The crowd erupted in applause and shot to their feet. Darius clapped and cheered so loudly that his palms hurt. Skylar grabbed Raquel's hand and thrust it up, screaming her joy to the vaulted ceilings while Raquel grinned and covered her face behind her knuckles. They walked down the aisle, followed by the best men and bridesmaids in a line. Cain returned to the podium, smiling down at the Martyrs with his fingers laced at his waist.

Darius turned along with everyone else to watch the procession go by. Something swooped overhead. A blur of blue and red. His heart flipped as he followed it.

Sparkie landed on Thorn's shoulder at the back of the room. She stood away from the rest of them, half hidden in shadow and absolutely striking in a smooth, backless dress that flowed down her body like liquid silk. Her arms wrapped around her chest, her fingerless gloves disappearing against her gown. Straight, black hair framed her face like satin curtains and dropped along her collar, making her plunging neckline look deeper than it actually was. A thoughtful look tempered her sharp features as she watched the wedding party walk by. For a moment, Darius was swept up in the enchantment of her, and he couldn't tear himself away.

Then, Thorn's dark eyes flashed up and caught him across the crowd. He smiled. She smiled, too.

CHAPTER SEVEN

Food lined the kitchen counter, boasting a delicious selection of thyme roast chicken, seared prime rib, and vege-
tarian pasta coated in artichoke pesto that made Darius's
mouth water. Raquel and Skylar were already seated at a central table with a crystal flower garland, their wedding party
on either side. The rest of the dining area was first come,
first served. Darius and Chris grabbed an empty table at the
far end. As he took his seat, Chris's eyes narrowed.

"You okay?" she asked.

Darius reached for the water pitcher beside a bottle of
red wine at the center of the table and filled his glass. "What
do you mean?"

"I mean *this*." Chris took the dull end of her fork and
pointed it at Darius's mouth. "You've been smiling since we
got in line. What are you suddenly so happy about?"

"I dunno," he said with a shrug as he filled her glass, too.
"I just like weddings. It's a… nice break. You know?"

"Mmm," Chris agreed, but she lifted her chin and
frowned like she wasn't convinced. For a minute, the two
of them quietly ate as the rest of the Martyrs grabbed their
food and wandered around the dining area. Motion without
an aura caught Darius's attention, and his head snapped up

as Cain paused at the other end of their table.

"Good evening," he said, his eyes crinkling with an indulgent smile. He held a plate of food in one hand. "May I join you?"

Darius covered his mouth while he worked through a piece of meat. "Absolutely," he said when it was tender enough to speak around. He gestured his knife forward, and Cain pulled out a chair.

"That was a beautiful ceremony," Chris said.

"They are beautiful people," Cain said, "which made my job all too easy." His eyes moved over Darius's shoulder, and his smile widened. "Speaking of beautiful, my dear, that gown is stunning."

Darius spun in his chair as Thorn paused just behind his back. One slender brow arched, but she didn't say anything, like she saw no point in acknowledging the compliment because she knew it was true.

And, god, was it true.

It was all Darius could do not to stare. Up close, he could see more detail. The black fabric looked so soft and supple that he ached to run his fingers across it. It slid along her skin as she moved toward the seat to Darius's left. He pulled it out for her, and the corner of her mouth twitched up in a smirk.

"Thank you," she said, putting her plate and a glass of scotch down before lowering into the chair. She crossed her legs, and a slit up the side of her dress slipped open, exposing a length of pale skin from her ankle to thigh. Her calf accidentally brushed against Darius's knee as she adjusted, making him inhale a quick breath that stuck in a cough at the back of his throat. He focused on his meal again, catching Chris in the corner of his eye. She was staring at him, and her eyes went wide when he glanced at her. Heat bloomed across his cheeks as he gently kicked her feet under the table.

"Last I heard, you weren't sure you would make it," Cain commented.

"I didn't think I could." Thorn drew her hair around one shoulder, which left Sparkie out in the open on her back. His wings pulled close to his body.

"What in the world could be more important than attending the first Martyr wedding in nearly ten years?" Cain asked.

Thorn raised her scotch and took a sip, frowning over the rim. A smudge of scarlet lipstick clung to the glass as she drew it back.

"We still have four Sins to destroy."

Cain scoffed as Chris leaned forward. "Were you working the Greed case?" she asked, propping her elbows on the table. Her shawl draped around her, catching at the crook of her arms.

"Mulligan got me the list of donors signed up for Bently's fundraiser next month," Thorn said with a nod. "I went by a few of them and planted Sentries to see if Claytor ever shows up in person. It's a long shot, but getting to him before the event would be easier for us."

"Absolutely," Chris said. "Fewer people means fewer potential casualties if the plan falls through."

Darius frowned. "What plan?"

"Part of our operation against Claytor," Thorn said. "We want to plant a tracking device on him, but Alan is—"

"Ah, ah, ah!" Cain interrupted, waving his hands between them all. "No! Not today. Today is not a day for this Sin business. It's a day for celebrating."

His eyes snapped from Thorn to Chris and back again. Chris shifted awkwardly in her chair, but Thorn watched Cain with a bemused indifference. She adjusted her gloves before grabbing her fork off the table, stabbing a piece of chicken, and popping it into her mouth. Before she or anyone else had a chance to say anything, a lukewarm aura bounded toward their table.

"Hey!" Mackenzie said, grinning as she pulled the chair out beside Cain and plopped into it. Her blue hair was styled nicely, matching her short, tank-top dress, and she'd accessorized it with a pair of flats and a handful of clumsy bruises dotting her shins. She didn't have a plate of food, and she seemed wholly unaware of the moment she'd interrupted as she rubbed her palms together and took a wild look around the room.

"Okay, John and I are running a bet on the Underground's next new couple. He's got his eye on Porter and Westmoreland from the Discovery Unit, but let's be real… DuPont is one we should be looking at, right?"

Thorn shook her head. "What the hell are you talking about?"

"DuPont!" Mackenzie said. "He's young, he's hot, he's *vital,* not to mention *killing it* in a three-piece suit. He's already got a great ass, but in *those* pants? Even *I* wanna get in them."

Chris let out a loud, uncomfortable laugh. "Jesus, Mackenzie…"

"All right, we can just say he's 'easy on the eyes,'" she corrected, flicking a wrist. "Is that HR compliant enough for you? My point is, I *guarantee* DuPont's gonna swipe up some cute new thing before Saint Patrick's Day, so I put my bet on him. What d'ya think? Am I throwing money down the drain here?"

Chris glanced over her shoulder, where Gabe and a couple of other TAC officers sat nearby. The background music transitioned to a more upbeat number, and people drifted to the dance floor. The same group of women from their classes lingered behind Gabe's back. He laughed at something Conrad said, and Chris's cheeks darkened another shade of pink.

"I really don't know," she finally said.

Mackenzie leaned across the table. "C'mon! You work with him! You're telling me he hasn't shown interest in *anyone?*"

Chris shook her head, and Mackenzie groaned.

"Fuck! You've gotta give me *something* to go off of! John's beaten me in our last six bets!"

"Why are you taking bets on who's going to pair off?" Darius asked as he grabbed his water glass.

Mackenzie shrugged and raised her hands to indicate the courtyard. "I mean… why would I *not*? It fits the mood!" She laughed as she reclined back in her chair. "John struck down all my other romance-related ideas. This was the only one I could get him to agree to."

"I'm almost afraid to ask what the other options were," Chris said.

"Most of it was innocent," Mackenzie answered. "Who's had the longest relationship… gone on the most dates… has the highest body count, if you know what I mean."

Mackenzie winked, and Thorn rolled her eyes. Cain chuckled to Mackenzie's right.

"Sounds like good fun," he said.

"Right?" Mackenzie said, holding a palm out toward him. "Thank you! But John said it was 'inappropriate' and 'he didn't want to think about other Martyrs' sex lives.' So boring."

"For once," Thorn said with a smile as she brought her scotch to her lips, "I agree with Waters."

"Oh, calm down," Mackenzie said. "We wouldn't be looking at *you*. Your list of conquests is a hundred and fifty years long. No one else could even compete!"

She laughed, but none of the others did. An awkward quiet overwhelmed the table. Thorn's smile instantly dissolved like bitter salt in warm water. Darius and Chris exchanged a quick, uncomfortable look while Cain cleared his throat and grabbed the bottle of Zinfandel. He popped the cork with an expert hand. "Wine, anyone?"

"Yes, please," Chris said, turning her stemless glass right-side up like somehow it could shield her from a barrage of verbal bullets. He poured her a healthy serving as Thorn put her scotch back on the table. It slammed against the surface, and her fingers tightened around the rim until they turned white. Sparkie's wings trembled behind her back.

"Twenty of those years were out of my control," Thorn said, the words struggling from her mouth like she resented the fact that she had to say them at all. Suddenly, the room felt colder, and Darius's chest caved in. He knew Thorn's possession had been traumatic, but from the outside, it was all too easy to forget everything Wrath had stolen from her—or forced upon her.

Thorn didn't have the luxury to forget.

Mackenzie frowned. "Obviously, that's not what I'm talking about."

"Then what are you talking about?" Thorn pressed. She had to raise her voice to be heard over the music, but her strangled tone made it clear that she was fighting not to shout. "Is that what you think I do? Fuck around and add notches to my bedpost so people like *you* can't loop me into your stupid games?"

Mackenzie's eyebrows shot high on her head, and she leaned back, crossing her arms. Her fingers rapped against her bicep. "No," she argued, "but you're not a goddamned *nun*, are you? Jesus, Thorn, stop being so sensitive. It was just a joke."

"It's not fucking funny," Thorn snapped.

Mackenzie laughed again, but this time, the sound was cold and callous. "Yes, it *is!* Anyone else would think so!"

"I don't," Darius cut in.

Mackenzie's focus flashed to him, and her jaw dropped. "Wow, okay," she said, throwing up trembling hands. "I get it. I'm the bad guy. Fine." She pushed away from the table and got to her feet. "Thanks for the help."

She stomped off, her tiny frame quickly disappearing in the crowd of Martyrs standing around tables as dinner wrapped up. Thorn shifted, and Darius worried she was going to follow after Mackenzie. Cain seemed to think the same. He reached out and wrapped his fingers around hers.

"None of this, either," he said. Thorn turned to him, ready to fight. Cain was nonplussed. "No talk about the Sins, and no worrying about what we did when we were one."

Thorn said nothing as she tore her hand out of his and threw the rest of her drink down her throat. She sucked in through her teeth as she put the glass back on the table without letting go. Her fingertips tapped against it—from pointer to pinky and back again. Darius glanced at the side of her face curiously. She didn't catch his eye, but her shoulders rolled upward, backward, and eased toward the ground. Sparkie shuffled, raised his wings, and vaulted to the ceiling, where he disappeared behind the lights. The gust made Darius's napkin flutter on his lap.

"Well," Cain went on after a moment. He got to his feet and straightened his suit jacket. "I, for one, will not let one woman's poor judgment ruin my evening, and I did not help orchestrate this whole affair to sit at a table all night. Come, now. Everyone up."

He held a palm out to Thorn. She frowned at it without saying a word. Darius, however, stood, too.

"Come where?" he asked.

Cain looked him over incredulously, as if the question were offensive. "To dance, of course. This is a wedding, after all. Come, come."

Chris rose from her chair, but Thorn shook her head. "I don't—"

"Of course you do," Cain cut her off. He pried the empty glass from her fingers, put it back on the table, and all but lifted her on his own. When she was standing, he provided her with an arm to hold. At first, Thorn stared at him, the furrow to her brows going even deeper, but when she glanced at Darius, the coldness melted. She shook her head, rolled her eyes, and linked her wrist through Cain's elbow.

"See," he said, leading the way through the tables. Chris and Darius followed. "That wasn't so hard, now was it?"

"Shut up," Thorn said, but there was no venom in the words, and Cain let out a deep, rich laugh.

The dance floor hummed as dozens of other Martyrs

twirled to the music. Cain took Thorn's fingers, spun her to face him, and guided her into a beautiful, quick-paced two-step with graceful poise. He moved fluidly, and Thorn seemed as naturally adept at this as she was in everything else she did. Darius watched them for a moment before he turned to Chris. She was smiling at him.

"What?" he asked as he put a palm at her waist.

Chris took his other hand and laughed.

"I don't know," she said with a playful shrug. Her shawl slipped, and she adjusted it as her eyes darted over Darius's shoulder to where Thorn and Cain were dancing. "I just like weddings."

She looked at him again, and he couldn't stop the corners of his mouth from pulling into a grin.

For the next few minutes, they danced. Chris had no idea what she was doing, so Darius walked her through the steps. It wasn't long before the room was full of moving bodies, the heat from their auras hovering like an afternoon haze. It was clear who here had taken Cain's classes and who hadn't, but it didn't seem to matter. Every face Darius saw in the crowd was smiling.

Elijah and Colette swayed without concern for the tempo, forehead to forehead, while they whispered beneath the music. Parker and her father awkwardly shuffled and laughed in the corner. Madison danced with a group of women, center-stage between them while her focus trained in Darius's direction. Even Kit bounced on his heels with a crowd of people, a beer bottle in his hand. He met Darius's eye, and he raised the drink. Darius smiled back. A flash occasionally brightened the room while Caleb darted through moving bodies, his camera up and ready.

And sometimes, Darius caught a glimpse of Thorn, still among them yet apart from them, like a light shone just for her. As Cain held her hand, all the anger and bitterness drained away from her expression, her eyes awash with joy and a radiant smile across her painted lips.

Midway through a waltz, when Cain's back was turned

and Darius could see Thorn's face over the curve of his neck, Cain murmured something against her ear, and that smile disappeared. She faltered, a glimmer of worry darkening her eyes. Chris's grip slackened in Darius's hand, and she followed his gaze. Thorn's went hollow, unblinking for a few seconds, before she nodded, just once, and Cain nodded, too. Then he spun her away from a presence Darius didn't need to sense to know it was there.

Alan. He stood on the far side of the room, leaning against an empty dining table. His mouth tightened into a sharp line behind his black goatee as he considered Cain and Thorn. Darius paused, and Alan glanced up. When their eyes met, Alan straightened his spine and walked away. Darius watched him go until—

"Ouch!"

His heel landed on Chris's foot. She stumbled backward, and Darius barely managed to catch her before she fell. Her shawl furled to the ground as he pulled her upright again.

"Jesus, sorry," Darius said. He held her by the shoulders and looked down, where the black suede on her toe was scuffed. "You okay?"

"Yeah, I'm fine," Chris said, laughing through a wince. She turned to get her shawl, but Gabe had beaten her to it. He broke away from his group and knelt behind her to grab it from the tile. As he stood up, Chris's cheeks, already flushed from dancing, went darker.

"Thank you."

"No problem," Gabe said. Instead of handing the shawl to Chris, he draped it over her outreached forearm. She stood there, dumbfounded, but Gabe didn't walk away, and she did not turn back around. His eyes darted to Darius before he focused on Chris again and flashed his signature, crooked smile. "It gave me the excuse I was waiting for."

"Excuse for what?"

"To ask you for a dance."

Chris's lips parted in surprise, and she looked to Darius and then past him to where Madison was dancing across the room. "Oh. Well, Darius and I—"

"I need a break, actually," Darius cut in. He put a hand on her back and gently pushed her forward as he tilted his head at the shawl. "Want me to take that to the table? It keeps slipping anyway."

Chris grabbed the garment and hesitated, her fingers holding tight to the fabric. Then, she nodded, and she passed it off to him.

"That would be great."

"Awesome," Darius said. "Have fun."

As he walked away, Gabe swept Chris to the center of the dance floor. He took her by the waist and pulled her close—much closer than Darius had been dancing with her—and Darius smiled as he dropped her shawl onto the back of the chair beside his. Then, he looked back out at the crowd.

From a distance, the scene was somehow more impressive than being immersed inside it. A sea of bodies, of lives, full of love and laughter and light, so tightly tied together that Darius couldn't feel any single person apart from the others. He peered through bobbing heads and bare shoulders, hoping to catch a sign of Thorn again, but she and Cain had disappeared. Alan was gone, too.

Not Madison, though. Her eyes had fixed on Darius the moment she saw him leave the floor. His stomach twisted uncomfortably as he moved to take refuge by the dessert table and started piling pastries onto a plate, calculating how many he'd need to eat to get out of dancing for another hour. Behind his back, he felt Madison's warm energy make a beeline right for him.

He sighed. God, he was being ridiculous.

Darius was about to go back and face Madison like an adult when suddenly, she paused. He turned around.

Thorn was coming up behind him. She walked through the tables silently, moving like the wind—powerful and unstoppable. Behind her back, Madison lingered at the edge of the crowd. Thorn didn't seem to notice, or maybe she just didn't care. She stopped in front of Darius, and the corner of her mouth turned up in a smirk.

"I don't think you're getting your date back," Thorn said. The dim bulbs caught her face in shadow. Triangles of soft light highlighted her high cheekbones and the tip of her nose. She turned her head just enough to indicate the dance floor as Madison disappeared onto it.

Darius laughed and put his full plate on the table. "I'll live."

They both looked back. Chris was glowing, and Gabe watched her like he knew it—like the light pouring off her came from a star, and he was grateful just to be in orbit.

"I'm glad you got her to come," Thorn said. She crossed her arms around her chest, and they rose and fell in a low, slow breath. "I haven't seen her this happy since before her mother died."

"I was worried she'd be miserable," Darius admitted. "When I picked her up, she was so uncomfortable."

Thorn turned to him with a frown. "Why?"

"Her scars, I think. She didn't have a dress that covered them."

"What?" Thorn sounded genuinely surprised, and she looked back up. Her eyes sharpened on Chris. "She has nothing to be embarrassed about."

Darius's eyes darted to Thorn's forearms. "Yeah, I wonder where she picked that up…"

He indicated the fingerless gloves extending to Thorn's elbows. She waved him off. "These are just to protect my *Peccostium*. They're fireproof and cut-resistant—"

"Good thing, too," Darius interrupted. "Who knows which of the Martyrs out there has a knife strapped to their thigh? Probably quite a few of them, actually." He laughed, and Thorn's mouth broke into a half-smile, but it flickered on her lips.

"It's different," she tried again, but this time more quietly. "Chris got her scars out on the field. They're a sign of how hard she fights and how much she's survived."

Thorn held her left arm up, palm facing the ceiling, and ran her fingers from her wrist all the way down, following the fibrous lines of old acid burns Darius knew were hidden behind the black fabric. She shook her head.

"Mine aren't."

Darius watched her in the dark, taking in her somber expression. "That's not true."

Thorn glanced up, and he nodded toward her arm.

"Just because the monsters you fought were inside your head doesn't mean they weren't real. Cover your scars if you want, but if Chris doesn't have anything to be embarrassed about, neither do you."

For a moment, Thorn stared at him. Her attention moved from his eyes to his mouth, and he smiled. She raised a brow as she grabbed the edge of her glove and gently peeled it away. Her forearm opened up to the room, smooth skin shifting to tight scars before finally exposing the black *Peccostium* beneath her wrist joint. When she pulled the other glove off, too, she folded them together.

"Better?"

Darius wanted to say something clever, something meaningful, but the right words escaped him. Instead, he swallowed hard and nodded. "Much better."

Thorn's eyes sharpened in that deadly, serious way of hers, as though she could peer past Darius's body and directly into the depths of his soul. She brought her hand to his jacket, clasped the lapel with slender fingers, and pulled him toward her. Darius's breath hitched, and he was caught, spellbound, so close that he could smell the inviting scent of vanilla and sandalwood on her skin. As she slipped her gloves into his pocket, he leaned in, like he expected her to whisper in his ear. And she did, with a voice as rich and smooth as a shot of espresso.

"Dance with me."

He pulled back, jaw slack, and looked at her, half expecting this to be a dream, a joke, *something*, but Thorn didn't step away. Darius's heart came alive in his chest. Without a word, he held out a hand. Thorn considered his palm, her gaze carving a path from his wrist back to his face, dark eyes glistening, and her lips parted just enough for Darius to catch the pink flash of her tongue behind her teeth. His stomach swirled at the sight.

Then she dipped her fingers into his.

Whatever Cain had taught Darius disappeared somewhere between the dessert table and the dance floor. The moment Thorn wrapped her hand around his shoulder, everything else melted away. He held her close, his palm at her waist, her skin cold beneath his fingertips. It was like they were alone in the room. All Darius knew was the feeling of her—the pressure of her fingers against his skin, the musical sound of her laughter in his ear, and the way the glass bulbs overhead reflected in her irises, creating galaxies of warm light in the deep, endless black.

For several minutes, or hours, or lifetimes, they danced like that, too caught up in the music to do much of anything else. Then, the beat slowed, and a soft, quiet melody took its place. Dancers began to move away. Martyrs without a partner headed back to the dining area for food or drink. Darius caught Mackenzie apart from them. She and Kit were coming out from the elevator. He returned to the party, but her aura moved along the far wall, headed toward her quarters. Thorn must have sensed her, too. A breath rippled through her body. It lingered beneath Darius's palm.

"Are you okay?" he asked. "After what happened earlier?"

"I'm fine," Thorn said. Her jaw tightened, but there was honesty in her eyes. "I know how Mackenzie is. She can be tactless, tasteless… I just didn't realize that nerve was so raw."

"Why?"

"Because she's right," Thorn murmured. "I turned one hundred and forty-six in December. *One hundred and forty-six.* All I have is a list… I can't even remember most of their names. Only two people ever really meant anything to me, and I fucked it up both times."

Darius frowned. "I'm sure that's not true."

"I got one of them killed," Thorn said. "And Simon was so disgusted by who I'd become that he wanted *me* dead in the end."

"Wait," Darius said, his mind triggering on the name. "Simon Reed? The doctor who…"

He paused, not wanting to bring up old, painful memories, but Thorn nodded.

"Tried to pull the plug on me after I did this and got myself shot in the head." She raised her left hand, indicating her scars, before she put it around Darius again. This time, she drew closer. When she sighed, her warm breath poured against his throat. "That's the one. I don't blame him. He watched me break down after Donovan died and saw how many people I was willing to hurt for revenge. I would've wanted to pull the plug, too."

"Thorn," Darius started to say, but she cut him off.

"So, yeah." She cleared her throat. "Mackenzie hit that nerve, but it's not her fault."

"She was out of line," Darius said.

Thorn shook her head. "No, she really wasn't. She doesn't know *any* of that. I don't talk about it. It's unfair for me to get upset when people don't understand what I've gone through if I haven't given them the chance."

A smile teased at Darius's lips. "That sounds like something Cain would say."

Thorn gave a dark chuckle. He felt the tremor of it in his chest. "That obvious?" When Darius nodded, she did, too. "We just talked about it. He says I'm still young. That the first three hundred years are the hardest. God, I hate even saying that out loud." Her fingers dug into Darius's shoulder and against the back of his palm, like she needed the reassurance that he was still there.

"The truth is, Darius, events like this are hard for me," she went on quietly. She looked around at the Martyrs. Their laughter and warmth swirled the courtyard, echoing back in a way that seemed infinite. "I feel so… *stuck*. I have watched generations of people grow here. Celebrate new milestones, move onto new chapters… and I'm just doing the same goddamned thing I've done every day for a century."

"Did Cain have any advice for that?" he asked.

"The same thing I've heard him say a thousand times before," she said.

"Which is?"

"To live like I'm human," Thorn said. "To get attached, feel deeply, and embrace the end, whenever it comes. However it comes. But I don't know if I can. I'm so fucking sick of always being the person who has to say goodbye."

Darius's stomach dropped, and he glanced at Thorn to find her already watching the side of his face. He wondered then how many times she'd looked at him just like this— like she'd peered into her future and couldn't imagine him within it. After a moment, she pulled back, putting more distance between them, an invisible wall she could safely hide behind.

Darius wished he could comfort her—that he could tell her she wouldn't always feel so trapped.

But he couldn't, and she knew it.

———

Darius closed his door, and he felt cold.

After hours surrounded so closely by warm, human energy, being alone sent a shiver across his shoulders, like he'd stepped into an air-conditioned building after a jog in the sun. He paused over the threshold, looked around his room, and drew in a breath that turned into a yawn.

God, he was exhausted.

When he and Thorn had decided to leave, the party was still roaring. Even at two in the morning, music pushed across the courtyard, the heavy bass rattling the walls and pulsing through Darius's feet until they'd passed the first turn in the eastern block of rooms. He couldn't remember the last time he was up this late on purpose, for *fun*.

He walked toward his bed, loosening the top buttons of his shirt as he went, and sat down. Months ago, he'd taken the time to order some simple decor for himself—forest green bedding, industrial table lamps, an abstract art piece of the Williamsburg Street Bridge made by a local artist—just so the space didn't feel so sterile. He stared at the bridge as he untied his laces, and his tired mind wandered.

Three years ago, he associated that bridge with home.

Darius kicked his shoes off and lined them up nicely by his bedside table. Three years ago, he hadn't even had a bedside table—or shoes without holes in them—and he certainly never would have imagined attending a wedding like this one.

He got to his feet and walked to his dresser. His arches ached, but in that good way, and he stretched them as he shrugged his suit jacket off his shoulders. When he laid it across his dresser, a lump in the pocket made him pause. With a frown, Darius reached inside. His fingers closed around a thick, familiar fabric. Where had he felt that before?

Darius pulled it out, and his heart skipped a beat: Thorn's gloves. He lingered there for a moment. Her perfume still clung to them, and he could detect the slightest scent of her in the room. He closed his eyes, shook his head, and put them on the dresser.

There had to be a line here—somewhere between the insurmountable pain of Thorn's past and a present she didn't know how to embrace. He wasn't sure exactly where it stood, but he did know he'd hedged close to it tonight.

With a sigh, Darius finished getting ready, and he tried hard to think of something, anything, other than her. He put on pajamas, brushed his teeth in the bathroom down the hall, and finally threw himself into bed. From here, he couldn't hear the music in the courtyard, but he got a sense of the party from the feeling of energy fluttering around. It must have been dying down. Martyrs were drifting, pulled like paper on the wind in different directions.

As he turned off his bedside light, some of that energy moved in this direction. Darius recognized Chris and Gabe among them. They walked with a group of other Martyrs before separating and heading toward Chris's room. Minutes later, they paused outside her door, and the edges of their auras merged together. Darius chuckled to himself.

Then they went inside, and the humor died. There were moments he never wanted to intrude upon, and *this* was one of them.

Closing his eyes, wishing he could close out his Virtue senses just as easily, Darius began to meditate. His focus followed, and the plane of Martyr energy blurred around him, becoming indistinct and ill-defined as Darius worked to clear his mind. That was better.

Better, but not perfect. He was too tired, and his thoughts wandered. Flashes of work and the new Virtue in New York City. Memories of his childhood and life before the Martyrs. Thorn. Her face or her voice or the way her skin felt cool against his whenever they touched.

After a few minutes, he quit fighting it, and Darius drifted off to sleep, counting the flecks of light reflecting in her eyes.

CHAPTER EIGHT

Nearly all the snow from the previous weeks had melted, leaving grimy mounds of packed, muddy ice behind in the gutters. Even so, the cold was bitter and biting, and hazy winter clouds cast New York City in dreary shadows. As he glanced north on Broadway, Darius zipped his coat up to his throat, shoving his gloved hands deep into its pockets. His breath lifted around his head in a cloud of condensation.

Mackenzie stormed out of the stairwell behind him.

"I can't believe I missed it!" She bounded up to Darius's left, practically giddy. Her puff jacket extended past her knees, making her look like a bright blue marshmallow with a pair of denim twigs sticking out the bottom. The garage they'd parked in rattled as other cars rumbled through it, and Mackenzie shouted, probably not to be heard but because she just felt like shouting about this. "DuPont and *Chris!* Did that happen? *Really?*"

Darius chuckled and glanced to his left right before darting through a gap in traffic to cross the street. Mackenzie stuck to him like a child eager for sweets. "I told you," he said. "I don't know."

"They were just dancing," Kit said with a shrug as he and Madison followed. Mackenzie rounded on him in the middle of the road, earning a chorus of honks as she forced their whole group to stop.

"Dancing!" she exclaimed. Darius grabbed her by the elbow and pulled her the rest of the way across while she squealed.

"How the hell didn't you notice?" Darius asked with a laugh.

Mackenzie waved her hands in broad, dismissive circles. "I had a lot of other stuff going on. The real question is, how did *you* not tell me they were *dancing?*"

"People dance at weddings all the time," Madison said, almost defensively. "It doesn't mean they're into each other." Her voice raised an octave on the final word, like she was suggesting something else—about *someone* else. They'd been driving through the city all morning, and so far, Madison had made a handful of prying comments that no one else seemed to pick up on.

Darius wasn't playing the game.

"It also doesn't matter," he said. "Can we *please* focus?"

Madison looked at him, and her brows twitched upward. Darius pretended he didn't notice as they hopped onto the far curb. Traffic blasted by, and Mackenzie ignored the volley of swear words and middle fingers thrown her way. Kit flipped them off in return as she turned to Darius.

"I am focused," she said. "You're Chris's best friend. She'll tell you. You've gotta ask her."

Mackenzie peered up at him from beneath navy bangs with bright-eyed insistence. Darius shook his head.

"I'm not going to."

And he didn't need to. He knew Gabe had gone into Chris's room, and he knew he'd still been there in the morning when Darius woke up. It had been three days, and Chris hadn't said anything to him. He figured when, and if, she wanted to confide in him, she would.

"Aw, come on!" Mackenzie said. "If they get together, I win the bet!"

Darius cast her a dubious look. "A bet against *John.*"

Mackenzie's delight teetered, bouncing between realization and reservation, and she slowly nodded. Her tongue piercing slid against her teeth as she pulled it between them. "Fuck. You're right. God damn it, even if I win, I lose!"

"Well," Darius began with a sigh as they reached the intersection where Broadway, Columbus, and 65th met. He looked east, where he could see Central Park's naked trees poking through traffic a block away. "Do you think maybe it isn't the best idea to make bets on your friends' personal lives?"

"Jesus, you're still on that?" Mackenzie snapped behind him. "I guess we're just gonna drag up all my sins first thing in the morning."

Darius frowned. "What?"

He turned to see her glaring at him, hands on her hips, but she didn't respond, instead shoving past him to stomp down 65th. Darius glanced at Kit, who just shrugged, before he followed her.

"Hey, what was that?" Darius asked as he came up to Mackenzie's side. He tried to put a hand on her arm to get her attention, but Mackenzie pulled away. "What's wrong?"

"I'm just sick of always being set up to be the bad guy."

"Mackenzie, no one thinks you're the bad guy."

"Sure, whatever. Lewis!" Mackenzie suddenly shouted, turning to Madison and Kit while she walked backward. "You got the map?"

Madison grabbed her phone and unlocked the screen. "Right here." Mackenzie held her palm out, opening and closing her fingers until Madison dropped the device into them. Then she barreled forward without any concern for the people who had to walk around her on the sidewalk as she flicked through their plan for the day.

"Returning to the scene of the crime," she huffed. "We've checked here before."

"But not at this time of day," Darius said.

"Yeah," Mackenzie said, but she didn't sound optimistic about it. Truth be told, Darius wasn't, either. "All right. Let's get on it, then."

She darted down the street, moving between other pedestrians like they weren't there at all. Darius tried to catch her eye, but Mackenzie made a point of not looking at him. By the time they reached the park, he gave up. At the corner of 65th, Darius looked across the street, his eyes shifting between indistinct civilians hidden behind heavy winter clothing. There were *so* many people. He could easily walk this whole damned city on foot and never meet the same one twice. His heart sank.

How the hell were they going to find a Virtue here? The only clue they had was at this intersection…

"Any tingly Virtue feelings, Jones?" Mackenzie asked. "Or is this just a fat waste of our time?"

Darius sighed and ignored her. "Let's start with the park," he said, glancing both ways before he crossed Central Park West. "Then we can zig-zag through the neighborhoods…"

"On foot?" Kit groaned. He lumbered stiffly onto the curb and grabbed a plastic box out of his pocket, where the painkillers Dr. Harris had prescribed were kept. He tilted one into his palm and tossed it into his mouth. Darius gave him a useless, sympathetic shrug.

"Yeah," he said. "I'm sorry, but I want to be thorough. Something felt off the last time I sensed this Virtue, but it was gone too quickly for me to tell what it was. I don't want to miss anything again."

"If you *ever* feel it again," Mackenzie said with a snort.

Darius threw her a sharp look. "Hey, if you don't want to be here, you're more than welcome to wait in the car." Her eyes widened, and she blinked, shocked. When she opened her mouth to argue, Darius held up a hand to stop her. "Look, I want you to stick around, but we're supposed to be working. Being cranky with me isn't helping, and I don't deserve to be treated this way. Let's finish up here so we can go home, and you can have it out with Thorn like you clearly want to. Sound good?"

For a few seconds, it looked like Mackenzie was going to keep fighting. Her nostrils flared, and her tongue piercing clattered angrily against her teeth. At last, though, her shoulders rose and fell in a sigh.

"Okay," Darius said. "Let's go."

The walk started off cold and quiet, and not just because of the weather. Mackenzie staunchly refused to speak while they walked around the ballfields, the playground, and the pond. By the time they reached the Wollman Ice Skating Rink, though, her sourness seemed to break. They approached a coffee cart near the front kiosk, and Mackenzie rubbed her palms together.

"Jesus, it's freezing out here. Anyone else want a mocha? My treat."

Darius raised a brow. "The Martyrs pay for everything."

"It's just an expression," Mackenzie said. "Now shut up, and let me make things better by pretending to pay for a cup of coffee."

Darius smiled. "I'll take a flat white."

Several minutes later, their hands wrapped around hot paper cups, they found themselves walking through the mall. Even in forty-degree weather, booths and tables lined the walkway, filling the space with arts, crafts, and curiosities. People pushed around them, giving Darius the illusion of warmth as their human energies hovered in the air. He was reminded of the Williamsburg Bridge Street Market. The rituals were the same—men and women bartering what they had for what they could, no matter the time of the year or the state of the world, because it was all they could do to survive. He'd met quite a few vendors who had started in Central Park before their luck ran out and pushed them further south, out of their overcrowded studio flats and into the projects on the Lower East Side. He wondered how many of these people were sitting on the fine edge of that blade right now, and he wished he could whip out his Martyr credit card to purchase all their merchandise and make their lives a little easier.

"This is insane," Mackenzie said. She waved her phone in Darius's face. "D'you know how many people live in New York City right now? Almost fifteen million! There's no way in ever-loving fuck we're going to find the Virtue this way."

"You guys found me," Darius said, clinging to hope even as his stomach twisted.

Mackenzie shook her head as she shoved her device into her puff jacket pocket. "It took *forever* to find you," she argued. "That old Virtue felt you in The Bronx right around when I joined the Martyrs—*eighteen years ago*. I heard talk about this Virtue in the city as soon as I became a part of the thing. We had people looking for you for as long as I could remember. I thought you were a myth."

She laughed, elbowing Darius lightly, but not so lightly that her mocha didn't bubble through the mouthpiece in her lid. Mackenzie took a sip and frowned.

"What are you thinking?" Darius asked.

"Not sure, but we've gotta do something different," she said. "There has to be a better way."

"If there is," Darius said, "I don't know it."

Mackenzie sighed. "God, I wish Lina were here. She was great at thinking through stuff like this."

A brush of tears glistened behind Mackenzie's lashes, making her blue eyes brighter and the shadows beneath them darker. Darius's chest constricted, and he laid a palm on her shoulder. She glanced up at him before clearing her throat, rubbing her eyes with the tips of her fingers, and letting out a groan.

"Anyway, I'll bug Nicholas. Maybe he's got some ideas bouncing around in that over-inflated head of his."

She winked, but this one looked more somber than usual, and started toward Bethesda Fountain.

They spent the rest of the afternoon traversing the lower half of Central Park with nothing to show for it. Darius dragged them from the Met to Belvedere Castle, up through the Great Lawn, and as far north as the southern shore of the reservoir. He leaned against the wrought iron fence and looked out at the water, heaving a sigh.

"We're officially north of Lincoln Square," Kit said. He stood to Darius's side and shifted uncomfortably as he put his weight against the fence, too. "If we wanted to check out those neighborhoods, we've gotta go back south."

"Sounds good," Darius said, but it didn't sound good. It sounded like more hard work without any reward. He turned to Kit to see the man stretching his back. "How are you feeling?"

"Stiff but good," Kit said. "Meds should kick in any minute now."

A twinge of guilt made Darius frown, but there was nothing he could do about it. He glanced up to Mackenzie, who was chatting with Madison a couple of yards down the fence line. "Hey, how do you feel about heading back to the car? Take it through the neighborhoods instead of walking."

Mackenzie's face lit up. "You serious? I'd sell a kidney on the black market to get out of this cold."

Madison and Darius laughed as Kit pushed away from the fence. "We can take the C train," he said. "There's a stop at 86th."

"Fucking excellent," Mackenzie said.

Kit led them out of the park and back into the urban reality of New York City. The intersection at 86th and Central Park West swarmed with vehicles and pedestrians alike, their energy warm and inviting but not at all what Darius was looking for right now. As they crossed the road, he felt it in every direction—including above, in the apartment complex, and below, on the subway. When he'd first come back to New York after Initiating Kindness, all of these auras would have overwhelmed him, but now it faded into the background, as normal and inconsequential as the white noise of the market had been.

Halfway across the street, Darius felt a train barreling toward him. The movement of hundreds of warm bodies deep below the ground surged in and away from him so quickly that he hardly had the time to focus on them. He'd felt the sensation dozens of times before, but this time, something about it clicked.

There and gone in an instant.

He grabbed Mackenzie's wrist with a gasp.

"Oh, my god," he said. This time, she was the one who pulled him to the far side before traffic crashed into him. Cars laid on their horns, but Darius ignored them. "Mackenzie! I know why the Virtue's energy felt so off. I can't believe I didn't figure this out before."

She frowned. "What the hell are you going on about?"

"The subway," Darius said. "The Virtue was riding the subway that night."

Her eyes went wide. "Holy shit," she said. "Do you know what this means?" Darius shook his head, and Mackenzie did, too. "Me neither, but it's somewhere to start! Way the fuck better than 'there's a Virtue in New York.' C'mon! We've gotta talk to Wolfe."

Nicholas bit into an egg salad sandwich and frowned at the subway map on his phone.

"Whelp," he said from the corner of his mouth. The word came out muffled around his lunch. "This fucks up my whole theory."

Darius leaned across the table to look at the map, too. Mackenzie, sitting on his other side, picked at her food absently while her foot tapped on the ground. The afternoon crowd was in full swing, so they'd taken a table near the edge of the dining area, and even then, they were surrounded by other Martyrs. Off-duty TAC officers, researchers, and nursing staff buzzed around, and at the nearest table, Caleb pored over a laptop with a cup of coffee.

"Yeah," Darius said. "It means the Virtue might not be in Lincoln Square at all."

"They could have come from literally anywhere in the city," Nicholas confirmed. "Damn it." He took another bite and leaned back in his chair, considering the tall ceiling. All the wedding decorations had been taken down and put away, so it was back to vaulted concrete and bright daylight bulbs.

"It also makes me wonder what kind of person we're looking for," Nicholas said after a moment. "A local out with all the bullshit happening makes sense. First responder, same thing. What day of the week was this again?"

"Uhm." Darius squinted one eye closed as he thought back. "It was a Sunday—well, early Monday morning."

Nicholas lifted a hand into the air in indignation, chewing around his annoyance. "See, that's what I mean. Who the *fuck* is riding the subway at three a.m. on a *Monday?*"

Darius sighed. "I don't know. Anyone who works nights? Healthcare, hospitality, housekeepers…"

"Alcoholics," Mackenzie added. When they turned to her, she shrugged. Her chipped nails tapped against her bicep. "Most bars have their last call at two."

"Great," Nicholas said. "I'll just get a list of all the hospitals, clinics, hotels, restaurants, and bars in the city. That'll narrow it down." He swore under his breath and pushed his empty plate away, brushing the crumbs off his fingertips. Caleb glanced at their table. "Do we at least know if it was going north or south?"

"No," Darius said.

"Perfect," Nicholas said. "We've got a Virtue in New York, who could be *anywhere* in New York, and all we know is that they ride the subway and, at least once, were up at three in the goddamned morning on a Monday." He groaned and ran his hands down his face, raking his strawberry-blonde stubble with his nails.

"Uh, excuse me?" Caleb cleared his throat and raised a hand. Nicholas turned around while Mackenzie and Darius looked over his shoulder. Caleb twisted in his chair to face them more fully. Behind him, his computer screen glowed with a filmstrip view of photographs from the wedding. "Why don't you just check out the subway stops?"

Nicholas frowned and crossed his arms. "Why?"

"Most people live their lives by patterns," Caleb said. "If the Virtue was on the subway at three in the morning, they probably ride the subway a lot. Probably even that same train."

Darius and Nicholas exchanged a curious, impressed look before Nicholas grabbed the fourth chair from their table and pulled it out, tilting his head at it and indicating for Caleb to join them. Caleb grabbed his computer in one hand, his coffee in the other, and sat down between Nicholas and Mackenzie.

"So," Nicholas said when Caleb was settled. "You were saying…"

"Uh, yeah. Basically everyone has patterns, right? Think about this place." Caleb gestured around the courtyard. "We've all got routines and schedules and things we do every day. It's like that in New York, too. It might not look like it, but when you pay attention to people long enough, you start picking it up."

"Which is what you do," Nicholas said.

Caleb nodded. "Yeah. It's how we try to identify a Sin's new host. Like, right now, I'm watching a few people in Lust's old circles that I think are good candidates for a new possession to see if they have any sudden changes in behavior or schedules or anything like that. Anything that breaks their routine."

"A three a.m. subway ride is a pretty wild routine," Mackenzie countered with a frown. As she spoke, she leaned against Caleb's shoulder and peeked at the photographs on his screen. Caleb's pale cheeks went pink, but she didn't notice.

"Well, we don't have enough information to say if it's routine or not," Caleb said, "but even if that ride was a one-time thing, the Virtue has to be comfortable with the area if they're riding the subway at three in the morning. I'd bet it's their regular line."

Darius nodded and turned to Nicholas, who shrugged in

agreement. "It gives us somewhere to start, at least," Darius said.

"We'll have to work out the details with Chris and Gabe to see how our extended TAC patrols would change," Nicholas said. He glanced at Mackenzie for confirmation, but she'd started tapping through Caleb's pictures and didn't acknowledge him. Nicholas focused on Darius again. "But camping out near subway stops will be a hell of a lot easier than walking around."

"Yeah, but you could draw attention," Caleb said. "The people who know the area really well will start to notice. It's weird when some guy sits at the same park bench for eight hours."

"The man's got a point," Nicholas murmured. "We could—"

"AH HAH!"

Mackenzie jumped to her feet, nearly tripping over them, and barely managed to catch herself by putting an arm entirely around Caleb's shoulders. The both of them tilted to the side, Caleb bracing against the table as Mackenzie pointed at his computer screen. "I *knew* it! Look at this! Look!"

She leapt up, grabbed Caleb's laptop, and spun it on the table. Then she ran in an awkward circle to Darius's side. Her tiny body all but slammed into him. "You can't tell me this is *just dancing!*"

Chris's face glowed from the monitor, a larger, central photo surrounded by a mosaic of smaller thumbnails. The focus was entirely on her, only showing the back of Gabe's head while they swayed arm in arm. Even the background beyond her was a swirling mix of color and light, truly isolating Chris in a way that felt surreally familiar to what Darius had personally experienced that evening. It was hard to tell how close they were from this angle, but her eyes fixed on Gabe so ardently that Darius was struck with the sensation that he was intruding on a private moment.

But he had to admit, it was pretty damning evidence, and

he wasn't sure he could talk his way out of this one.

Nicholas saved him the trouble.

"McKay," he snapped, and then he *literally* snapped, holding his hand in front of Caleb's computer to draw her attention. When she finally looked at him, he threw his shoulders up in a universal "what the fuck" gesture.

"Sorry," she said, still bouncing and anything *but* sorry as she tore herself away from Darius and crossed her arms with a sheepish grin. She shrank into her chair and held a palm up for Nicholas to continue. He watched her, exasperated, for a moment longer before he shook his head.

"As I was saying," he continued, "we could walk a circuit. We're focusing on…" He paused, grabbed his phone, and navigated to the subway map again. "…the A and B lines beneath Central Park West, and we know the Virtue made it as far south as 66th Street. We could start at Columbus Circle and walk up to the 81st Street Station, then turn around and come back down."

"You say '*we*,'" Mackenzie said, her eyes going narrow, "but I don't see *you* out there walking a million miles every day."

"Yeah, it probably would have to be every day, too," Nicholas said, ignoring the jab. "Or, at least, more often. If we're trying to figure out whether or not this commute is part of the Virtue's routine, we have to be there pretty consistently."

"Gee, you're really selling me on this idea," Mackenzie said.

Darius leaned forward on the table. "*I'm* sold," he said. Caleb's computer was still turned his way, and he absently looked at the wedding photos as he spoke. One of the thumbnails caught his attention, a flash of black and green. His heart flipped, and he stumbled over his thoughts as he looked back to the rest of the table. "On walking, going down more often, whatever it takes to find this Virtue."

"Great," Nicholas said, only this time, he sounded like he meant it. Darius glanced back at the screen as Nicholas slapped his hands on his thighs. "This feels like a solid plan. I'll start writing it today so we can bring it up at the next leadership meeting."

"Sounds good," Mackenzie said. She stretched back in her chair, her spine cracking between her shoulder blades as she bent it over the metal. Then, she got to her feet. "I'll go find Kit and let him know what's coming. Maybe I'll chat with Chris, too… About… TAC assignments."

She winked at Darius, and he rolled his eyes. As she sauntered off, Nicholas stared after her.

"Has she always been like this?" he asked. "I can't get her to focus on fucking *anything*."

Darius shrugged, and finally, he gave in to temptation. He tapped the right arrow button on the keyboard, and the photography program flipped to a new picture. This one showed Conrad, Seth, and Kit shotgunning cans of imported beer. "I always figured it wasn't about forcing her to focus on something specific but finding something she *could* focus on."

Darius hit the key again. Another picture. Alan speaking with Raquel and Skylar by the head table.

"I think it's been hard without Lina," Caleb said. Darius glanced up to see him watching the elevator doors slide shut behind Mackenzie's back. A glint of affection flickered in the hurt across his face.

"Yeah," Nicholas agreed with a sigh. "That's a good point. Losing people can mess you up for a while… especially losing them like that."

The memory roared into Darius's mind, and suddenly, he was overwhelmed by the stomach-turning smell of charred human flesh. Lina had died seconds before Darius had been able to heal her. He'd never forget the hollow, lost look on Thorn's face when he'd opened the door to find her clutching Lina's lifeless hand…

He tapped the keyboard, looked down at the screen, and paused.

He'd rather remember this. He and Thorn captured in

time, frozen mid-dance. Her delicate fingers wrapped around his, his palm pressed flat to the small of her back. He recalled this moment vividly, like it played on repeat. He had just caught her at the end of a spin and dipped her back on the return. She'd thrown her head back in a laugh so radiant and free that it wrinkled the bridge of her nose and showed off a sliver of pink gums above her teeth. God, he'd never seen her look this happy.

He'd never seen himself this happy, either. While she laughed, he just watched her, soaking her in. Darius suddenly realized he was lucky Mackenzie stopped snooping before she'd found this one, too.

Nicholas's voice snapped him back to the present. "Darius?"

His eyes darted up. Nicholas and Caleb watched him. "Sorry." He shook his head as he gestured down to the computer. "Caleb, man, these pictures are incredible."

He scrolled forward a few paces, paused the roll on a photo of the brides, and turned the laptop back around.

Caleb chuckled and ran his fingers through his platinum hair. "Thanks."

Nicholas snagged the computer and started looking through the images, too. He let out an impressed whistle. "Holy shit. Can we get copies? I wanna print some of these for Skylar and Raquel before they get back from their honeymoon."

"I mean, yeah. Just let me know which ones. They're also on the server, so you can download whatever you want."

Across the table, Nicholas and Caleb pored over the laptop, talking now about brides and weddings instead of Sins and Virtues. Darius, meanwhile, grabbed his phone out of his pocket and started going through the server.

He had never had photographs of any of the important people in his life. Everything was digital, saved on old data chips rotting away in a landfill by now. After his father died inside the slide in St. Mary's Park, Darius had kept his old phone for as long as he could just to turn it back on and stare at the image on the lock screen: a family portrait of Ayda and Garret Jones with a bright-eyed, unbroken Darius, back when Ayda had been alive and Garret had been sober. Well, sober enough.

This was more than one sentimental picture on an old, dying device. There were hundreds of photographs here, and he found gems among them. He and Chris in the front row with Alan. Skylar and Raquel at the altar. Mackenzie laughing with John. And, of course, the one of him and Thorn. He downloaded them all.

CHAPTER NINE

Finding safe locations for TAC to stand by was one of the hardest parts of organizing an operation like this.

It had to be perfect: close enough to the scene without being so close that any Sins present would immediately notice suspicious auras, subtle enough that people walking by on the streets or through buildings wouldn't get uncomfortable and call the authorities, and large enough for Martyrs to carry weapons, armor, and other offensive gear just in case things went wrong.

These locations were even harder to find in the goddamned Financial District.

While all of Manhattan was busy, the Financial District boasted vaulting towers, narrow streets, and enough tourist traffic to fund the rest of the island for an entire year. The city had poured money here, building higher, extending further, and packing as many bodies into a half square mile as it possibly could. The cold energy pulsed with a life of its own, hungry and demanding.

The Financial District was more than the central hub for New York's commercial prestige: it was an international powerhouse. People came from around the world to do business and get steeped in the Sins' evil, bringing that corruption and Influence with them across oceans to incite policy and violence in other nations.

The Sins hadn't had to take over the world to dominate it. They just needed to take over the city that dominated the world.

That, more than anything, made planning an operation in the Financial District complicated. Thorn wasn't sure how the hell they could avoid casualties if violence broke out.

She walked down Greenwich Street, her hands shoved deep into the pockets of her kevlar bike jacket, as she created a mental map of her options. Couldn't have people armed and armored on the streets. There were too many witnesses, and Cain couldn't hold Influence long enough to disguise them during Bently's event. She could park SUVs along street corners, but construction narrowed the roads. Huge concrete blocks choked the traffic as it moved south, leaving no room for anyone to stop.

They'd have to go in disguise.

Thorn considered the construction trucks. The color. The make. The size and how many people she imagined she could shove in there with full TAC gear and M4 rifles. Not enough—not for a situation where trying to plant a bug on Greed could send a room full of Puppetted moguls in their best evening wear into a bloodthirsty rage of Sin panic.

Delivery trucks would be better. She turned the corner and headed back toward Trinity Place, where the Mezzanine event space overlooked the street below. Thorn gazed left and right, wondering if Greed would be able to sense her team's auras at the foot of the building and know that something was going on.

Then again, there were so temany goddamned people here that maybe he wouldn't notice hers at all. A current of pedestrians pushed around Thorn, their energy a cool draft behind her back that sent a tickle down her spine. She frowned and looked over her shoulder, where a woman peered at her from a park bench inside a fenced-off plaza across the street. When Thorn met her eye, the woman turned away, but the feeling that something was off didn't fade. Thorn pulled her hood over her head and turned down the alley beside the venue.

For the next few minutes, Thorn walked in circles around the block, noting locations for delivery vans to pull up to the building and calculating how many TAC units she wanted to bring. When she started hunting for the best place to establish Darius and the rest of the medical team, her heart twinged.

How far was far enough to guarantee nothing could happen to him? *Could* she guarantee that? Or was she leading him and the rest of the Martyrs on a suicide mission?

Alan's doubts wormed their way into Thorn's thoughts, finding the weak points and devouring them until she was left full of holes. Maybe he was right. If this went south, it wouldn't just claim Martyr lives. A lot of people would die here. Darius's face flashed through her mind, so vivid that she could make out the day-old stubble across his chin, and when she pressed her eyes closed, she could almost feel his palm against her back. A warm flush rushed across Thorn's cheeks.

Darius had been interrupting her thoughts more than usual, like he'd found an open window to her mind. She never should have listened to Cain—never should have asked Darius for that goddamned dance. It was *never* just a dance. It was a dream and, at its core, a delusion… a *distraction* Thorn couldn't afford right now.

Was she really hesitant to run this operation against Anton Claytor because it was risky… or because it could put *Darius* in danger?

Thorn turned around and stormed up Broadway, making her way to where she'd parked her bike a few blocks away. As she did, an alert pinged on her phone—a coded message from an unknown number sent to the public line she used exclusively for the people she Programmed in the city. A location marker and two letters: AH.

The pit of Thorn's stomach dropped so quickly it stole her breath with it, and she scrambled to her map. The icon flashed on the screen, underlining a name Thorn recognized because she'd been there barely a week ago planting Sentries in the hopes of finding Greed. Crave Media LLC: the advertising firm promoting Mayor Bently's campaign and overseeing his events.

Autumn Hunt was there.

Thorn leapt onto her bike and tore through Manhattan, weaving between slow traffic and angry pedestrians whose middle fingers turned in her direction as she headed north. Part of her considered calling for backup, but she didn't want to get people riled up if it turned out to be nothing… Not before she did a little bit of reconnaissance on her own first.

Fifteen minutes later, Thorn pulled onto the sidewalk and gazed up at the high-rise. Crave Media's headquarters looked down at her from the third floor. She scanned the auras inside, focusing on their distinctiveness to see if she recognized any. She didn't. Wrath was gone. Thorn's eyes narrowed.

What the hell was Autumn Hunt doing at Mayor Bently's advertising agency? She didn't usually dig her fingers into this kind of industry. Thorn could only imagine one other possibility.

Wrath was going to be at this event.

She grabbed her phone, ready to call Alan and let him know, but she paused.

If he thought there was even the shadow of a chance that Autumn Hunt would be there, Thorn was sure he would call it off.

Thorn pulled her lower lip between her teeth, her nails tapping against the back of her device, while Alan's name started back up at her from the screen.

Then she shut it down, slipped it into her pocket, and rolled off the curb.

It might not have been a million miles like Mackenzie had complained about, but it was still a lot of walking.

Seventeen blocks separated Columbus Circle from the Museum of Natural History, and while the distance didn't feel very long on its own, it certainly did after walking it repeatedly for six hours a day, three days in a row.

Darius was relatively certain half of his team wanted to kill him.

"My feet are going to fall off," Mackenzie said as they sat down at a coffee shop just off Central Park West. "And when they do, I'm gonna hit you with them."

She groaned and shrugged her puff jacket off her shoulders. Kit sat to her right and Darius across the table. The shop bustled with people filtering in from the streets as the sun started to go down. They'd made the turn into March over the weekend, and the first signs of spring showed in days that were getting just a little bit longer and a sky that wasn't quite as bleak.

"It's not *that* bad," Darius said. Mackenzie threw him a dirty look, and Kit didn't look at him at all, shifting uncomfortably in his chair.

"I agree," Madison said. She'd gone to grab water from the station by the pick-up counter and placed a tall glass in front of each of them. As she slid Darius's toward him, she watched him with a playful smile. "I'm having a good time."

"Well, good for you," Mackenzie said.

Madison laughed. "A little cardio never hurt anybody."

She flashed Darius another look, and he awkwardly shifted in his seat. "I suppose so."

Mackenzie ignored them. "I'm starting to think Claytor was full of shit with this routine thing," she groaned.

"It's only been three days," Darius said.

"Three days should be enough if his stupid theory was right."

"Alan told us to give it to the end of the week," Darius

said. "If we haven't made any progress by then, we'll come up with a new plan."

With a sigh, Mackenzie lifted her glass, but she didn't drink. Instead, she swirled the water, watching ice chips twirl in circles before putting it down again. She looked exhausted, her dark blue hair a sharp contrast to her pale, washed-out skin. As the barista came to the table, dropping off two black coffees, a mocha, and some complicated latte with a set of ingredients that made it seem more like a science experiment than anything safe for consumption, Mackenzie ran her hands down her face.

"We knew this wasn't going to happen overnight," Darius said. Mackenzie peered at him through her fingers. "New York is a big city."

"We better not be walking the whole thing," Kit said, picking up his coffee. He grabbed Mackenzie's mocha and slid it to her across the table. "I don't think my back could handle it."

Darius frowned. "We could always request another TAC guard—"

"No," Mackenzie cut in, so fast that the rest of them snapped to look at her. "It's fine. We'll make it work. Sore feet and all."

"Well," Darius said, "maybe I can help. Here."

He laid his hand face up on the table. Mackenzie's brow raised as Kit looked down at his palm with a frown. "Here what?"

But Madison understood. Her lips curled in a smile, and she ran her nails along the inside of Darius's fingers before she laced hers between them—much more intimately than he'd been expecting. Darius cleared his throat and adjusted his grip to something less personal, and then, he opened himself up. Their energies mingled instantly, and he felt the tenderness in her heels reflected in a shadow of tension along his. He pushed a little healing power into her, and the sensation disappeared. When he was done, Madison didn't pull back, so he drew his hand away.

"Mmm. I don't know that I'll ever get used to that," she said. The apples of her cheeks blushed, and she nudged his elbow with hers. "Thanks."

"Ooh, my turn!" Mackenzie said.

She thrust her hand across the table and grabbed Darius's so quickly that he hardly had time to prepare. Her fingers felt cold, and they shook as he gripped them. The second Mackenzie's lukewarm aura met with his, Darius felt so much more than sore feet. Within seconds, he got a dizzy sense in his head that he hadn't experienced before. Healing energy didn't localize just in her heels and the balls of her feet; it coursed through her body like it was following the current of her circulatory system. When Darius pulled away, he felt a momentary sense of nausea.

"That was weird," he said. "Are you okay?"

"What happened?" Kit asked, his voice sharp enough to catch Darius off guard.

Mackenzie waved him away with a quick flick of her wrist before she answered Darius. "I'm good, yeah."

"Are you getting sick?" he pressed. "I got this… all-over feeling that you weren't doing well."

Mackenzie's eyes widened, and she glanced at her palm. She wasn't as shaky now. "You can do that with healing?" When Darius nodded, she did, too. "Well, I mean, I did wake up feeling achy and tired today. I just figured it was from all the walking."

"That's amazing," Darius said. He looked down at his own hands. Now, his fingers were quivering, and he flexed them to get the blood pumping again. "I've heard Virtues can heal sickness, but I've never actually done it before."

Mackenzie laughed and ran her fingers through her hair, pulling the blue strands out of order. "Well, you better keep that one under wraps. Dr. Harris will never let you leave the hospital ward if he finds out you can cure the common cold. You better know, though, I'm coming for you the next time I get sick."

She winked, and Darius laughed. Then, he turned to Kit

and reached out a hand. Kit stared at it warily before curling his nose and shaking his head.

"Nah. I'm good."

"C'mon, Kit," Madison said, propping her elbows on the table and leaning into them. "It's super fast."

"And it feels great," Mackenzie said. "Better than morphine."

But Kit shook his head again and held his palms out. "Seriously, I'll live. You might be able to heal a virus, but you can't do shit for old injuries, right? And *that's* what's hurting me."

Darius was confident he'd be able to ease at least a little of Kit's discomfort, but he didn't press the matter. Instead, he wrapped his hands around his coffee.

"We'll figure out a way to make this easier on you," he said as he took a sip. "We can take more breaks or hang out a bit longer before moving on. The subway runs under this whole street. As long as we're somewhere on Central Park West, I should feel if the Virtue is on any of the trains."

"Sounds good," Kit agreed. He grabbed his coffee, too, and Mackenzie finally started drinking hers. Darius realized it was the first thing he'd seen her consume all day. A guilty surge dropped into the pit of his stomach. This was taking a bigger toll on them than he realized. They were literally getting sick and tired out here in the cold. Though he wouldn't admit it out loud, Mackenzie's frustrations triggered his own uncertainty. He'd been hoping to know more by now, hoping that three days *would* be enough to sense the Virtue. Now, he wasn't so sure.

The four of them enjoyed their drinks and talked for a few more minutes before Darius glanced at his watch. Four thirty.

"I think it's time to call it a day," he said as he stood up and grabbed his jacket off the back of his chair. The rest of them followed suit. "Get some rest before we're back at it in the morning."

"You don't have to tell me twice," Mackenzie said. She

zipped her puffy jacket up to her throat and pulled the hood on, leaving nothing but her heart-shaped face open to the elements. Madison looked her over and laughed.

"It's not *that* cold out," she said.

"Says you!"

They left the coffee shop and stepped onto the sidewalk. The sun had disappeared behind buildings hours ago, but occasional lines of light broke through the glass and steel, coating them in a warm, orange glow. Central Park stretched out on their left, across a river of vehicular traffic overflowing from rush hour. Darius looked around, ignoring the ache in his arches he hadn't been able to heal on himself as he took in the city.

Ever since he'd joined the Martyrs, this place had felt different. Dangerous. With the Sins and their networks infesting every aspect of infrastructure here, Darius hadn't been able to walk these streets without worrying that he was being watched. It always felt like a monster was lurking around the next corner, waiting for him to drop his guard.

He didn't feel like that now, and it wasn't because of the two armed TAC officers walking behind him or the gun clipped against the small of his back. It was because the city *was* safer. This was a taste of what was possible when the Sins were finally destroyed—a peek at the future. The warmth of human souls pushed in around him, and Darius smiled.

Then something caught his attention.

Darius stopped where he stood, right at the 72nd Street subway station entrance, and turned around. Madison ran into him, and Darius grabbed her by the shoulders to steady her as he looked into the distance. His stomach flipped.

That magnetic pull roared by, tugging at his soul as it zipped under the soles of his feet. Darius's head spun to follow it, but it disappeared in the distance faster than he could blink. Madison's voice drew him back in.

"Darius?" Her hands wrapped around his face and turned it toward her. Her thumbs were warm against his cheeks. "Hey, are you okay?"

He suddenly realized how close they were, and he stepped back, pulling out of her palms as he turned to Mackenzie. His mouth twisted into a smirk, then a smile, then a fully-fledged grin.

"It's here," he said, looking south down Central Park West. "The Virtue is here."

For the next two days, Darius and his team constantly shifted. First, they kept to the same basic strategy, focusing on the distance between 72nd Street and Columbus Circle. Again, at approximately a quarter to five, Darius felt the Virtue zip by underfoot.

Next, they came in later in the day, and this time, they camped out aboveground at the Columbus Circle station. There, it had slowed to a stop under Darius's feet. His heart leapt to his throat as he watched the stairs, waiting for the Virtue to ascend them, but seconds later, it shot south and disappeared further into the city.

On the third day, Darius sat inside a bistro on the corner of 8th and 50th, picking at a Reuben sandwich. It was half past four, and it took all of his self-control to keep from staring out the windows as he waited for that magnetic Virtue allure to fly by again. His feet tapped anxiously on the tile as Madison stabbed at her salad with her fork.

"Looks like Caleb's routine theory is pretty sound after all," she said, smiling as Mackenzie sat back down across the table.

"Looks like," Mackenzie agreed. She sniffled, grabbed a napkin, and blew her nose, groaning as she crumbled it up and tossed it onto her empty plate. "Hopefully, we're on the right line, though. It could have switched trains at Columbus Circle."

"I don't think so," Darius said. "I didn't get the idea that it moved at all when the train stopped at Columbus. It'll be here."

Kit returned to the table, too, back from a bathroom break. "It is Saturday," he said with a shrug. "Most people have a different routine on the weekends."

The hope in Darius's gut twisted, and he finally turned to look out the window. According to his watch, they had another fifteen minutes to find out.

Those minutes passed in a blur of conversation that Darius didn't focus on. While Mackenzie and Kit laughed across from him, he watched the world outside, observing pedestrians pushing by on the sidewalk and drivers turning on headlights as the sky overhead grew darker and the shadows from nearby buildings deepened.

"You're not going to speed it up, you know," Madison said.

Darius glanced back to find her smiling at him.
"What?"

She pulled a strand of dark, wavy hair behind her ear. "You keep looking at your watch," she said. "You're not going to make time go by any faster."

He laughed and scratched the back of his head. "Too bad, huh?"

"I don't know," Madison said with a shrug. She looked out the window, too, and her knees brushed against his under the table. The last light of day shined softly against her face. She seemed to have put extra care into her makeup today, which made her eyes shine brightly and her skin look especially smooth. "I wouldn't mind slowing it down a bit."

She stole another glance at him. Darius's face tightened into a conservative smile, and he faced the table, tuning into Kit and Mackenzie's conversation.

"If they are, they're keeping it super quiet," Kit was saying with a shrug. "I hardly see them in the same room."

Mackenzie shook her head. "I don't buy it. They're hooking up. They've *gotta* be. I'll have to check their schedules... see if we can't see where they're sneaking it in."

"Still obsessing over Gabe and Chris?" Darius asked.

"Weren't you going to ask her about it?"

"I *did* ask her," Mackenzie said, "but she wouldn't say anything! Then I asked Holly if I could take a peek at the internal cameras, but—"

"That's not an invasion of privacy at all," Darius cut in.

"Well, she didn't let me," Mackenzie went on, pouting her lower lip as she wrapped her arms around her chest in a huff. "And since *you* won't tell me what you know, Kit and I have had to get… creative."

Darius raised a brow while Madison laughed. "So you're trying to catch them red-handed?" she asked.

"I'm *going* to catch them," Mackenzie countered, a mischievous glint in her eye. "It's only a matter of time before they slip up… or someone *else* will slip up." Her attention shifted to Darius, and she stuck her tongue between her teeth.

He chuckled, but Mackenzie was right. In the two weeks since the wedding, Darius had felt Gabe visit Chris in the middle of the night more times than he was comfortable thinking about, and he'd started planning late-night meditation sessions in the pool room to avoid feeling like he was poking his nose into business that wasn't his. They were bound to get caught. Eventually.

But he wasn't going to be the reason why. He opened his mouth, about to insist *again* that Chris still hadn't said anything to him, but a familiar tug beneath the ground pushed the thought away. Darius sat pin-straight in the chair as he spun toward the window. Mackenzie leapt to her feet.

"Code Virtue," she said, pulling her coat on and glancing at her phone. "Right on time, too. Where's it at?"

"Stopped," Darius said. He zipped his jacket to his throat and looked across the street, where he could see the 50th Street Station subway entrance. Bright green lights atop the posts flicked on in the growing evening, giving him something tangible to focus on. The Virtue's pull was below the ground, and that magnetic force began to shift. Darius's heart skipped into a faster rhythm. "They got off the train!"

He twisted around. Mackenzie's blue eyes shot wide, and Madison's jaw dropped.

"What do we do now?" she asked.

Darius strode past her. "We figure out who they are."

He burst onto the street, drawn by the feeling of the Virtue moving upward. The sensation of it cut through steel and concrete, past the horde of hot energy coming off of human souls pouring out of the stairwell, as clear and crisp as a floodlight in the darkness. Mackenzie and the rest followed behind Darius, but he paid as little attention to them as he did to the men and women pushing around him on the sidewalk. Someone gave him a hard shoulder, and he was knocked so far to the side that he stumbled into Mackenzie.

"Hey, watch it, pal!" the man shouted.

"You watch it!" Mackenzie yelled back.

Darius ignored both of them. He reached the intersection and peered across, looking for a gap in traffic and wishing he'd thought to wait on that side of the road. He had a view straight down the steps, and a crowd surged up it. He craned his neck and stepped forward. Warm fingers wrapped around his wrist to keep him from walking right off the curb.

Then, through dark cars with flashing headlights, through hurried people on the street, through the hot fog of human auras, Darius found him.

A Black man skipped up the steps two at a time, a set of high-tech headphones clamped to his ears. A thick, stylish crop of short locs sprouted up from the top of his head, transitioning into a clean fade by his ears. He couldn't have been more than twenty-five, and he strode onto the sidewalk with a charming bounce in his step. Eyes moved toward him, drawn to him, just as Darius was, and the Virtue smiled whenever he caught someone's gaze. He stopped at the corner, looking to cross it in the opposite direction, headed west on 50th.

"What is it?" Madison asked. Her fingers tightened

around Darius. "Did you find the Virtue?"

He nodded. The man across the street looked down at his phone, his head bobbing to music as he waited for the light to change. Suddenly, he paused and looked up, like he sensed someone's focus on him. His manicured brows drew in over warm, mahogany eyes, and he slowly spun on his heels to take in his environment. He moved over Darius at first, and then, he tracked back. Their gazes met across the road, and the new Virtue smiled at him, too.

"Yeah," Darius said. "I did." Mackenzie had tucked up next to Madison, leaning around her shoulder to hear Darius over the sounds of the city. The Virtue's light changed, and he walked off without so much as a look back over his shoulder.

CHAPTER TEN

"This is Lamar Verrette," Alan said.

He stood at the narrow end of the conference room and tapped a tablet in his hands. Mackenzie, Nicholas, Chris, and Darius all looked up as a photograph filled a massive, paper-thin screen pulled down on the wall behind his head. Alan gestured to it with a wide, sweeping motion. "He is a Virtue."

Darius stared into Lamar's face. He seemed even younger here than he had in person. His arms were wrapped around a couple of friends, all laughing against the backdrop of a crowded dance floor. They were attending some event in matching, rainbow-themed outfits. Lamar himself had a deep v-neck that showed off lean muscle on his chest, and he beamed a smile so wide and bright that it outshone the multicolored lights behind and above him.

"Awe," Mackenzie said, propping her elbows on the table and tilting her chin into her palms. "He's a wee babe."

"He turned twenty-four last August," Alan confirmed as he took his chair. "Mr. Verrette was born in 2068 in East Harlem, briefly attended New York University between '87 and '89 before dropping out, and has worked as a bartender at a nightclub in Hell's Kitchen since. He seems to have a solid network of close friends, a healthy relationship with his parents, and a thriving romantic life."

Nicholas leaned back. "We know a hell of a lot about a guy we just found yesterday."

"Miss Andrews tapped into the security feeds inside the subway station," Alan said. "When Darius identified Mr. Verrette in the footage, it was as simple as running his face through a database of New York residents. Once we had a name, everything else was easy to find."

"Seems like a massive invasion of privacy, but okay."

"This was all publicly available from his *own* social profiles and online presence," Alan said.

"It's hard to have any claim to privacy when you post your whole life on the internet," Chris agreed.

"Now, identifying Mr. Verrette is only half the battle," Alan went on. "We must decide how best to approach him. Until today, our strategy for introducing new Virtues to the Underground has been purely theoretical. This is our first opportunity to put it to the test."

Nicholas frowned. "What's the strategy?"

"Trick them into liking us," Mackenzie said with a shrug as she drew her legs up beneath her.

Nicholas's frown only deepened, and Darius sighed.

"We're not tricking anybody," he said, throwing Mackenzie a look that she returned with a sheepish grin. "We make contact and then work on establishing a real relationship before we ever tell them about all this." He opened his arms around the room. "That was our plan for you, but it… didn't work out that way."

"Hah!" Nicholas scoffed. "No, it sure as fuck didn't. How long is this relationship-building phase supposed to last?"

"It depends," Darius ventured.

"Very much, I imagine," Alan said. "Some Virtues are more receptive to learning what they are than others."

Then he glanced at the door right before it swung into the room. Darius jumped at the sudden movement and spun around as Thorn strode in. He smiled at the sight of her. God, his face almost ached with how much he'd missed that feeling. In the two weeks since the wedding, Thorn had been so busy planning their operation against Greed that she all but disappeared. He saw her at meetings or in the fleeting moments when he was up early enough, or working late enough, to catch a glimpse of her as she came and went from the Underground. Darius sometimes wished he hadn't passed his combat assessments just so he could go back to those grueling training days for an excuse to spend time with her.

Thorn unzipped her kevlar bike jacket with an impatient sigh as she closed the door. The elastic holding her hair back from her face had fallen loose, letting windswept strands fly free, where they clung to her cheeks and throat. Sparkie held onto her shoulders, and as she shrugged her jacket off and took the chair on Darius's other side, he disappeared down the nape of her black tank top.

Mackenzie clicked her tongue.

"That's two meetings I've beaten you to in a month," she said, a cynical smile tugging at the corner of her mouth. "I don't *ever* want to hear you complain again."

Thorn's attention snapped to her, and Mackenzie stared back, the levity in her thin and fragile. One of Thorn's slender eyebrows threatened to arch upon her head, but she said nothing as she looked at Alan instead. Her focus was immediately drawn to the young man on the wall behind him, and her expression tightened.

"That's him?" she asked. Darius sensed a note of frail hope in her tone.

"Lamar Verrette," Alan repeated. "We were just discussing our next steps. At this point, I believe our best option is to build rapport."

Thorn nodded, but Nicholas leaned across the table and laced his fingers on top of it. "Just to play devil's advocate… Why not just tell him? We have a Virtue right here with us." He jutted his chin in Darius's direction. "That magic is pretty hard to ignore once you've seen it in person."

"We do have more means of crafting a convincing argument than we once did," Alan agreed. "But the stakes are still much too high. The human mind is capable of disregarding all kinds of evidence in order to cling to a desperate sense of stability and familiarity. We run the risk of Mr. Verrette making things more complicated for us if we tell him before he is ready to hear it. Best case, he simply leaves the city. Worst case, he speaks too openly about what we have told him, and the Sins track him down."

Nicholas's eyes darkened. "You say that like it's happened before."

"It has," Alan said.

"Great."

"So," Mackenzie said, "we go the friendship route. The next question is, who are we sending in?"

"Darius," Thorn said. He glanced at her, and she was already watching the side of his face. When their eyes met, his heart beat a little harder. Thorn lingered for a moment before she considered the rest of them. "Virtues are naturally drawn to one another, even before they've Initiated. That's what all our research has indicated, at least. Darius has the best chance of building a quick connection."

"Speed is not the goal," Alan said, casting Thorn a hard look. She returned it with a brighter fire, and Sparkie peered out from behind her hair.

"No," she agreed. "It's about who's the best person for the job. That's him."

She laid a palm on Darius's shoulder. His pulse leapt a few beats, and part of him worried she could feel it racing beneath her fingertips.

"This is riskier than reconnaissance," Alan said, his eyes narrow. Thorn drew her hand back and crossed her arms. "Whomever we send in will revisit the same location multiple times as this relationship is fostered. They must have a whole identity formulated to match this false life while they gain Mr. Verrette's trust. It seems more in line for a Gray

Unit operative. Mr. Claytor, perhaps?"

"No, it should be Darius," Nicholas said. "Take it from a guy who used to be a Virtue. Plus, he's Kindness. It's impossible not to like him, even if you wanted to."

He threw Darius a smirk, and Darius chuckled. From the corner of his eye, he caught Thorn smiling, too.

"I also think it's important to remember the strategic advantage we could get here," Chris said. She held a hand toward Lamar Verrette's photograph. "There are only two Sins active right now. Statistically speaking, this Virtue stands a good chance of being Patience or Charity. Imagine what this war would look like if we managed to take either Wrath or Greed out permanently."

For a moment, a silence settled around them. Thorn's eyes moved back to Lamar's face, taking it in with a reserved, hopeful reverence. Everyone else did the same. Everyone but Alan. He cast a quick, mournful look in Thorn's direction before he caught Darius watching him. Then, he straightened his back, and his expression neutralized again.

"If we are sending Darius," he said, drawing focus back, "then additional precautions must be taken. This will take multiple points of contact before a proper relationship has been built. The more often we are settled in one location, the more likely we are to stand out and attract the wrong kind of attention."

"We can get more TAC units on patrol in the area whenever we send Darius down," Chris said. "I'll talk to Gabe about it when we're done here."

"I'm sure you will," Mackenzie said. A coy smile stretched across her face. Darius was confident Chris would break, but she didn't so much as blush when she turned to face Mackenzie.

"He's my assistant director, so… yeah. I will."

"We should also send additional guards in the club with him," Nicholas said.

"*Additional* guards?" Mackenzie raised her brows until her piercing disappeared behind navy bangs. "You mean besides me, Kit, and Madison? We can handle this."

"Can you?" Nicholas asked. "Alan's right. We could draw attention. I know there is a significantly smaller risk of running into Sentries with only Wrath and Greed out there right now, but if we did, we'd be leading them to *two* Virtues. No offense, but you're not exactly the most experienced security team in the Underground."

Mackenzie scoffed, covering her heart with a hand. "Offense *taken*."

"I have full confidence in Mackenzie's team," Chris said. *"Thank you."*

"But one or two more operatives might be a good idea," she went on. Mackenzie's face fell. "We'll want to spread our efforts out. We should have people posted at each exit, someone on the street, and another with Darius as a personal guard. That should be our most experienced operative."

"I'll do it," Thorn said. Everyone in the room turned to face her. Her gaze moved up, considering the young Virtue on the screen with a slow breath before she looked back to Alan. "I have the most experience with security, with the Sins, with the city. I make the most sense for the biggest impact while using the fewest resources."

While Darius and Chris nodded, Mackenzie's jaw tightened, and she remained doggedly silent. Nicholas said, "I thought you avoided being seen in the city with other Martyrs? Wouldn't this… defeat the whole point?"

"I do that to make sure the Sins or their Sentries can't identify our people," Thorn said, "but they already know who Darius is. Anyone Programmed to recognize me has been Programmed with his face, too."

Nicholas tilted his chin with a concurring frown, but Alan shook his head. "You are currently building a case for a strike you want to plan against Greed," he said. "I am not sure you need this kind of distraction."

Thorn leaned back in her chair, straightening her spine to sit as tall and proud as Alan was. "I can handle both jobs," she said, "and keeping Darius safe while we bring in this new Virtue is a higher priority. Wouldn't you agree?"

Alan's jaw clenched, but he nodded regardless. "Of course."

"Good," Thorn said. "When do we go?"

"According to Miss Andrews's research, Mr. Verrette works the same shift Wednesday through Sunday, from 5:00 p.m. to 2:00 a.m.," Alan said. "We should plan for our first contact at the start of his next work week and make regular appearances from there."

"Sounds good," Nicholas said. "I'll get a report written up by Monday."

"I look forward to it, Mr. Wolfe." Alan got to his feet. "Before we take our leave, I want to stress one thing. We have found our fifth Virtue, and that is *incredible*. What once seemed impossible is now a reality, and it deserves celebration and recognition. But this is also far from over. We must not get complacent. Stay diligent. Stay aware. Stay focused. Is that understood?"

His eyes moved around the room, landing on each person one by one until he reached Thorn. He held her there longer, and his chest expanded in a quiet breath. Once they all nodded in agreement, he excused them, and as the rest of the team got to their feet, Alan swept from the room as quickly and quietly as a shadow chased away by the day.

"Speaking of celebrations," Mackenzie said as she bounced toward the exit. "Raquel and Skylar got back from their honeymoon this afternoon. Cain's throwing a party in the courtyard. Who's going?" She glanced at all of them, her mouth open in a wide grin. Darius noticed that she made a point to avoid Thorn's eye.

Chris frowned. "*Another* party? How many of those do we need?"

"It's not really a party," Nicholas said. He pulled the door open and held it for them. "It's just dinner, but Caleb and I got a bunch of their wedding photos printed into a book, and we wanted to surprise them with a little wedding gift."

Thorn chuckled as she closed the conference room door behind them and locked it with her code. Sparkie crawled out of her top and clung to her shoulder. His wings unfurled with a leathery hiss.

"That's uncharacteristically thoughtful of you, Wolfe," she said.

He rolled his head toward her. "What can I say? I'm an evolved man. Whoa, where the hell do you think you're going?"

While the rest of them had started down the hallway, Thorn took a step in the opposite direction, toward the directors' offices. She paused.

"I have to—"

"No, you don't," Nicholas cut in. Thorn blinked, and Sparkie's head tilted to the left. "Come downstairs, have some fucking gyros with us, and look at wedding pictures. Then you can do whatever bullshit work you think won't survive two hours without you."

Darius's eyes widened, and he cast a glance at Chris to see her watching Thorn with a suppressed smile. Mackenzie's mouth tightened on her face, her tongue piercing clacking against her teeth. She stomped down the hallway, and Thorn's attention flashed up to her before it returned to Nicholas.

"You really have evolved," she said with a smirk, but she stepped back to join them. "Since when do you prioritize anything over work?"

Nicholas chuckled. "Who says I do? I helped plan this dinner. It *is* work."

They reached the elevator just as the doors slid open. Mackenzie hardly glanced at them as she stepped inside. They filed in behind her. Thorn was the last one, and when she turned around, she hit the button and backed away until she and Mackenzie stood side by side. Neither acknowledged the other, and as soon as the lift opened, Mackenzie bolted out. Nicholas followed after her, but Chris hesitated.

She cast Thorn a serious look as the rest of them stepped into the courtyard.

"Are you two still fighting?" she asked.

"We were never fighting," Thorn said. She strode away, Sparkie's wings flared behind her head like a warning signal.

Nicholas insisted this wasn't a party, but Darius wasn't sure what else to call it. A bustling mass of human energy hovered around the kitchen. Nursing staff, researchers, TAC officers, and maintenance crews gathered around, eating Mediterranean finger foods from trays in the center of their wrought-iron tables. Mezze platters, dolma plates, and bowls of smoky baba ganoush filled the air with an aroma that made Darius's mouth water.

Skylar and Raquel sat in the middle of the dining area, both beaming and bronzed, pouring over a photo album as Nicholas plopped into a chair across from them. Thorn cut through the room in a razor-straight line and found Cain standing near the back, a glass of red wine perched delicately in his slender fingers. Darius watched her from across the crowd as she slipped behind the counter and disappeared into a back pantry. He took a deep breath that got lodged in his chest.

A hard hand slapped against his back, throwing it loose. He spun to see John, a broad smile stretched across his face, and he wrapped an arm around Darius's shoulders.

"Hey, man!" John said. "I heard the news! You found *another* Virtue?"

Darius laughed and gave John a proper hug.

"Yeah, we did," he said. "Just yesterday."

"That's incredible!"

Within minutes, people realized Darius was there, and news of the new Virtue whispered through the pack like a warm wind. He and John found themselves surrounded, pushed and pulled into different conversations. Darius moved through the current gracefully, happily enveloped in the Martyrs' energy. Virtues could not heal themselves, but sometimes, he felt like this was enough. This, right here, was all the healing he needed.

Soon, they landed a seat at the table with Skylar and Raquel, and the dialogue moved to the upcoming Virtue mission.

"I'm surprised Thorn's going," Skylar said. "She's not really a security officer…"

John snorted. "No, but she *is* a control freak." He'd picked up the album and was absently flipping through it when he suddenly paused. His eyes shot open, and he looked up to Darius. "And she'll certainly keep *you* safe."

A quick smile lifted his face as Darius craned his neck to see what photo John had found, but all he caught was a flash of green and black as John turned to a new page. Warmth rushed to Darius's cheeks. "Yeah, she insisted."

John laughed. "I'm sure she did."

Then he looked down at the book, and the smug look on his face dissolved instantly. The photograph of Chris and Gabe looked up at him. Raquel and Skylar caught each other's eye just before Raquel cleared her throat and reached for the album, snatching it out of John's hands without looking at him.

"She probably wants to see this new Virtue up close," she said as she closed the cover. "I mean… can you imagine if he's Patience?"

Raquel glanced across the room, and Darius followed her gaze to see Thorn at the counter with Holly. A bittersweet flurry of emotions knotted up in his stomach.

He *had* imagined Lamar Verrette might be Patience. Hell, every single Martyr here probably wondered what would happen when they finally found the Virtue who could destroy Wrath and free Alan and Thorn from its corruption forever.

But he doubted any of them thought about it as often as Thorn herself.

She sat on one of the stools, Sparkie curled in her lap, while she talked with Holly and swirled a glass of scotch in tight, elegant circles. Darius remembered what she'd said at the wedding—that she felt stuck, trapped in an immortal body while the rest of the people in her life moved through time in a way she never could.

That would all come to an end if Patience destroyed Wrath. Darius's stomach swam at the possibility.

He quietly excused himself, leaving John, Raquel, and Skylar, and made his way through the crowd. Thorn didn't spot him coming, too absorbed in her conversation. As he neared, he heard her say, "Simmons has a contact within the Pentagon? Really?"

"Really," Holly said, "and they got us what we needed."

"Confidentially?"

"Of course." Holly waved her hand with a dismissive huff. "What do you think? That I'm just spreading Martyr secrets? I know how to keep my hands clean."

Thorn chuckled and raised her scotch to her lips just as Darius asked, "Is this about your new weapon?"

The moment he spoke, Thorn startled, and Sparkie jolted up on her lap. Darius winced an apologetic smile, placing a hand on her shoulder as Holly nodded.

"Yep." She adjusted her thick glasses before she shoved her hands deep into her hoodie's front pocket. "Simmons tracked down the tech we needed for a louder blast in a smaller package. We're building a prototype now."

Darius pulled a stool out on Thorn's other side. "Sounds like you're getting close. Are you trying to have it ready before that event Greed is going to in a couple of weeks?"

"Hah!" Holly barked a laugh and shook her head. Her boyish hair swished around the top rim of her glasses. "I wish we could have it ready by then, but no. We'll have to test the prototype, perfect it, and train my AI to delay detonation if any of our people are too close before it's battle-ready. We won't have all the bugs worked out for a month or two. I'll let you know when we're good for more field tests." She smiled at Thorn, who responded by taking another sip. Then, she hopped to her feet, losing a couple of inches in height as she did so. "Anyway, looks like the newlyweds finally have a spot open at their table. I better go say hi… "

With a smile that was half grimace, Holly made her exit. Sparkie scurried up to Thorn's shoulder as Darius raised a brow. "I thought you were supposed to be having dinner, not working."

Thorn brought her glass to her mouth, tilting it just enough for the amber liquid to pour over her bottom lip and onto her tongue. Darius's throat ran dry, and he swallowed.

"You've been too busy talking to have dinner," Thorn countered. Darius smirked, and they considered the room. Holly had joined Skylar and Raquel at their table, flipping through the photo book. Conrad and Amelia made their way over from the gym, and Gabe walked out shortly behind them, damp and freshly showered. As the three of them merged with the group, Chris looked up from her conversation with Nicholas. She and Gabe locked eyes with each other, smiled, and resumed what they were doing without a hitch. Darius laughed.

"What's so funny?"

He glanced at Thorn to find her watching the side of his face. She seemed closer now, and Darius caught the smell of vanilla and sandalwood washing toward him. Their knees drew together beneath the counter, never touching, but Darius felt the shadow of that touch anyway, like the air around them was charged.

"Oh, I was just thinking about Mackenzie's bet," he said. Gabe and Chris were still not speaking, acting as though the other wasn't there at all. Mackenzie, who was talking with Caleb, snapped between the two of them like a pendulum that had been swung too hard.

Thorn scoffed, downed the rest of her drink, and set the glass back on the counter. "Chris better watch it. McKay's not going to give up until she finds proof that she won the fucking thing."

"Wait, *you* know she won?"

"I do," Thorn confirmed.

"Man, Chris hasn't admitted anything to me yet," Darius said. Thorn's lower lip slipped between her teeth, and she cast Darius a knowing look from the corner of her eye. He frowned. "What?"

"Ah…" She took a deep breath and forced out an awkward laugh. "Chris hasn't talked to me about it, either. It's hard to keep secrets down here. I think *you* know what I mean."

It dawned on him, and Darius felt a warm flush bloom across his cheeks. "Oh… Yeah. Yep." He cleared his throat and scratched the back of his head. "I know exactly what you mean. To tell you the truth, I've felt a little creepy about it. Sometimes, I wish I could just turn this sixth sense off."

Thorn nodded, her mouth pulling into the shadow of a smile that fizzled on her face. She reached for her glass again and shifted it between her fingers. Sparkie shuffled anxiously on her shoulder. "Sometimes," she said after a moment, "I wonder if I'll miss it when it's gone."

A hole opened up in Darius's chest—a tiny fracture of the emptiness that would consume him once his Virtue was obliterated alongside Envy. He pushed the thought away and forced a smile as he nudged Thorn's elbow.

"Did you just say 'when' it's gone?" he asked.

Thorn let out a soft, humorless laugh. "Don't get ahead of yourself, Jones."

But Darius was already ahead, and he planned on staying there. "I like that you're starting to believe we'll destroy Wrath," he went on. "That's a huge change from feeling like this would never happen for you."

This time, Thorn only nodded. It was just as empty as her laugh had been. Darius leaned forward.

"You won't miss it. You're going to gain a lot more than you lose."

His breath caught on the last word, and the joy melted off his face. Darius quickly looked down at his hands, hoping Thorn wouldn't notice, but a soft weight instantly landed on his shoulder. Sparkie. The lizard pressed up against his neck, winding the length of his body across Darius's shoulders like an embrace. Goosebumps rose along his skin as he turned to Thorn again.

She hadn't moved, sitting with the same poise and power as before, but her expression softened. A warm wave of gratitude moved through his chest. Behind their backs, the Martyrs still laughed and talked, but Darius felt like time slowed down, and he realized he didn't want to share it with anyone but Thorn. He had to claim these little moments wherever he could.

"All right," Darius said, taking a breath and stretching back. Sparkie perked up and leapt to Thorn. "I think I'm all partied out. Wanna get out of here?"

For a moment, Thorn seemed stunned. She blinked, her half-empty eyes narrowing. "I have work to do."

"I know," Darius said. "What is it?"

Thorn crossed her arms. "I was going to finish writing up my plan for our operation against Greed, plus I missed the first half of that meeting, so I wanted to look into Verrette and start thinking about what our first contact is going to look like."

"Well," Darius said, "I can't do much for the strike on Greed, but I know a lot about Verrette. That is, if you'd like some help…"

The corner of Thorn's mouth pulled into a smirk. "I would."

They got to their feet and walked around the edge of the crowd, disappearing without anyone saying a word. As Darius hit the elevator button, he cast a final glance back at the courtyard. On the far side of the dining area, pulled away from the rest of the Martyrs, he spotted Cain. As soon as the old Forgotten Envy caught Darius's eye, he grinned.

CHAPTER ELEVEN

Lamar Verrette worked at a nightclub nestled deep inside the basement of a pre-war building in Hell's Kitchen. During off hours, Darius never would have spotted the place. A heavy, steel door stood against a brick wall, and the only indication that it led anywhere interesting at all came from the sign above the frame. In the daylight, the boxy, metal plaque read "The Eros Project," but at night, a bright blue light illuminated it from within, casting the shadow of a bow and arrow lurching upward onto the building.

Darius and Thorn approached from the east, walking along 49th Street. They'd dropped the rest of their team off by the entrance, ensuring they arrived separately and that security could get in place. The nearest "parking lot" was over a mile away. The gravel plot was locked behind flimsy chain-link fences, and a seedy guy in a pop-up booth demanded ridiculous fees to drop their car off. The sun had set just over an hour ago, bringing with it the bitter bite of a cold night, and a twilight sky outlined the surrounding city in a handsome, navy glow. Though Darius couldn't see him, he knew Sparkie flew the skies, keeping an eye on the neighborhood while the rest of them were below ground.

As they neared the club, Darius shivered and rubbed his

hands together before plunging them deep into his jacket pockets. A velvet rope extended along the side of the building, keeping the young men and women waiting to get in clumped together in a tight, human mass. Even a block away, Darius could see that the line extended nearly fifty feet from the entrance. The warmth from those souls drew him in. So did the Virtue's pull, and his stomach twisted in excited, anxious knots.

Darius glanced at Thorn.

Where he was feeling the cold, she seemed immune to it. Thorn stood with the same poise that she always did, wearing nothing but her bike jacket over a tight-fitting red top. Her eyes scanned the building, the crowd, the city. The nearer they came, the more anticipation wound around her spine, holding her in a grip that refused to let go. Darius's heart plummeted.

He knew, without having to ask, that Thorn couldn't sense the Virtue.

At last, her focus flashed to him, and something in his expression must have given that away. Thorn's mouth pressed into a line, and whatever hope she'd held disintegrated as her shoulders slumped toward the ground. All she managed to ask was, "Where?"

"North side of the building, about sixty feet in, give or take." Darius tilted his head toward his right and down into the ground, beyond the crowd of young partiers shivering in short skirts and high heels. They reached the end of the line, and he turned to see Thorn watching the brick wall. She drew a slow breath and held it for a moment before it whispered out in a sigh. Darius mirrored the gesture, disappointment coiled around his stomach like a snake.

"I don't see McKay, Lewis, and Garfield," Thorn said. Her voice constricted, slightly higher pitched than Darius was used to. She coughed, low and deep in the back of her throat. "Can you?"

For a second, Darius watched her, wishing he had something he could say to make this easier. When she cast him a look, he stretched over the crowd to search the wave of people in front of them. "No," he said. "I can't feel them, either. We're all jammed too close together."

"Not a surprise," Thorn said. "They better get right into position when they're allowed in."

Her tone was shorter than Darius expected. "I'm sure they will," he said. "They signed off on the plan, too."

Thorn nodded, but she didn't seem convinced, and she crossed her arms. More people filed in behind them—more bodies, more energy, surrounding Darius in a hot cloud of human aura that alleviated at least some of the cold. Every few seconds, they'd take a half step, inching forward like a single organism. It went like that for a while. Shuffling. Pausing. Waiting. The crowd around them laughed and shouted, and people started to bounce to the music pulsing through the open nightclub door. The music wasn't the only thing getting louder. As they approached, that Virtue signal resonated strong and clear. Darius could sense it moving inside with a busy, bustling energy. He craned his neck to see how much longer they had to wait.

"Nervous?" Thorn asked.

He scoffed. "Yeah, I am. I've never been to a bar before… and I don't know if you noticed, but the last couple of times we've done this, things haven't exactly gone according to plan."

Thorn's grim expression cracked a bit. She'd dressed up to fit in tonight—just a little more effort put into her makeup and outfit than usual—and her red-painted lips slipped open to expose white teeth in a soft smile.

"I have noticed," Thorn said. "It's one of the reasons I wanted to be here."

"It's one of the reasons I'm glad to have you here," Darius responded. Thorn's eyes narrowed, curious, maybe even challenging him to say more, and he shrugged. "Or, should I say, I'm glad to have *Teagan Love* here."

At that, Thorn let out a loud, gloating laugh. She wore a small satchel around her hips that dropped along the top of her thigh and strapped to her leg, and she dipped her hand into it to grab her wallet.

"You don't have Teagan Love here," she said, flashing her ID at him between two fingers like she was brandishing a cigarette.

"What!" Darius snatched the plastic and squinted at it in the dark. His jaw dropped. "Evelyn Dawson? When did that happen?"

Thorn chuckled and grabbed her license back. "A couple of weeks ago."

"That's so unfair," Darius said with faux resentment. Thorn smiled again. God, he was happy to see that smile.

"Are you finally getting sick of *Dante Stone?*" she asked as they took another half-step forward. "Didn't anyone warn you not to let McKay pick your name?"

"Yes, they did," Darius said, "and they told me I wasn't allowed to change it! Why are you?"

"I didn't have a choice."

Darius frowned. "The Sins figure it out?"

Thorn nodded, and the humor in her expression faded. She drew a strand of long, black hair behind her ear. "Jacob told them. It was in his manifestos. Besides, I'd held onto it for too long. People were starting to notice."

He didn't know how to respond to that, and for a few seconds, they sat in silence. Thorn didn't look back at him. She focused instead on the crowd, growing ever smaller ahead of them. After a moment, Darius said, "If you don't mind me asking—"

"No."

"What?" He laughed. "I didn't say anything yet!"

"You want to know what my name was before the possession," Thorn responded, and the laugh suffocated in Darius's mouth. "Every time I change my alias, someone asks me that. Locke, McKay, even Chris. And every time, I tell them no. It wasn't just my name. It was *Wrath's* name, and I don't want to talk about it."

Darius shook his head. "I don't care about *that*," he said.

"I want to know about the name that actually matters to you. The one *you* picked. Where did 'Thorn' come from?"

A flash of genuine surprise wiped the cynicism from Thorn's face, and she blinked as she stared at him. At first, he thought she was going to reject that question, too, and he was prepared to walk away from it, but then she frowned and looked out at the sky.

"It was my father's name," she said at last.

"Wait, really?"

"More or less," Thorn said with a nod, still gazing starward. "His legal name was Benjamin Rose, but his brothers-in-arms called him Thorn."

"Brothers-in-arms?"

"He was a soldier in World War II," Thorn said, "and he built a reputation for being impossible to kill. According to my mother, he had a knack for surviving shit that no one expected him to come back from. One day, one of his squad mates joked that he should've been named 'Thorn' instead of 'Rose' because he was such a pain in the ass. It stuck. They even got custom dog tags made. I still have them."

Darius stared at her. "That's incredible."

She shrugged. "It just felt right."

"Because you're impossible to kill?" Darius asked with a smirk. "Or because you're a pain in the ass?"

Thorn laughed. "Maybe a little bit of both."

The group ahead of them was allowed through, and they stepped up. A huge bouncer with a pale, freckled face stood before them, his vibrant orange hair held back in a ponytail. A frizzy beard extended well below his collarbone, clashing against his blue button-up and black vest. He asked them for identification and the fifty-dollar cover fee, and he compared Thorn to her card for several long seconds before he switched to Darius's. When he read the name "Dante Stone," one of his bushy brows raised. He passed the ID back and stepped aside to let them through. Darius heard Thorn snicker.

"Oh, shut up, *Evelyn*," he said. He placed his palm

against the small of her back to guide her ahead. Thorn's head spun toward him, her hair pouring over her shoulder in a silky, black wave as he leaned in. "After you."

Her eyes moved between his before traveling downward, taking him in, and she relaxed beneath his touch. Then, she stepped through the open door and into the hallway.

As soon as they were inside the building, electronic dance music pumped under their feet. The bass pulsed into Darius's heels, vibrating all the way up his body as they made their way toward a stairwell. At the bottom, it opened up to a massive space. Darius and Thorn paused in the doorway.

The entire basement had been converted into a club, extending so far beyond them that Darius could hardly see the far wall through the people and flashing lights. Bodies pressed together, wearing so little clothing that, for the most part, it was all skin. It even smelled of people—musky and warm, though not unpleasant, and not surprising with how many of them were crammed down here. Darius took his coat off. The atmosphere was so saturated in hot, human auras that he was already beginning to sweat. The Virtue's pull tugged more firmly at him.

Suddenly, a light hand touched Darius's back. Fingertips traced up his shoulder blade until Thorn's palm rested near the crook of his neck. Even through his shirt, the cold sensation of her skin was a relief down here. She leaned around to speak to him, her cheek almost directly against his ear, but all Darius could make out was the deep, inviting drone of her voice.

"What?" he yelled.

"Where is he?" she replied, this time shouting to be heard. When she pulled away, strands of her hair clung to his stubble, tickling his throat, and he shook his head to remember what the fuck he was even doing here. Darius tilted his chin toward the far end of the room. Thorn nodded, and they started walking.

Even though the club was packed with young, half-naked men and women wearing sequined tops, short skirts, and layers of metallic makeup, Thorn commanded a striking presence. She moved apart from the music, holding herself with a confidence that dominated the room. As they pushed through the crowded dance floor, people leered after her. Their eyes toured her body like a bus full of sightseers gazing at the Statue of Liberty for the first time. She was absolutely magnetic—so much so that even with the Virtue drawing Darius in, she was all he could focus on, too. When they reached the bar, she shrugged her jacket from her shoulders, revealing thin, crimson straps against a strong back. He had to tear his eyes away, forcing himself to look for Verrette. Two doors stood at either edge of the wall of alcohol, and the Virtue was on the other side of the one on the right.

"He's in the back," Darius said. Here, the music was quieter and the crowd thinner. People dotted the L-shaped counter, swiveling around in barstools or standing between them as they ordered. Most customers cleared out as soon as they had a drink in their hands, but others lingered at the counter to chat. The bar itself was surrounded by a handful of tall tables, where other groups sipped on expensive but beautifully crafted cocktails while they laughed and talked. A raised lounge area lined the opposite wall, full of dark corners where Darius could feel energies converging more than he could see the people hiding there. He took a breath, trying to decide if it was his own impatience or Thorn's tugging at his gut.

At last, a pair of barstools opened, and Darius jumped in. He pulled one out for Thorn before grabbing the second for himself. As she sat down, Thorn draped her jacket across the back, pulling at her fingerless gloves to make sure they were securely in place. Then she leaned toward him, speaking quietly like she was resting words on his shoulder.

"Lewis and Garfield are by the front entrance," she said.

Darius looked back to see the two chatting just inside the doors. He couldn't believe he hadn't noticed them when he came in. "And Mackenzie?"

"I sense her by the emergency exit."

Darius nodded as he spun around again. Verrette still hadn't emerged from the back room. A different bartender came by, and while Darius declined, Thorn asked for a scotch. When the woman placed it in front of her, Thorn drew it across the black marble counter.

"Gray Unit 101," she said, lifting her drink. The amber liquid caught the flashing lights. "Order something. You're here to *blend in*."

She tilted her head, raised the glass higher, and took a sip.

Darius frowned. "I don't drink."

"Good," Thorn said. "Pretend to drink."

"How the hell do you expect me to do that?"

Thorn laughed. "Darius, you're here with a Forgotten Sin who processes alcohol too efficiently to get drunk. Trade glasses with me."

She downed the rest of her scotch in a smooth swallow, caught the bartender's eye, and waved her down for another. When the woman came to refill Thorn's glass, Darius asked for one of the same. Seconds later, he held the tumbler in his fingers and lifted it to take a whiff. Even the smell of it burned, and the bridge of his nose wrinkled.

"Ugh, how does anyone drink this stuff?"

"Practice and poor impulse control," Thorn said. She stared into her scotch thoughtfully, reading it like tea leaves. "No one likes the taste of alcohol at first. We just convince ourselves that it will solve some problem or another." Thorn shook her head and raised her glass again. "It doesn't, but we're really fucking good at lying to ourselves."

She tipped a taste into her mouth, and her tongue slipped out to lick the remnants from her lips.

"All I ever saw were the lies," Darius said. He tried his hand at swirling his drink, too, just to give him something to do with it. "A drunk driver killed my mom when I was ten, and Dad died in a slide with a fifth in his hand."

Thorn watched him with a somber, understanding frown. She drew a deep breath and put her tumbler on the bar.

"After my father died, my mother did nothing but drink," Thorn said. "It's how she dealt with her grief… and with me. I wasn't an easy kid. I disappeared on her as soon as I was old enough to leave the house, and I didn't see her again until I escaped Wrath. By then, she was…" Thorn paused, circling the rim of her glass with her middle finger. She scoffed. "I can't even remember. In her early seventies, I think. She'd been institutionalized for over a decade. The doctors said her early onset dementia was probably alcohol-induced brain damage."

She glanced down at her scotch, shook her head, and slid it across the counter toward Darius. The imprint of Thorn's lipstick clung to her glass. He ran his thumb against it, smudging it, and for the first time in his life, he was tempted to take a sip.

"This is a great conversation to have at a bar," he said instead, clearing his throat. Thorn smirked, and Darius watched her lean back to look across the room. Had anyone asked him yesterday if he could imagine Thorn in a club like this, he would have laughed, but now that they were here, she looked like she belonged. It reminded him of every other undercover operation they'd ever gone on together, from the gala in Washington to the farm down in Georgia. Somehow, Thorn could shape herself into whatever she needed to be, into whomever she needed to be, to get what she wanted. How many years of practice and false lives had given Thorn that skill?

Before he had the chance to wonder any more about it, the Virtuous pull tugged at his chest. Darius's focus snapped to the wall of liquor, a gaudy glass array with bottles of every shape, size, and color, as Lamar Verrette's energy moved behind it. Without looking at her, without thinking about it, Darius tapped the back of his knuckles against Thorn's thigh. She caught on and spun toward the bar.

The door to a storage room swung open, revealing shelves of beer, baskets of citrus fruits, and stacks of drinkware… Then Lamar Verrette stepped into the club.

If Darius thought Thorn blended in here, Verrette was born for this. The instant he crossed the threshold, a bright, vibrant smile filled his face, and he took a moment to look around the room and admire the scene before he jumped into work. He was shorter than Darius, and more slender, but clearly in great shape. Like the rest of the employees here, Verrette wore a navy button-up with a black vest, kept open in a deep v that stopped halfway down his sternum and flaunted a smooth, toned chest. He hugged the bartender on duty, wrapping his arms around her middle in a brotherly way, and made his way to the register.

Thorn straightened in her chair. "All right, Jones. You're up."

She threw her drink to the back of her throat with such prowess that it drew the attention of a couple of people sitting down the counter. She held out the glass, and he traded it out again. Her fingers wrapped around his, her mouth curving into a half-smile. A nervous flutter moved through Darius's chest as he nodded.

Thorn let go, and she got to her feet, wandering to one of the tables nearby. She pulled out her phone and pretended to browse, but Darius could feel her focus on him as he looked back to Verrette. The flutter grew to a flurry, and he took a deep breath to calm his pounding heart. The bass from the music behind him didn't help.

When Verrette glanced up from the register, his dark, warm eyes moved around the bar. They landed on Darius, and he paused even before Darius had the sense of mind to raise his glass. The Virtue's full lips stretched back into that grin, and he sauntered his way over.

"Hey there," he said as he reached the countertop across from where Darius was sitting. He leaned onto it, arching his back in an almost feline way as he clasped his hands together. Up close, Darius could see a delicate brush of navy eyeshadow glistening against his umber skin, and he'd painted his lash line in thin, black pencil. Verrette tilted his head at Darius's empty glass. "What's your poison?"

"Scotch," Darius said. Then, remembering how Thorn had ordered it, he tacked on, "Neat. Please."

Verrette's brows drew together in a beguiling frown. "Ooh, a *real* drink." He winked, Darius laughed, and Verrette grabbed the tumbler. "Let me get that for you."

He walked back to the liquor shelf with fluid grace and refilled the glass. As he returned, he considered Darius with a more obvious curiosity. He put the drink down and pushed it forward, his blue-painted nails flashing in the scattered light.

"There you go. Let me know if you need anything else."

Darius nodded, and Verrette disappeared down the bar to help another customer.

For a few minutes, Darius sat there with nothing to do but swirl his drink. Verrette moved constantly, tag-teaming with the other bartender as they took in wave after wave of parched dancers coming in for refreshments. Whenever Darius caught Verrette looking in his direction, he acted like he'd just put the drink back on the counter. Jesus, he felt ridiculous. He turned to find Thorn, but the table she'd been sitting at was empty.

"How'd it go?" a familiar voice hummed by his ear.

Darius startled, nearly splashing his scotch onto his lap as Thorn sat down again. He exhaled a harsh sigh and shook his head. "Jesus, Thorn," he managed through a laugh. "A little warning next time."

An amused smile settled on her face. "Here," she said, swapping out the drinks. Hers was already empty. "Ask for a sparkling water next."

"Why?"

"Because as far as anyone here is concerned, you just downed four ounces of top-shelf liquor in less than half an hour," Thorn said. "Unless you want to start acting like you're drunk."

"I don't," Darius replied.

"Didn't think so." Thorn smirked again and moved to leave, but Darius touched her hand to stop her. She froze halfway out of her stool.

"Wait," he said. "I clearly don't know what the hell I'm doing, and I could use some on-the-job Gray Unit training from a master."

Thorn frowned. "If I'm here, he might not stop to talk to you."

"The whole point of this is acting like we belong, right?" he asked. When Thorn nodded, he shrugged. "Then who comes to a club like The Eros Project alone on a Wednesday just to sit at the bar all night?"

She hesitated, and her painted lips pressed together. "Someone pretty desperate," she said. Darius laughed, and she did, too. "Maybe if you look desperate *enough*, he'll feel guilted into talking to you."

"Oh yeah," Darius said. "That's what we want. A pity friendship."

"Bartenders make decent therapists."

"C'mon, Thorn," he implored. "Sit back down. I'd rather look like the luckiest guy in the room than the loneliest."

Thorn blinked, her half-empty eyes glinting, and her mouth parted. He realized he was still holding her hand, and he squeezed it once before tilting his head toward the counter. The pulsing party lights in the room made it hard to tell, but he thought he saw a blush of pink cross her cheeks. She pulled her hand back to swipe a strand of hair behind her ear, but she did sit down.

"Fine," she said. "But *I'm* going to need another drink."

"What problem are you trying to solve?" Darius asked with a coy smile.

"Shut up, *Dante*." Thorn raised her empty tumbler, and Verrette caught her eye across the bar. Darius couldn't help but smile as they ordered another round—scotch for Thorn and seltzer water for him. As she took her first sip, he admired the way the glass pressed against her bottom lip, the way the line of her throat extended, as she tilted her head back. She caught him watching from the corner of her eye, and when she turned toward him, he held up his drink.

"Cheers," he said, clinking his glass against hers. "On a successful first contact. What do we do now?"

Thorn took a deep breath, looked back at Verrette, and shook her head. "I don't know. We've never made it this far. If this were a standard Gray Unit operation, we'd make ourselves present as often as possible and let it develop naturally."

Darius nodded and watched Verrette, too. The young man danced behind the counter, absolutely radiating a sense of enthusiasm and life that Darius found refreshing. He poured cocktails like he was crafting a piece of art, the whole time with a smile that infected the room around him. People weren't just getting drunk off the alcohol. They were saturated in his Influence, the power his Virtue poured into these walls and anyone lucky enough to be inside them.

"Yeah," Darius said. "We can be patient."

He glanced at Thorn. The smile on her face flickered.

———

Barren highway sprawled out for miles, a stretch of US 9 as isolated and cold as Thorn felt driving down it at one in the morning.

The SUV plowed forward smoothly, its electric engine running silent even at eighty-five miles per hour. The only noise in the cab came from heat hissing out of the air vents and Mackenzie's knee impatiently bouncing. Thorn cast a look in the rearview mirror, where she could see the Irishwoman pressed between two sleeping TAC officers in the center seat. When she caught Thorn's eye, Mackenzie quickly averted her gaze to stare out the window over Garfield's head instead. The sound of her tongue piercing against her teeth joined the hissing and the bouncing.

A vise pinched Thorn's chest as she focused back on the road. Sparkie, wrapped around her throat, held tighter. She couldn't tell if she was furious or hurt. Fury felt more manageable, more familiar, but the bruising wouldn't fade. Either way, Thorn didn't want to deal with it. Not now. Not when there was so much else on her mind.

Like tonight.

Overall, the operation had been a success—the most seamless first contact they'd had with a Virtue since Thorn had met Teresa Solomon at a school event with Donovan over seven decades ago. Though Verrette hadn't talked with them more than refilling their drinks and wishing them a good night when they'd finally closed their tab at midnight, there had been no Sins. No violence. No complications.

Well. *Fewer* complications.

Thorn's stomach twisted, and her heart skipped a beat as she glanced at Darius curled up in the passenger's seat. His elbow rested at the seam between the door frame and the window, angled perfectly for the heel of his palm to press against his chin and keep him propped up and passed out against the glass. He breathed evenly. A fog of condensation pulsed just beyond his open lips, shrinking and growing with every inhale and exhale.

Thorn's jaw clenched. Maybe Alan had been right. Maybe this assignment was a distraction.

Or maybe it had just been another fucking letdown.

Freehold Township blew by them in a blur of dull, yellow lights, and several minutes later, Thorn pulled onto a smaller road shooting off the main highway. The gas station came to life in the distance, a single point of bright light surrounded by naked winter trees. She drove into the empty lot. Below them, the Underground stretched out, the Martyrs' energy a cold blanket beneath the earth.

As Thorn stopped the SUV at the car wash entrance and rolled down the window, she sensed the first signs of life. Madison Lewis lifted her head and stifled a yawn, and Garfield's cold energy moved at Thorn's back. Darius, however, didn't budge. Thorn was content to let him sleep for as long as she could, but Lewis peered around his chair and grabbed his shoulder, shaking him gently. When he didn't stir, she tickled at his neck with long nails.

Darius startled, drawing Sparkie's attention. The lizard's head popped up as Darius opened his eyes, bright green against his warm, olive skin.

Madison giggled. "We're back, sleepy head."

Thorn's jaw clenched, and she fought the instinct to roll her eyes.

"Great," Darius responded. He pressed his fingertips against his eyes with a sigh.

Thorn turned out the window—ignoring Lewis and Darius, Mackenzie and Garfield, everyone—as she swiped her access card through the credit slot. The car wash came to life, dim internal lights turning on as the drop-down door slowly rolled upward. The second she had the clearance, Thorn drove in, and she stopped a little rougher than she'd intended. The whole vehicle lurched forward.

That seemed to wake Darius the rest of the way up, and he glanced at her as Garfield swore. Thorn felt Darius's attention on the side of her face, and Sparkie watched as his mouth tightened in concern. The ground beneath them rumbled and moved, slanting into the earth. Thorn inched forward until they were on the descent and brought them deeper into the Underground.

The closer they got, the more distinct each Martyr's energy became. Every single one of them was downstairs, tucked quietly into their rooms. As they hit the landing and parked by the doors, Thorn sensed that this floor was empty—a vacuum of nothing compared to the sea of cold bodies below her.

"Hurry up, will you?" Mackenzie grumbled, tapping her knee against Garfield's. He seemed the least aware of them; his eyes were glassy and bloodshot, and he stumbled over his weaker leg as he climbed out of the SUV. Thorn frowned as she stepped down from the vehicle.

"You good, Garfield?"

"Yes, ma'am," he groaned, stretching his back with a wince. "Just tired. I'll be right as rain after some shut eye."

"Go on inside," Thorn said as Lewis and Darius got out of the car. When they shut their doors, the sound echoed through the garage. "All of you. I'll handle the gear."

Garfield nodded, and Mackenzie was already well on her way, having walked halfway to the door before Thorn had even finished speaking. Thorn stared after her as Lewis followed suit. Darius, however, hesitated. He stood by the tail light as Thorn came to the back of the vehicle.

"You sure you got this?" he asked, a yawn stretching out the final word. He'd wrapped around himself as he shivered in the cold garage, and his dark brown hair splayed up in a messy fray on one side of his head as though it had been pressed up against a pillow.

"I'm sure," Thorn said. She smiled, or she tried to, but she could tell it didn't fill her face. Darius's eyes, tired but perceptive, moved between hers. A tiny crease between his brows showed his worry, but he nodded.

"Okay. I'll talk to you tomorrow, yeah?"

"Yeah."

He smiled. "Goodnight, Thorn."

"Goodnight, Darius."

He walked away, heading to the entrance by the elevator, and Sparkie peered after him while Thorn opened the back. She waited until Darius had disappeared through the glass doors and out of sight before she closed her eyes and leaned against the hatch, her arms above her head, as she fought down the urge to scream. Her fingers tightened around the metal, and her throat was so tense it ached. She knew exactly what Darius would say:

"What do you see?"

His voice rang out in her head, as loud as though he was standing right beside her and just as warm as it had been the first time he'd asked her to do that stupid exercise with him. She could practically see him sitting across from her in the back of the pool room, cross-legged on his towel, as he held up a hand and tapped his fingers against his thumb. He was damp after a shower, skin silky and hair ruffled like he'd done nothing more than scrub it dry.

"What do you hear? Smell? Feel? Ground yourself in your environment so you can better control your anger."

Thorn drew in a deep breath and settled into the space around her. She saw the black weapons cases, thick and heavy, as she pulled them out of the SUV. She heard the echo of the door snapping shut and her boots thumping against the concrete floor as she dragged the cases into the Underground. She smelled the signature cocktail of the tactical room—stale metal, earth, and musk—when she opened gear closet number four. She felt the Martyrs below her stretched out in an icy sheet. When she reached the hallway, she paused.

While Thorn appreciated knowing her people were safe here, she didn't feel like being surrounded by so much coldness tonight.

With a sigh, she made her way toward her office, ready to collapse onto the couch and go the fuck to sleep. Sparkie arched on her shoulder, his wings quivering as his tiny mouth stretched wide in a yawn.

When she opened the door to the lounge between her office and Alan's, however, she paused. The room was dark except for a sliver of yellow light coming from beneath his door.

Thorn's stomach twisted up as all the work she'd done to mellow her emotions lit up like a small flame. She knew why he was still awake—knew that he was waiting for her to get back so he could talk to her about Lamar Verrette.

And, if she was honest with herself, she wanted to talk to him, too.

Thorn strode to Alan's door in three steps, and she pulled it open.

Sure enough, her uncle was sitting behind his desk, a book laid out on its surface, but he wasn't looking at it. His focus landed on Thorn the second she walked in, and he took his reading glasses off, placing them on the wood. Rae's ears fixed in her direction.

For a moment, Alan and Thorn stared at each other. His eyes were leaden, full of concern and curiosity. Each vertebra in his spine rolled into place as he squared his shoulders and took a shallow breath.

"Well?" he asked at last.

Thorn simply shook her head.

Another stretch of silence. Alan's sharp chin tilted downward in a ghost of a nod, and his lips turned into a narrow frown behind his trimmed goatee. When they opened again, it was with a sigh. "I'm sorry."

"I should have known better than to get my hopes up," Thorn murmured, all the fury and hurt and tension in her body swirling in a familiar feeling of loss that she'd spent the whole goddamned evening fighting to ignore. She shut the door behind her and fell into one of the plush chairs in front of Alan's desk. Sparkie wound around her throat, his wings laying across one shoulder as he pressed as close to her as he could. Thorn felt her pulse beneath his jaw.

Alan closed his book, set it aside, and got to his feet. Rae stood, as well, and Alan walked around the desk to take the other chair. He leaned toward Thorn, propping his elbows on his knees. "It was a reasonable expectation given our circumstances."

With a scoff, Thorn pressed her fingertips against the bridge of her nose. "I wanted him to be Patience, Alan. God, I wanted it *so* badly."

Her uncle shifted uncomfortably in his chair before he murmured, "I know."

Thorn looked up at him again, finding him watching her down his strong nose with a somber expression. Rae padded up, hesitated, and then gently laid her chin on Thorn's knee. The contact startled Thorn, and she stared at the wolf, looking right into those bright, intelligent blue eyes. Rae rarely displayed Alan's need for connection so openly, and Thorn ached to close the gap—to finally cross over that fucking divide Wrath had carved between them. After decades of fighting and healing and growing, they were so much closer now. Thorn knew that no matter how often they argued, no matter what they disagreed upon, Alan was neck-deep in this pit with her.

Sparkie unwound himself from Thorn's throat, slithered down the front of her body, and landed with a thump in her lap. Then, he touched the tip of his smooth, scaly nose to Rae's, and the wolf breathed a sad sigh against him. The sensation sent a tickle across Thorn's cheeks. She inhaled slowly, feeling her lungs expand, pushing against her ribs and opening up around that aching hole stuck in the middle of her chest. She placed a palm flat against it.

"Hey, Alan?"

"Yes?"

"What was it like? Feeling Patience?"

Alan's whole body bristled, and Rae's ears laid back against her skull. She withdrew from Sparkie, lifted her chin from Thorn's knee, and stepped backward. Alan shook his head.

"You know I don't like discussing this," he said, the words cold and distant, as though they themselves had walked away, too.

"I know."

"Then why are you asking?"

"Because," Thorn said, the bitterness thinning her voice, "I need to convince myself that this is a good thing. That Verrette being some other Virtue, destined to destroy some *other* Sin, is a goddamned blessing. That feeling Patience is… I don't know. Worse than whatever the fuck I'm feeling right now."

Alan stared at her, his throat tight, jaw clenched shut. He took a deep breath that flared his nostrils, and he held it for a moment. Then, he said, "Feeling the Virtue is… remarkable. Unforgettable. But it certainly cost me."

Thorn frowned. "What do you mean?"

"When you get a taste of what freedom would look like," he said, "you chase it. Like an addict chasing a high. And addicts take a lot of risks to get that high, Thorn. They will sacrifice a *lot* of things that matter to them."

She watched him, and he did not look away. Rae sat back on her haunches, and a low, contrite whine rumbled in her throat.

"Are you ever going to tell me what happened?" Thorn asked.

Alan didn't answer right away. First, he looked down at his hands, which he wrung in his lap. Then, he nodded. Slowly. "Yes. Of course. But not today…" His voice trailed off, and Thorn's chest constricted. She understood what it was like to have bodies in your past that you wanted to keep buried. God knew she had a few herself. More than a few. Before Alan had the chance to continue, Thorn grabbed his fingers and gripped them tightly. He looked back up.

"I'm sorry," she began.

Alan squeezed her hand to stop her.

"Thorn," he said. "Have faith in yourself. You will find Patience someday, I promise, and you will be a stronger person than I ever was."

She nodded. Alan's mouth tightened into a smile, but it didn't reach his eyes.

CHAPTER TWELVE

After two weeks, four visits, and dozens of glasses of scotch Darius didn't drink, he was starting to feel like they weren't getting anywhere.

It was always the same. First, they drove into the city and dropped Mackenzie, Madison, and Kit off to secure the area and start manning the exits. Then, Thorn and Darius would park their vehicle, walk to the club, and head straight to the bar where they hung out, hoping to catch Verrette's attention and strike up a conversation. So far, all Darius had managed was three meaningless dialogues about traffic, the weather, and how he didn't know one of the artists blaring over the speakers. It went like that until sometime between midnight and two, whenever Thorn decided to pile them all into the SUV and head back to the Underground.

Darius knew this was a long game, but the only thing he'd really figured out about Lamar Verrette was that he had an impressive menagerie of friends around him. He was practically a public figure at The Eros Project, coming around the counter to hug people so often that it was a miracle he managed to work at all.

"Man, he knows *everyone*," Darius mused, speaking loudly enough to be heard over the music. He and Thorn sat at the far end of the bar, tucked away in the corner. She glanced over her shoulder to where Lamar had his arms wrapped around a couple of gorgeous girls in short skirts and crop tops leaning over the counter.

"He's a Virtue," Thorn said. She turned back to Darius, crossing her legs as she did so. "People are drawn to him. Think about your market and Samira's farm."

Darius raised a brow. "Nicholas was a Virtue, too, and he didn't have people like this."

Thorn laughed, tilted her glass of scotch into her mouth, and poured a splash over her tongue. She put the tumbler back down with a snap. "I'm telling him you said that."

"He won't disagree," Darius joked, and he glanced back up as Verrette moved down the far wall. The young Virtue busied himself with a martini glass and a metal shaker, bopping his narrow hips to the rhythm of the music. While Darius watched him, Verrette threw a look his way, and their eyes met. Darius smiled awkwardly and turned back to Thorn.

"I feel like such a creep…" He grabbed his glass, which Thorn had drained thirty minutes ago, and spun it between his fingertips on the bar counter. "I'm just staring at the guy from across the room."

"Welcome to the Gray Unit," Thorn replied. Her wrist revolved in delicate circles, sending the liquor swirling at the base of her drink. She watched it absently. "Movies always make Intelligence look like a glamorous job, but the truth is, a lot of the time, all you do is fucking wait."

"Yeah," Darius said with a chuckle. "Eva told me the same thing."

At the mention of Eva, Thorn's dark eyes moved up to Darius's, catching his gaze and holding it with an empathetic curiosity. Then, she lifted her scotch to her mouth. "She was a great agent," Thorn said, breathing against her glass. Condensation collected around it, making it appear frosted until she tilted back and washed it away with a final mouthful of amber liquid.

A pang of stale grief came back to life in Darius's chest—part of him that always lingered, just under the surface, for those he'd loved and lost to this war. He felt Thorn's focus on him as he looked around the room. It was busier tonight than he was expecting. Nearly all the seats at the bar were full, and people forced themselves between bodies to get a chance to order before disappearing again. Behind them, all the tables had been claimed by groups of giggling women, co-ed parties, and a couple that appeared to be on a date. Darius tried to imagine Eva in this environment and wondered how she would have done connecting to Lamar Verrette. It didn't work. She would have hated this even more than Thorn did. All these people, all these wasted resources. It felt so goddamned excessive. More than that, though, Eva wouldn't have been able to do this job, and not just because she hadn't been a Virtue…

"Darius?"

Thorn's voice drew him back, and he turned to see her leaning over the counter, her back curved toward him and her hands a breath away from where he gripped his empty glass on the surface. She didn't speak, didn't ask him the question Darius knew she wanted to ask, but he saw her concern plainly in her gently sloped brows and the soft frown on her lips.

He didn't want to talk about this. Eva was gone.

"I was just thinking," he said, clearing his throat and putting his glass back down, "I'm doing this all wrong."

Thorn shook her head. "How?"

"I'm supposed to act like I'm in the Gray Unit, right?" Darius asked. When Thorn nodded, he did, too. "Well, the Gray Unit agents have a good reason for being where they are. Usually, it's a job. Alexis works in dispatch to stay aware of what the NYPD is doing. Caleb's a photographer for the news stations. No idea what Peter does."

"He's an admin assistant with one of Anton Claytor's biggest firms," Thorn answered.

Darius raised his hands. "Exactly! And Eva was looking

for Sloth, so she integrated into the homeless communities he targeted. For all of them, it wasn't just about blending in. They really belonged."

Thorn's eyes narrowed, and she pulled her lower lip between her teeth. "We can't get you a position in the city, Darius."

"I'm not saying we do," he argued, "but we need to be more than just a couple of people who hang out at the bar and drink all night. I want a reason to talk to him."

"Do you have any bright ideas?"

Darius shook his head. "No. I don't want to lie to him."

Thorn frowned. "That's what the Gray Unit *does*."

"I get it," Darius said, "but there has to be a way to just… bend the truth." At Thorn's skeptical look, he waved a hand between them. "I'll think of something."

"Well, you'd better think fast." Her eyes darted over his shoulder to the far end of the bar. Darius felt that familiar magnetism move, drawing nearer, and he turned around as Lamar Verrette reached them. The Virtue bent at the waist, leaning over the countertop as he propped his chin on the heel of one palm. His warm, mahogany eyes caught Thorn and looked her over.

"You know," he said, his silky voice rich and inviting, "I have *never* seen anyone drink straight scotch the way you do, honey. You don't even wince. What's your secret?"

His full lips opened in a handsome smile as he reached for Thorn's empty glass. He pulled it out of her fingers and dragged it across the bar. This time, he'd brought the bottle with him, and he filled her tumbler with a smooth, expert hand.

Thorn laughed—a deep, vibrant laugh that Darius knew was in part an act, but she was so convincing that even he couldn't tell what was fake and genuine anymore. "No secret," she said. "Just a lot of practice."

"You don't look old enough to have the practice," Verrette teased, winking as he pushed the glass back toward her. Then he turned to Darius and tilted his head playfully.

"Now, do you want one, too, or should I just give it to your girl since she's the one drinking it anyway?"

Darius's jaw dropped, and Thorn froze with her scotch held halfway to her mouth. Verrette's gaze swung between them, and his eyebrows raised in a giddy wave. At last, Darius managed to breathe out an awkward laugh.

"How'd you know?" he asked.

Verrette gave a mischievous smirk as he grabbed Darius's tumbler out of his hand. He spun the glass around until a faint lipstick smudge faced outward. "Red isn't your color, honey," he said, tapping a blue-painted nail against it. His attention dipped slowly, moving from Darius's eyes to his mouth and back again. "It's *hers*, but somehow, all your glasses keep getting pretty little kisses all over them. I'm not here to judge whatever game you've got going on, but there's no shame in ordering something with a little more flavor if you don't like the straight stuff. We don't assign drinks by your gender here, sweetie. Sex on the beach is a classic for a reason—because it's *damn* good."

For a moment, Darius gawked, not sure what to say. "Sex on the beach?" he stammered at last.

"It's a cocktail," Thorn said.

Verrette laughed, and his eyes narrowed curiously. "Good god, you *don't drink*, do you? I knew there was something about you… Give me a second. I've got just the thing."

He twirled away and headed back to the wall of liquor. Darius spun toward Thorn.

"What the hell do I do now?"

Thorn shrugged. "You've got him talking. Keep him talking."

Darius didn't have the chance to respond. Verrette came back his way and put a tall glass on the countertop: a light tonic with muddled cherries and limes suspended between chunks of ice. A mint leaf varnish balanced on the rim.

"What is it?" Darius asked.

"A cherry mojito," Verrette said. "Virgin."

"Meaning there's no alcohol," Thorn clarified.

"I knew *that*," Darius responded, throwing her a look. Thorn's tongue ran along her upper lip, drawing Darius's attention to the thing that had gotten them caught in the first place. Heat rose to his cheeks as he turned back to Verrette and held out a hand. "Thank you, uh…"

"Lamar," the Virtue said, grabbing Darius's fingers in a tight but delicate grip.

"Darius. And this is Thorn."

Thorn's eyes widened, and Darius sensed her staring at the side of his face as Lamar drew his hand back.

"You're very welcome, *Darius*. Like I said, we don't assign drinks by gender, and we certainly don't want to pressure you to drink if you're sober, but…" Lamar paused, leaning further into the counter. His mouth pushed out in an inquisitive pout. "Why are you at the bar if you don't drink?"

Darius glanced at Thorn, who just watched him with her eyes piercing and lips pressed together, before he turned back to the Virtue and said the first half-truth he could think of. "I'm hoping to meet somebody."

Lamar's brows shot up as he raised a hand, thumb extended, to point directly at Thorn's chest. "You walked into The Eros Project with a goddess like *this*, and you're here to *meet somebody?*"

Darius's heart skipped a beat while Thorn poured the whole glass of scotch down her throat without looking at him. "Oh, we're not—uh, that's not what I meant."

Lamar laughed and popped a hip out behind him. "Oh no? Then what *did* you mean?"

"It's a long story," Thorn answered. A sharp edge hardened her tone, and she shot Darius a quick look. Lamar turned to her, no more put off by her mood than he had been by anything else.

"The best ones usually are," he replied with a smile. He opened his mouth to pry further, but his attention shifted over Darius's shoulder, and that smile disappeared. A darkness settled over Lamar's entire body. His jaw tightened, and his warm eyes glistened like the sky before a storm.

"Excuse me," he murmured. Then he strode along the bar, whispered something to the other bartender, and hurried into the club. His coworker quickly typed a message on her phone before holding it up, as though to record something over Darius's shoulder. Her face had gone pale and serious.

Darius and Thorn exchanged a look before they spun around. Lamar stopped at a table directly behind them, where the young couple sat. The woman was about to take a sip, but Lamar swiped the glass out of her hand so smoothly that the surface didn't even ripple.

Then he turned to her date. "Sir, you need to leave."

The woman pulled a wisp of teal hair behind her ear. "I'm sorry, is something wrong?"

"We'll talk about it later, sweetie," Lamar said, his focus never straying from the man across the table. He was a burly guy, easily carrying sixty pounds of muscle on Lamar, and his whole face flushed a deadly red. Thorn's left hand wandered to her satchel. Darius grabbed it to stop her from drawing a weapon. "Sir, I won't warn you—"

"Fuck off," the man cut in. "Can't you see we're busy here?"

Lamar's mouth pulled into a dangerous smile—a smile that was more about slicing throats than making friends. "Why don't you show me what's in your pocket, big guy?"

The man sneered. "What are you, some kind of pervert?"

Lamar held up the woman's drink, dipped his pinky in, and swirled it around a few times. When he drew it back out, the blue nail polish changed color, going black within seconds. Lamar's jaw clenched. "There's enough Rohypnol in here to down a bodybuilder. You tipped it into her drink when she was looking at her phone."

Darius's jaw dropped, and Thorn's hand tensed so hard

inside his that he might as well have been holding a steel rod. The woman beside Lamar sat stunned, and all the color drained from her face as she stared at her date, trembling like she'd almost been hit by a city bus in a busy intersection. Lamar placed a palm on her forearm.

The man, however, snarled. Darius caught the glisten of sweat beading his hairline.

"You're a *fucking liar!*" he yelled. Behind his back, the massive, red-headed bouncer moved through the crowd, a tiger coming in for the kill.

"Sir," Lamar went on with the same smooth composure he'd had from the beginning, "one way or another, you're leaving this—"

"I didn't spike her fucking drink!"

Lamar cocked his head to the side and put the glass on the table. He pushed it forward with two long, delicate fingers. It stopped just shy of the man's clenched fists.

"Then drink it."

The crowd around them stilled. If the club music wasn't so loud, Darius was sure he'd hear the rumbling of whispers and rumors around him. At last, his nose curling furiously, the man stood up. He hulked over Lamar, his shoulders broad enough to eclipse the flashing lights. His thick chest expanded in a deep breath, and for a moment, Darius was sure he was going to start throwing punches. Thorn must have thought the same thing. She got to her feet, her hands clenched at her sides, ready to go. Darius rose beside her.

But before she jumped in and made a mess of the guy on the nightclub's tile floor, the bouncer lurched forward. He grabbed him by the arm, fingers digging so deep into his tricep that he dropped with a yelp.

"Mickey, get him out of here," Lamar said.

"Oh, it's my lucky day," the bouncer said, glowering down at the man in his hands. "Not yours, though. C'mon, asshole. Let's go make some calls. You ever been arrested before?"

As he dragged the guy away, Lamar turned back to his

date, and all the darkness Darius had seen in him washed away.

"It's all right, honey," Lamar said. Silent tears had filled her eyes and were now pouring quietly down her cheeks. Lamar eased her to her feet. "It's okay. Well, no, it's not. It's absolutely horrible. Do you have anyone here with you? Anyone you can call?" When the woman shook her head, still not speaking, Lamar beckoned to the other bartender. "Faith, can you be a sweetheart and take her to the office? Call Jace for a ride so we can make sure she gets home safe and sound."

The other bartender stopped recording and helped Lamar guide the girl around the counter. Once she was safely tucked away, he made his way back to Darius and Thorn.

"Give me a few minutes," he said. His voice lacked the laughter and light he had carried, but he smiled nonetheless, and that smile was still charming. "I am *very* curious to hear these long stories about the people you're hoping to meet. I just need to file a report on this… situation first."

Darius nodded, and Lamar vanished. Thorn's hand touched lightly between Darius's shoulder blades.

"We need to go," she said. Her dark eyes sharpened as she glanced toward the front entrance. Around them, the rest of the room melted back to normalcy—men and women returning to drinks and dancing like nothing had happened—but Thorn's focus was fierce and serious. "We don't want to be here when the cops show up."

Darius frowned. "Gluttony's Programming is gone."

"But Wrath's isn't," Thorn answered. "It's not worth the risk. You can continue this another night. It will give you a chance to figure out what the fuck you're going to tell him— besides our real names."

She shot him a hard look in the dark, and Darius let out a short laugh as she guided him away from the counter. Another set of people immediately swooped in to take their empty stools.

"I told you, I don't want to lie to him."

Thorn sighed and shook her head. "And I don't want you to get yourself caught and killed," she growled. "Let's go."

She dragged him out of the club, collecting Mackenzie, Madison, and Kit on the way. Darius looked over his shoulder, waiting for Lamar to come back out to the bar, but before he did, people swarmed around it, and Darius couldn't see a thing.

Thorn soaked a rag in a glass of water and squeezed it in her fist. With a sigh, she wiped away the trail of blood dribbling down her throat. Droplets flowed along her neck and pooled in the crevice above her collarbone.

"Well," she said as she pulled the rag away and looked at the red streaking across it, "Simmons was right. Our TAC helmets can't compensate for the new device's higher volume."

Chris leaned back in her chair across the table. "It's only a problem when you're too close to the weapon."

Thorn scoffed. They'd just wrapped up another round of testing, where she'd gotten to experience their latest sonic disruptor prototype firsthand. Simmons had managed to create something both small enough to be thrown and powerful enough to disable Puppets for twenty meters without killing anyone, which was precisely what Thorn wanted. The only problem was, when they tested the weapon at close range, the sound wave had overpowered Thorn's noise-canceling protection. She couldn't decide what was worse—having her eardrums blown out or listening to Holly Andrews and Taylor Simmons bicker about how to fix it.

"We can't risk this happening on the field," Thorn said. Sparkie perched on the table, and he peered up at her as she moved to the other side of her neck, making sure she didn't miss any spots. She had, the drier stuff sticking stubbornly to her skin. Thorn rubbed it harder. "But Andrews is starting to train her new AI program to delay detonation until we're at a safe distance."

"I'm sure she'll get it," Chris said. "This whole thing is pretty incredible. We'll be able to prevent so much damage."

Thorn nodded as she dipped the rag back into her water glass. "It's too bad it won't be ready for another couple of weeks. It would come in really fucking handy tomorrow."

"Hopefully, we won't need it," Chris said, but she shook her head with a sigh. "I feel good about the plan, but I've never tried to run this kind of operation. I'm a little nervous."

A knot wound in Thorn's stomach. She wanted to comfort Chris, tell her everything would be fine and the mission to plant a tracking device on Anton Claytor would go exactly as they planned, but experience had taught her all too often that she couldn't predict things like that. Especially not if her suspicions were correct and Autumn Hunt made an appearance. The knot in Thorn's gut yanked tighter.

"Me, too," she said. "We'll have to be really careful. Really diligent."

Chris nodded, and her focus drifted up toward the room behind Thorn's back. It was too early for lunch and too late for breakfast, so the courtyard was mostly empty. A few lingering Martyrs came and went, their cold energy passing through as they headed toward one of Cain's studios or back to their quarters. One of those energies approached Thorn's shoulder, and Chris's eyes lit up.

"Here you go," DuPont's deep voice rumbled by Thorn's side, and he put a hot cup of coffee on the table next to Sparkie. He had another for Chris. When she took it, her fingers brushed against his in a way that seemed intentional. Thorn's gaze slowly traveled up to Chris's face as she smiled and pulled a strand of yellow hair behind her ear.

"Thank you," she said. When she met Thorn's eye, she cleared her throat and took a sip. Either the coffee was warmer than Chris expected or a soft blush flooded her cheeks. Thorn looked back down at the rag, her jaw tight.

"Of course," DuPont said as he sat to Chris's left. A warm smile lifted his clean-shaven cheeks as he reclined, crossing one ankle over his knee and propping a muscular arm upon the back of his chair. His cognac eyes lingered on Chris for a moment longer before he looked at Thorn and frowned at the cloth in her hands. "How're you doing?"

"Fine," Thorn said. With the blood cleaned up, she tossed the rag onto the table beside her coffee and lifted the mug. The rich, bold aroma washed over her. She closed her eyes, breathing it in. When she touched the cup to her lips, it was almost too hot to drink, but Thorn did anyway. The inside of her mouth tingled, healing before it even had the chance to hurt.

"Good," DuPont said with a nod. "What'd I miss?"

"We were just talking about tomorrow," Chris said.

"What about it?"

"About how dangerous it's going to be," Thorn replied. "Greed is paranoid. He'll have his guard up and probably a handful of actual guards surrounding him. Getting close is going to be difficult."

Chris nodded. "How's Cain feeling about being the one who has to do it?"

"He's freaked out," Thorn said, "but he understands why we need him. The Sins can't sense his aura, and since Envy still hasn't repossessed, he's the only one of us who can use his Influence without them immediately knowing about it."

DuPont frowned. "Maybe you can't use your Influence, but they can't sense *you* either," he argued. "Why don't you plant the device?"

"They know me," Thorn said, and her chest constricted. Sparkie shifted anxiously from foot to foot before he leapt to Thorn's shoulder and slid behind her hair. "Anton Claytor will have Sentries looking for me all around the goddamned venue. I can't go in."

She fucking hated that. The idea of sending her team into this thing alone, being forced to watch from the street where all she could do was pray that it went smoothly while being ready to run in, guns blazing, if it went wrong, made her sick. She swallowed another mouthful of coffee, letting it burn all the way down her throat.

DuPont ran his hand across his chin with a groan like he knew exactly what they were risking by not having Thorn there. "We'll make it work. I mean, worst case scenario—"

"A lot of people die," Thorn cut in with a scoff.

"What's the second worst, then?" DuPont pressed.

"Cain can't get close enough," Chris answered. "We put all this time and energy into this event and walk away with nothing."

DuPont raised a hand in her direction. "See? The second worst-case scenario is just a draw."

Thorn's teeth clenched, and she looked down into her coffee, wishing it was scotch—wishing she could feel it. "That's our most likely outcome," she admitted, "but if we do get this thing planted, we might actually stand a chance at eliminating Anton Claytor. We have to take the risk."

She glanced up at them, thankful they seemed at least as convinced of that as she was.

"And this new Virtue has a fifty-fifty shot of being Charity," Chris said. She caught Thorn's eye, and the two stared at one another in silence. Not long ago, Chris would have never dreamed of finding a Virtue and destroying a Sin. Hell, Thorn wouldn't have, either. The possibility was still unfamiliar. She wasn't sure if she should trust it. Sparkie's tail twitched against her collar, and she raised a hand to still it.

"How is that going?" DuPont asked. "You and Darius have been working on connecting with him for a while now."

Thorn sighed, suddenly swimming in a new set of worries she'd been trying to ignore. "We're making progress. Darius officially introduced himself the last time we went down. Honestly, he got there faster than I expected."

Chris shook her head. "Isn't that a good thing?"

"It is." Thorn paused, looked into her coffee, and watched the dark reflection of her face staring back from the black. "But he's making it complicated. He doesn't want to lie to Verrette. I'm not sure how we can move forward from here."

DuPont sucked a breath through his teeth and leaned forward. "Yeah, that's tough, but he's a resourceful guy. If anyone can figure it out, it's Darius."

Thorn nodded, but she didn't say anything. Chris's focus zeroed in on her, and DuPont glanced between them before he spoke again.

"Anyway. Seth and Conrad are up in the garage, camouflaging our vans as delivery vehicles for the mission tomorrow. I'm gonna go give them a hand."

"Need help?" Chris asked.

DuPont's mouth curled in a charming, lopsided smile. "Nah, we've got it. You should hang out, relax, take a break…" She laughed, and DuPont's smile deepened as he shook his head. "You know what I mean. I'll see you at the debrief tonight?"

"Yep," Chris said. "Six sharp."

"Can't wait." With that, DuPont tilted forward like he was going in for a kiss, but he stopped just shy of it being undeniable. He cast Thorn a look over his shoulder, cleared his throat, and got to his feet. As he headed toward the elevator, Sparkie peeked out from the strands of Thorn's hair to watch him, but Thorn watched Chris. Her green eyes tracked DuPont until his energy started climbing upward. Then, she looked to Thorn and busied herself with her coffee.

A silence settled between them—Chris avoiding Thorn's eye to get out of having a conversation about this, and Thorn not sure how to start the conversation in the first place. At last, she simply said:

"I like him."

Chris's chin snapped upward, and she hardly had the time to mask her surprise. She stared at Thorn, and Thorn smiled. The shock melted from Chris's face, replaced by that pretty blush on her cheeks, and her lips curled up softly.

"Yeah," she said. "I do, too."

Thorn wanted to tell Chris how proud she was of her. How happy she was that Chris was smiling like this again. That seeing her treat herself as a woman and not just a weapon was the biggest relief Thorn had ever fucking experienced.

Instead, she reached out and wrapped her hand around Chris's fingers on the table, hoping that was enough for her to understand everything Thorn didn't have the words for.

CHAPTER THIRTEEN

Mayor Bently's fundraising event had kicked off just as the sun dipped below the buildings to the west, casting the whole neighborhood in cool, blue shadow. A line extended from the Mezzanine's ground-floor reception, full of wealthy donors with dubious morals. They funneled through the open door on a river of cold energy. Men and women huddled together for warmth or pulled luxurious fur jackets around themselves as they waited. A guard posted inside the building checked everyone for weapons—digging through purses and inspecting the guests with pat downs that seemed downright violating—before he led them through a metal detector and into the building.

Thorn sat in the back of a large, white van around the corner. From the outside, it appeared as nothing more than a Mercourier Delivery Services vehicle parked in the loading zone, its hazard lights flashing. Inside, though, the whole back had been gutted beyond the second row, bench seats replaced with floor-mounted stools and windows hidden behind paper-thin monitors. Thorn tapped on one of the screens, opening an array of video feeds, and she selected the reception area. The entire camera view filled the display. Thorn zoomed in further, narrowing on the security setup.

"Fuck." She glanced over her shoulder to where Chris was helping Peter Mulligan and Cain get ready. "You can't go in armed."

"*What?*" Cain breathed, looking every bit as frazzled as Thorn knew he would be in a situation like this. He'd opted for a more subtle black and gray suit instead of the flashier, fancier items he would have worn if he wasn't trying to keep a low profile, and he tugged at his bowtie anxiously. "Why on earth not?"

"They're checking for weapons," Thorn said. "Look." She gestured to the feed, and Cain shuffled over. "There's a metal detector by the door, and they're running any other belongings through this x-ray. You might be able to Influence the guard to ignore a pistol, but we can't fool the machines. It's better to be safe."

Cain huffed and shook his head so sharply that his slicked-back hair almost bounced out of place. He pulled his jacket off to remove the holster strapped to his back. Mulligan did the same. He'd dressed up in a similar suit and tie and somehow managed to tame his strawberry blonde curls into a stylish mop.

"If we were playing this 'safe,'" Cain grumbled, "we wouldn't be doing something so foolhardy at all." He handed his weapon to Chris and drew in a shallow breath. "What about the tracking devices? You think they won't be a problem?"

"No," Thorn said. She gestured to Chris's partner, Seth Graves, and he handed two leather, bi-fold wallets to her. She opened one, showing Cain's fake identification, a couple of paper bills, and a small stack of business cards. She tapped on them.

"Andrews embedded the trackers into these," Thorn explained. "Ultra slim, ultra covert, and they're designed with some kind of material that should mask the device. Just put this in the tray while you go through security, and you should get it back without a problem. Even if the guard searches through it, he won't find anything."

She passed a wallet to both Mulligan and Cain. Cain snatched his and shoved it in his pocket.

"Well," he said, shivering as he put his jacket back on like a bird ruffling its feathers, "I'm glad *you* feel confident. I wonder if you would still be so calm if you were in my shoes."

"I would be." Thorn tried on a smile to see if she could get Cain to do the same, but he just shot her a sharp look that made it clear that he'd never let her live this down if he managed to get out of this in one piece. Thorn exchanged a dark look with Chris. "Don't worry. I'll be with you every step of the way."

With that, Sparkie leapt from the van's dashboard and onto Cain's shoulder. The Familiar wound his way along the inside seam of the suit jacket and disappeared, his body and wings pressed flat between Cain's shoulder blades. Cain's eyes narrowed, but his lip did twitch upward.

"In spirit," he said.

Thorn chuckled. It felt tight and uneasy in her throat.

"Your goal," she said, now looking between Cain and Mulligan again, "is to get one of these devices on Anton Claytor's person—somewhere he won't immediately find it. His suit jacket is probably the best option. I'm hoping he drops it off at the coat check. That would make our job a hell of a lot easier. But if not, Andrews suggested handing him a card or slipping one inside his pocket."

Cain scoffed. "Impossible!"

"We'll see what we can do," Mulligan said.

"The goal might be to plant a device," Thorn continued, "but the priority is *you*. Be careful, don't rush, and if an opportunity does not present itself, let it go. I don't want anyone dying tonight. Is that understood?"

Mulligan confirmed as Cain said, "You certainly don't have to tell me twice."

"Good. Now go." Thorn opened the back of the van to the brisk March air. Mulligan leapt out first, and he stood up tall as he straightened his jacket and smoothed the seams of his slacks. Cain hesitated, breathing out a sigh as he glanced at Thorn one last time. She grabbed his shoulder and held it fiercely. He relaxed under her touch just enough to nod. Then he was out, and the two of them were gone. Thorn watched her team disappear down Exchange Alley until Mulligan's energy faded into the background of city noise and Cain's salt and pepper hair vanished.

Thorn shut the door and tapped into her coms earpiece.

"We're officially moving in," she said.

Chris took the stool to Thorn's left. Unlike Thorn, who wore plainclothes with a vest and gun tucked beneath her jacket to make it easier for her to jump in without drawing attention, Chris and the rest of her TAC patrols were fully decked out in the standard uniform of beige cargo pants and black turtlenecks with plates of body armor on top. Thorn squatted beside her as Chris typed a few keys, and the screens divided, filling with various video feeds, chat windows, and a corner frame where Holly Andrews stared back at them from her webcam.

"Everyone ready?" Thorn asked.

Names and positions sounded off in her ear. TAC units listed a half dozen locations around the Mezzanine. DuPont at Rector and Trinity. Carter on Greenwich. Davis on Broadway. Then, at last, Darius chimed in.

"Medical at Morris," he reported.

Thorn's heart skipped a beat, and she glanced up at the map to see just how far away that was—to calculate again, like she'd calculated a hundred times already, if that was far enough away. She closed her eyes and sorted through the sensation of civilian energy on the street until she found Skylar Fulton and the medic guard to the South.

It would have to do.

Thorn opened her eyes again. "Claytor, you've got your people ready to scramble the police?"

"They're all waiting on my signal," Alexis confirmed. Her mic caught the background sound of her work—phones ringing, voices droning, the crackle of radios. "Just say the word."

"Roger that," Thorn said. "Any sign of Greed on the cams, Andrews?"

"Not yet," Holly replied, "but Bently's schmoozing with a bunch of other political suits already, and there seems to be a lot of extra security. Check the corners."

Thorn squinted at the camera feeds. Sure enough, tall, broad men in matching suits with matching statures watched the party from the perimeter, hands clasped behind their backs.

"Greed probably hired bodyguards," Chris said. "We should assume they're all armed."

"You hear that, Cain?" Thorn said.

"I am counting my blessings," Cain grumbled, "and my days."

Mulligan chuckled, the laugh pouring through Thorn's earpiece and bringing a smirk to her mouth, and Chris shook her head with a tense smile. For the next few minutes, they watched as Cain and Mulligan made their way to the front of the line. The second Cain's figure appeared in the ground floor reception area's camera view, Thorn's spine straightened. As he spoke to the guard, she heard his voice in her ear and felt the vibrations of it through Sparkie's body pressed up against his back. She held her breath.

"Good evening," Cain said. "Lovely night, isn't it?"

He dipped his hand into his pocket and drew out his device to display the event ticket Holly had managed to get for him. The guard did little more than grunt in Cain's direction as he scanned the screen. When that was done, he held out a plastic dish.

"Wallet, phone, keys," he said.

"Yes, of course."

Cain dropped his belongings into the basin, glanced at the camera in the corner, and approached the metal detector. Thorn could feel his nerves in the way his body trembled beneath Sparkie's belly. He walked through without incident, and the guard did a pat down that barely missed the

Familiar lying flat between Cain's shoulder blades. Seconds later, his wallet and phone back in his hands, Cain ascended the stairs to the Mezzanine, and Thorn nodded.

"We're in," she said as Mulligan followed on Cain's heels.

Hundreds of people filled the venue space; men and women in deliriously expensive clothing made of silk, cashmere, and embroidered jewels chatted around standing cocktail tables and plates of hors d'oeuvres. The dining rounds had been removed, opening up much more floor space than Thorn had seen when she'd first looked over the venue. She recognized a few people here—nine-figure business owners and politicians with enough clout to make waves every time they so much as sneezed.

Mayor Richmond Bently clearly wanted to dominate the room. He'd dressed in a sleek Italian suit that showed off the new body he'd bought for himself, even though he had declined all reports of cosmetic surgery circulating in the less reputable New York papers. He stood near the presentation stage on the southern edge of the room, speaking with his new police commissioner, Adeline Faust, and a collection of other officials he'd put in place since winning his last election.

But there was a massive gap between wanting to dominate the room and actually doing it. Too many high-powered people filled the space for him to be the most influential one. Thorn thought she recognized one of the matriarchs from the Davis family, who commanded so much money that she might have had more tucked away in secret accounts and investments than even the Martyrs did. She saw businessmen, lawyers, diplomats, celebrities… And, standing near the large, floor-to-ceiling windows was a man who looked familiar. Thorn frowned as she took in his face: the blonde hair, symmetrical dimples, and a smile that charmed the people around him. Something about him tugged at her, but she pushed it to the back of her mind.

All these people, and not a single sign of Anton

Claytor—or Autumn Hunt.

The next several minutes passed in a tense quiet as Thorn's field agents integrated themselves. Mulligan quickly found a table to join and people to talk to, and soon, he was laughing with a plate of stuffed mushrooms and a pretty, older woman hanging on his every word.

Cain, on the other hand, made a direct line for the bar, and he stood there with a glass of red wine in his palm as he took in the room. Thorn felt him draw a deep, shuddering breath. If she knew Cain, he was calculating ways to escape and places to hide.

"Greed's here," Holly announced. "Northeast corner of the room."

Cain's body went rigid. Thorn's eyes flicked to the correct video feed, and she instantly spotted a head of platinum blonde hair above the crowd. Anton Claytor stepped out from the hallway leading to the back rooms and emergency exit behind Cain's shoulder. Thorn's stomach dropped.

"Move in, Cain," she said. "He's coming up on you. Get in the crowd so he doesn't realize you don't have an aura."

The Forgotten Sin practically leapt away from the bar, scurrying into a throng of people and weaving his way to the far side of the room. He glanced back, and the minute he spotted Greed stepping over the threshold, he sucked in a breath. His heart pounded so fast that Sparkie could hear it through his back. Thorn leaned in, her eyes glued to the screen as she watched Greed take in the space, hoping he didn't stop on Cain—hoping he hadn't realized someone just as unnatural as he was had slipped into the crowd.

As much as Cain was their only chance at using Influence and getting close, he was also a damned red flag. If Claytor paid close enough attention or caught Cain alone, he would know without a doubt he wasn't human, and that would get him killed.

But Greed didn't notice Cain at all. His sharp, blue eyes swooped right by him as his head swiveled around. He adjusted his suit jacket before he walked along the bar. Thorn let out a sigh of relief.

"Check out the guard," Chris murmured. She arched forward in her stool, fingers steepled together as she stared at the display. A big, bald, barrel-chested man loomed over Claytor's shoulder. He wore a pair of dark sunglasses, which obscured his eyes and made it difficult to tell if he was being Puppetted or not. His expression was stony, serious, and impossible to read. A concealed pistol disturbed the back of his suit jacket, making it stick out at an odd angle.

"Let's assume he's a hired hand," Thorn said as Claytor talked with the bartender before grabbing a martini off the counter. "Greed's easily got the power to keep a couple of Puppets locked in for a few hours without wearing himself out, but I doubt he'll waste his energy. If he's worried about being attacked, he'll preserve it for a real fight."

Claytor's eyes darted around again as he took a sip of his drink. Thorn's stomach twisted. A Sin with anxiety in a room full of people was a volatile combination. Heightened nerves meant a short fuse, and Greed could do a hell of a lot of damage if he got spooked. She felt like she was watching a nature documentary. Claytor was a cornered viper, winding himself into a position to strike and bury his fangs into anyone who crept too close.

Thorn's mouth ran dry, and she swallowed against it.

"Okay," she said, adjusting her squat to rest on her knees. "Hold back for a bit. I want Claytor to relax before we try anything. Mulligan, keep doing what you're doing. Cain, get somewhere Sparkie can disengage. I want to follow Greed. Then I need you to stop acting like you've got a goddamned gun to your head and make small talk with literally anybody there. I don't care who. You look like you're about to have a stroke."

He snorted indignantly, raised his wine to his lips, and emptied the glass in three large gulps. As he returned to the bar for a refill, Claytor walked to where Mayor Bently and the police commissioner were still speaking. Bently did a double take when he noticed Claytor, and he forced a cordial smile.

Cain reached the counter and asked for more wine. As the bartender filled his glass, Sparkie slid down Cain's back and wriggled his way to his hip. Cain slipped a hand into his pocket, casually opening his jacket as he did so, and Sparkie followed the line of Cain's leg to the ground. The Familiar wedged beneath the barstools and slipped around the counter, disappearing from sight. With his drink full again, Cain merged back into the crowd and found his way into a group near the staircase where he could easily keep an eye on Greed.

Sparkie, meanwhile, tucked his wings tight against his body and slithered into the attached kitchen, where two chefs were prepping a new round of salmon mousse canapés and caviar cups. He kept to the edge of the cupboards, and Thorn watched the video footage to make sure no one was looking in his direction as he scurried up a beam and to the ceiling. Once there, he was out of sight of the cameras, the attendees, and Anton Claytor. Thorn sighed as her Familiar positioned himself right above Greed's head.

She closed her eyes and focused on what Sparkie could hear.

"…and it really is a tragedy," Bently droned. "All this business with the slums in Manhattan is quite unfortunate for our image. They're spilling into more neighborhoods. Tourist revenue was expected to grow by six percent last year, but we only managed to make it to three. This problem is, quite literally, losing us money."

Anton Claytor snorted. Thorn's eyes snapped open again as she found him on the security feed. His bodyguard was still tucked close to his shoulder, ensuring the rest of the guests kept a respectable distance.

"What are they talking about?" Chris asked.

"Politics and money," Thorn murmured. "The only two subjects assholes like this care about."

"Surely, there's a solution here," Claytor was saying. "That percentage of revenue loss is unacceptable."

Bently's mouth opened for a moment before he cleared his throat and straightened his back. "Of course, there's a solution," he said. Claytor's cold eyes moved onto him. "Adeline and I are working on a new program to clean up this mess—"

"Bland campaign promises," Claytor interrupted, his voice flat and uninspired, as he waved the mayor away with a sharp flick of his wrist. "Give me something *concrete*, Bently. Something I can *truly* believe in."

Bently's face went red, and his jaw slammed shut. Adeline Faust crossed her arms over her navy dress uniform.

"Excuse me," she began, tone hot and defensive, "Rich is—"

"It's fine, Adeline," Bently cut in, casting the commissioner a quick look. "He's right, of course. When we have the details put together, Mr. Claytor, we'll be sure to reach out to you. You have invested a lot in my campaign, and I am forever grateful for your continued trust *and* patience. And speaking of investors…" Bently glanced at the watch on his wrist so quickly that Thorn knew he didn't care what the time read. "…There are quite a few here tonight. If you'll excuse me."

Anton's lips thinned into a humorless smile as Bently cleared his throat and made his way to the speaking dais at the southern end of the room. The mayor raised his glass and struck it with a thick, gold ring on his pointer finger. The chime rang around the venue, silencing the chatter, and Bently lit up in a wide smile that showed off his whitened teeth.

"Thank you all for coming tonight," he said. In true politician fashion, he projected loudly enough for Mulligan's and Cain's mics to easily pick up the words. To Thorn's left, Chris touched her earpiece as Bently went on.

"My, what an incredible turnout. There is nothing better than standing in a room of my peers… other than, perhaps, standing in a room of supermodels, but sadly, they all declined my invitation."

His grin widened, and a rumble of laughter moved through the crowd. Thorn rolled her eyes as Holly's voice sounded over their channel. "Wow. Who the hell votes for this guy?"

"Too many people," DuPont said. "He won by a landslide in the last election."

"Gross."

Bently kept talking, pouring more of the same bad humor and baseless promises Thorn had heard from hundreds of politicians over the years. She ignored him and instead focused on Anton Claytor. He backed away from the podium, standing far enough from the rest of the crowd not to get lost within it without being so far he seemed misplaced. The Sin didn't even pretend to listen to the mayor's speech. His sharp eyes looked around the guests while he sipped his martini. He held so tight to the body of his glass that the bones in his knuckles stood out hard and white against his pale skin. Every time someone moved, whether it was a caterer walking trays of appetizers between the cocktail tables or an attendee scratching their nose, Claytor's attention snapped to them like he expected someone to pull out a gun.

"God, he's freaking out," Thorn murmured. She pinched her tongue between her teeth. "We might be here for a while."

"Oh, lucky me," Cain murmured against his wine as he raised it to his mouth.

For the duration of Bently's speech, Greed observed the room, and the Martyrs observed Greed. Thorn pressed her steepled fingers against tight lips. After Bently, several city council members came to the stage to praise the mayor, boasting about defunded programs, tax cuts to the wealthiest one percent, and other policies his administration supported. All the while, Anton Claytor's cold, calculating gaze circled the guests. Cain and Mulligan diligently watched the stage, never so much as glancing in Claytor's direction. After over an hour of people talking about all the things fucking wrong with this city like they were the goddamned heroes sent to fix them, Thorn spotted the first sign of a change. She straightened up.

"Look at that."

Greed pulled his phone out of his pocket and looked at the screen. He typed something, waited for a response, and then looked out again.

Suddenly, Mulligan's voice came over the channel.

"Influence," he murmured. "I feel it."

"As do I," Cain whispered. Nerves tightened the words.

Thorn's eyes widened. "He's trying to weed out anyone resistant to it." Her heart pounded, fists clenched as she leaned forward against them. She looked around the room, focusing on every guest, looking for a common thread. "He suspects we have people here… Shit!"

A simultaneous rustle moved through the crowd as attendees began putting glasses and appetizer plates on the tables, the bar, or even the floor at their feet. Mulligan caught on immediately. He set his food down as soon as the people he was with began to do it. Cain, however, froze with the hallmark stare of an animal caught in a trap.

"Put your wine down, Cain!" Thorn hissed into her mic.

He did, but maybe too late. Anton Claytor looked his way, and he scowled. People around the venue then moved their hands up to cover their mouths with their fingertips. Mulligan followed, and Cain was right behind him, but he cast Claytor a look, and Thorn swore under her breath.

"They've marked him," Chris said. She got up from her stool and started gathering her gear.

A guard moved away from the back exit just as Claytor took a step toward the crowd. DuPont ordered his team to get ready. The monster in Thorn's stomach flared to life.

Sparkie bolted from the ceiling and crashed headfirst into the wall of liquor behind the bar.

The collision sent a cascade of glass bottles and crystal drinkware tumbling from one shelf to the next, dragging more to the ground in a waterfall of shards and spirits. It all smashed to the tile floor, and a wave of shock tore through the crowd so intensely that even the Martyrs winced at the sound. Thorn's teeth gnashed together, and she closed her eyes against the pain of sharp edges cutting against Sparkie's wings and body as he yanked himself out of the wreckage and darted beneath the cabinets. When he was in the clear, she sucked in a harsh breath and looked at the screen again.

"Cain," she said when she spotted his salt and pepper head dip behind the mob as people gasped and swarmed toward the kitchen. "Get out of there. You've been compromised. Mulligan, follow the crowd. Act natural. Don't draw any attention to yourself. When Cain is clear, I need you out, too."

"What about the tracking—"

"Not now, Mulligan," Thorn snapped, swearing under her breath at this complication, at this mission, and at herself for dragging them here in the first place. "We need to get you both to safety and—"

"Thorn," Holly cut in. The tension in her voice sliced through Thorn's thought process like a guillotine. "We have a problem."

"What?"

"Security is locking and barricading both exits."

Thorn scanned the feeds, her jaw pressed so tightly shut that the muscles in her face groaned under the pressure. Sure enough, the man running security in the ground-floor reception had gone to the door and bolted it shut, and now, he stood there with two other armed officers.

Cain froze where he stood, surrounded by people, and murmured, "What do I do?"

Thorn had no fucking idea. She frantically searched the venue for a sign of Anton Claytor and found him stumbling toward the kitchen and the emergency exit beyond it. A server tripped on his way to help clean up the mess, landing on top of the Sin and covering him with a greasy shower of buttered oysters. Before Thorn could speak, an icy, evil beacon came to life in the back of her mind. Her stomach plummeted.

"Oh, *fuck*," she breathed. Panic built in her throat, and the world around her began to fade to gray. "Wrath."

Chris's eyes shot wide. *"What?"*

"Hold back," Thorn said, shaking her head, feeling her whole body shake with her as the fire in her core roared. She moved toward the rear of the van, tore the door open, and shouted to Chris as she leapt down to the asphalt. "Wait for my orders to come in. Claytor, get ready to cut off police communications."

"Thorn, wait!" Chris started, but Thorn had already shut the door, and she headed up Broadway.

Wrath's Influence pulsed in intermittent waves of wicked power no further than Liberty, if Thorn had to guess, which was too goddamned close for comfort. Part of her wanted to run that way—to cut the bitch off and plant a bullet in her head right there in the middle of the fucking street—but right now, she had two people trapped like wounded divers in a tank of sharks. Her heart racing, her focus drawn north, Thorn swore as she made her way into the alley. She was so caught up in her thoughts that she hardly registered the icy aura of someone around the corner, and she almost ran right into him.

"Jesus," she breathed, "sorry, I—"

"No, it's fine—wait, Teagan?"

Thorn froze, her mouth dropped open, as a man considered her from over the top of a smoldering cigarette. His handsome face lit up in a smile.

"Teagan Love, right?"

Thorn stood stock still, so shocked to hear someone use her old pseudonym that it took her a second to realize who it was. The man from the party who had looked so familiar. He held out a hand, his smile stretching until the dimples pinched into his cheeks came into full focus.

"You don't remember me, do you?" he asked. "Connor Amoretto? I was at the press conference at City Hall six years ago when we had that fiasco with the subway attacks."

Still, Thorn only stared. Her brain filled with a confusing mess of information. Wrath's beacon started to move away, and the com device lodged in her ear was a cacophony of voices—orders flying between the TAC teams and Chris asking her what was going on. Thorn pinched her eyes closed, vaguely aware of Sparkie darting through feet inside the Mezzanine until he reached the emergency hallway. He leapt for the wall, latched onto a fire alarm switch, and suddenly, blaring sound filled the room—and Thorn's head.

"I'm sorry," she said again. Chris shouted something about Greed exiting the venue, Alexis announced she was scrambling police responses, and Holly reported the guards backing off from the door, but the tickling sense of danger in Thorn's brain refused to fade.

"Thorn, who the hell are you talking to?" Chris asked.

"Connor Amoretto?" Thorn said aloud. "No, I don't remember you."

Amoretto's tongue slipped out of his mouth, wetting his full lower lip as he pulled it between his teeth. "Is everything okay?"

"No. I need to get to—"

"The mayor's event," Amoretto cut in, and again, Thorn gawked at him. He tilted his head back toward the venue. Somewhere inside, Sparkie found Cain and climbed into his suit jacket. Amoretto kept talking. "You're covering it for… what paper do you work for again?"

"The Brooklyn Register," Thorn answered.

"I didn't see you up there," he said with a frown. He brought his cigarette to his lips, paused, and held the pack out to her. Thorn nearly reached for one on instinct alone before remembering where she was and shaking her head instead. Amoretto returned the pack to his pocket with a shrug as he let out a stream of gray smoke. "Couldn't land a ticket, huh?"

"Mulligan's clear," Chris's voice chimed in Thorn's ear.

"You know Bently doesn't like the press." Thorn side-stepped a bit, craning her neck to look over Amoretto's shoulder where she could barely make out the entrance to the Mezzanine in the alley. People poured from it, but she couldn't spot Mulligan among them. In the distance, further north, Wrath's Influence pinged one more time and disappeared.

Amoretto laughed, drawing Thorn in again. His deep voice was a sultry rumble that was almost infectious, and he turned to keep in line with her. "Don't I. I was promoted to lead manager for his campaign a couple of months ago. But I'll tell you what… It's not Bently who doesn't like the press. It's that snake he works with, Anton Claytor."

All of Thorn's attention homed in on Amoretto with a snap. "Anton Claytor?"

"Yeah. Something's not right with the guy," Amoretto said with a frown as he ran his thumbnail against his lower lip. "He dropped off the face of the earth about eight months ago then suddenly comes crawling back out like he owns the place, and apparently, it's not the first time this has happened. No one I've talked to knows a damn thing about him."

Thorn's eyes narrowed. "What do you think's going on?"

"No clue," Amoretto said. He drew in a fresh mouthful of nicotine and breathed it out in a sigh. Suddenly, Thorn felt Peter Mulligan's energy climbing safely into the van around the corner behind her. The knot in her stomach loosened a bit as Amoretto went on. "But Bently does whatever Claytor wants. It's like he has no choice, like Claytor's got some crazy dirt on him. I've been looking into it."

"You have?" Thorn asked. He nodded, and she shook her head. "Well? What have you found?"

"Not a lot," he replied, and he scratched the back of his neck. "I'm actually glad I ran into you. I can't do a lot of digging without risking my job, but that's what journalists do, right? You think there's a story here?"

"Cain's out," Chris said.

Thorn nodded, the relief flooding her so intensely that

her hands and feet felt numb.

"You do?" Amoretto said.

Thorn blinked, closed her eyes, and shook her head again as she focused on what was happening in front of her. "I'm not sure. It's not my area of expertise."

Movement in the alley drew her attention, and Thorn looked past Amoretto's shoulder as Cain hurried toward her. He was soaking wet, hair and shoulders saturated from the Mezzanine's sprinklers, and when he saw her, he slowed his step to a more natural pace. They locked eyes, and he raised his brows, jutting his chin forward.

"I'm sorry," Thorn said as Cain slipped around her. "I've got to go. Good luck with your investigation."

Amoretto watched Cain walk by, shocked at the state of him, but he got his bearings back before Thorn walked away. "Wait!" He stuck his cigarette in his mouth and reached into his pocket, pulling out a business card and forcing it into her hand. "If you decide you want to look into this Claytor thing, give me a call."

He smiled at her, his piercing, blue eyes zeroed on her face. Thorn forced a smile and left without another word. When she turned her back on him, she felt Connor Amoretto's gaze following her.

As soon as she rounded the corner, she broke into a run and leapt into the back of the van. Chris was already in the passenger seat, Seth behind the wheel. The second Thorn was inside, he tore into traffic without waiting for the doors to close behind her. She groaned and ran her hands down her face.

"Jesus," she breathed against her gloves. "What a fucking disaster."

"Well," Mulligan said, his voice coy. "Not completely."

Thorn dropped her hands and frowned at him. "What do you mean?"

He grinned.

"I got the device on Greed."

CHAPTER FOURTEEN

The Martyrs returned to the Underground in waves. First, the medical van pulled into the garage, followed by all the TAC patrols. Gabe, Conrad, their partners, and other officers moved through the loading area while they unpacked their gear. Skylar slipped inside as Darius held the glass doors open, and he glanced back. Tightness stretched across his chest. He took a deep breath and felt upward, hoping to catch a sense of the people sharing Thorn's vehicle moving down the ramp.

"Darius," Alan's voice called behind him.

The Martyr leader stood across the waiting room just outside the hallway to the back offices. Holly squeezed past him, and Darius sensed Mackenzie's aura in the conference room. Alan tilted his head in that direction, his shoulder-length hair draping like curtains around his chin. "We are getting ready to debrief. Are you coming?"

"Yeah," Darius said. He shut the door, and they headed down the hallway together.

"That was quite an operation," Alan mentioned. "Did I hear correctly that there were no casualties?"

Darius nodded. "There might have been a few civilians hurt, but all of our guys made it out in one piece."

"Excellent," Alan said as he opened the conference room.

Holly and Mackenzie weren't alone. Nicholas sat just inside with his back to the door. He turned around as Darius and Alan made their way in.

"Good job out there today," he said with a smirk.

Darius chuckled. "I didn't do anything, but thanks." He walked around the table to where Mackenzie and Holly were already sitting, but he didn't join them. Adrenaline still coursed through his system, and he knew he'd just fidget if he sat down right now. Instead, he grabbed the back of his chair and leaned forward. "It went a little off the rails, but everyone's okay."

Mackenzie forced out a quick, strained laugh. "That's a rarity, isn't it?"

"More than I like to admit," Alan said coldly. He moved to the head of the table. Like Darius, he remained standing. "We are fortunate Greed is more interested in self-preservation than violence."

The door to the conference room flew open again, and Thorn strode through it. The second Darius saw her, the tension in his chest loosened. Chris and Peter Mulligan followed behind her. A frown settled onto Alan's thin lips as Chris shut the door.

"Where is Cain?" he asked. "I made it very clear that I want him here for this debrief."

"I know," Thorn said, running her fingers through her hair. Black, silky sheets poured between them as she shook her head. Sparkie clung to her shoulder and gazed around the room. "He said he'd be right up."

Alan's frown deepened, and an angry glint flashed across his half-empty, black eyes. "What is so important that it must be done *now?*"

Thorn threw her hands up, exasperated. "I don't know what to tell you, Alan," she said as Peter plopped into a chair beside Nicholas, and Chris made her way around the table.

"The guy *did* nearly get caught," Holly said. She scooted

her chair forward as Chris walked behind her to take the empty spot on Darius's other side. "Give him a minute."

"He might just need to cool off," Darius agreed. He hadn't even been in the building, and he still felt wired after the hour-long drive back. "A lot went down in that room."

Peter nodded and laced his fingers behind his head. They disappeared in a messy, damp fray of strawberry blonde curls.

"There was a minute there where I thought we wouldn't get out," he said. "Especially when I heard Wrath was nearby."

Thorn's eyes darkened as she and Alan exchanged a quick, hard look.

"It's weird as fuck that she was so close and didn't make an appearance, though, isn't it?" Nicholas asked.

"She's probably afraid Thorn would try to kill her again," Mackenzie said.

Thorn's throat went rigid, and she crossed her arms. Her fingers dug into her biceps as Sparkie slid behind her hair until nothing but the end of his tail laid flat against her breastbone. Darius watched her, and he heaved a deep breath. "Whatever the reason," he said, and Thorn looked up. Their eyes linked across the table. "Wrath didn't show up, and we did what we set out to do. I'd call today a win."

The tension in Thorn's expression melted, and Sparkie peeked around the far side of her throat. Darius managed a smile. At the head of the table, Alan nodded.

"Yes." He took a deep breath and forced his shoulders to relax as he finally took a seat. Darius followed suit, pulling his chair out as Thorn settled across the table. "Thanks to Mr. Mulligan's quick thinking, we now have a tracking device on Anton Claytor."

Nicholas blew air between his teeth. "How the hell did you manage that?"

A sly smile stretched across Peter's face. "One of the servers dropped a whole tray of oysters all over him."

"What kind of oysters?" Nicholas asked.

"Rockefeller," Peter said with a snicker. "A bunch of people rushed in to help get him cleaned up. I just… offered a hand. When I got close enough, I slipped the tracker into the inner pocket."

Mackenzie's brows shot up. "Pretty fuckin' slick, Mulligan."

"Did anyone see you?" Darius asked.

"It was so insane in there that no one was focusing on me," Peter replied.

"The biggest thing we'd have to worry about is the Sins checking the camera footage," Holly said. "When you look at it, it's pretty clear you were up to something. It would be a shame if someone downloaded and corrupted all their server files…"

She grinned as Mackenzie nudged her with an elbow and laughed. Alan's chin tilted in a soft nod. "What is our next step, Miss Andrews?"

"We wait to get the data back," Holly said. "I set the devices up to send a continuous signal from the moment of activation so we can map where he's going. Thanks to interference from the buildings and all the signals going through the city, it's not one hundred percent accurate, but it can get us a good fifty-foot range."

"Fifty feet is incredible," Thorn said. "We should have no problem pinpointing him with that."

"Exactly," Holly agreed. "Now it's just a matter of how much data we're going to get. Running nonstop means the battery will drain in approximately a hundred hours."

"That's less than five days," Nicholas said.

"Right," Holly said. "Which is perfect. Considering he got himself covered in a healthy dose of sea snot—"

"Sea snot *Rockefeller*," Nicholas cut in, which sent Mackenzie and Peter into a round of giggles.

"—I'd bet he's going to get his jacket washed. Hopefully, he'll empty his pockets first. The next couple of days are going to be crucial."

Thorn's expression pulled together in a thoughtful

frown, but before she could speak again, Cain walked into the room. She spun in her chair as he kicked the door open with his foot because both his hands were taken. In one, he carried an open bottle of wine, and in the other, a tall, stemmed glass half-full of merlot. He'd changed out of the damp formalwear he'd had on for the event, instead wearing tight slacks and a button-up shirt left open a couple of inches below his collar.

"Sorry I'm late," he murmured with the distinct air of someone who was not sorry at all. He cast Alan a look and raised his glass toward him. "It has been quite a day, and I needed a bit of a... refresher before I am forced to relive it."

He took a drink and came to Thorn's other side. As he put down the bottle and pulled out his chair, Alan's lips pursed. He caught Cain with a hard stare.

"We typically debrief immediately following a mission," he said. Cain simply took another sip of wine. "I will let this instance go, as you have been out of the loop of our operations, but in the future, I expect you to join us promptly."

"Oh," Cain said, settling into his seat, "that shouldn't be a problem, as I will refuse to be a part of such things in the future. Covertly using my Influence as we had when hunting down Wrath is one thing, but being trapped in the same room as the Sins is another entirely."

Thorn's mouth twisted compassionately, maybe even regretfully, and she said, "Cain—"

"No, no," he interrupted as he raised a hand. It shook between them. "My dear, please. Do not appeal to my sensibilities or my affection for you. I was woefully under-prepared, and we all know this fiasco could have been avoided had I simply not been there at all. No. No, I don't think I'll be doing things like this again, but thank you for the... *opportunity*. I have *missed* being involved."

His jaw tightened, and though he raised his wine again, he didn't seem capable of opening his mouth to take another drink. Darius saw the same panic he'd watched on the cameras coming back, haunting him like a shadow. When Cain met his eye, he tried to smile, and the Forgotten Sin seemed to relax. At last, he brought the glass to his lips.

Peter cleared his throat. "Honestly, I don't think we would have managed to get this done without you." He leaned forward to look around Thorn. Cain refused to look back. "All that chaos helped me get close to Greed, and your Influence on the guards is the only reason they opened the doors."

"I appreciate the flattery," Cain answered curtly.

Alan heaved a sigh and laced his hands on the table. "Enough," he said. "What matters is that we successfully planted a tracking device on one of the Sins, a feat that we have *never* accomplished before, and we must determine our best course of action. Miss Andrews, you were saying?"

"Right," Holly said. "The next few days are critical. My team is looking at the information we're getting back from the tracker right now, and we should have an idea of where Greed is moving soon. Since we don't know how long that data will be relevant, we've got to act fast."

"What kind of action are we talking about?" Nicholas asked. He propped his elbows on the table and leaned into them. "Do we want to attack *now?*"

"No," Chris said. "Rushing an offensive strike will just get people killed. We want to figure out where he goes. Hopefully, this will help us identify his patterns, and we can spend more time planning a real operation after that."

"Might not be enough," Mackenzie said with a shrug. "Wrath has had how many hideouts? I'd put money down that Greed has more than one place he skulks off to when shit hits the fan."

"Yes, that is very likely," Alan agreed. "The tracking device is a victory, but we must not assume it will be the windfall we need to successfully kill Anton Claytor. It is a tool, potentially a highly valuable one, but that is all. Mr. Mulligan, how are you faring with integrating into his circles?"

"Slowly, sir," Peter said with a sigh. "I've been at one of

his main firms for a while now, but it takes time to get people talking… especially since he's been MIA. Not a lot to see when nothing's happening."

"Maybe not nothing," Thorn said. "This man approached me today. He recognized me by my old alias and asked me to look into Anton Claytor for him."

She reached into her pocket and drew out a business card. With a flick, she tossed it onto the table, where it spun to a stop a foot from where Darius was sitting. He frowned as he picked it up, and Mackenzie peered over his shoulder to look at it, too. "Connor Amoretto?" he said, glancing up at Thorn.

"Holy shit." Mackenzie grabbed the card and let out a low whistle. Amoretto's headshot took up half of the back, and Mackenzie's eyes widened as she admired his flawless skin, bright eyes, and dimpled smile. "Is he single?"

"He's the new manager for Bently's reelection campaign," Thorn said.

"And an aspiring underwear model," Mackenzie added.

Holly took out her phone and started typing as Darius shook his head. "Why did he want you to look into Anton Claytor?" he asked.

"Because he's picked up on the fact that Claytor plays by his own rules," Thorn said as she crossed her arms. "I also got the impression that he might have seen Influence at work. He told me Bently does whatever Claytor wants him to do."

"You said he recognized you?" Holly asked. When Thorn nodded, she went on. "Did he say where from?"

Thorn's eyes pinched shut as she thought back. "Ah… a press conference six years ago about the—"

"Subway shootings?" Holly cut in.

"That's the one."

Holly adjusted her glasses as she read her screen. "It tracks. This 'Connor Amoretto' was an account manager with Crave Media back then… He'd just started working with Bently's campaign." She considered Thorn from across the table. "Do *you* remember *him?*"

"No," Thorn said, "but I talked to a lot of people at that event."

Nicholas leaned forward so he could see her around Peter. "What were you even doing there?"

Thorn let out a hard scoff. "Seeing how fucked we were," she said. "Those shootings were between Martyrs and some of Lust's Puppets. It was one of our messiest run-ins with them in years. I was there to run damage control and make sure certain details never got out."

"God, it was such a bitch to cover up," Holly murmured as she sank back into scrolling through information on Amoretto.

"So," Alan said, and he cleared his throat to regain control of the room. They all turned toward him. Cain tilted his head back, pouring the last mouthful of merlot down his throat as Alan went on. "Claytor has an interest in what Mayor Bently is doing."

Cain laughed, the sound of it sudden and harsh. "Of course he does," he said as he lifted his wine bottle and poured another healthy serving into his glass. Alan's expression tightened, and the muscles on his neck went rigid. "Greed, Pride, and Lust, more than any of the other Sins, have always had their fingers dipped into political pockets. It's just a matter of how deep those fingers go."

"Maybe we should talk to Amoretto," Chris said. "If he's starting to suspect Claytor, he might have information we could use."

"Probably not," Nicholas said. He shook his head as he sat back in his chair again. "I'm sure he just suspects Claytor of bribery or blackmail—you know, the normal kind of evil we expect from politicians and billionaires."

"That may be true," Cain said, "but digging into Greed will certainly put him in danger, regardless of what he suspects. Claytor will have no qualms with silencing anyone who gets too close to him."

"Yes," Alan agreed. "We should monitor this situation.

Mr. Mulligan, see what you can find out about Mayor Bently's relationship with Anton Claytor, if such a thing exists. As for Mr. Amoretto, if we start to suspect he may be a target, or if we think he may have information that will be valuable to us, we can make contact."

"I'll see what I can find out about him," Thorn said. She leaned across the table and reached for the business card. Mackenzie's blue eyes flashed mischievously as she dropped it into Thorn's palm.

"Can I help?" the Irishwoman asked.

Thorn rolled her eyes. "No."

Mackenzie pushed her mouth into a pout. "Fine. Keep all the good ones for yourself. I'm sure this guy will make a nice notch for your bedpost."

Thorn froze, her eyes wide and jaw dropped open. Darius's stomach fell. He exchanged a stunned look with Chris before both of them stared at Mackenzie. The whole table turned to her, too shocked to say anything for the half-second it took for Thorn's hand to curl into a fist. "Jesus, McKay, what the *fuck* is your problem?"

"Aw, c'mon!" Mackenzie laughed. "An underwear model gives you his card, and you really think it's just about work?" She indicated Thorn's knuckles, now pressed so firmly against the table that Darius thought he could hear the wood groan beneath them. "Grow up, Thorn."

Thorn got to her feet, but at the exact same moment, Cain grabbed her arm, and Alan said, "Miss McKay, that is *enough*. This is an inappropriate conversation, and if you cannot help yourself, you may leave."

A tense silence filled the room. Nicholas, Holly, and Peter sat awkwardly still, with confused frowns across their faces as they glanced from Thorn to Mackenzie to Alan and back again. At last, Mackenzie scoffed, shook her head, and flung back in her chair, pulling her legs up beneath her like a child sitting in the corner.

"Yes, sir," she said. Her piercing clicked against her teeth. When she began picking at her chipped nail polish,

Darius saw her hands were shaking.

Alan turned back to the table as though nothing had happened.

"Now," he said, "to revisit this question, what happens next? Miss Andrews, since Cain missed the beginning of our debrief, would you care to enlighten him on what we can expect from the tracking device?"

The rest of the table slowly settled. Thorn sat back down as Cain withdrew his hand from her forearm and returned it to the glass of wine beside him. Holly dove into explaining the specifications and complications of the data they hoped to get. Everyone else watched her, but Thorn stared at the far wall with blank-faced coldness. Darius saw a glint of old hurt behind her black eyes that made his chest twinge. Her jaw was clenched so tightly that it looked painful, and she crossed her arms around her chest like it could provide a wall between her and the rest of them. Sparkie was still hidden behind her hair, but his long tail wound around Thorn's throat, a blue slit against her pale skin.

"We did all this work to get *maybe* five days of data?" Cain said when Holly was done. "I nearly got myself caught, killed, maybe even tortured, for just *five days?*" He scoffed. "Thank the gods! I was worried this had been a waste of our efforts!"

"Five days should be plenty," Holly countered. "Even narrowing down just one location of interest would make this worth it."

Cain snorted as he downed another mouthful of wine. Nicholas threw him an agitated look before he spoke to Holly.

"What do we do with these 'locations of interest?'"

"Scope them out," she said, "and bug them if we can. I'd love to get a listening device inside, and we should try to link to the cameras. If there aren't any installed already, we'll want to put in some of our own."

"That's not going to be easy," Nicholas said.

"It is not," Alan agreed. "It will demand a lot of time and

careful planning, particularly because we will know, without a doubt, that a Sin frequents these locations. Thorn, I want you leading this operation." She turned toward him, her brows drawn in, her mouth a fine line. Alan went on. "You know the technical aspect of installing any surveillance devices we might want, and your ability to sense Anton Claytor will help ensure you do not get caught."

She nodded, and Alan looked at Chris. "Miss Silver, please assign another TAC guard to accompany Mr. Jones and his team on their visits to The Eros Project for the foreseeable future."

Darius's stomach flipped as Thorn's eyes sharpened. "Wait, what?" she asked. "Why the hell do we need another guard?"

A soft frown turned on Alan's lips. "Because *you* will have your hands full. Identifying locations of interest, setting up surveillance devices, and trying to track Anton Claytor is a full-time job."

For a moment, Thorn just stared, and Darius glanced at her from across the table. Sparkie peered around her throat, his beady eyes locked in Darius's direction.

Cain shook his head. "Certainly, she could manage both. This work with Greed can be done during the day while providing a guard for Darius is strictly a night job. I see no overlap."

Alan's eyes narrowed. "Neither of these tasks should be taken lightly," he said. "They each require a keen attention to detail."

Cain scoffed, tilting his wine glass in Thorn's direction. "Of which she is more than capable."

"This is not a question of capability," Alan began, but Cain cut him off again.

"No, it's a question of who is best suited for the job, isn't that right?" He shook his head and leaned against the table. "It might have escaped you, Alan, but Darius is not the only person building *rapport* with a Virtue in that club."

"Thorn is not there for the Virtue," Alan said. His voice

grew louder and more incensed. Nicholas cast Darius a frustrated look across the table. "Her job is to provide security—"

"Which she is also the best suited for," Cain cut in.

"Cain," Thorn started, but he barreled over her.

"Removing her from this position isn't only illogical. It's foolish."

"She is not a security attachment," Alan argued. "She is the head of our Intelligence Department, and as such, her focus should be on locating Greed."

Thorn's eyes slashed from Cain to Alan. Her fingertips drove into her biceps, leaving deep dimples in the skin. "Can I—"

Cain interrupted her again. He threw his hands up and exclaimed, "Pigeonholing Thorn as simply *one thing* is—"

"*SHUT UP.*"

Thorn slammed an open palm on the table. The slap resounded sharp around the room and heralded a static quiet. Alan and Cain both stared at her as she focused on Chris. She pried her teeth apart to say, "I want an experienced TAC guard to replace me."

Chris's lips slipped open in surprise, but she slid into the expression with a graceful nod. "Of course."

Cain, however, shook his head. "Thorn—"

"It's fine, Cain," Thorn snapped.

"No," he insisted, and his voice softened. "Respectfully, my dear, it's not. You are as much a part of this undercover operation as Darius is, and you deserve to see it through. Isn't that what you *want?*"

Thorn didn't answer, but her dark eyes flicked in Darius's direction. Sparkie disappeared down the back of her shirt.

"All I want is for Verrette to join the Underground," she said at last. "Darius doesn't need me."

Darius's heart dropped. He wanted nothing more than to tell Thorn that wasn't true, that he *did* need her, for more than she could know, but all he did was stare at her, and she stared back. Cain's jaw slammed shut, and he watched Thorn with a disappointed, pained expression. Darius thought he was going to challenge her, but the next time his mouth opened, it was to swallow another gulp of merlot. Nicholas cleared his throat, and the table turned to him.

"If we're done being fucking children here," he said, and his eyes flashed between Alan and Cain. Cain seemed nonplussed, but Alan's mouth tightened dangerously. "I agree that we have plenty of people who can help with security, but no one else can handle the Greed situation like Thorn can."

"Besides," Mackenzie chimed in, "we've been to The Eros Project plenty of times now, and Kit, Madison, and I've got the security down. There's no reason to worry too much about anything going wrong."

She looked around the table, her gaze gliding past Thorn like she wasn't there. Cain nodded, downed the rest of his wine, and sucked in a quick breath through his teeth.

"I suppose that settles it," he said as he got to his feet. "Alan knows best, as usual."

Cain didn't wait for anyone to respond as he stepped away from the table, grabbing his glass and the bottle as he did. He pinned the merlot beneath his arm as he opened the door, and he allowed it to slam shut behind him. When he was gone, Alan heaved a sigh as he laced his hands on the table. Darius glanced at Thorn. She refused to look at him, but he could see cold disappointment written in her downturned eyes.

CHAPTER FIFTEEN

The Eros Project felt dimmer without Thorn.

Darius paused when he walked into the main room. Electronic music blasted at him, and for the first time in the weeks he'd been coming here, Darius found the wave of human auras obnoxiously muggy and confining.

A woman's hand landed halfway up his back, and fingers hovered awkwardly at the boundary between friendly and sensual. Darius tensed as Madison shouted directly into his ear to be heard over the noise.

"You okay?"

He glanced at her. Every time they'd come to the club, Madison wore casual attire suited for dancing and partying to fit in, but tonight, she really overdid it. Even on a cold, late March evening, she'd chosen a short skirt and high heels that showed off long, slender legs, and her navy top had such a deep neckline that it seemed to be more skin than satin. The whole look was impractical, both for the weather and a potential run-in with the Sins.

"Yeah." Suddenly aware of how tight his shoulders felt, Darius headed across the room. By now, he was starting to recognize the few regulars who showed up almost as often as he and Thorn had, but as usual, most of the crowd was brand new. One of the fresh faces was Conrad Carter. Darius spotted him as they walked by, planted near the front entrance with a wad of chewing tobacco pressed against his lower lip. When he caught Darius's eye, he jutted his chin out in a nod. He looked so damned out of place that Darius wondered if replacing Thorn with him hadn't been a mistake.

Hell, he'd been wondering that ever since they'd climbed in the car, and Mackenzie let him know that Madison was his bodyguard tonight.

Her energy followed him so closely that he could still tell her apart from the rest of the hot bodies taking over the room. Her bare arm brushed against his as she leaned in.

"I'm *so* excited to meet Lamar," she gushed. "Officially, I mean. It's crazy that I've been here every night but haven't talked to him. It practically feels like you're taking me to meet your friends." She threw her head back in a laugh, her eyes lingering on Darius.

"Well, I can't say we're friends, but he's a good guy," Darius said as he looked over the heads of people mashed up against the counter. Lamar's Virtue tugged at Darius's core, moving back and forth between customers. The idea of sitting at the bar with Madison made his stomach turn. What would Lamar think of him showing up here with a new woman? He didn't want to imagine. "There's a couple of spots open at the far end. C'mon."

Madison sat first, swishing her hair around her shoulder to expose her open back. Darius grabbed the stool beside hers and moved it over enough to put some distance between them. Lamar was leaning over the counter on the opposite side of the bar with his hips popped back and his legs crossed gracefully at the ankle. Madison watched him for a moment before she propped an elbow on the counter and bent toward Darius.

"So, how's this usually work?" she asked. "You just sit here all night, drinking and talking?"

"That's the idea, yeah."

Madison's lips curled into a smile as she tilted her chin into her palm. "And that's effective?"

"It's all we've got so far," Darius replied with a shrug.

Lamar's energy moved as he made his way to the far wall to craft a drink. He glanced around the counter, and his dark eyes flashed to Darius almost immediately, like he could sense him in the room. Lamar smiled, but that smile warped into confusion as he spotted Madison over Darius's shoulder. He wrapped up the cocktail, handed it off to a woman on the corner, and headed back to the prep station. Minutes later, he sauntered up to Darius with a clear drink in his slender hands. Red and green garnishes stood out inside the ice.

"Darius," he said as he slid the mojito across the bar. "Here you go, handsome. Made just the way you like it."

He winked, and Darius thanked him and took a sip. The refreshing cherry and lime flavor washed over his tongue, bringing a cool, welcome relief to the heat inside the club. When Darius put it back down, Lamar propped a hand on his hip and considered Madison with a coy smile.

"I don't recognize you." His lip pinched into a playful pout. "But I'm going to go out on a limb here and assume you don't drink scotch." He narrowed his eyes, and the blue shadow on his lids made them feel even more perceptive.

"Madison," she said with a laugh. She pulled a lock of brown waves behind her ear. "And no, I don't, but I'd love a Long Island iced tea, please."

"You got it," Lamar said. He glanced at Darius, amused, before he disappeared to make Madison's cocktail.

"I probably should have clarified," Darius said when Lamar was out of earshot. He raised his glass. "We *pretend* to drink. Don't want to be impaired on the job."

Madison's mouth slipped open, and she nodded. "Oh… Yeah, that makes sense. Well, then, I guess this is my first and last for the night." She grinned, and Darius chuckled as Lamar's Virtue drew closer.

"Here you go," he said as he placed a highball glass on

the bar top and slid it to Madison. "One Long Island iced tea. I put an extra lemon wedge in there for you."

"Thank you so much," she said, her smile as bright and friendly as ever. Her fingers wrapped around the glass, and she used her tongue to expertly pull the straw between her lips.

"Of course," Lamar said. He grabbed a crisp, clean cloth from his shoulders and wiped the condensation off his hands as he considered Darius with a playful seriousness. "I'm glad you came in. After you left in such a hurry last time, I thought I might have scared you away."

Darius laughed. "No, not at all. We had an emergency that we had to handle."

Lamar's brows drew downward. "Oh, I hope everything's okay."

"It is," Darius said. "Thanks."

The Virtue bowed his head in a soft nod. "I hope you stick around tonight. When things slow down, I'd love to hear all about the kind of person a man like you is looking to meet in a place like this. I have a feeling the story has only gotten *longer*…"

Lamar's eyes flashed toward Madison, and he looked at Darius like he knew what that meant. Heat rushed across Darius's cheeks, and he scoffed.

"You have no idea."

"Can't wait," Lamar said with a smile. He flung the towel across his shoulder and got back to work. As soon as he walked away, Madison elbowed Darius in the arm.

"Look at you," she said. "Why didn't you tell me how close you already are? He knows your drink!"

Darius shrugged. "He made this up for me last time I was here," he said. "It's really not a big deal. I'm just glad he remembered who I was."

"How could he forget? I mean…" Madison scooted her stool nearer to his, leaned forward on the bar, and laid her arms on the surface in a position that accentuated her cleavage. Darius gave an exasperated sigh and cast his gaze around the bar, but he could still feel Madison's eyes moving downward, lingering on his mouth, his neck, and the hand wrapped around his glass. "You leave a lasting impression."

The side of her calf pressed up against Darius's shin. He brought his drink to his lips as he searched for Lamar again, praying he'd be back soon with another mocktail to rescue him.

He wasn't. The first half-hour was so busy that Lamar hardly had the time to refill Darius's drink, so he and Madison filled the time with meaningless small talk.

The second half-hour was just as busy, Lamar just as distracted, but the Long Island iced tea had kicked in. Madison hedged closer and closer to Darius. Soon, she was near enough that their knees bumped beneath the bar every time she laughed, and her hands were inches away from his above it. Her sharp, floral perfume wafted between them, thick enough that Darius could taste it.

"So, what do you think about Mackenzie's bet?" she asked. The last time Lamar had tended to them, he'd given them both a water, and Madison brought hers to her lips. "She seems to think you know if Gabe and Chris are a *thing.*"

Darius shook his head. "She looped you into bugging me, too?" He threw Madison a sideways glance. "Like I told her, I'm not getting involved."

Madison's pink lips pushed out playfully. "She's recruited more than half of TAC into finding out, but most people don't seem to think they are."

"Oh no?" Darius lifted his glass to his mouth.

"No…" Madison ran her tongue against the bottom of her teeth. "No, a lot of them think Chris is sleeping with *you.*"

Darius froze, his body suddenly cold. Madison stared at him with twinkling, curious eyes.

"*What?*" he finally managed to ask. "Who thinks that?"

Madison placed a hand on his forearm. The sensation sent ants crawling across his skin. "Well, maybe not a *lot* of them," she said. "It's mostly Conrad. He's been saying it as long as I've been here."

Darius scoffed. "Jesus, Conrad needs a new hobby."

A giggle rolled from Madison's mouth. "I mean… can you blame him? Chris *was* your date to the wedding, and you two are obviously really close…"

"I'm close with a lot of people I'm not sleeping with," Darius said.

Madison paused. Then, she leaned so deeply over the bar that her breasts threatened to spill from her blouse. "So, you're not…"

"No," Darius snapped. "I'm not seeing *anybody*, not that it's any of Conrad's business. Why the hell are we still talking about this?"

He took a drink of his water, hoping that was the end of it, but Madison's face lit up. She dragged her lower lip between her teeth as she inched even closer, and the hand on Darius's arm squeezed more tightly. "I'm sorry. I shouldn't have said anything. Conrad's got a big mouth."

"He's not the only one." Darius eased out of her grip as he got to his feet. "I'll be right back."

Madison frowned and moved to stand, too. She was unsteady in her heels, wavering slightly. "Where are you going?"

"Bathroom," Darius said. It was at least half-true. He needed a little space to breathe just as much as he needed to empty his bladder.

"I'll come with—"

"It's fine," Darius cut in. Madison's bright eyes widened, and her lips opened, the bubblegum pink gloss shining under the nightclub lights. He shook his head and sighed. "Mackenzie is already there. I'll have a guard."

Madison tilted forward and gently placed a palm on his bicep. "You sure?"

Darius pulled away again. "Positive."

"Oh," Madison muttered. "Okay. Well, I'll be here when you get back."

As Madison sat down, dejected, Darius looked over her

shoulder to see Lamar watching them. He forced a smile, tilted his head toward the bathrooms, and made his way across the club. Even at the edge of the room, The Eros Project swarmed with dripping heat, but Darius knew that wasn't the only thing making him uncomfortable. He pulled at the neckline of his t-shirt, frustrated with this whole damned evening.

A narrow hallway in the other back corner led to the emergency exit and three individual bathrooms. As Darius approached them, he looked around. No sign of Mackenzie. With a frown, he searched the nearby auras…

Kit and Mackenzie were tucked inside one of the bathrooms.

Darius's cheeks flushed with a heat that had nothing to do with his bad mood or the warm, human energy saturating the club. He swore and closed his eyes as he tried to distract himself with thoughts about anything other than sex and the Martyrs having it as he rushed into an open lavatory and quickly shut himself inside. Before he'd even opened his fly, he felt Kit's aura move back into the club. Mackenzie followed moments later, and they both disappeared within the throng of warmth from the crowd on the floor.

Darius exhaled a sigh. Jesus, this was the last thing he needed to deal with right now.

Minutes later, his bladder empty, hands washed, and mind once again scarred with the intimate details of his friends' lives that he would rather not know, Darius walked back into the room. Kit was gone, but Mackenzie swayed along to the music at the edge of the mob, a glass of non-alcoholic seltzer water in one hand. A pink flush rushed across her face, and her short, blue hair looked like it had been tugged out of shape. Darius pushed that thought to the back of his mind. When she spotted him, her eyes went wide.

"Jones!" Mackenzie exclaimed as she threw her hands in the air. Her water spilled, trailing down her arm and dripping off her elbow. She watched it dribble onto the floor with a dramatic frown. "Ah, fuck! Guess I had that coming." Then she laughed and grabbed Darius in a damp hug. More water sloshed from her cup and hit the concrete floor behind him. "Where's your cute bodyguard?"

"At the bar," Darius said. "Everything good over here?"

"Everything's great," Mackenzie said immediately, too quickly, as she shook her head. She didn't make eye contact, instead turning to look out at the room. "Just trying to 'fit in' while I watch this exit. Kit and I have a bet on how many people are gonna get sloppy drunk and end up crying in the bathroom. So far, I'm winning—"

"Where is Kit?" Darius cut in as he looked around, too. "I thought I saw him heading this way a while ago."

Mackenzie shrugged. "Haven't seen him." The lie flowed off her tongue as liquid as water. "Usually, he holds out by the front doors since there is *way* more traffic up there, but he'll come and relieve me when I've gotta pee or something."

"Does he usually go *in* the bathroom with you?"

Mackenzie's whole body froze, and her head swiveled in Darius's direction. Her mouth dropped open, and her bright, blue eyes went wide.

"Did you…" she began, but Darius sighed and raised his hands.

"Look, I don't want details," he said. "Your romantic life isn't any of my business."

Mackenzie's cheeks flushed a deep pink. "You shouldn't be peeping!"

"I wasn't!" Darius defended. "But you shouldn't abandon your post to hook up in the bathroom! If Thorn finds out, she's going to be pissed. You could lose your spot on this team."

Her face went redder, and she shifted from side to side with a rapid, nervous energy. "You're not gonna tell her?"

"I should," Darius said, and his stomach swirled with irritation—at how this evening was turning out, at Madison's prying and Mackenzie's carelessness, and at the fact that

Thorn wasn't here. He sighed, biting it back, willing himself to look at this with grace instead. "But I won't. Not this time. Just make sure it doesn't happen again, all right? We can't risk it."

Relief flooded through Mackenzie, and she nodded. "Right. Right, of course. Look, Darius, I'm sorry."

"It's fine," Darius said. He didn't want to deal with this right now. "Really. Just… do your job, okay?"

She nodded again. Faster this time. "Yep. You got it."

"Good. I'll uh… I'll see you later."

With that, Darius headed back to the bar, and Mackenzie's aura slowly melted into the rest of the club. When he was well beyond her, he groaned and ran his hands down his face. The idea of going back to Madison was almost worse than imagining what Kit and Mackenzie had been up to. He considered taking a lap around the club to clear his mind. Maybe he'd go talk to Conrad and tell him to keep the rumors and whispers to himself for once in his god-damned life.

But that seemed like more emotional labor than he was willing to do right now, and he was supposed to focus on Lamar. With a sigh, he made his way to the bar. The minute he was close enough to see Madison sitting at her stool, the hairs along the back of his neck whispered, and an aura approached him from behind. A strange aura—fractured and small and weaker than any Darius had ever felt before.

"Darius Jones?" a familiar, oily voice shouted over the music. "I heard you were dead!"

A hot stone fell into the pit of Darius's stomach as he spun around. His jaw plummeted toward the ground.

A man ambled toward him, one thick fist shoved into his front pocket while the other held a dry martini in sausage-like fingers. His bald, dimpled head reflected the bright colors from the club lights behind him, giving him the distinct look of a pale potato at a rave. His black suit and yellow tie stuck out here, way too overdressed to blend in, but he seemed more concerned with looking good than disappearing in the crowd. A massive bodyguard loomed over his shoulder. He glared at Darius with tiny, squinted eyes.

The last time Darius had seen them was at a tiny park on the East River when he'd been negotiating for a bottle of antibiotics to save a little girl's life.

"Max Douglas," Darius said. His lip curled into a snarl, and his hands clenched at his sides. "What the hell are you doing here?"

Max smiled a wormy, twisted smile and used his glass to gesture around the club. "Working, obviously."

"Still pushing overpriced medication to people who can't afford it?" Darius asked.

"That was never a big corner of my market," Max said, dismissing the comment with a wave. Gold rings pinched between his knuckles like thick strips of twine wrapped around hunks of meat. "But it *is* a fulfilling one. I save lives with my services, Jones. That's more than I can say for you..." He paused, and his deep-set eyes narrowed as he looked Darius over. "Last I heard, one of your friends showed up bloody back on the market. What was his name... Peter? Paul?"

The stone in Darius's gut churned. "Saul."

Max snapped his fingers. "Yes! That's it!" A malicious grin pried his round face open, and Darius's shoulders pulled back. The guard crossed his arms and fixed Darius with a scowl as Max went on. "Yes, rumor has it Saul told people that your little orphanage was destroyed, and then he disappeared. Haven't seen any sign of him since he got him-self tied up in those bombings a while back... I hope you're keeping better company these days, Jones. He was *bad news.*"

Years' worth of life came at Darius in vibrant color. Memories of Saul—of boarding up doors and windows, stocking the cellar with food, wrestling with kids before tucking them into bed each night—flooded him, catching in his throat and stopping the rage bubbling up from it. He hardly had the sense to notice another aura approaching them until a hand touched his shoulder.

"Is everything all right?" Madison asked.

Her voice drew Darius out of his head. She pressed close to his side, her right hand tucked inside her purse behind her back. Max's jaw dropped, and his tongue darted out to wet his lips as he admired Madison's body with uncomfortable, obvious intention.

"Ooh," he said. "Who is this? You've got yourself a pretty little thing here, haven't you, Jones?"

Madison bristled. "Excuse me?"

Darius threw his arm out and stepped in front of Madison to stop Max's eyes from wandering over her the way a hungry man admired a buffet. "Ignore him," Darius said. He spoke to her, but his eyes never left Max's smug face. "He's just a rat who thinks he's a king. Come on."

He grabbed Madison by the elbow and guided her back to the bar. She glared over her shoulder, but Darius didn't turn around—not even as Max's tainted energy followed on his heels, the bulk of his personal guard behind him.

"I am a king in that market you used to care so much about," Max shouted over the pulsing music. "They'd be lost without me, but they're getting on just fine without *you.*"

Darius ignored him. Behind the bar, Lamar glanced up. He frowned, and his mahogany eyes flashed over Darius's shoulder. Max kept talking.

"I can't wait to tell them you're still alive," he sneered. "They were so broken when you disappeared. Had a memorial and everything. I wonder how they'll feel knowing that the real reason you abandoned them is because you'd rather fuck wealthy women in Hell's Kitchen than rot on the streets with them."

The anger exploded. Darius spun on his heels and punched Max Douglas right in the face. His knuckles collided with the soft, squishy flesh on Max's nose, and he felt a crack beneath them as Max flew back, howling.

His guard rushed forward and took a wild swing at Darius's head. Darius ducked, deflected the blow with the back of his hand, and twisted around to grab the man's wrist. He yanked his arm back and pinned it behind his shoulders, forcing it upward until it pulled on the joint. The guard let out a deep, guttural cry as Darius shoved him forward. His knees cracked on the concrete, but he leapt up and came in for another round. Darius avoided the second strike just as easily as the first, and he thrust the heel of his palm under the man's chin, slamming his jaw together and sending his head snapping back. This time, when he roared, blood dribbled between his teeth and painted them a deep, cherry red. He grabbed a martini glass out of a woman's hand and reared back.

Darius ducked without thinking—without pausing to realize that a crowd had gathered, that energy pushed in on all sides, that a Virtuous pull was coming at him from behind. He ducked, and the glass sailed over his head. Someone shrieked, and the guard's face blanched as tight fingers wrapped around Darius's shoulder, yanking him back. He stumbled into Madison. Lamar stepped between him and Max.

"What the hell is *wrong* with you?" the Virtue shouted, not at the drug dealer and his bodyguard but at Darius.

Darius's mouth dropped open. Lamar gripped one hand around his forearm as he glared at Darius. His navy sleeve was torn, sliced by broken glass, and soaked in a mix of clear tonic and red blood. His eyes sharpened dangerously, and they cut from Darius to Max and back again.

"Get *the hell* out of my club," he hissed.

Max and his guard immediately took off, covering their mangled faces with open hands, but Darius's heart skipped a beat. "Lamar," he said. "I can explain."

"You heard me," Lamar said, shouting this time. His spine straightened, and he pointed toward the exit. "Go! Before I have Mickey call the cops."

Despite the pounding music and whispering guests surrounding him, Darius couldn't hear anything through the rush of gray noise suddenly filling his ears.

"But I—"

"*Get out*," Lamar interrupted, "and don't come back."

The colors, the lights, the details of the room started to fade as shock dropped down Darius's body like a flow of ice water. Warm fingers wrapped around his hand. Madison's voice broke through the fog.

"Come on," she said.

He allowed himself to be led away. As Madison grabbed the others, Darius followed like a shadow. Her fingers held tight to his through the crowd and up the stairs until they finally hit the street. Mickey frowned as he watched them push through the exit.

The late March evening was still crisp, clinging desperately to a winter bite that refused to die when the sun went down. Sharp air surged into Darius's lungs. It woke him up, and suddenly, the rage in his stomach was enough to warm him again. He tore his hand out of Madison's and pressed his knuckles against his forehead.

"Fuck!" he roared. Mickey startled, and the guests waiting in line to get into The Eros Project jumped. Darius stormed down the street, ignoring the staring, the whispering, and the Martyrs' auras running up behind him.

"What the hell happened?" Conrad asked. His deep, gruff voice grated on Darius's nerves like sharp shards of glass.

"I screwed up," he snapped. Shame cinched around his throat, and Darius tried to swallow past it.

———

They arrived at the Underground before 9:00 p.m., early enough for Martyrs to still be tewake. As Conrad parked by the glass doors, Darius felt Dr. Harris's warm energy in his office in the hospital, a couple of researchers tucked back in their headquarters, and people walking through the courtyard below—all normal, relaxed, and completely unaware that Darius had just fucked over their chances of getting close to Lamar Verrette.

While the rest of his team went downstairs, he walked listlessly down the hallway on the top floor. He passed tactical, the R&D headquarters, and the conference room until he made the first turn to the Martyr directors' offices. Name plaques adorned the doors—McKay, Silver, Wolfe, and Jones. He opened his and stepped inside.

It still reminded him of Abraham.

When the old counselor had left, Darius had gotten his office, and he hadn't changed much since he'd moved in. Blue walls, taupe couches, and handsome wooden furnishings gave the room a comfortable, calm vibe. The overhead bulbs had been removed, and instead, the space was lit by standing lamps that made it feel more lived-in and soft. The bookshelf on the left wall had once been full of photographs and belongings from Abraham's life, but now it housed dozens of binders and books from Teresa Solomon's old library. Darius lowered himself into the desk chair with a groan, turned on his computer, and opened the Martyr reporting app.

For several minutes, he stared at his screen. The cursor blinked at him like it was laughing, and when Darius finally worked up the energy to type, all he got out was the date. He swore and dipped his head into his hands.

God, he couldn't believe he'd messed up *this* badly.

It took over an hour and a half for Darius to finish writing his incident report, and when he was done, he waited another thirty minutes before he submitted the electronic version to the system. Hitting enter felt like admitting to a crime—like confessing some big sin to a priest so a god he didn't believe in could pass judgment, and Darius knew that god wouldn't be kind. He sat there for a moment, letting the events of the evening wash over him, and he took out his phone.

Thorn was at the top of his favorites list now. He'd attached the photograph of the two of them dancing to her contact, and he stared at it. His eyes lingered on her face, and the memory of her laughter made his chest ache. He wished he could go back in time and live that moment again. His thumb hovered over the call button, but he hesitated.

She didn't need to deal with his bullshit tonight.

With a sigh, Darius slipped his phone back into his pocket, shut down his computer, and locked his door as he left for the evening. When he made his way down to the second level, it was well past lights out, and the bulbs above the courtyard were dimmed to just enough to see by. All around him, Martyrs tucked into their rooms. Hot auras, nestled in beds, cast out a blanket of warmth that extended twice as far as it used to. As Darius turned into the eastern block of rooms, he felt Chris and Gabe as they lay quietly in her quarters, wrapped closely together.

Darius followed the hallway on autopilot, twisting and turning by habit on the path to his room. Suddenly, though, a knock rang through the corridor, and Darius paused as an orange glow from an opening door poured through the ingress of another passage ahead of him. He frowned. There was no energy coming from that direction. As he edged closer to the corner, he heard Cain's voice in the dark.

"Alan," he said, full of mock kindness and genuine surprise. "To what do I owe the pleasure of this… midnight visit?"

"You know damn well why I'm here, Cain."

Alan's tone caught Darius off guard, and he froze where he stood just outside the flood of light. It seemed that Cain had only opened his door wide enough to stand in the frame, and he did not welcome Alan inside. Their shadows, long and slender across the tile, sprung up on the opposite wall. The one Darius recognized as Alan's stiffened as Cain let out a sigh.

"If I did, that question would have been quite pointless, don't you think?"

"I don't have time for your games," Alan snapped. "You may have charmed everyone else, but I will not be manipulated."

"You think I'm charming? Why, Alan, I'm flattered."

"You will *stop* what you are doing. Right now."

"What exactly do you think I'm doing?" Cain asked.

"Sticking your nose where it does not belong."

"You're going to have to be more specific—"

"Leave Thorn alone."

Darius's heart jumped into his throat. Cain's shadow shifted. When he spoke again, it was softer.

"If you're talking about fighting to keep her on the Virtue mission—"

"That, the wedding, this relationship she can never have—all of it!" Alan cut in. Like Cain, he kept his voice down, loud enough for Darius to hear him but not so much that his words would carry through the concrete walls and wood doors down the hall. "You know what's at risk here, but you keep pushing her toward something that will tear her to pieces."

"I keep pushing her?" Cain let out a deep, throaty laugh. "That's a bold accusation coming from you."

"*You* are setting her up for pain and failure," Alan said. "*I* am protecting her."

"From what?" Cain asked bitterly. "Having friends? Falling in love? Being *happy?*"

A knot in Darius's chest tightened, and he inched closer to the wall, pressing his back against it as Cain went on.

"That's not protection, Alan. That is annihilation. Maybe not quickly. Maybe not all at once. But robbing her of what makes her inherently human will destroy her more than being possessed by Wrath ever did. Why can't you see that?"

"What *I saw*," Alan answered with a voice like ice, "is what happened when Donovan was killed, what she became. You were not here for that—for *her*. You did not see how broken she was after the Sins murdered her son. I barely managed to get her back."

"She found her way," Cain said.

"What about the next time?" Alan hissed. "What happens if she explores this infatuation? If he is killed? What if she falls into that darkness again? Are you willing to risk losing her forever?"

"It doesn't matter what I am willing to risk," Cain said. His shadow moved, one arm raising upward. "This is not about *me*, Alan, and it certainly isn't about *you*. Thorn has the right—"

"Thorn does not understand what is at stake here!"

Cain paused. Darius heard the sharp intake of an indignant breath and then a short scoff behind it.

"And whose fault is that?" Cain's tone grew heavy with scorn. "You have been so obsessed with keeping her safe, keeping her close, that you've lost sight of what really matters." He paused again, and his shadow shook its head. "You're driving a knife into the fragile connection you've finally built with her."

"You know nothing of my relationship with my niece," Alan said. "You have undermined it from the beginning."

A bitter laugh erupted from Cain's mouth, so loud and sudden that Darius jumped.

"I may have been possessed by Envy, but you, my friend, *reek* of it," he snarled. "I undermined *nothing*. All I ever did was treat Thorn as a human being rather than a bomb. Can the same be said for you?"

Alan rushed forward. Both his and Cain's shadows disappeared, and Darius heard the distinct sound of a body slamming against the wall. From somewhere inside Cain's room, Crescendo cried out a short, mewling yowl. Darius resisted the urge to peek around the corner.

"How *dare* you?" Alan growled. "Everything I've done, I have done because I love her."

"Of course you do," Cain spat. His voice was tight with effort, like he was struggling to speak past a fist around his windpipe. "But love is not enough! You have tried to control her because you're terrified of losing her. But you *are* losing her, Alan, and you're running out of time. The longer you wait to trust her with her own life, the more she will hate you for it."

Cain grunted, and Darius heard Alan take a couple of steps back.

"You don't understand Thorn as well as you think you do," he said.

"I understand that she deserves more credit than you have ever given her," Cain responded. "Allow her the chance to embrace who she is—*all* of who she is—or she really will slip away from us, Alan, and it will be your fault."

"Leave her alone, Cain," Alan said. He took another step away. His shoes thudded against the tile. "Stop meddling in her life."

"It's not meddling when you've been invited in," Cain called out.

Alan turned and headed in Darius's direction. Darius's chest constricted, and he scrambled backward. One of the bathrooms was two doors behind him, and he slipped inside just as he heard Alan turn the corner. He crouched close to the ground, waiting until Alan's shadow strode past in the dim light coming through the crack beneath the door. He gave it another couple of minutes before he finally walked back into the hall.

The light from Cain's room was gone, but his cat sat at the corner. Darius froze. The Familiar's bright, orange eyes focused on him, and his fluffy tail twitched once before he stood up and disappeared. Cain's door opened one last time, just long enough for Crescendo to disappear inside, before it snapped closed and stole the light.

CHAPTER SIXTEEN

"So, what did Alan say?" Chris asked.

Darius was so caught off guard by the question that he forgot what he was doing for a moment. The medicine ball Chris threw hit him square in the chest. He barely managed to catch it, stumbling back a few steps and nearly losing balance. Chris's eyes widened as he rubbed a hand flat against his sternum.

"What?"

"I wanted to know what Alan said," Chris repeated.

They were the only two training in the gym, surrounded by dull silence punctuated only by the occasional thud of the medicine ball as they tossed it back and forth. Darius watched her for a moment.

"What Alan said about what?" he got out at last as he hurled the ball back at her.

Chris caught it without missing a stride. "Your report," she said with a frown. "Didn't you have a meeting with him this morning?"

Relief trickled down Darius's spine. The report. That's right.

"Oh, yeah," he said with an awkward chuckle. Chris threw the ball back. "He wasn't happy."

Though Darius hadn't been able to tell why. Not completely. Alan had certainly been less than thrilled about Darius losing his good standing with Lamar Verrette, but there was a snappiness to his mood that didn't feel like it had anything to do with Darius at all—like Alan was standing on a bed of nails and any annoyance was enough to push him off-kilter.

"Are you being reprimanded?" Chris grunted as she caught the ball again. Sweat blossomed along her chest. Beads of it followed the fine lines of old scars before soaking into her black tank top. She wiped her forehead with the back of her hand as Darius shook his head.

"No. I offered to do a stint with Stevie's crew, but he said he wasn't going to punish me for responding to very natural, normal human emotion."

The irony of that wasn't lost on Darius. His jaw clenched as Chris provided a conceding half-nod.

"Well, that's good," she said. "I don't think anyone could blame you. I want to punch that guy in the face myself."

Darius sighed. The fury from the night before turned over in his gut, spoiling like old milk. "I'm mad I let him get under my skin. Getting close to Lamar is going to be that much harder."

"What's the plan now?"

"We still have to figure that out," Darius said. Chris's phone blared with a timer, and when he caught the ball a final time, he propped it under one arm. He drew in a deep breath as he turned to the bench behind him to grab his shirt, and he used it to wipe the sweat off his face. A wall of floor-to-ceiling mirrors stretched out around him, and Darius caught his reflection. When the medicine ball slammed into him, it left a red halo against his olive skin. Sighing, he tossed the ball onto the padded floor and grabbed his water instead. "Alan's going to talk to Thorn about putting Caleb on the case."

Saying Alan and Thorn's names in the same sentence put a sharp, sour sting in Darius's mouth. He washed it away with a swig of water as Chris stepped up beside him.

"What does Thorn think?"

"I don't know," Darius said. "I haven't talked to her."

Chris's eyes flashed in his direction as she lifted her water bottle from the bench. "Why not?"

He took a deep breath and held it for a beat. The truth was, he wasn't sure how to talk to Thorn right now, and not just because of what had happened at the club.

"She's busy following up on the tracking data on Greed," Darius said at last. "I didn't want to throw off her focus."

Though Chris didn't respond right away, Darius felt her attention on the side of his face as he took another drink.

"Why don't you call her?" she asked. He lowered his bottle and glanced back. Chris gave him a soft smile. "No one is going to understand getting so angry that you lose control more than Thorn will."

Darius's heart flipped. The idea of Thorn losing control made him uneasy, but he forced a smile onto his face anyway.

"I know," he responded.

"But you're not going to."

"Probably not."

Chris sighed. "You should take a chance."

Her focus lingered on him, bright-eyed and curious. The unspoken understanding in her expression let Darius know she wasn't talking about the situation with Max Douglas anymore. A heartsick surge made his throat tighten, and he swallowed through it.

"It's not that easy," he said after a moment. Chris's lips pressed together, and her chin tilted in a thin, sympathetic nod. Before she could say more, Darius sensed a pulse of warm energy heading toward the gym from across the courtyard. Conrad Carter was leading the pack, and suddenly, Darius remembered *another* uncomfortable moment from the night before.

"Oh, uh…" He cleared his throat and threw his shirt

around his shoulders like a towel. "I wanted to warn you: Mackenzie's got TAC on the lookout for Gabe's latest love connection…"

Chris froze with her water halfway to her mouth. A pink tint that had nothing to do with their workout flooded her cheeks as she ran her tongue along her upper lip.

"Love's a strong word," she said.

Darius slipped into a grin before he could help himself. "Is it the *wrong* word?"

She laughed, shook her head, and drew a few loose strands of blonde hair behind her ear. "Does there need to be a word for it right now?"

For a moment, Darius was caught up in Chris's smile—the way her eyes crinkled at the corners, the lines of pain and experience pulled into joy and hope, and how her lips stretched so wide open that they revealed a sliver of pink gums above her teeth. Without putting more thought into it, except that, god, no one deserved this more than she did, Darius wrapped his arms around Chris and drew her into a tight embrace. She stiffened at first, but then her body relaxed.

"God, you're so sweaty," she teased. Her hands linked behind his back, and she rested her chin on his shoulder.

"Sorry," Darius said, but he wasn't sorry, and he didn't pull away. "I'm just happy that *you're* so happy."

Chris melted further against him. "Thank you."

The double doors to the gym swung open. Conrad froze on the threshold, one meaty hand gripped tight around the handle. Darius caught his expression in the mirror over Chris's shoulders: Conrad's dark eyes opened so wide that they appeared to be little more than brown circles swimming at the center of pools of milk. Darius held Chris a little longer, a little tighter, and smiled against her hair.

It wasn't much, but maybe he could give her a few more weeks of peace and privacy before Mackenzie managed to expose her.

Conrad cleared his throat. "We, uh… we've got the

room booked for weight class."

Darius wiped the smirk from his mouth as he finally stepped back from Chris and turned toward the door. More people filed in behind Conrad: Seth Graves, Deidre Cummins, Charlotte and Andre Davis, and a half dozen others… including John. His lips tightened into a frown, and he adjusted a gym bag on his shoulder as he looked Chris over. Her spine straightened.

"I saw the sheet," she said, tilting her head at a schedule tacked to the wall by the door. "It's all yours."

She leaned down to gather her things, and Darius followed suit. He pulled his shirt on over his head as they walked across the room. Conrad gawked after them, and while John forced a smile when he met Darius's eye, he didn't look at Chris at all.

***

Max Douglas dominated Darius's mind. No matter what he did to clear it—breathing exercises, grounding practice, affirmations—within moments of closing his eyes, that smarmy, arrogant face crept in again. And then, even more upsetting, it faded into others.

First, the men and women of the market: Jalal, Mrs. Miller, and Miguel. Then, the orphanage. Saul, Juniper, Eva, and Thad. The children. He remembered Sophie and Aren and little Lindsay, so sick and so small. The ghosts of them stalked Darius's thoughts, making it almost impossible for him to focus on anything else. Max hadn't just touched a nerve. He'd set it ablaze, and even twenty-four hours later, Darius was still burning.

"Damn it," he groaned. He tilted his head back until it thudded numbly against the concrete wall, and he opened his eyes. Bright, sterile light glowed around him, where it bounced off blindingly white paint and reflected from the surface of the pool. The water was as still as glass, perfectly untouched, practically begging for a familiar body to slip in and break it.

Darius's focus shifted to the women's locker room, and his stomach twisted with the fleeting hope that the door would open.

Thorn hadn't set foot in the Underground for two days, but it didn't seem to matter. Phantom sounds and movement disrupted Darius's meditation almost more often than thoughts of Max and the market did. With every imagined interruption, he'd glance across the room, wishing it was her.

And then he'd hear Alan's panicked voice like a siren in his ear:

"What if she falls into that darkness again? Are you willing to risk losing her forever?"

A painful vise held Darius's heart and squeezed. He forced his chest open, inhaling deep. When he released it in a low, quiet stream, he shook his head.

It was no use.

Darius got to his feet, gathered his things, and made his way through the lockers and into the gym. This late at night, it was as empty as the courtyard beyond it. No, wait. The courtyard *wasn't* empty. Darius felt a solitary point of human energy tucked away by the kitchen, and he frowned as he strode through the double doors.

The dim lights overhead were hardly bright enough to see by, but John's aura was unmistakable. He'd taken one of the tables near the elevator, and the harsh glow from his phone screen glared up against his face, making it the only part of him visible at all. He glanced across the vast room as Darius turned off the gymnasium light.

Darius couldn't see his expression from here, but he knew it wasn't good.

John didn't move as Darius made his way toward him, and when he grabbed a chair at the table, John just watched with a tired, numb stare. His deep eyes pooled in an exhaustion Darius knew was more emotional than physical.

"Hey," he said as he sat down. "You okay?"

"Yeah," John said. He took a slow breath as he looked down at a half-drunk bottle of beer in his hands. His phone lay face-up next to him, and photographs from Skylar and Raquel's wedding were displayed on the screen—a grid of happy memories and smiling faces that didn't mirror the look John wore right now. Chris was among them, wrapped around Gabe like a garment. John sighed. "It's just been a shitty day."

Darius's mouth pressed together. "Wanna talk about it?"

"I don't know what there is to talk about," John replied. "This is just how it goes, you know? One of you moves on. I always knew she'd be the first. Didn't think it would happen so fast."

His eyes glistened in the dark, and Darius leaned onto the table. "Did she talk to you?"

"No," John said as he shook his head. "She didn't have to. Chris and I were together for a long time. I know her. I know this look." He indicated the picture of her and Gabe dancing on his screen, and his jaw clenched before he flipped the device over so he didn't have to look at it anymore. "If it hasn't happened already, it will soon. And don't worry," he added, raising a palm toward Darius like he could read his mind, "I'm not going to hound you like Mackenzie. The less I know, the better."

Darius nodded. "I appreciate that."

John lifted his beer to his lips again and took a tiny sip, just enough to give him something to do. Darius could tell he wasn't really into it—that he wasn't drunk or trying to get drunk, but maybe just hoping it helped solve this problem long enough to get some sleep tonight. By the dark circles under his eyes, he needed it.

"I didn't think it would suck this badly," John muttered.

Darius frowned. "What do you mean?"

"All I want is for her to be happy," John said. He made to take another sip, thought better of it, and put the bottle back down with a dull thunk. "And if that doesn't include me, fine. I never wanted her to stick around if she didn't want to, if she didn't want *me*…"

His voice trailed off, and he stared at the label on his beer without reading it. The muscles on his jaw flexed and relaxed, like he was chewing on a thought, before he finally shook his head.

"But, god *damn*, Darius," he said, his voice stinging around the words. "I had no idea seeing her happy with someone else would make me this fucking miserable."

John pressed his fingertips against his eyes, and his shoulders drew up in a breath that he held onto like a lifeline.

"You still love her," Darius said. John lowered his hands and peered over them. "That doesn't go away just because the relationship ended."

"I suppose," John said with a sigh. "It's hard as hell loving her and not getting to be with her."

The vise in Darius's chest tightened again, and he looked down at his hands on the table. His fingers laced together in a white-knuckle grip.

"I wish I could help," he murmured, "but I don't think there's an easy fix for this kind of thing."

John let out a scoff. "There's not. Trust me. I've been looking."

"I'm sorry."

"Don't be," John said. He leaned back in his chair. "I went into this with my eyes wide open. I always knew we might not make it. We both knew it. This life is hard. It pulls on you. Pulls you apart. Chris and I talked about it for a long time before we decided it was worth taking the chance anyway."

"Do you still think it was worth it?" Darius asked.

John frowned, almost incredulously. "Yes," he answered. "Hell yes. Every goddamned second. Even though it hurts like a son of a bitch right now, if I knew it was going to end this way, I'd do it all over again. It was worth it. *She* was worth it. He better know that."

Suddenly, John's ocean eyes glistened with tears. Before

Darius could say anything else, he swiped his phone from the table, shoved it into his pocket, and got to his feet.

"Anyway," he said, clearing his throat as he picked up the half-full beer bottle. "That's enough moping for tonight. I'm gonna crash." He took a step back but paused when Darius stood up, too. His expression softened into a sad smile. "Thanks, man."

Darius stepped around the table and grabbed John in a tight, affectionate hug. As they pulled away, he said, "Any time."

His eyes gleaming again, his throat tight and hard, John walked away. He poured his beer down the drain, tossed the bottle in the recycling bin, and went to his quarters in the western block of rooms. Darius headed to his own, the silence of the night pressing around him. When he sat on his bed a few minutes later, he pulled his phone out, navigated to his contacts, and stared at Thorn's name. He tapped the call icon and raised the device to his ear. It rang once, twice, three times. He started to think she wasn't going to answer, and a weight grew in his chest.

Then, her voice snapped through the receiver.

"It's late," Thorn said without a hello. A line of panic made the words quick. "Is everything okay?"

"Yeah," Darius said, and he let out a chuckle as he ran his hand over his mouth. "Yeah, sorry. I didn't mean to worry you. I just had something I wanted to talk to you about. Do you have a minute?"

CHAPTER SEVENTEEN

A silver monstrosity of a building jutted into the night sky over Thorn's head. Every one of its faces rippled with architectural waves, creating a dizzying illusion of steel movement. Highlights and shadows organized themselves in an abstract display some considered "art," and while most of the windows were dark, a handful glowed with sterile, LED light bright enough to see from the sidewalk below.

Thorn pulled her helmet off, locked it onto her bike, and frowned at the high-rise. "Son of a bitch lives one god-damned mile from the Mezzanine," she grumbled.

"Makes sense," Holly Andrews replied in Thorn's ear-bud. Her voice was muffled, like she was speaking around a mouthful of food. "Over ninety percent of his regular haunts are in the Financial District, and the area is known for wretched excess… seems perfect for Greed."

A slow breath expanded between Thorn's lungs. She looked at a map on her bike's dash display, where a winding, yellow line looped through the Financial District, starting at the Mezzanine Event Space before eventually settling here. As far as she could tell, the device was still actively sending a signal.

"Do you think he's in there right now?" she asked.

"No clue," Holly said. "But we know he was on Friday. Mulligan says he hasn't seen any sign of him since Bently's dumb event, and he hasn't triggered the facial recognition software I have combing feeds from all over the city… I wouldn't be surprised if he's holed up inside, waiting for things to cool down."

Thorn nodded as she turned back to the building. "What do we know about this place?"

A rattling of keystrokes poured into her ear.

"Besides the fact that it's high-end as fuck?" Holly asked. "Let's see here… Built in 2010, remodeled in 2046 and again in 2070… The first five floors are used as a private school. Wow, the tuition rates are *insane*—"

"Andrews," Thorn cut in.

"There are over nine hundred rental apartments," Holly went on. "They range from tiny studios to four-bedroom units, but there are a couple of ridiculously huge penthouses on the upper floors. I'd say Claytor is probably in one of them, but there's always the possibility he took a smaller unit to avoid standing out."

"Is there any record of him in the leasing agreements?"

"Nuh-uh," Holly said, chewing again. "I went through all the public lease information I could find. No one by the name of Anton Claytor lives here. At least, no one who would openly sign the name Anton Claytor onto anything the Martyrs could so easily track down. Half the penthouses are owned by LLCs."

Thorn sighed, swung her leg off her motorcycle, and stepped onto the sidewalk. Sunday night left the streets more empty than usual, and only a few pedestrians crossed her path as she walked along the building's edge. She found the apartment entrance tucked around a corner near a landscaped pedestrian thoroughfare. At this hour, a well-dressed and—Thorn presumed—well-armed doorman stood inside the front hall, his hands clasped behind his back.

"Remind me," Thorn murmured, pulling her hood up to hide her face from the doorman as she walked by. "What's security like here?"

Holly let out a laugh. "As you can imagine, it's pretty top-notch. There's always a guard at the front door—sorry, a *concierge*—and tenants need an access card to use the elevators. Emergency exits are locked twenty-four-seven and only open during an actual emergency, otherwise alarms will sound and send an alert straight to the NYPD. They've got cameras in every common area, including the stairwells and parking garage, and, though I haven't been able to actually prove it, I suspect they also have guards walking the premises. Call it a hunch."

With Greed living here, it was more than a hunch.

"So, we need to tap into the cameras," Thorn said.

"Yep," Holly replied. "They have an insane security system, too. Tons of protections stopping an outside entity from getting in. I could do it on my own, but that takes time we don't have."

"And *this* will help?" Thorn asked as she stopped beneath the naked branches of a maple that was just beginning to bud. New growth full of baby leaves sprouted along thin switches in the sky. She leaned against its trunk and dipped her hand into her satchel to grab a data chip. Sparkie curled inside the bag, and he peered at her with a curious, tilted head. Thorn turned the chip around in her fingers. The thing was hardly the size of her thumbnail, unmarked and unassuming.

"If you can get it plugged into their main computer terminal," Holly said. "You up for a challenge?"

Thorn's eyes narrowed as she looked up at the complex. "Hardly a challenge."

She lowered her hand back into her satchel, and Sparkie delicately grabbed the chip between two rows of razor-sharp teeth. He scurried out, flattening his wings as close to his body as he could before scaling the maple to the topmost branches. Thorn wished there was more leaf cover to conceal him, but when she glanced around, she didn't spot anyone looking in this direction.

Over her head, a bough rocked back and forth as Sparkie found his balance. When they were certain no one was paying attention, he spread his wings and vaulted into the sky. Thorn's stomach vaulted with him, her breath caught in her throat as the sensation of air rushing by her body threatened to steal the very air from her lungs. For a moment, she allowed herself to close her eyes and just *feel*.

Even after almost one hundred years with half of her soul incarnated outside her body, Thorn had never gotten over the sensation of flight. She hoped she never did. The risk, the exhilaration, the absolute *freedom* of wind beneath wings she didn't have, pulling her up, up, *up*, so high above the city that the view made her stomach plunge and head swim, was one of the few things about being a Forgotten Sin that had ever allowed Thorn to feel more human than not.

Sparkie scaled the side of the apartment complex, surfing along waves of steel and glass as eddies propelled him faster. His wings shot wide, catching a draft and dragging him in a wide arc around the corner to avoid lit windows. Seventy-six stories later, he pulled them back into his body and looped in a single, joyful arc at the crest of the structure before he spotted a ventilation output shaft on the roof. He flew right into it.

Thorn opened her eyes again.

"We're in."

She pushed herself off of the tree to walk the perimeter. Now, all the feedback she got from Sparkie was dark and warm as he drifted down a long duct all the way to the main floor. "You sent blueprints?"

"Right to your phone," Holly replied.

Thorn pulled them open, toggling the three-dimensional floor plan with her finger and thumb. The schematics were detailed enough to show every room on the ground level. The security station sat in the middle, a digital brain at the center of an artificial nervous system.

"Perfect," Thorn said. Sparkie was still descending—by

her estimation, halfway down. "And we just plug this into the server?"

"Yep," Holly said. "In the most hard-to-reach port you can find."

Thorn nodded as she hit the corner and turned again. Sparkie finally found a bottom point and landed lightly on his claws inside the aluminum duct. Thorn had no way to orient where exactly he was, so he chose a random shaft to follow until he could see light through the slats of an open vent. He pressed his scaly nose to the metal.

Mail room. Thorn glanced down at her phone again, ignoring pedestrians walking by as she traced the path from Sparkie's location to the vent leading to the security office. He scampered off, following her train of thought the second it happened, and found himself outside the right room. He peered inside.

It wasn't all that unlike their own security headquarters, but instead of being buried beneath the ground with Holly and her team of four diligently at work, a single officer sat behind the computer. Thorn rolled her eyes.

"I thought you said this place had top-notch security," she said.

"It does," Holly replied.

"The man watching the cameras is passed the fuck out with a full cup of coffee in his hands."

Holly laughed. "Oh, *that* is embarrassing. It's easy to fall asleep on the job when the most excitement you see is rich people fighting over the line to the garbage shoot. Can you get in?"

Thorn paused and pinched her brows together as Sparkie tested the vent panel. It was loose. With enough force, he would easily be able to push it out. "Yes," Thorn said, "but not without making a bit of noise and losing access to my escape. You sure you'll be able to get into the cameras with the chip planted?"

"Absolutely," Holly said.

"Good. Because you'll have to scrub us from the

footage."

"Whatever it takes to get us in before this line on Greed goes cold."

Thorn glanced at the complex entrance. She was a few meters up the road, and while she couldn't see the doorman, she could sense his energy just inside. "I'll let you know when it's done."

Sparkie stepped back, squared his tiny little feet on the metal duct beneath him, and pulled his wings tightly to his body. Then, he rushed forward and barreled into the vent. Both he and the panel tumbled into the security office with a crash.

By the time the guard jumped awake, spilling coffee all over himself, and found a dusty grate lying haphazardly on top of an ancient copier, Sparkie was out of sight. He squeezed himself behind the network server just as the man said, "What the *fuck*…"

Thorn's heart pounded. Sparkie scurried off to slip the chip into a port in the back of the server. Before he'd finished, the security officer had replaced the vent.

"We're good," Thorn said.

"Aw, yeah!" Holly chimed in her ear, but Thorn hardly heard her. Sparkie peeked around the edge of the server. The guard grumbled as he looked down at the coffee staining his pants and swore again. He opened the door and stepped into the hall. Sparkie followed, turned in the opposite direction, and darted down the central corridor toward the front office.

Thorn covered the lower part of her face in the crook of her elbow, ran at the entrance, and crashed her shoulder into the glass doors.

It wasn't enough to break them—just rattle them on their hinges and make the doorman jump. Then, Thorn sprinted off, and he hurried outside after her. On his heels, Sparkie slithered into the open air. Before Thorn had even turned the corner, her Familiar was skyward again.

"There you go, Andrews," Thorn said as she threw a leg

over her bike. "Anything else you need from me?"

"Not today," Holly replied. Thorn pulled her helmet on, and the call automatically redirected to the com system inside. "I'm going to tap into their camera feeds, and then we'll see if we can spot Claytor. I want to know what floor he's stopping at so we have a better idea which unit he's in."

"Great," Thorn said. She opened the satchel strapped to her thigh. Sparkie dove into it and disappeared inside. Thorn snapped it shut again. "Then I'm going to get the hell out of here."

"Roger that," Holly said.

They disconnected. Thorn engaged her engine and tore away from the curb. She glanced down at the display on her dash for the time: ten after ten. For a fleeting moment, she considered returning to the Underground—sleeping in her own room rather than one of the studios the Martyrs owned in the city—but she decided against it. Not because it was too late but because a break from the Underground was exactly what she needed right now.

Or, more specifically, a break from the people in the Underground. Certain people.

One person.

Her empty chest quaked, and Thorn ground her teeth together. Fuck, she knew better than this, but here she was, playing the game again like it could have any other outcome. She'd let herself get so wrapped up in it that her focus on taking down the Sins had started to slip. Alan was right: anything else was a *distraction*.

So Thorn pushed away thoughts of the Underground, of nightclubs, of warm hands on the small of her back, and made her way toward the nearest Martyr apartment. She was halfway there when a bright beacon of evil energy lit up her mind like a wildfire on the horizon. Her stomach dropped.

Wrath was using her Influence.

That was another benefit of staying in the city. When Thorn was in the Underground, she was too far away to get a read on where Hunt might be when her Influence came to life, but here, in the Financial District, Thorn could esti-mate. She frowned.

If she wasn't mistaken… Wrath was in The Bronx. Thorn hadn't sensed her so far north since Sloth had been blowing people up. What the hell was she doing there *now?*

The wildfire grew, and Thorn changed direction. Alan called her, just as he always did when she was in the city and he felt Wrath's Influence, but Thorn ignored him, just as *she* always did when he insisted on checking in on her like he didn't trust her not to get herself killed. She made her way toward FDR Drive and was about to turn up the on-ramp when her phone rang again. Frustrated, she went to cancel Alan's second attempt when she looked at the corner of her visor display and realized it *wasn't* Alan.

Her heart jolted, and she pulled over to the side of the road. For a few blind seconds, she stared at Darius's name on the caller ID. All thoughts of getting some distance and taking a break dissolved under more urgent worries. Across the city, Wrath's Influence tempted her to follow.

And she ignored it.

Thorn tapped an icon on the dash. "It's late." She tried to keep her tone even, but her stomach was tangled with knots. "Is everything okay?"

Darius's voice carried through on a chuckle that made Thorn long to turn right the fuck around and head back home. Jesus, why was she doing this to herself?

"Yeah," he said. "Yeah, sorry. I didn't mean to worry you. I just had something I wanted to talk to you about. Do you have a minute?"

Thorn hesitated. Wrath's evil called her north, taunting her. Sparkie wriggled in the satchel clasped to her leg as she glanced in that direction.

"If it's a bad time," Darius began to say, but Thorn cut him off.

"It's not." She pulled back into the light, late-night traffic before turning around and heading distinctly *away* from The Bronx. "I'm just on my way to the apartment. What's up?"

This time, Darius was the one who hesitated. Thorn heard him draw in a slow breath. Before he answered, she went on for him.

"Is this about what happened at The Eros Project the other night?"

"So, Alan did talk to you," Darius said.

"He did," Thorn replied, "and I read your report."

"Did you decide to send Caleb in?"

"Yes," Thorn said, biting back her frustration. Caleb was good, but he wasn't *Virtue* good, and she had her doubts this would work. "His first shift is tonight."

Darius paused again, and Thorn waited with him. The streets of New York flashed past her in the dark—cold energy, cold air, cold steel. At last, Darius laughed a second time, and even though it was full of shame, it was still the warmest part of Thorn's evening.

"Honestly," he said, "it's just nice to see that you were wrong for once."

Thorn frowned. "*I* was wrong? What the hell about?"

"You said that I didn't need you."

Thorn's stomach flipped, and her grip tightened on her handlebars.

"That I could manage the Lamar situation on my own," Darius went on. "Well, look what happened. I punched a guy in the face and got banned from the club."

Now, humor lit the words, and Thorn felt a smirk tug at her lips.

"And you think none of that would have happened if I had been there?"

"I do think that, yeah," Darius said.

"You're right," Thorn agreed. She turned onto another street. The brick face of her apartment building stood at the far end of the block. "I would have punched him first. Trust me, you were way better off without me."

The second those words slipped from Thorn's mouth, her breath caught in her chest. She tried to lighten it with a laugh that she knew lacked any kind of substance. Darius chuckled, too, but his was even less convincing. Afterward, dead air filled the line. Thorn thought she heard Darius shifting, like he was getting comfortable or maybe mustering up the courage to say something more important.

"I'm sorry," he muttered at last. "You worked so hard to help me out, and I just screwed everything up."

Thorn shook her head. "There's nothing here that can't be saved," she said as she stopped outside the parking at her complex, but she didn't go in. "Verrette clearly sensed something special about you."

"Maybe," Darius said through a sigh. "I feel like I could get him to understand, you know? Like, if I had a shot to talk to him again, I could fix it. I just don't know how to get that shot."

Wrath's Influence flashed again, but this time, Thorn didn't look northward. Instead, she pushed that temptation away and turned her focus to the west. Her lips pressed down in a frown.

"We'll figure something out," she murmured as she pulled back into traffic. "Hey, I just got to the apartment. I should—"

"Right," Darius cut in, clearing his throat. "It's pretty late. You should go."

"I'll call you tomorrow?"

Another pause. "I'd like that," Darius said. She heard a smile on his words. "Goodnight, Thorn."

He hung up first, and the sounds of the city surrounded her. Thorn's jaw clenched as Sparkie squirmed in her satchel again.

There wasn't a lot that Thorn could offer Darius—nothing worth offering, at least. A bloody past. A broken soul. A bad attitude that got her into more trouble than it was worth. He didn't need *this*, didn't need *her*…

But maybe, just maybe, she could get him that shot with Lamar.

Thorn made her way through Manhattan, and she didn't stop until she reached Hell's Kitchen.

The Eros Project was one of the only places still booming this late on a Sunday night. Even hours after opening, a line still extended along the building, and inside, bodies bounced to the beat of loud techno music. The hot condensation of their sweat stood out in disorienting contrast to the sensation of their cold souls filling the floor with icy energy. Even the bar was crowded. Thorn forced her way between two people too drunk to care and searched for Lamar Verrette.

He stood at the far end of the counter, leaning over in a serpentine curve as he and a tall, slender man with platinum blonde hair poured over a camera. Lamar laughed and pointed at the view screen, which made Caleb Claytor's mouth open in a boyish grin. Thorn couldn't help but feel a blossom of pride swell in her chest. One night in, and the kid already had the Virtue talking.

Too bad she was here to ruin it.

She bent across the counter and propped her elbows beneath her to get more leverage. For a moment, she thought coming back without Darius would make this more challenging for her—Lamar seemed to home in on Darius's Virtue every damned time he entered the club, whether he realized it or not—but within minutes, the young bartender glanced over his shoulder, and his eyes caught Thorn. The smile on his face immediately tightened. The muscles in Thorn's brow twitched downward.

Then Lamar turned away from her. He made a comment to Caleb, who glanced across the bar, too. He barely managed to disguise the shock on his face when he noticed Thorn sitting there. He busied himself with his camera as Lamar sauntered along the counter.

"Thorn." Lamar's voice cut through the noise. His dark eyes were sharp, and the smirk on his face felt perilous, like they were playing a game of chess, and she had just moved her queen into a trap he'd been planning for six moves.

"Can I get you a scotch?"

Thorn shook her head. "I need to talk to you."

"Oh?" Lamar frowned, pouting his full lips out with theatrical emphasis. "What do we need to talk about?"

"I think you know."

Thorn stood perfectly still as Lamar considered her slowly. He took a long breath, pressed his tongue against the back of his teeth, and finally said, "My break is in ten."

"Okay," Thorn said. "Then I'll take that scotch while I wait."

Lamar's eyes narrowed, but he moved to the back of the bar anyway and returned with a glass. Thorn raised it in thanks and wormed her way onto one of the few open stools. For the next several minutes, Lamar's energy tanked. Where Thorn was used to seeing him jovial and lively, it was like a storm had darkened his mood, and Thorn had a feeling the storm was named for her. When he was finally ready, he caught her attention and tilted his head toward the back office. Thorn poured her drink down her throat and followed him behind the counter.

The tiny room hardly had the space for one desk covered with paperwork, branded coffee mugs, and an old computer. As he shut them inside, blocking out the beat of the music, Lamar paused.

"Are you comfortable with me locking the door?" he asked.

"Go ahead."

He turned the latch. Thorn hadn't taken the chair, content to stand at the other end of the room where Lamar was just far enough away that he couldn't reach out to touch her, not that she worried he would. The two of them were roughly the same height. With her boots on, Thorn might have been taller. Lamar's mouth pressed together, and he took a deep breath that stretched across his chest. In the bright bulbs in the office, his makeup was even more dramatic. Deep, stunning strokes of blue eyeshadow popped against his dark skin.

"Well," Lamar said, throwing his hands between them. "Out with it."

"It's about Darius," Thorn began, but Lamar let out a high-pitched laugh.

"*Darius?*" he challenged. "Or do you mean *Dante?*" Thorn's eyes widened, and Lamar nodded. "Mmhmm, that's right, honey. I talked to Mickey about the incident, and he had no idea who Darius was. Did know Dante Stone, though. Weird, isn't it, how they look exactly the same? I don't like being lied to."

Lamar crossed his arms and popped a hip. Thorn's lips slipped open as she sucked in a shallow breath.

"Darius didn't lie," she said. "Not to *you*, at least. I was pretty pissed about it. He was *supposed* to lie."

At that, Lamar scoffed. "What the hell does that mean?"

"You want to know why we've been coming to The Eros Project?" Thorn went on. "The real reason? Darius didn't lie about that, either. We did come here to meet somebody. *You.*"

She let that hang for a moment. Lamar froze to the spot, but his fingers tightened around his biceps as he watched Thorn with a calculating stare. His eyes darted between hers like he was trying to guess her next move.

"Why me?"

"I'm not the person to tell you that," Thorn said. Then, she gestured around the room. "And this isn't the place to have that conversation."

Lamar glared at her for another dense moment. "You are out of your *mind*," he said at last. "Why the hell should I listen to anything you say? You two show up here, stalk me at work, cause a scene…"

His voice drifted off, and he finally looked away from Thorn. She waited a moment before she said, "But for some reason, you feel a connection to us—a pull to *Darius.*"

Lamar's gaze snapped back to her face. This time, he seemed more surprised than angry. "How the hell can you know that?"

"I know a lot more than you think," Thorn said, "and if you want to hear it, you're going to have to give us a chance."

At first, Thorn thought he was going to tell her to fuck off, but then, Lamar's shoulders rose and fell with a sigh. He stepped up to the desk, grabbed an old receipt, and scribbled something onto the back.

"One chance," he said as he delicately brandished the note toward Thorn. She took it. "I pick the place and time."

"All right," Thorn said. She slipped the paper into her satchel. "Come alone."

"Hah!" Lamar shook his head. "Don't get any crazy ideas. I'll be alone, but all my friends have my location, and they'll call the authorities if they don't hear from me."

A single brow arched on Thorn's head. "You think we're a threat?"

Lamar paused. "No," he said. "But I've been wrong before."

CHAPTER EIGHTEEN

The sun sank lower in the sky, eclipsed by distant buildings and nearby trees. A chill settled over Darius's shoulders, and he pulled his jacket tighter to keep the breeze out. Early spring still settled into crisp evenings, so fewer people walked through Central Park than he expected. Men and women wandered the Conservatory Garden leisurely, the warmth of their souls wafting toward Darius like an early summer wind that wasn't quite strong enough to do him a damn bit of good. Somewhere to the west, a Virtue flickered into range. An anxious grip wrapped around his chest.

"Lamar's coming," Darius said.

He looked across the park table, where Thorn sat with pin-straight professionalism. Her eyes flicked up to meet his, and she lingered there. The intensity in her black irises somehow made Darius more nervous. So did the kevlar bike jacket zipped up to her throat and the gun she carried in the satchel at her side. Sparkie circled overhead, his silhouette indistinguishable from the bats flapping between branches.

"Do you know what you're going to say?" Thorn asked.

"Yeah," Darius said. "Yeah, I think I do."

A single, slender brow curved up on her forehead. "If you tell him everything—"

"You'll have to Program him," Darius cut in. "Alan made that clear, and I agree. We can't risk that he'll talk about it and get himself caught."

Thorn's expression darkened. "And killed."

Suddenly, the air felt colder, and a shiver ran down Darius's spine. He tore his eyes away from Thorn and focused on his hands on the wrought iron table. Where hers were softly held together, fingers interlaced, his clenched so hard that his knuckles ached. He forced them apart, placed his palms flat, and stretched forward.

"We should've made Cain come with us," he said.

"At this point, I don't know that I could convince Cain to leave the Underground if the damned place was on fire," Thorn said.

Darius nodded, but the motion felt hollow. "I just don't like the idea of you using your Influence," he said. "The last thing we need is Wrath showing up."

"She won't," Thorn said. Darius glanced up at her again. Her attention was still trained on him with the same sharp focus she always wore. It felt more personal today. A knot in his chest relaxed as she went on. "Don't worry. I know how to be careful."

Thorn smirked, and Darius returned the gesture. He looked back down at the table. Their hands were so close, just a breath apart. It would take little more than a sigh to touch her. He curled his fingers into a gentle fist and drew back. Almost like an instinct, or a recoil, Thorn did the same.

"Thanks for making this happen," Darius said.

Her face softened further as her smile stretched into an elegant curve. "Just don't fuck it up again," she said. Humor tugged at the corners of her eyes. Discouragement, too, like she wished she could have done more.

Darius laughed and took a moment to consider the garden just to give him something else to focus on rather than the woman sitting in front of him and the sensation of Lamar's Virtue growing stronger. They'd chosen a table on the third tier out from the central fountain, far enough back that they were left alone and undisturbed. Darius had never visited this area before, but Thorn warned him that the city had stopped caring for the northernmost edges of Central Park decades ago, instead pouring time, energy, and money into the southern areas where tourists were more likely to visit.

The neglect was starting to show here. Bushes and trees were wiry and overgrown, flowerbeds hinted at a winter with little maintenance—last year's dead greenery still tucked beneath the early growth of spring—and even the fountain looked old and crusted. Three delicately crafted bronze maidens danced in a circle around a jutting stream of cloudy water, their faces pocked and patterned with dark green tarnish. It dripped down their faces and throats like emerald tears.

"How close is he?" Thorn asked.

Darius glanced over his shoulder. Lamar was still out of sight, but now he was near enough that Darius could get a sense of him. He squinted as though it would help him spot the kid through the trees.

"If I had to guess, he's crossing East Drive," Darius said. "Looks like he really did come alone."

"No, he didn't."

Thorn's dark eyes swept the garden. Beyond the civilians sitting on benches or admiring the fountain, a handful of Martyrs in plainclothes dotted the area—TAC agents here to provide a higher level of security. They played the part of regular citizens, keeping to themselves to avoid drawing attention to Thorn and Darius.

But other people *were* paying attention to them. Thorn leaned forward and tilted her head across the way, where a young Asian woman sat at the table opposite theirs on the circular path. When she caught Darius and Thorn looking in her direction, her head flicked down, and a veil of vibrant, scarlet hair obscured her face.

"She's been watching us," Thorn murmured. "And the man back there?" Darius spun around, where another person leaned back against a metal arch leading to the garden. "He hasn't taken his eyes off you since you sat down."

A knot formed in Darius's chest. "Great…"

"I'm not surprised," Thorn said as she sat up straight again. "We brought our guard. Can't blame him for bringing one of his own."

Her attention then moved away from Darius and focused behind his back. Lamar's Virtuous draw was so close it was undeniable, and Darius could feel the shape of his body now—how his arms were pinned to his sides, bent at an angle that implied his hands were shoved deep into jacket pockets, and he walked with a smooth, elegant swagger that was just a little too fast to be relaxed. Darius took a breath to ready himself, and at last, he rose to his feet. When he turned around, Lamar paused just out of reach.

"Hey," Darius said. "Thanks for meeting us."

Lamar smiled, but his expression didn't soften, so it looked strangled on his face. He'd come without his signature makeup, and his locs were pinned beneath a neat, navy beanie. "Something told me I'd regret it if I didn't."

Darius let out a laugh. "I know the feeling." He turned back to the table, finding Thorn still seated, and pulled out the chair he'd been in for Lamar as he grabbed the one in the center. Lamar glanced at the woman across the circle before he joined them.

"My roommates think I'm absolutely out of my mind," he muttered, adjusting his denim jacket.

Thorn smirked. "I don't blame them."

Lamar sighed and shook his head. "Look, I'm gonna be upfront with you. I know I said I'd come alone, but they wouldn't let me. I told them to keep back, but…"

His eyes flashed across the garden again, where his roommate busied herself on her phone.

"It sounds like you have good friends," Darius said.

"I do." Lamar's shoulders relaxed, and he took a long, even breath. When he spoke this time, he sounded less tense. "They've seen me through some dark places, and they don't want me to end up in those places again."

Thorn and Darius exchanged a look, and Lamar glanced between them. He pulled his lower lip between his teeth.

"Anyway," he went on after a moment, "you got me down here, in the cold, after casually stalking me for three weeks. This better be good." He crossed his arms. "Let's start with the part where you said you were at The Eros Project looking for *me*."

Darius leaned forward onto the table. "I'm ready to tell you that, but I have to be upfront with you, too." He glanced at Thorn, who nodded, before he continued. "This is going to be... hard to believe, and it could get you killed."

A dense silence dropped around them. Even the birds in nearby trees quieted, like they were trying to listen in and their own song was too distracting. Lamar's eyes opened wide. His focus passed from Darius to Thorn and back again before he laughed. When they didn't laugh back, the sound choked deep in his throat. "You're serious?"

"If you're not okay with that, I understand," Darius said. "We'll leave right now, and you won't see us again. But if you want to know more, we have ways to guarantee you won't be able to talk about this—to keep you and the people you love safe."

Lamar scoffed. "What? How can *anyone* guarantee that? Are you feds? US Marshalls? Am I in danger?"

"We're not feds," Darius said.

"But you *are* in danger," Thorn added.

More silence, heavier this time. Lamar's hands wrung in his lap, and he watched Darius with a wide, calculating stare. From his periphery, Darius could see that Thorn maintained a calm composure, and he consciously worked to keep himself equally poised. He failed. His heel tapped on the concrete underfoot. After a moment, he cleared his throat.

"Look, I know this is—"

"Insane?" Lamar cut in. "Yeah, you're damn right it's insane."

His voice drifted off as his eyes moved around Darius's

face, like he was trying to read some hidden message written in the lines.

"I don't believe you," Lamar said at last, but he didn't look away, and his voice fell to a murmur. "But why the hell do I *want* to believe you?"

Darius provided a soft, sympathetic smile. "Because the second I walked into your club, you felt like you knew me, and you can't explain why. But I can."

Lamar glanced at the table behind Darius's back, where his friend was now glaring at them with a stare that could kill. He sighed. "Well, then," he murmured. "Start explaining."

For the next hour, Darius talked about the Sins, the Virtues, and the Martyrs. He explained, as best he could, what the history of this corruption looked like in the world and how long it had been ingrained in the fabric of human development. When he got to the details of the Sins and their powers, Thorn filled in the blanks, and Lamar listened to them both with an increasingly skeptical look painted across his face. Slowly, his eyebrows rose, his mouth slipped open to reveal a sliver of white teeth, and his arms wrapped around his chest. By the time Darius was done, the sun was lower, the evening colder, and Lamar seemed stunned into silence.

"So, you're trying to tell me that *you* used to be a Sin," he started, tilting his head at Thorn, "and *you're* one of these Virtues," a nod in Darius's direction this time, "and you think *I'm* one, too?" Lamar planted a palm flat against his own chest.

"I know you are," Darius said.

"Because it… calls to you?"

"That's right."

Lamar laughed. "Oh, honey," he said. A cold rush flooded over Darius's body as Lamar shook his head. "You had me going for a minute there. I've lived in New York my whole life, and that's one of the most creative pitches I've ever heard. Are you working on a show? I hate to tell you this, but not *all* queer folks are into theater. It's not my thing, but I know some people. What about Mickey? You know, the bouncer? He loves this stuff."

"What?" Darius shook his head. Beside him, Thorn shifted silently in her seat. "No. No! This isn't some story. If the Sins find you, they'll—"

"I've heard enough," Lamar cut in. He moved to stand, but before he did, Thorn laid her right hand bare on the table and slashed a blade across it. Lamar's eyes shot open as her palm filled with blood. He shoved his way back, nearly toppling off his chair, but he managed to catch himself before he fell. "What the hell are you—"

The question died on his lips as Thorn's cut began to heal. He watched her torn flesh stitch itself back together, entranced, and his jaw dropped.

"Jesus, Thorn," Darius murmured as Thorn set the knife beside her glove, both neatly folded on the table. "You couldn't have been more subtle about it?"

He glanced around the park. Most of the civilians had disappeared, and the Martyr guards still acted like they were civilians themselves. Lamar's roommates, however, were now both sitting at the table across the fountain, poised like alley cats ready to pounce.

Lamar's voice drew Darius back.

"What the ever-loving hell did I just watch?"

"Accelerated healing," Thorn said. She dipped her left hand into her satchel and drew out a folded black tank top, which she used to dab the blood away. When she opened her palm again, the cut was little more than a pale pink line against her skin.

Lamar continued to stare. He pulled his chair back to the table, leaned forward, and looked more closely at Thorn's healed hand. After a moment, he closed his lips and met her eye.

"Can you do it again?"

"No," Darius started to say, but Thorn had already raised the knife and flipped it open. She dragged the blade against the heel of her hand, piercing the skin with the point and slicing a vibrant red incision open, before she folded it up and slipped it into her pocket with the casual nonchalance of someone who had just pulled out their phone to check the time. Even in a situation like this, seeing Thorn wounded made Darius's chest ache, so he looked around the park to make sure no one else was watching. Thankfully, his body seemed to obscure Lamar's roommates from seeing the show. All the while, Thorn's eyes trained on Lamar, sharp and curious, as he watched the second cut heal as smoothly as the first.

Then he didn't speak. Not for a long time. He drew his hands in front of his face and pressed his fingertips against his mouth before he looked at Darius.

"And *you* can heal *other* people?" he asked.

"Yes," Darius said.

"Even other Virtues?"

"Anyone but Sins and Forgotten Sins," Darius said, gesturing in Thorn's direction. She picked up her spare shirt and wiped her palm again.

"Show me."

Lamar opened the snaps on his left sleeve cuff, rolled it up to his elbow, and laid his arm on the table. A days-old gash from the martini glass Max Douglas's bodyguard had thrown tore through his skin, the wound edges puckered and pursed. Around it, an abstract scribbling took over most of his forearm. At first, Darius thought it was a tattoo, but upon closer inspection, he realized Lamar had doodled on himself in permanent marker. And beneath the marker…

Darius's heart sank.

Dozens of healed, razor-thin scars lined the inside of Lamar's arm, scratching horizontally across his skin. Ink sank into them, following the tracks like black rivers on earthen plains. Thorn's lips opened in quiet surprise, and a low, compassionate breath softened her expression.

"Well?" Lamar said.

Darius's focus snapped back to his face. He cleared his

throat and reached forward, but then he paused.

"I have to touch you," Darius said. "Is that cool?"

"Do whatever you've got to do."

Darius gently pressed the tips of his fingers directly against Lamar's cut. Their energies blended. Lamar's soul seemed eager, ready for Darius's to come pouring in. Healing power tingled from Darius's core, following through his hand and into Lamar's flesh. The wound immediately began to come back together. Within seconds, all that remained was a clean swatch of skin, free of blood and ink.

When he drew back, Lamar stared at his own arm in awe. He ran his fingertips over the space where the injury had been. His hand trembled. "My god," he murmured. Then, his face snapped back up, and a rush of panic glistened in his eyes. "What do I *do?*"

Thorn began to pull her glove back over her hand. "Your Virtue won't activate until you Initiate it," she said. "So, you have a decision to make."

The color drained from Lamar's face, leaving him ashen. "How long do I have to decide?"

"As long as you need," Darius said. "I'm not trying to force you into our war. This is *your* life. We'll support whatever you choose to do. I just wanted to make sure you *had* a choice."

"But, the Sins. You said I'm in danger!"

"Only if they find you," Thorn said. "And there is *always* a risk that they might. Right now, though, they don't seem to have any idea you exist."

Lamar looked back down at the clean spot on his healed skin. "So… which one am I? Which Virtue?"

"Either Chastity or Charity," Darius said. "We won't know until you accept it."

"*If* you accept it," Thorn added. Lamar stared at her, and she opened her satchel. "Here." She packed away her bloodied shirt and pulled out a red card with nothing but a number on it. "If you need anything, reach out to me. In the meantime, we need to make sure you and the people you care about are safe."

"Oh," Lamar said with a scoff as he tucked Thorn's card into his jacket pocket. "Don't worry. I won't tell anyone. No one would believe me anyway."

He breathed into a nervous smile, but his expression fell when Thorn and Darius exchanged a dark look. Thorn laced her fingers on the table. "This isn't the kind of thing we leave up to chance."

Lamar frowned for just a moment. Then, it dawned on him, and he slowly nodded. "Oh… You have those other Sin powers, too." He shuffled in his seat. "Will it hurt?"

Darius shook his head. "Just a headache, which is… better than the alternative."

Lamar's throat tightened, and he swallowed through it. "All right," he said. Strength poured back into his voice. Fragile at first, but when he squared his shoulders, it fortified. "Let's do it."

It took Thorn less than sixty seconds to Program Lamar, making it impossible for him to talk to anyone who wasn't a Martyr about what the three of them had discussed, and then they parted ways. Lamar immediately walked across the Conservatory Garden, where his roommates swept him up with soft embraces and whispered questions. He glanced back at Thorn and Darius one final time as they moved him through the park.

Darius lingered just long enough to watch Lamar disappear into the trees before Thorn pulled him away.

"So," he said, "how does it feel to be wrong again?"

Thorn's eyes flashed to him. "What the hell are you talking about?"

"You put this all together so I could get Lamar to understand what we're doing here."

"You *did* get him to understand," Thorn argued.

"No," Darius said. "I didn't. *You* did."

Thorn blinked, and her pace slowed. Darius smiled as he tilted toward her, nudging his shoulder against hers. "I couldn't have done this without you."

Her lips tightened into a smirk, and she focused on the path ahead like she was trying to hide it from him. "Don't start celebrating yet," she said. "Verrette might understand what we're up against, but that doesn't mean he'll want to be a part of it."

Darius nodded. "We'll just have to wait and see."

"We could be waiting for a while."

Thorn's phone rang at two in the morning. Her studio was pitch black; curtains closed against a seventh-floor window kept the city lights out but not the sounds. Sirens wailed in the distance, and cars honked on the street below. Thorn sat up, and Sparkie stretched his wings out on the pillow beside her as she grabbed her device from the table to see Holly's face glowing from the screen. When she answered, Thorn pressed her fingertips against her eyes.

"Andrews," she said. "This had better be an emergency."

"It… might be?" Holly's voice came through on a stifled yawn. "I just woke up to an alert saying our new Virtue got himself landed in the hospital. I figured you'd want to know."

A cold pit opened up in Thorn's stomach. *What?* She flung her sheets away and jumped out of bed. The vinyl flooring was cold beneath her bare feet as she strode across the studio. Her Familiar vaulted after her and landed deftly on the dresser drawer as Thorn pulled it open. "When? Which hospital?"

"Sinai," Holly said. "He was just admitted."

The pit grew deeper. The Sins had Sentries planted in every single ER in Manhattan, hoping to catch injured Martyrs dragged in by well-intended good samaritans. It didn't happen often, but it *did* happen. That was how Thorn had met Simon. Seven decades ago, she'd been strapped to one of his medical cots, bleeding and furious, until Wrath had shown up and made a mess of the whole goddamned unit.

Thorn had saved his life. He returned the favor by saving hers.

"What was Verrette admitted for?" Thorn asked. She put her phone on speaker, laid it on her dresser, and grabbed a pair of leggings.

"His intake says he's got a fever of one hundred and four."

Thorn froze. The possibilities of what that meant fluttered through her head like moths around a candle flame. She finished getting dressed in a daze. Moments later, Holly cleared her throat.

"Maybe you should call him and make sure everything is okay."

"I can't," Thorn replied. She sat at the edge of the bed and pulled on her boots. "I don't have his number."

Holly yawned again. "Yeah, you do."

Thorn snatched her phone up and navigated to her contacts. Lamar Verrette's information had been added to the list.

"What the hell would we do without you, Andrews?"

"I don't even want to imagine," Holly said, but her tone got serious. "I also don't want to imagine what the Sins would do to Verrette if they found him there. Do you think they know what to look for in an Initiated Virtue?"

A knot tightened around Thorn's throat. "I don't know," she said, "but we're not going to wait to find out. Can you wipe him from Sinai's system?"

"I can," Holly said. "Can you get him out of the building?"

Thorn grabbed her jacket, threw it around her shoulders, and zipped it to her throat. Then she dug through a separate drawer, pulled out a black beanie, and put it into her satchel. Sparkie leapt inside just before she snapped it shut. "We're about to find out."

The moment she and Holly disconnected, Thorn called Lamar, but he didn't answer. He also didn't answer the second time, as she was sprinting down the stairwell, or the third, when she reached her bike in the parking garage. She'd been staying at the Martyr apartment in Midtown East, which made Mount Sinai just over three miles away. There was so little traffic at two in the morning that Thorn made the trip in less than ten minutes. Madison Avenue was practically deserted, and she parked her bike on the street corner outside the emergency room doors.

Sinai was one of the largest hospitals in the city, which meant the Sins would have spent a lot of time Programming in the people who worked here, and Thorn wasn't about to take chances that either Wrath or Greed had Sentries looking for her. She tied her hair back in a low ponytail, hid the length of it down the back of her jacket, and covered her head with her beanie. Then, she pulled her hood up and walked into the building.

Before she did anything else, Thorn made her way to a self-serve station just inside the door. It was stocked with boxes of disposable face masks, rubber gloves, and other personal protective equipment. She grabbed a mask, put it on, and took a quiet breath to steady herself.

This would have to be good enough.

A handful of people lined the waiting room. A drunken man with an ice pack pressed against a lump rising on his brow line. A senior woman with no apparent reason for being there who kept anxiously looking at her watch with tears streaming silently down her face. A middle-aged couple with their daughter huddled in a corner. The girl was just old enough that the corruption of the world was starting to tint her soul. She had a subtle coldness—the beginning of an aura that Thorn had to fight to feel. If Thorn had to guess, the kid was just a year or so older than she'd been when Wrath started its possession. God, sometimes she forgot how early her life had been ruined until it was staring her in the face.

The girl seemed to sense Thorn's eyes on her. She glanced up, and Thorn immediately averted her gaze and made her way to the counter. The receptionist hardly looked up from her computer. "Hello," she said in a tired, monotonous drone. "What brings you to the ER today?"

"I got a call that my friend was admitted," Thorn said. "Lamar Verrette. I wanted to see him."

"Mmm." The woman clacked away on her keyboard with inch-long, turquoise nails that looked impossible to type with. "Verrette. Yes, he's here. What's your relationship?"

"I'm one of his roommates," Thorn lied.

"All right, let me just call and make sure you're cleared to go back. What's your name, sweetie?"

Thorn hesitated for half a second, her mind cycling through her options until she landed on one Lamar would recognize. "Dante Stone," she said. *Thank god for this mask. It hid the look of disgust across her face.*

The receptionist looked at Thorn more critically now, her brown eyes narrow. One drawn-on brow raised as she picked up her phone and hit a few buttons. After a brief pause, she said, "I have a visitor for Mr. Verrette here. His roommate, a woman named Dante Stone… Yes, that's right. Thank you." She hung up, hit a button under her desk, and the double doors to Thorn's left swung open. "Mr. Verrette is in room four."

Thorn made her way into the emergency department. The hall buzzed with cold energy as doctors, nurses, and technicians made their rounds. Glass doors and white curtains were closed as far as Thorn could see, but she sensed patients hiding behind them. Some rooms were full of frantic movement that Thorn could feel through the walls, but most were calm. Room four was one of those. Thorn pulled the door open and slipped through the curtain to find Lamar Verrette lying on the bed in nothing but an undershirt and a pair of boxer briefs. He startled when she walked into the room, and then, his face broke into a smile.

"*You're* not 'Dante,'" he said with a laugh. "What are you doing here?"

The kid was coated in sweat. It glistened in beads against

his forehead and cheeks, and his blue tank top was so saturated Thorn was hard-pressed to find a dry spot on the fabric. Now, with his arms bare and the overhead hospital lights blaring down on them, his scarring was more apparent beneath his drawings. It extended inside his left forearm almost as far as Thorn's own. The Asian woman from the park sat on Lamar's right, and she caught Thorn in a piercing glare as she closed the door behind her.

"Checking on you," Thorn said. "I tried to call."

"Oh, my phone is piled with everything else over there," he said, weakly gesturing to a folded stack of clothing on a table by the door before he let his head fall back onto the pillow. He didn't seem surprised that she'd found him here or that she'd somehow gotten his contact information. "Sorry to scare you. I was just going to sleep this off, but Naomi found me and—oh, this is my friend, Naomi." He indicated the woman. "Naomi, this is…"

Then Lamar stopped, like Thorn's name was heavy on his tongue—her Programming hard at work. She turned to Naomi and nodded in acknowledgment.

"Evelyn," she answered.

Naomi frowned and crossed her arms. "Evelyn? Dante? How many names do you have?"

Lamar laughed again. It sounded exhausted. He ran his hands down his face and sighed through them.

"I told you about her," he mentioned. "From the club, remember?"

"Yeah," Naomi said, her voice protective and cold. "With the guy who punched someone."

At last, Lamar's humor fizzled, and he pressed his full lips together. While Naomi continued to glare with a ferocity Thorn couldn't help but respect, Lamar shook his head.

"Hey, Mimi," he said as he sat up. Naomi turned to him, and he touched a hand to her shoulder. The contact made him wince, but he held on. "I've gotta talk with her alone, okay? Just a few minutes, I promise."

Naomi's expression sharpened, and she offered a

concerned frown as she pulled a silky strand of vibrant red hair behind her ear. "I'll get some coffee. You want anything?"

"God, *yes*," Lamar said with a groan. "An iced caramel latte with extra caramel. And extra ice."

"Sounds good." Naomi smiled at him, wrapped him up in a quick hug that made him grimace, and walked away. She threw Thorn another glare for good measure before she shut the door. When her energy wandered off, Lamar sighed.

"Sorry about her."

"Don't be," Thorn said. "She's a good friend."

"She's worried as hell about me," Lamar said. "I can't say I blame her. I put her through a lot today—meeting you guys at the park, not telling her a damn thing about it, and then spiking a fever so hot they want to test me for all sorts of rare diseases. I can't exactly tell her what's *really* going on, can I?"

He let out a chuckle and fell back onto the mattress. Thorn's jaw tightened. "So, you really did it?" she asked. "You really accepted your Virtue?"

Lamar cracked an eye to look at her. "You sound surprised."

"I am," Thorn admitted. "I've never seen someone embrace it this fast."

His lips widened into a grin. "Not even *Darius?*"

He watched her with a coy look, and Thorn raised a brow.

"Look," she said, waving her hand to get back on track. "We've got to get you out of here. The Sins have people planted in all of the hospitals in Manhattan. If they find you, they *will* kill you."

Lamar's grin melted off his face. He sat up again. "They said I might need fluids."

"We have a medical suite in the Underground," Thorn said. She grabbed Lamar's pile of clothing off the table and handed it to him. "Let's go."

"Whoa, hold up," he said, setting his things aside. "I'm not going *with* you."

Thorn frowned. "You accepted your Virtue."

"I did," Lamar said, "and I want to help you fight this thing, but I'm not giving up my life for it. What would happen to my friends? My family? Everyone I have here if I went to this headquarters of yours?"

He watched her, and for a moment, all Thorn could do was watch back. Her mouth parted as she took in a slow breath through her mask. "You leave them behind," she said at last. "Or we can bring them with—"

"Absolutely not," Lamar cut in. "It's dangerous."

"It's *war*," Thorn countered.

"Our war," Lamar said. "*My* war. Not theirs. But there's no reason I can't fight that war here, in Manhattan. You said it yourself that the Sins have no idea I even exist."

Thorn's teeth clenched. "If they *do* find you, they'll target everyone you love to get to you."

"If," Lamar said. "I'm not uprooting my whole life for an 'if.' I'm staying in the city. Not *here*, though. I *hate* hospitals."

Lamar began to get himself put back together, and all Thorn could do was stare. When the nurse came by, Lamar informed her that he was checking himself out, and he signed the digital release absolving Sinai of responsibility for him declining care. On the walk to the front, Lamar called Naomi and asked her to meet him at the entrance. When he and Thorn stepped outside, he opened his arms to the cold night air.

"Ah, that's better." He tilted his head back and let out a sigh. Thorn moved to his side, removing her face mask, and he looked her over. "Thank you for this. It's… incredible."

He gazed around again, like he was seeing the city through a new lens. He considered the buildings above them, the street behind them, the cars passing by with a smile across his face. Thorn had never experienced this— the awe-inspiring moment when human beings suddenly lit up with an otherworldly sensation. The first time she had felt the aura of a person's soul, she'd been trapped inside her own body, watching a Sin at the reins.

"This won't last forever," she said.

"I know," Lamar said with a nod, "so I'll enjoy it while it does. Which Sin am I going to destroy?"

He turned back to her at last. "That depends," Thorn said. "Are you Chastity or Charity?"

A passing car flew down Madison Avenue, its lights reflecting against Lamar's face as he shook his head. "I don't know."

Thorn frowned. "The name should have come to you when you Initiated it."

Lamar's eyes widened. The levity in them faded to confusion and then concern. "Is *that* what that was?"

"Yes," Thorn said. Lamar's crestfallen look made her pause. "What's wrong?"

He didn't answer right away. His attention drifted over Thorn's shoulder, where Naomi's energy drew toward the emergency department doors. "I heard a name," Lamar murmured, "but it wasn't either of those."

A weight of shock fell into Thorn's stomach. "What was it?"

"Consent."

Thorn's mouth opened, but before she could ask anything else, Naomi walked out of the building.

"I think leaving the hospital is a mistake," she said, and she threw Thorn a hot look as she handed a massive, iced coffee to Lamar. "But if you won't stay, I'm dragging your butt home and getting you to bed. It was nice meeting you… whatever your name was. Let's go."

Naomi linked her arm with Lamar's, making him wince, and practically dragged him down the street. He threw Thorn an apologetic look over his shoulder as they trudged down Madison. She watched them, her mind on fire.

As far as Thorn knew, there were only three Virtues left, and Consent wasn't one of them.

CHAPTER NINETEEN

The percussive clacking of keyboards greeted Darius as he walked back into the R&D headquarters with a full thermos of coffee and a stack of paper cups. Researchers filled the workstations on each wall while Nicholas and Thorn sat at one of the round tables in the center of the room. Nicholas dragged a hand through his blonde hair.

"An *eighth* Sin," he grumbled. He wet his thumb against the inside of his lip before he turned another page in the binder he was holding. "There's no way there's an *eighth* fucking Sin out there."

"How else can you explain this?" Thorn asked without looking up from the report in her hands. She'd kicked back in her chair, propping the heels of her boots up on the table. Sparkie perched on her shoulder and peered down at the document. His head moved in perfect sync with her eyes as they read.

"I don't have an explanation," Nicholas said. "Doesn't mean there isn't one."

"We know there used to be more than the seven we've had to deal with," Darius said as he approached the table. Thorn's eyes flashed to him as he set the thermos and cups in front of her, and she pulled her feet down to make more room. "It's not impossible that we've missed one of them."

While Darius poured each of them a steaming cup of coffee, Nicholas shook his head. A worried knit tied his brows together. "If we missed one, we could have missed more. Fuck, I wish this were whiskey." He grabbed one of the cups, grumbled a thank you, and took a sip.

Darius laughed as he sat down on Thorn's other side. "It's two in the afternoon."

"It feels like six," Thorn murmured. She lifted her coffee to her lips and sighed against it. Her breath sent a ripple across the surface, and steam wafted toward her face, making her tired eyes look heavy. Darius was sure she hadn't slept since Holly had woken her up, and it appeared that even immortality didn't completely take the edge off of sleep deprivation. "I could use a drink myself."

Thorn tossed her report onto the table, and Darius took it. Dozens of pages with hundreds of names—deities, demigods, warriors, rulers, leaders, and celebrities from every eon of human history. Threads of the seven he knew laid a clear map through the millennia, but others frayed out at the edges, connected to spirits long dead and forgotten that the Martyrs could only guess at.

"The ancient Egyptians worshiped over fourteen hundred gods or godlike people," Nicholas said. "And the Greeks had hundreds. Titans, gods, heroes, you name it. Any of them could have been Sins, and we haven't even started looking at the Eastern religions and myths. I don't know where the fuck to start."

He slapped his binder down on the table and swore. Darius's eyes wandered down the list again. There were a lot of opportunities for Sins to hide in history, and the idea that one had made it to the end of the twenty-first century without being discovered made his stomach tight and uneasy.

A warm energy approached the door, and Darius glanced back as it opened. Parker Boseman walked into the room with Cain on her heels, peering over her shoulder. His eyes landed on Darius with a magnetic focus, and a smirk lifted on his face.

"Good afternoon," he said, his voice silky. He pulled a chair out on Nicholas's other side and glided into it. "My, the Underground is rife with rumors today, isn't it? I heard some *very* interesting things in my pottery class just now…"

Darius looked at Parker, who gave a guilty smile and an apologetic shrug that made her tight ringlets bounce. He chuckled, and Cain's expression glittered. Thorn's sharpened with the distinct air of someone who wasn't in the mood for games.

"Out with it," she said.

"They say we're dealing with the *eight* deadly Sins now." Cain grimaced and shook his head. "That doesn't roll off the tongue, does it?"

Thorn closed her eyes and pinched the bridge of her nose. "What do you know?"

"I know it is an absolute crime that you would not reach out to me with this concern before throwing yourself into needless research," Cain said. He placed a hand over his heart and gave Thorn a false, offended look. "Certainly my *six hundred years* of experience is worth more than simply teaching art classes."

With a sigh, Thorn placed her cup on the table and glared at Cain. "You specifically stated that you didn't want *anything* to do with management when you came back. Morale, remember? You wanted to focus on Martyr *morale*."

"And yet I still get dragged into dangerous missions because *you* want to take advantage of my unique skills and abilities," Cain argued with a shrug. A single brow arched on Thorn's head as he smiled and held up his hands. "I am simply here to help."

Nicholas scoffed. "Good. We could use it." He put his coffee down and reclined in his chair, arms crossed. "What are *your* thoughts on this eighth Sin?"

Cain's eyes twinkled as he considered Nicholas. "I think it's interesting that your first assumption is that we were wrong about the *Sins* and not about the *Virtues.*"

Darius propped his elbows onto the table with a frown. "What do you mean?"

"The Martyrs is not the first organization dedicated to eradicating the Sins that I have been a part of," Cain said. "I was a key player in the Order of Light, which was searching for Virtues and hunting down the Seven centuries before any of your ancestors had even dreamed of coming to this god-forsaken continent. With the Order, my primary function was the discovery and recruitment of others like me."

Nicholas shook his head. "What does that have to do with this?"

"Because in my *decades* of work there, I never once met a Forgotten Sin that had not been possessed by one of the original seven we have been fighting," Cain said. "And I have met *many*. There have always been more Forgotten Sins than Sins in the world. Even if an eighth Sin had eluded us, I surely would have encountered one of its abandoned vessels over the years."

Darius nodded, but Nicholas's eyes narrowed. "You can't be one hundred percent sure of that."

Cain shrugged. "The Order had more information than the Martyrs can even fathom. Pity it was destroyed in the Inquisition. I lost many friends, many other *Oblitus Peccatum*, and millennia's worth of knowledge."

"You said we're wrong about the *Virtue*," Thorn said, fixing Cain with a hard stare. "How?"

"Information on the Virtues has always been notoriously difficult to find," Cain said. "Even the Order struggled to learn more than what we know today. Our understanding of the Virtues is extremely limited, which means we are more likely to make mistakes there. Tell me, which one did our young friend say he was?"

"Consent."

Cain's eyes widened, his spine went straight, and he drew a reverent breath. When he spoke, his voice was deep in wonder.

"Fascinating. Sadik and I wondered about this, but I

never imagined I would live to see it—"

"Cain," Thorn cut in. "What the hell are you talking about?"

He shook his head. "I don't believe we have an eighth Sin… Thorn, my dear… I believe you've found Chastity."

Thorn's lips parted, and she and Darius shared a shocked look. Nicholas, however, frowned. "How do you figure that? Consent and Chastity are practically *opposite* values."

Cain provided a conceding nod. "That is, in fact, the point." At Nicholas's confused expression, Cain sighed. "Much like the Sins, our current understanding of the Virtues came from a man named Gregorius Anicius, or Pope Gregory I. You may already notice a distinct… flaw in his credibility: the papacy. He was aligned with the *Catholic Church*. While some argued that Gregory was well intended, we now understand that the Sins themselves were heavily involved in the growth and power of the Church. That alone means we ought to be critical of things taught and supported by even the most enlightened men and women within that institution."

"So," Darius said, "you think this pope was wrong about Chastity?"

By now, the clattering of fingers against keys had tumbled to a stop, and Darius was acutely aware of warm souls bending toward them, like Cain's voice was a vortex sucking in the energy of the room. Cain seemed to sense it, too. He focused on Darius with a theatrical intensity.

"I do," he said, louder to indulge the research staff now listening in. "Consider it: one of the single most damaging lies propagated by Christianity is that of *purity*. The villainization of sex and sexuality has promoted more dissent and conflict within human societies than nearly any other value, and in the grand scheme of our development, this particular concept is relatively new. Ancient Egyptian, Roman, and Chinese civilizations were largely open in their views, and modern repression of sex can be linked to Western influence by the Church. Pope Gregory may have succeeded in passing down knowledge about the Sins, but the *Sins* succeeded in bastardizing one of the Virtues so thoroughly that even the name Chastity has been enough to evoke disdain for centuries."

Nicholas's brows drew together. "Are you saying *Lust* is actually the Virtuous half of this thing and Chastity is… the bad side?"

Cain scoffed, waving the idea away with a swift flick of the wrist. "Absolutely not. I'm saying that the Virtue Chastity never even existed. Instead, we have been searching for *Consent* this entire time without ever realizing it."

"Why would the Sins change the name?" Parker asked. Her voice pierced through the room, and her tawny cheeks warmed as everyone spun toward her. Cain smiled.

"Because it is nearly impossible to find something if you are looking in the wrong place," he said. Then, his head swiveled back to Thorn, and the light in his half-empty eyes flickered. "Lust is so much more complicated than a sexual *desire*, but a desire for sexual *control*. It is, and has always been, about power."

Thorn's jaw hardened, and she drew back to her full height, arms crossed. Sparkie slipped behind her hair.

"Hmm," Nicholas started, slowly nodding as he considered Cain. "It's a good theory."

Cain's positivity fractured, and his mouth strained to keep his smile. "It's more than a theory."

"Right," Nicholas agreed. "But I still want to look more into it. Thanks, Cain. This gives me a great place to launch off from."

He got to his feet, thumping a grateful palm on Cain's shoulder as he turned to his team and set them out on looking at Lust and Chastity—at *Consent*—in particular. Darius took a deep breath and focused back on Thorn again. Her eyes were distant, gazing out beyond Cain's head without really seeing, lost in thought. From the expression on her face, it wasn't a pleasant one. Darius gently nudged her with his elbow, and she snapped back to the present. When she looked at him, he smiled.

"This is way better than tracking down an eighth Sin," he said.

Thorn nodded, but the rigidness in her shoulders held hard as stone.

"It also doesn't help us," she said. "Lust hasn't taken a new host, so I guess we're keeping our focus on removing Greed from the picture. This does make me wonder, though…"

She drifted off, and Darius leaned toward her with a frown. "What?"

"If the Sins were able to demonize Consent so much that we never even knew its name," Thorn went on, "what else could they have done to hide the other Virtues from us?"

She glanced across the table, where Cain simply watched them. Darius got the feeling he wanted to say more, but he kept his thin mouth tightly shut.

Exactly five days after Peter Mulligan had planted a tracking device on Greed, the signal stopped.

Information shone down on Thorn from Holly's mosaic of computer screens—everything from tactical reports, camera feeds, artificially enhanced algorithms, and all sorts of technical shit Thorn had never felt compelled to learn. She steepled her fingers and pressed them against tightly closed lips as she focused on the one display that interested her at all: a map of the Financial District, cut into pieces by the bright yellow path their tracking device had carved through the neighborhood. The final point, where the device had been when the signal disappeared, sat in the middle of an industrial park outside Newark. Thorn swore.

"He trashed the jacket," she murmured.

"Yep," Holly confirmed. She tapped a few keys, and the entire six-screen setup filled with the satellite image of

Lower Manhattan. "After it stopped at that apartment, the device followed a crazy path through the city before heading to the Essex County incinerator. We got nothing."

With a sigh, she leaned back in her chair and slipped her fingertips beneath her thick-rimmed glasses to rub her eyes.

Thorn glared at the aerial view of the building she and Sparkie had broken into just days ago. "Have you seen Claytor at the apartment at all?"

Holly shook her head. "He hasn't been in or out since we tapped into the camera feeds. Either he hasn't been home *or* he's found a way to work around me. I doubt that's true, so I'd guess he tossed the coat before moving somewhere less… conspicuous."

She gestured widely at the ugly high-rise on the screen. Thorn's head dipped in a nod before she abruptly shook it instead.

"Fuck."

Thorn flung herself back and threw her hands behind her head. Holly's team at the far end of the tiny room shifted uncomfortably, peering at Thorn over the tops of their computer screens as she chewed her lower lip. Holly spun in her chair to face her, her short legs pulled beneath her body as she twirled her thumbs in her lap.

"There has to be something valuable in here," Thorn said after a moment. She scooted forward and pointed at the looping, yellow line. It flowed along New York's streets, traversing several blocks of the Financial District in a winding pattern, clearly a garbage truck route. "Can you show me the path it took between the event and the apartment?"

"Yeah, just a sec." Holly twisted back to her computer and hit a few commands. A toolbar appeared at the bottom of the center screen, and she dragged the cursor backward. All at once, the icon zipped away, tracing dizzying circles until it landed at the corner of Spruce and William. A complicated pattern still colored the Financial District streets.

"That's a lot of movement," Thorn said.

"My guess is that he was afraid he was being followed,"

Holly said, "so he took the extra-long way back to his closest apartment."

She slid the icon across the progress bar at the bottom of the screen, and the yellow path snaked its way around the streets again. It lingered over a different building, snagging Thorn's interest.

"What was that?" She sat forward again and indicated that part of the map. "He stopped here. Can you tell me how long?"

Holly frowned and clicked open a separate dialogue box. "According to this, he spent about two hours there."

Two hours... Something about the street felt familiar. Thorn hedged toward the edge of her chair. "That's a significant stop if he was worried about being followed. Where is it?"

"Let me see..." Holly highlighted the address, dropped the map to a smaller size, and opened a new window. The building's front face filled a separate display. Thorn's mouth slipped open as Holly said, "Businesses at this location include AIM Accounting Corporation, The Law Offices of Jensen and Jensen, Lifelock Insurance—"

"Crave Media," Thorn cut in.

Holly twisted around. "Yeah. How'd you know?"

Thorn's jaw tightened, and she thought back to the alley outside the Mezzanine Event Space. "Connor Amoretto," she said. "The man who wanted me to look into Anton Claytor for him. He works there."

"Oh, shit." Holly's eyes widened behind her glasses, the thick lenses magnifying them even further. "They're managing Mayor Bently's campaign."

"And Amoretto seemed pretty convinced Claytor had some kind of power over Bently," Thorn confirmed.

"Seems a little convenient that Claytor would hide out there after the catastrophe at the event," Holly said. "Do you think Mr. Mayor was with him?"

Thorn took a deep breath and shook her head. "I don't know, but I do know how I can find out."

Holly raised a brow. It disappeared behind her boxy, boyish bangs. "Bringing Teagan Love back from the dead?"

A smirk pulled across Thorn's lips. "Just for one night. I want to see what this Amoretto guy can tell me about Greed."

Thorn sat at a table on the side patio of a little hole-in-the-wall burger joint in East Harlem. From the street, this place didn't look like much. Grungy, brick walls. Weathered, wood tables. The sharp, distinct smell of frying oil. Quiet, unassuming, and a little less crowded than areas in central Manhattan—perfect for meeting someone known to have contact with the Sins.

A black camera lens looked down on Thorn from the corner of the building, where someone back at the Underground was keeping tabs on her to call for backup if anything went wrong. Once Connor Amoretto agreed to meet, the security team swept the area and searched for any sign that Greed was getting ready for an ambush. They found nothing. No increased civilian movement. No shady characters. No sign at all that anything was amiss.

A cold energy moved toward the building, and familiar anticipation crawled up Thorn's spine. When Amoretto strode around to the patio, his deep blue eyes swept the occupied tables until they landed on her. Thorn watched for any sign of Sin Influence. A look, an emotion, a move for a phone to alert Greed that he had Thorn here with him right now.

But he simply admired her. His wide mouth cracked a charming smile that pinched handsome dimples into his freshly-shaven cheeks. Thorn stood up as he approached.

"It's Connor, right?"

Amoretto laughed, a deep, rich sound. "That's right." He shook her hand with vigor. His grip was stronger than Thorn expected—almost strong enough to sting—and he held on just a second too long. "Teagan, thank you for meeting with me. I've been hoping you would call every day for a week now."

His smile stretched, flaunting perfectly straight, perfectly white teeth. Thorn gave a dismissive chuckle as she lowered herself back down and shrugged her jacket and satchel from her shoulders. She hung both off the back of her chair while Amoretto took the seat opposite hers. His eyes traveled down her body, from her neck to her breasts to her hands, lingering on the fingerless gloves covering her forearms. When she pulled them beneath the table, he looked around the patio instead.

"Interesting choice of venue," he said. His upper lip curled like he disapproved of what he saw. He stuck out, his navy suit as strange here as Thorn's typical black would have been in a Sunday school choir. "You know, it's not too late to go somewhere more upscale." His attention landed on Thorn again, hungry and piercing. "My treat."

Thorn lifted her menu with a snap and hid her disdain behind it. "I like this restaurant."

Amoretto laughed again. "Of course. I apologize. It's a habit."

A brow arched on Thorn's head. "A habit?"

He shrugged, but his gaze held Thorn in a thirsty grip. "When I'm out with a woman, I want to give her the best—especially when she's so stunning."

That gaze wandered again, drinking Thorn in, and her jaw tightened. Mackenzie's words cut through her like a piece of shrapnel. Another man. Another notch. Another waste of goddamned time.

"This isn't a date," she said. "We're here to talk about Anton Claytor."

Amoretto grinned a Cheshire grin that gave Thorn the distinct impression that he wanted to sink those sharp teeth right into her.

"As I said, a habit."

The waitress returned, dropping off glasses of water and

taking their orders. Thorn asked for hot coffee and a plate of mozzarella sticks while her guest made an elaborate display of ordering a complicated burger with so many personalizations that it no longer represented anything offered on the menu. Thorn's chest crackled with coals of anger and indignation. She swallowed a mouthful of ice-cold water to drown it out.

"So," Amoretto said as he leaned onto his elbows and arched toward her. He was taller than Darius by maybe an inch, but somehow, that inch felt like miles. "What made you so interested in looking into Claytor all of a sudden? Not that I'm complaining, mind you, but you seemed ambivalent about it when we last talked."

Thorn's spine straightened, and she pressed it into the back of her chair to get a little distance. "Not ambivalent. Just busy."

"Weren't we all?" Amoretto sat up again, dipped his hand into his jacket pocket, and drew out a pack of cigarettes. As he pulled one from the box, he offered it to Thorn, and she declined with a shake of her head. "When I was outside talking to you, things went to hell at the event."

"I heard," Thorn said.

He frowned, the cigarette dangling from his mouth as he lit the tip. A knowing curiosity flashed over his eyes. He pulled the smoke back and ran his tongue across his lower lip. "You did?"

Thorn nodded. "I have my sources."

That cat-like smile stretched across Amoretto's face again. "I'm sure you do. Well, the *public* story is that there was an accident, but Rich, I'm sorry, *Mayor Bently*, is convinced someone tried to assassinate him."

"What would make him think that?" Thorn asked.

"You know politicians," Amoretto said with a shrug. "They always think they're more important than they actually are." He sucked in a mouthful of nicotine and blew it in Thorn's direction. A cloudy haze dangled between them before a spring breeze whisked it away. "But I have to admit, the entire situation was a little strange…"

His voice dissipated as he brought his cigarette back for another drag. Thorn's eyes narrowed. "You don't think what happened at the Mezzanine was an accident?"

"I don't know," Amoretto replied. "But I *do* know that Claytor booked it out of there so fast you'd think someone was holding his family hostage."

"Have you seen him since then?"

"No. He seems to have disappeared—*again.*"

A dark twinge swirled in Thorn's stomach as the waitress returned with their food. Amoretto tossed his cigarette onto the ground and crushed it with his heel as she placed the plates in front of them. Thorn's mozzarella sticks wafted hot, savory steam into the air, and Amoretto's burger was piled so high that there was no reasonable way for him to take a bite without dripping sauce and oil all over himself. Part of Thorn relished the thought, and she hid a smirk behind her coffee cup as he asked the waitress for a knife.

When she walked away, Thorn lowered her mug and cleared her throat.

"So," she said, "I understand that Anton Claytor visited Crave Media before he went to his apartment after the event. You weren't back at the office yet?"

A shock of genuine surprise warped Amoretto's face for the first time. His eyes widened, and they darted between hers.

"How do you know where Claytor went?" he asked.

The waitress returned with a sharp, pointed steak knife and laid it beside Amoretto's plate before topping Thorn's mug with fresh, steaming coffee. Thorn refused to answer, instead taking a sip. Her tongue burned and immediately healed. Amoretto raised the knife and sighed.

"Your 'sources,' then," he mumbled, and for a moment, Thorn was relieved to see his bravado shrinking. The relief was short-lived. With a deep breath, Amoretto slipped back into his suave cadence. "Well, you're right. I was putting out fires at the Mezzanine all afternoon, but Rich went down to

Crave to chew out my team for not doing the proper inspections. Claytor was with him."

Amoretto pressed the top of his burger down. In a smooth, buttery movement, he sliced the blade through it and cleaved the whole thing cleanly in two.

"And no one talked to him while he was there?" Thorn asked.

"You don't *talk* to him," Amoretto said with a chuckle. "He's untouchable."

"So he just went down to yell at your team, and then he left?"

Amoretto shook his head. "I have no idea." He wiped the knife clean on his napkin and placed them both to the side. "Like I said, I wasn't there. Maybe you should ask your sources." Then, Amoretto's eyes glittered. "Do you have a guy planted in my company, Teagan Love? If you want to know more about me, all you have to do is ask…"

He fixed her with a coy look as he licked a line of sauce off the side of his thumb. His tongue moved delicately, with an expertise that made Thorn uneasy. The anticipation along her back flickered again, not because of Influence or Sins, but because the man sitting across from her reeked of intention, and Thorn wasn't in the fucking mood to fight this particular battle today.

"You told me that you suspect Anton Claytor is up to something," she pressed, forcing the topic. "That he might have power over the mayor. I'm just trying to understand how deep that goes. Does Claytor spend a lot of time at Crave's headquarters?"

"No," Amoretto said. "I usually see him in meetings at Rich's office. If I see him. Like I said, he's been absent for months now. Is that where your sources are? The Mayor's office?

A cold chill ran down Thorn's spine. She crossed her arms. "My sources aren't any of your business."

That feline smile came back, sharper than ever. "Oh, I seem to have hit a nerve." Amoretto leaned toward her, perched on his elbows, and laced his fingers beneath his chin. "If we're going to work together, I think I've earned a little give and take here. How do I know I can trust you?"

Thorn's upper lip curled. "This isn't about trust," she snapped. "*You* asked for *my* help, but it looks like I'm wasting my time."

She moved to get up, but Amoretto reached out for her. As he did, he knocked her mug, and coffee poured over Thorn's hands. It scalded against her skin, her *Peccostium*, and an intense wave of pain made her sink back into her chair with a hiss.

"Damn it," Amoretto swore. "Let me get that." A hint of desperation tightened the words—and anger, like a man who wasn't used to being told no. As Thorn pulled her left glove off to draw the heat away, he grabbed his napkin. "Here."

Amoretto took her fingers, flipped her forearm to the sky, and plunged his knife into the mark of the Sins beneath her wrist.

All Thorn knew was pain. It shot down her arm, deep into the thick tendrils of her scars, and through her bones, setting every one of her atoms on fucking fire until her muscles melted around them. A shrill, hoarse ringing filled her ears, so loud that she didn't realize she was screaming, too. Somewhere nearby, Sparkie plummeted from the sky. Thorn was only vaguely aware of him.

Instead, she stared at her hand—at her wrist pinned to the wood and at the blade sticking out from the *Peccostium*. Blood pooled around it, following the line of Thorn's arm and dripping onto her lap. She grabbed the hilt but couldn't even grip it without shaking, much less pull it from the table. Another jolt of pain made her cry out.

Across the table, Connor Amoretto laughed. Thorn's head swam with it.

"I wouldn't touch that if I were you." His voice was hazy. Thorn strangled the weapon with her fingers, still trying to wrench it free, but her hands felt like pudding.

Amoretto stood up and made his way to her. A thickness pushed on Thorn's head, tight at her temples. Dread pitched into the pit of her stomach as she recognized the sensation.

Influence.

She looked up, desperately trying to make eye contact with the waitress, with the other customers, with the people walking by on the street, but no one noticed her. She was alone here, trapped in plain sight.

"Oh, *fuck*," Thorn breathed.

Amoretto wrapped his hand around the base of her neck in a smooth, gentle caress, almost as though he were sorry for the hurt he'd caused. His thumb ran leisurely along the pulse point on her throat. Without warning, his fingers twisted into her hair, and he yanked her head backward. Thorn winced as he forced her to look him in the eye, to be violated by his gaze the same way she was by his touch. His expression burned with a carnal need she'd seen before—not in this face, in this man, but in dozens just like him over the decades. Nausea spun with the pain in her stomach.

"I've missed you," Lust purred.

"Fuck off," Thorn spat. She tugged on the knife again, but her arms felt even heavier than they had just seconds ago.

"Still as stubborn as ever, I see," Amoretto said. "You know, that's one of my favorite things about you. This would be so much less satisfying if you were easy." His eyes flicked up to the busy restaurant just feet away from them. "And so much less thrilling if we were alone…"

He grabbed the hilt and twisted the blade until he popped it out of the table without dislodging it from her arm. Another scream poured out of the deepest part of Thorn's chest, scraping against her throat until it was raw. When Lust released the weapon, her wrist slammed back down. Thorn grabbed at it, her fingers slipping on blood, and she struggled to breathe through a lump of bile threatening to climb into her mouth.

"Even superheroes have their weaknesses, don't they?"

Amoretto went on, indicating the knife. "Not everyone's is so… easy to manipulate." He leaned toward her, close enough for Thorn to see the smooth pores on his perfect complexion and breathe in the second-hand smoke lingering on his blazer. He let out a hungry, little moan. "Mm. I *like* this."

With his right hand still gripped tightly behind her head, his left moved to her face. Thorn tried to turn away from him, but he grabbed her cheeks and pinched them together until he pried her jaw open. Horrified, too weak to do anything else, Thorn gasped as Amoretto slipped his middle and ring fingers deep into her mouth. He forced them back so far that his knuckles knocked against her teeth, and she choked on him.

"No biting," he teased.

Amoretto laughed as Thorn retched and coughed, furious tears stinging the corners of her eyes. She tried to slam her jaw shut and cut those fingers off right at the joint, but she couldn't. With a hoarse groan, Amoretto drew his hand back.

"Jesus," Lust murmured. He admired the glisten of her saliva on his fingertips, sliding it against his thumb. "You feel as good as I remember…"

He grabbed her face again, but this time, he crushed his lips against hers. Thorn closed her eyes as his tongue lurched into her mouth, tasting her, invading her sanctity and her sanity as he held her tight.

Decades-old memories, endless, interminable days of them, surged to the forefront of her mind—memories of Lust wrapped around her, beneath her, on top of her. She was haunted by nightmares of his nakedness, his sadism, and his absolute fucking *delight* in fighting with Wrath for control over Thorn's body while Thorn crumbled within herself, locked away and powerless to escape.

She was gagging now. He laughed against her mouth, and when he pulled away, he dragged her lower lip between his teeth. The skin broke. Sweet, metallic blood coated her tongue.

"Fun as this is," Amoretto said, his voice grinding and famished, "I know your Martyrs must be close… My job is to deliver you to Hunt, but that can wait. How about a change in *venue?* I'll take you someplace nice…"

Lust lifted Thorn from the chair until her legs dangled beneath her. The second her weight hit her feet, she collapsed. He let her, stepping back as her knees crashed onto the concrete pavers. She tried to catch herself, but that damned knife was still pierced through her wrist, and the moment she landed on it, searing pain sent her sprawling forward. The side of Thorn's face scraped against the ground.

"You can't even stand," Lust said. The excitement in his voice was sickeningly, terrifyingly thick. *'Fuck.* This is better than I ever imagined."

He grabbed her by her hair again and pulled her to her knees. Thorn reached for the satchel draped on the back of her chair, desperate to get her gun, but the leather slipped in her bloodied fingers, and the firearm tumbled uselessly to the ground. Then, Amoretto was dragging her away. People surrounded them: the waitress, the cooks, customers, joggers, and anyone else unlucky enough to be nearby. She stared at them, aghast, to realize their auras were faint and fuzzy—so hard to read that she hadn't felt their approach at all. They flickered in and out, there and gone again, until they disappeared entirely.

Lust yanked her through the back exit of the patio to an alley behind the restaurant, his Puppets walking around them like a mindless entourage. Thorn's knees scraped along the asphalt, and she tried to look around, but even that motion was dizzying. The space was barren: no pedestrians on the sidewalks, no lurkers in cloudy windows, no transients tucked behind trash cans… and no Martyrs. Without her things, her phone, the only tracking device she had, they'd never find her.

For a horrifying moment, Thorn thought about Alan,

Chris, *Darius*. Her eyes stung.

She tried to kick. To thrash. To do fucking *anything* other than be dragged into hell. But every motion was feeble, every attempt wasted. Thorn screamed again, but even her voice felt used up—

A gunshot blasted through the alley. The ladder from a fire escape swung down and caught Lust on the back of his skull. He swore as half of his Puppets collapsed. The Sin glanced back.

Another shot, and he flew forward. A bullet ripped through his hip and sent him sprawling to the ground. The rest of his Puppets dropped, and Thorn crashed onto the pavement with them. A third shot. Lust roared.

Thorn sat up. She *tried* to sit up, but she couldn't use her left arm, and the muscles in her right folded beneath her. She was vaguely aware of Connor Amoretto hobbling away and a pair of hands landing on her back, turning her around.

"Jesus Christ, Teagan!"

Her heart skipped a beat as she looked into a face she never thought she'd see again.

"Jay," Thorn moaned through a wince.

He knelt beside her, a blue ball cap crooked over his auburn hair. His eyes were wide, and when he propped her up, his hands shook. An open wound poured blood from the webbing between his thumb and forefinger, and Thorn recognized her gun abandoned on the asphalt by his knee.

"What the fuck is going on?" Jay asked. He looked at the unconscious men and women on the ground. "What happened to them? What happened to *you?*"

Jay grabbed for Thorn's injured wrist. She flinched away from him.

"Don't take it out!" she gasped.

He gawked at her. The color drained from his cheeks. "We've got to—"

"No!" Thorn cut in. Her face felt cold, and she was suddenly aware of how much blood she'd lost—how much she was still losing. Still, she shook her head. "I can't go to the hospital."

"Teagan," he started, but she shook her head again. This time, the spinning was too much, and she emptied the contents of her stomach—a gruesome mix of black coffee and bile. It stung the cut on her lip. A cut that hadn't healed. Jay steadied her. "Teagan, you're hurt."

"I need my phone," Thorn said. "My bag."

"It's at the table."

"Bring me back."

Thorn tried to stand, but the knife embedded in her *Peccostium* sent torrents of pain through her nervous system, and she fumbled to the ground.

"Teagan—"

"I said bring me back!" she screamed.

Jay draped her good arm around his shoulders, grabbed the gun, and hoisted her up. Thorn hobbled beside him, but she could hardly make sense of her own body. Waves of pain, of adrenaline, of shock rocked through her, and by the time Jay lowered her into the chair, her jaw was chattering. She tried to pull her phone from her bag, but it slipped from her grasp.

"Here," Jay said as he got it for her. His hands trembled, and he wiped his fingers on his windbreaker, smearing streaks of Thorn's blood over the Mercourier logo. "What's your passcode?"

"Zero nine one nine," Thorn groaned. She wrapped her fist tight around her forearm, just below the knife, and felt her pulse in her palm. "Go to my contacts. Call Chris Silver."

He did, and instead of putting the phone on speaker, he held it against Thorn's cheek. Chris answered immediately.

"We're almost there," she practically shouted. Thorn looked around the neighborhood. Lust's Influence had vanished with him, and people were starting to approach. Thorn couldn't sense them, and when she tried to push them away again, she found she didn't have the power. Her stomach swirled. "Holly said you were attacked. Was

Amoretto Programmed?”

"No," Thorn hissed. She felt weaker than ever now. And cold. Too cold. "It's worse."

"What the hell do you mean?"

"He's Lust," Thorn said, ignoring the confused look Jay threw her. "Lust is back."

CHAPTER TWENTY

Darius wanted to hurt Connor Amoretto.

This feeling wasn't very familiar to him. Darius could count on one hand the number of times he'd wanted to harm someone else this viscerally. Derek Dane, Terrance Moore, Max Douglas—Sins and a man so awful he may as well have been one—made up the whole list. He didn't know what to make of the violent urges coursing through his nervous system, so he crossed his arms to keep his clenched fists close to his chest.

The drop-down screen on the far wall played security footage from the attack, and Darius watched helplessly as Amoretto spilled coffee onto Thorn's hands, stabbed his knife into her wrist, and grabbed her hair. When he forced Thorn's mouth open and slid his fingers between her teeth, Mackenzie gasped.

"This is *fucked up*," she breathed.

Like Darius, she was standing. They were *all* standing. Mackenzie covered the lower part of her face behind bony knuckles and chipped nail polish as she cringed at the display. Beside her, Chris's spine was pin straight, and she looked up at the ceiling as a brush of tears glistened in her wide eyes. Nicholas gripped the back of the chair to Darius's left.

Thorn screamed soundlessly as Lust kissed her and tormented her and dragged her toward the lot next door until they couldn't see her anymore. That was the worst part—not knowing what was happening and not being there to stop it. Darius's chest swirled with painful fire.

Then, a man wearing a blue hat and jacket paused by the patio.

"That's the guy who helped her?" Darius asked, surprised at the tightness in his voice. He cleared his throat and looked at Alan. Alan didn't look back. He stood near the screen, a pillar of black. The rage pouring off him was so palpable that Darius felt it in his gut.

"Yes." His voice was even more constricted than Darius's, and his dark eyes sharpened on the film as the man in blue watched a handful of Puppets follow the Sin through the patio. Then he leapt over the fence, rushed to the table, and grabbed Thorn's gun from the ground beneath it.

"Who the hell is he?" Nicholas asked. "And how did he resist Lust's Influence?"

"He knows Thorn," Alan said stiffly. "Or, he knows her as Teagan Love. He must have recognized her belongings. That and the blood on the table gave him an agenda directly contrasted with Lust's attempt to drive people away. Lust is also with a new host. His power is weaker than it once was."

"Still," Nicholas said, shaking his head, "the guy's got to have some natural ability."

Alan threw him a hard look. "That's not unheard of."

"What was he even doing there?" Mackenzie asked.

"He was delivering a package in the area," Chris said. Her eyes remained glued to the part of the screen where Thorn had disappeared. The man headed that way, too, and Chris swallowed hard.

The room went quiet again as they watched the footage for another agonizing minute. The second the man carried Thorn back into view, a flood of relief washed through Darius's body. He sighed and ran a hand down his face, his stubble catching at his fingertips like sandpaper.

"Did you bring him back?" Nicholas asked. "Thorn's friend? If Lust got a good look at him, he's fucked."

"We tried, but he refused to get in the car," Chris answered.

"Can't really blame the guy…" Mackenzie muttered.

"I am going to have Miss Andrews track him down and monitor him for signs of Sin activity," Alan said. "Right now, we have more pressing concerns. Lust's repossession, for one."

He spun to face them, and his jaw ground together as he took a deep breath. "Carlos Ruiz, its previous host, was killed nine months ago."

Nicholas whistled. "That's a *really* fucking fast repossession."

"Maybe faster than you think," Alan said. All eyes shifted to him. All but Darius's. His attention was glued to Thorn. The man pulled his jacket off to drape it around her shaking shoulders, and though Darius couldn't hear what he said, it was clear that he was speaking softly. A glow of gratitude warmed Darius's chest. Thank god—*thank fucking god*—she'd had someone there.

"What do you mean?" Chris asked. Her voice dragged Darius back to the present.

"Miss Andrews has been looking into Connor Amoretto," Alan said. "Six months ago, he was promoted to oversee Mayor Bently's campaign, apparently passing over several candidates with more experience and resources than he had. Many of his competitors mysteriously exited the company, and since then, Amoretto has been distant from his closest friends and family."

"Are they distant?" Mackenzie asked with a frown. "Or dead?"

Alan's head turned toward her in a slow, grim circle. "His mother has been unaccounted for," he admitted.

While Mackenzie swore, Nicholas said, "Three months. You're telling me it only took Lust *three months* to rip this guy's soul apart and glue itself in?" He threw his hands up. "That's insane!"

"He must have been harmonious with the Sin before," Chris said. She thoughtfully traced her thumb along her chin, and her eyes wandered back to the screen behind Alan's head, where the footage now showed her pulling up. She and the man helped Thorn into the vehicle, and the display went black. Chris sighed and turned to Nicholas. "When a host is harmonious, the possession goes faster."

"But Lust isn't known for taking harmonious hosts," Nicholas argued. Mackenzie raised a brow, and he propped his hands on his hips, glaring at her. "That's right—I *have* read everything Lina documented about the Sins." Mackenzie's shoulders drew up at the mention of Lina's name, almost like a flinch. Nicholas kept talking as though he didn't notice. "Their possession habits follow clear patterns. Lust's whole thing is choosing attractive hosts with status and power. As far as I can see, the only thing Amoretto had was good looks and money."

"We need more information, to be sure," Alan agreed, "but we must also move forward with what we know now. Mr. Jones, contact Lamar Verrette and explain the situation. If he insists on staying in the city, against our best judgment, I want him well-informed."

"Of course," Darius said.

"Now that we know his identity, Lust is certain to seclude himself further to prevent us from easily attacking him," Alan went on, addressing the rest of the room again. "We should expect him to disappear, as both Autumn Hunt and Anton Claytor have. Once Thorn is well enough, we can discuss how to reallocate our Gray Unit in the search for him, but I would appreciate your research department's help, Mr. Wolfe."

"Absolutely," Nicholas said. His eyes flickered up to the blank screen, and his mouth began to curl.

"So…" Mackenzie began, anxiously shifting from foot to foot. "How is she?"

Alan paused before he answered—like he had to pause or else he would explode. "She's managing."

"That injury will affect her powers, won't it?" Nicholas asked.

"Yes," Alan said. "Until her *Peccostium* heals, all of her Sin abilities will be muted and unpredictable."

Chris's shoulders drew up. "How long will that take?"

"I am not sure," Alan said. "Elijah has repaired what he can, but if Thorn refuses to follow up and get her wounds cleaned, it could slow the process. I would estimate several days, at least."

"Why would she refuse?" Darius asked.

Alan glanced at him. "Thorn prefers to heal alone. I think that is truer now more than ever."

He fixed Darius with a long stare, and for a moment, Darius was reminded of Alan's Familiar. A wolf, a pack leader, fierce and protective. He crossed his arms and stared back.

Darius wanted to hurt Connor Amoretto, but more than that—more *important* than that—he wanted to see Thorn.

***

She was stranded on an island.

For years, decades, damn near a century, Thorn had ridden the waves of human corruption, constantly pulled by the ebb and flow of cold, mortal souls. For the most part, she coasted, but sometimes the waters were so turbulent and wild that they overwhelmed her, drowned her, and it took everything she had not to get sucked under the surface. All she ever wanted was to find her feet on dry land.

But she had never stopped to think of how lonely land would be, and now, she was hungry to dive back into the sea.

Thorn's room was tucked into one of the furthest corners of the Underground. She'd chosen this one specifically because it had always given her a little distance from the

Martyrs' chilly energy, but she had never felt *nothing* before. At this point in the evening, she would usually get a sense of Kenia cleaning up from dinner, of TAC units training in the gym, of people heading back toward their quarters. Not tonight. Tonight, the space outside was a void, just as empty and terrifying as the hole in her own soul.

Thorn took a deep breath and swallowed a lump that had grown in her throat. She had never felt so… powerless.

Sparkie wound himself more tightly around her shoulders, his wings and tail slipping beneath her swooping neckline to lay flat upon her skin. He nuzzled his head against the underside of her chin. She hadn't realized how tight her jaw was, and she forced it to relax as she looked down at her left hand lying across her lap.

Elijah had fixed her up and put her in a wrist brace the color of clean snow that stood out against her blood-red lounge pants. She turned her arm around, tilting the inside to the ceiling. Slowly, Thorn dragged her nails along the old acid scars pouring from the base of her bandages. Her own skin felt distant—like it was separate from her, like she was once again trapped in a body detached from her mind.

She clenched her fist and twisted her wrist. Sparkie winced as the movement tugged at the wound piercing through her *Peccostium*. Rivers of pain flowed so deep into her nervous system that it left her breathless. Numbness melted away on a wave of hot fire, and Thorn closed her eyes as she felt it climbing up from her stomach like bile. Connor Amoretto's face filled her mind.

"Fuck!"

Fuck Connor Amoretto. Fuck Lust. Fuck *this*—the hole in her arm, the disruption in her powers, *everything*. Thorn jumped to her feet and strode across the room, pulling her good hand through her hair. It caught on knots she couldn't easily brush out with her left so *fucking useless*, and she cursed that, too. When she caught a glimpse of herself in the standing mirror in the corner, she paused. A purple bruise lifted on her cheek, and her lower lip was tender and swollen. A red cut sliced through it, just off from the center. Thorn shook her head to push away thoughts of Lust's teeth tearing against her skin before she got sick again.

She was going to *fucking kill him.*

A sudden knock made Thorn jump. Sparkie arched on her shoulders, his wings flared as she glared at the door. Nothing. She sensed *fucking nothing,* but she had a good idea who was paying her a visit. Again.

"Go away, Harris!" she shouted.

A voice on the other side chuckled—a voice that absolutely did *not* belong to Elijah Harris. Sparkie's wings snapped back to his body as Thorn's stomach flipped, smothering the rage.

"Guess again," Darius said.

Thorn froze where she was and stared at the brass knob like she expected it to turn on its own. Darius knocked a second time, more gently now.

"Thorn?" he called through the wood.

Her bare feet felt heavy as she moved toward the door. She opened it just enough to peek her head through, and the second Darius saw her, he smiled. Then his eyes slid away from hers, traversing her face. When they settled on her lower lip, his smile faltered, and Thorn self-consciously pulled the swollen spot between her teeth.

"What are you doing here?" she asked.

He indicated a fabric tote hanging off his shoulder. "There's a rumor you won't let Dr. Harris clean your wounds."

Thorn raised a brow. "If I won't let Harris, what makes you think I'll let *you?*"

The smile came back. That damned, charming smile. "I figured I'd bribe you with the scotch and coffee night you asked about a couple of years ago…"

He pulled the bag around, reached inside, and clumsily drew out a liquor bottle and metal thermos. Thorn's mouth parted in gentle surprise.

"Plus," Darius added, "you like me more."

Sparkie perked up on Thorn's shoulder before sliding down the back of her shirt. Her heart skipped a beat, so she crossed her arms around it. "Debatable."

Darius laughed, but before the sound fully escaped his mouth, his expression went more serious. "Honestly," he said, putting the items back, "I needed to check in. What happened yesterday…"

He stopped, and his jaw snapped shut. The fire in Thorn's gut swirled to life as a hot flush spread across her cheeks.

"Look, Darius—"

"It never should have happened," Darius interrupted, finishing his thought, his eyes never breaking from hers. "Not to you or anyone else. Ever. I'm sorry."

Thorn's eyes stung, and for a moment, she couldn't speak. Instead, she opened the door a little wider to rest her shoulder against the frame and pinched the bridge of her nose, exhaling a shaky sigh. "I appreciate it, but I'm not great company right now."

"So?" Darius asked. Thorn frowned, and he shook his head. "I'm not here because I want you to pretend you're okay to make me feel better. I'm here because I care about you. If you'd rather be alone, though, I understand. Whatever you need."

A foreign emotion stuck in Thorn's chest, and her heart began to race. She *didn't* want to be alone, trapped in this dark, empty box.

But Darius… he was the last person she should let in right now. She couldn't keep walking this line. It was stupid and dangerous, and it was going to *hurt*…

A few quiet seconds passed between them before Darius nodded. "Okay. I'll leave this here. If you need anything, text me. I'm just a couple of left turns away."

If he was disappointed, it didn't show. He flashed Thorn a compassionate smile and set the tote on the ground by her door. As he turned around, Sparkie whined. His body vibrated between Thorn's shoulder blades with a low hum.

She bit the inside of her cheek.

"Wait."

Thorn reached for Darius. When he spun toward her, his shoulder pressed into her hand, and her fingers wrapped around him. She swallowed against a dry throat.

God, this was so fucking stupid.

"I'd love a scotch and coffee night."

Darius's green eyes practically glowed, and his mouth widened into a grin so pure that, for a moment, Thorn almost forgot what a horrible idea this was.

"You sure?" he asked.

She opened the door and rolled her eyes. "Get in here before I change my mind."

Darius grabbed the tote and walked over the threshold. As Thorn closed them inside, he put the bag on her dresser and started pulling things out: the alcohol, the coffee, two mugs, and a first aid kit. He set the last beside Thorn's box of gloves.

"Oh!" Darius snapped his fingers, reached into his front pocket, and pulled out a neat, folded bundle of black cloth. "I keep forgetting to give these back."

He handed the bundle to her, and she pulled it apart. The set of gloves she'd slipped into his jacket at the wedding. Thorn ran her fingers along the thick, protective fabric. Fire retardant. Cut resistant. You couldn't stab a blade through these. Not easily.

Her stomach swirled with fresh anger.

"Are you okay?" Darius asked.

"I'm fine," Thorn said. She tossed these gloves with the rest and reached for the scotch. "And before you ask, no, I haven't done that stupid grounding exercise, and I'm not going to."

He laughed as Thorn threw him a smirk and uncorked the bottle. Without thinking, she lifted it in her left hand, and the moment she twisted her wrist to pour a drink, pain shot through her body. Thorn gasped as the scotch slipped from her grip and thudded onto the dresser. Amber liquid gushed from its mouth, flooding the wood and soaking into Thorn's bandages as she barely managed to keep herself standing.

"God fucking *damn it,*" she snarled. Sparkie writhed beneath her shirt and pulled himself out by her neck with a hiss.

Darius scooped the bottle up almost as soon as it fell. He unzipped the medical bag, grabbed a roll of gauze, and threw it onto the spill.

"Leave it," Thorn said as she drew back to standing, but Darius took the scotch again, poured a healthy dose into one of the mugs, and pushed it into her good hand. He held it there, his skin warm and reassuring.

"Stop," he told her. "I've got this."

Darius didn't give her a chance to argue as he returned to the medical kit and found more gauze. While he sopped up the mess she'd made, Thorn threw the drink to the back of her throat. It burned more than usual, and she sucked in a breath through her teeth.

"There," Darius said. He tossed the trash into his tote. "No big deal."

A tide of indignation crashed against the liquor in Thorn's stomach.

"It *is* a big deal." She lifted the bottle again, with her good hand this time, and delicately poured herself another two fingers. It was slow and clumsy. "Amoretto *stabbed* me clean through the wrist, and now I'm so goddamned useless I can hardly get myself a scotch without falling to pieces."

Thorn lifted her mug with a wince, shook her head, and took a sip. Darius simply watched her.

"And to make matters worse," she went on, like the alcohol had opened her throat and loosened her tongue, "I ruined all the progress we made tracking Greed by letting it slip that we knew about his apartment. Cain's identity is *fucked* since Lust saw him at the stupid event I forced him to go to, and I have no idea if he got a good enough look at Jay to hunt him down, too."

Her fingers tightened against the ceramic, and she stared at them. The bandages were tinted off-white from the alcohol. A cord of shame wrapped around her chest, and Sparkie let out an aching cry before he vaulted across the room and tucked himself beneath her pillow. Thorn shook her head.

"I am such a fucking *idiot*."

She lifted the scotch back to her lips but didn't have it in her to take another drink. Her teeth clenched together, so she cleared her throat instead.

"You're not an idiot," Darius murmured.

"Taking off my glove was a stupid mistake."

"Thorn." Darius took her gently by the arm, guiding her to face him. "It's not *your* fault someone lied to you and hurt you."

"But I—"

"It doesn't matter," Darius cut in. Thorn's side table lamps cast him in dim light that warmed every expression he made, and when his eyes traveled around her face again, she marveled at their tenderness. "It doesn't matter what *you* did or didn't do. None of this is on you. It's on *him*."

For a moment, all Thorn could do was watch him, acutely aware of how close he was standing. When she finally offered a quiet nod, Darius seemed to realize it, too. He cleared his throat and stepped away. A shadow of his touch lingered on her bicep.

"What *is* on you, though, is scotch," he added. "Which is great because now that you've got alcohol on your bandages, you can't really avoid replacing them."

He threw her a smile, and Thorn glanced at her hand. She found enough humor in this to merit a smirk.

"I'll see Harris first thing in the morning."

"Or I can just do it now," Darius said. "I'm already here, and it's good practice for my medical training." His voice drifted off, but he didn't turn back to the first aid kit. Again, his focus fell to the cut on her lip. Thorn hid it behind her scotch as she took another sip. "But there's something I wanted to test first if you're up for it."

Her brows drew together. "What is it?"

Darius raised his hand between them. "Healing you."

Thorn's eyes went wide, and she stared at him for a second. The hole in her chest ached at the possibility—and at the idea of Darius's energy moving through her body and putting it back together again. It felt so… intimate. Dangerously intimate. Sparkie fidgeted under her pillow as Thorn said, "You think it will work?"

"Your powers are disrupted," Darius said. "Not mine. I thought it was worth a shot. We can start small." He indicated the swollen spot on her lip. "If you're comfortable with that."

Thorn hesitated. A flash of memory pulled her out of the room and back to that patio in East Harlem. The sharp sting of Lust's teeth against her mouth nauseated her. Darius's voice floated through the haze in her mind. It coaxed her back in a deep, warm hum.

"It's okay if you're not," he was saying. Her attention zeroed in on him, and her bedroom swirled into focus. "We don't have to do this."

Finally, Thorn found enough sense to string a few words together. "It's fine. What do I need to do?"

Darius smiled and took a step toward her. "Just relax."

He was incredibly gentle. First, his fingers brushed against her temple as he swept a lock of hair behind her ear to expose the scrape from where she'd hit the pavement. He tilted her head to consider it, his eyes narrow and compassionate. Then, those eyes followed the hollow beneath her cheekbone before landing on her mouth. Thorn's breath caught in her throat as he laid his fingertips on her skin, soft against the wound, while his thumb grazed her lower lip. Heat radiated from him, his touch so electric that Thorn felt it flush across her face. She sucked in a short, quiet gasp between her teeth.

He lingered for one second. Two. Three. And just when Thorn thought she couldn't handle it anymore, Darius sighed and pulled away. She longed to move with him, but she stood rooted to the spot.

"Damn," he murmured. "I was hoping that would work."

He turned back to her dresser, and Thorn drowned the chrysalises hatching in her stomach with the rest of her scotch.

"Well, we can still check on your wounds, anyway," Darius said. He got himself a cup of coffee before folding the medkit and tucking it under his arm. "Come here."

Thorn didn't have a proper seating area in her room, so Darius laid the pack open across her comforter and sat near the head of her bed. Thorn poured another drink, her hand less steady this time than the last as she filled her cup with two more ounces of scotch. She came back around as Darius placed his coffee on the nightstand. He hesitated. The photograph of Thorn and Donovan that he had uncovered at Teresa's house looked out at the room. Darius considered it for a long time, and Thorn considered him.

"Teresa took that photo," she said. "Right after Donovan got his scholarship approval for the San Francisco Art Institute. He had a full ride."

Darius frowned. "He was going to leave New York?" he asked. When Thorn only nodded, he shook his head. "What happened?"

"He asked Teresa to go with him."

An icy rush locked Thorn's jaw together, and she sat beside Darius, crossing her legs beneath her. Sparkie slithered out from her pillow to hide in her lap.

"She didn't want to?" Darius asked.

"She didn't know *what* she wanted," Thorn snapped. Then, she took a deep breath, closed her eyes, and absently tapped her thumb against her fingertips. When she opened them again, Darius was smiling. Thorn cleared her throat and went on. "She told him she needed time to think about it, so he put off leaving. Wrath caught him before Teresa got her shit together. You know the rest from there."

He was one of the *only* people who knew the rest. Thorn glanced down at the acid scars on her arm bitterly.

"You make it sound like he was in love with her," Darius said.

Thorn's chest tightened. "He was."

"But I thought Alan and Teresa were together—"

She interrupted him with a sharp laugh. "Yeah. For months. Maybe a year. I don't know. When I found out, I lost it. She wasn't just Donovan's friend. He had feelings for her, and even if she didn't return them, Alan never should have crossed that line. So he cut it off. He claimed it was never serious, but I saw how he looked at her. Either way, it didn't matter. He knew that he and Teresa wouldn't have worked in the end."

She brought her drink back to her lips and poured a splash over her tongue. Darius shook his head. "Why not?"

"Because Alan's a Forgotten Sin," Thorn said. A painful bubble burst between her lungs. "And Teresa was a Virtue. They were just... too different."

She glanced into her mug, watching her dark reflection in the amber liquid rather than face whatever she'd have to see in Darius's expression. Movement told her he made himself busy—shuffling through the medical kit, pulling things out, and laying them on the mattress. Sparkie wrapped into his wings like a leathery cocoon and tucked deeper into the gap between Thorn's legs.

"I don't know," Darius murmured after a moment. "Samira and Leroy made it work. Let me see your hand."

She placed her injured wrist in Darius's palm. He began loosening the grip on the brace. The release of pressure on Thorn's *Peccostium* sent a chill down her spine, and goosebumps rose along her arms.

"Samira and Leroy work because she destroyed Gluttony and made him mortal again," she said.

The brace popped open, and Darius peeled it away from the gauze beneath.

"So his immortality was the only thing that limited

them?" he asked.

Thorn shook her head. "Not the only thing, but the biggest."

"Hmm."

Darius delicately unwound layers of scotch-soaked bandages, holding Thorn's fingers to keep her wrist straight and supported while he worked. She waited for him to elaborate. When he didn't, she asked, "You think they would have made it if Leroy was still a Forgotten Sin?"

"Honestly," Darius said with a shrug, "I don't think my feelings about this matter very much."

"Why not?"

He chuckled—a sad, resigned sound. "Because I'm *not* immortal. I can't imagine what it would be like living in Leroy's shoes. Or Alan's. Or yours." Finally, his eyes moved up to her. "It's a hard choice to make, and the call on whether it's worth it or not isn't up to me."

Darius focused on her hand again, his grip just as tender and steady as he continued to unwind the wrap. He took his time. Thorn found herself wanting him to slow down further—to extend their contact, prolong their closeness, steal a few more precious minutes to touch her. Her cheeks stung with heat. She tried to wash it away with another sip of scotch.

Finally, he exposed her wrist. It looked like fucking hell. Her skin was a patchwork disaster of purple bruising peeking between thick, white scars. An inch-long cut tore almost right through the center of her *Peccostium*, just missing the bone, tendon, and major arteries beneath the surface. He gently turned her hand over, and Thorn winced as a jolt of pain shot down her body.

"Sorry," Darius murmured. "Jesus, it went all the way through…"

On the back of her arm, a smaller incision pierced the skin. Elijah had cinched both up with some kind of dermal glue, so there were no stitches, but the wounds were swollen and raised into hot, red mounds. Darius's expression flashed with an emotion Thorn knew all too well but not one she saw him wear often: anger.

"What's wrong?"

He shook his head. "It's nothing."

Thorn raised a brow, and Darius let out a sigh that turned into a scoff halfway from his mouth.

"I was just thinking about how much worse this could have been," he admitted.

The muscles shifted along his neck as he swallowed, and a pit opened in Thorn's stomach. His fingers tightened around hers, his thumb gently stroking her knuckles as he turned her *Peccostium* to the ceiling again. Gingerly, he swiped a saline towelette around it to clear a slick build-up of wound drainage. A chilling, bone-deep sensation tickled through Thorn's body, and she had to bite her lip to keep herself from gasping.

Darius didn't notice. He was so fixated on cleaning her injuries that Thorn doubted he saw much of anything else. His brows furrowed as he patted the area dry, sprayed her with an antibiotic, and began the same process on the opposite side. When that was done, he applied fresh gauze and grabbed a new bandage. All the while, Thorn sipped her scotch just to give her something safer to think about.

"So," Darius said as he started binding the wound again. His voice came out low and quiet. "How do you know Jay?"

A cold rush spilled over the top of Thorn's head. Darius glanced at her.

"That's what you called him, right?" he asked. Like when he unwrapped Thorn's wrist, he seemed to move in slow motion. Painfully, exquisitely slow. "The guy who helped you?"

"Yeah. He's..." Thorn shook her head, struggling for an answer she was happy with. Her mind felt heavy, and her chest constricted. "He's a name on that list Mackenzie's so interested in."

She swirled her scotch, considered the last mouthful at the base, and shot it to the back of her throat.

Darius nodded. "It's clear he cares about you."

"I don't know how much he cares," Thorn said. "We didn't exactly end on good terms."

Darius's mouth pulled into a soft smile that lit up his face and made Thorn wish her drink wasn't empty.

"He cares enough to see through Lust's Influence," he said as he returned to his work. Thorn's eyes dipped down to their hands. Hers looked so small, so delicate, inside of his. "Most people can't resist it. You must have left a better impression than you realized."

Darius reached the end of the bandage and awkwardly tucked the edge together before replacing the brace. When he let go of her at last, Thorn's fingers buzzed, like they were starving for contact.

"I'm really glad Jay was there for you when you needed someone," Darius said, his tone bittersweet, but he didn't look at her. Thorn watched him for a moment, aching at his disappointment. She tilted her head, catching his gaze before it collapsed entirely.

"I'm glad you're here for me now."

His eyes grew serious and ardent, like he could stare into the depths of her broken soul for the rest of eternity. Darius reached forward, wrapped his hands around hers, and *fuck*, Thorn couldn't help but envision those hands at work elsewhere. Her mind swam with disjointed thoughts that she shouldn't be having.

This had been a mistake.

"I need another drink," she murmured.

Thorn pulled away, and she moved to stand. Sparkie tumbled from her lap to a dazed heap on the carpet. The instant she was on her feet, her head rushed with dizzying movement.

Before Thorn knew what was happening, her nightstand was barreling toward her, past her, and her shoulder slammed into the wall. She tried to catch herself, but when she put weight on her injured wrist, a bolt of excruciating pain shot through her body. Then, she was reeling again, falling apart—

A pair of arms wrapped around her before she hit the ground.

"Thorn?" Darius pulled her back to standing, but he didn't let go. "What happened?"

Panic rattled Thorn's heart. She was thrown back to when Lust had first driven the blade through her *Peccostium*. She hadn't been able to focus, to *function*. The room spun now just as the patio had then, and Thorn felt unsafe in her own skin.

"I don't know," she said. Her words seemed to blend together. Thorn shook her head. That made it worse, so she jammed her eyes shut. "Something's wrong. Everything is spinning. I need to see Dr. Harris."

Darius laughed.

His deep, rich voice made Thorn open her eyes again. He was close. *So* close. His hands held tight against her back, like he knew if he let go she'd just crumble to the carpet. Suddenly, Thorn was hyper-aware of them splayed out beneath her shoulder blades—of the pressure from every single fingertip firm against her skin. Her body tingled at the touch.

"Oh my god," Darius said. Still laughing. Still close. "You're drunk!"

Warmth flushed across Thorn's cheeks and sank beneath the surface, flowing down her throat like a fourth shot of scotch. It settled in her chest, her stomach, and *lower…* until her legs felt weak beneath her. Her lips opened in a silent gasp.

"Oh, *fuck*," she breathed. "This is so bad."

Darius laughed again, and Thorn melted further—a wax candle lost to a single, burning flame. "It's not a big deal," he said. "It'll wear off."

No. It wouldn't. *Fuck.* Her pulse was racing, hands shaking, skin on fire wherever they touched. She was in too deep now, and Thorn didn't know how to get out of this kind of hell. Her fingers dug into Darius's shirt, wrapping up in the fabric. His heart pounded beneath her fists, his chest so warm that Thorn ached to press herself against it. But she couldn't. She shouldn't.

Then his smile faded. As Thorn swayed in his arms, listing side to side as though they were dancing, Darius looked at her the same goddamned way he had at the wedding—tender and wanting. He stilled her, palms smoothed along the curve of her spine, and Thorn drew an inch further into his embrace until her thigh grazed the inside of his leg. When she took a shuddering breath, her breasts brushed against him. The rest of the world spiraled, but not Darius. His face was sharp and in focus, his body an anchor keeping her from drifting off to sea. Bright eyes traced the details of her hair, her cheeks, her nose, before lingering on her barely open mouth. Darius tilted toward her. Thorn's heart caught in her throat.

He had to leave. She *had* to ask him to leave.

"Darius…" Thorn whispered.

And she leaned in. A breath away. He sighed against her face. Soft and sweet with a subtle note of warm coffee. She imagined the taste of him on her tongue—

Darius stepped back.

"I should go," he murmured, like it was the last thing he wanted to do. His hands moved to her shoulders, and he steadied her on her feet. Thorn felt the sharp sting of cold air against her open mouth as she stared at him. "You need to sleep this off. Without your accelerated healing, tomorrow is gonna be rough."

"Oh," Thorn said. Her voice felt small. *She* felt small. "Right."

He smiled. Tried to smile. It looked sad on his face. Then he gently guided her back to her bed and made sure she was sitting before he gathered the things he'd brought. The scotch. The coffee. The first aid supplies. Darius tossed it all into the tote without looking at her, but Thorn couldn't look at anything *but* him. Sparkie clumsily climbed onto the mattress just as Darius reached the door. He paused, and a hot flush of shame poured across Thorn's cheeks.

"Call me tomorrow?" Darius asked.

She nodded.

Then he left, and Thorn was on her island again. No energy. No sound. No life. She fell back with a groan and covered her face with her hands. Sparkie slithered onto her chest and laid flat against her sternum. Her mind swirled with thoughts and dreams and fantasies of things she couldn't have until it made her feel sick. Or maybe that was the scotch. She didn't fucking know anymore.

CHAPTER TWENTY-ONE

Thorn didn't call.

Not the next day, or the one after that, or any between the night Darius cleaned her wounds to the morning her *Peccostium* healed and her powers returned. Exactly one week after Lust had stabbed her, Thorn was back in the city.

Darius was staring at his phone when Skylar said, "I fold."

She sighed and tossed her cards to the center of the table. Alexis scooped a pile of poker chips up with a grin while Caleb laughed.

"All right," John groaned, dragging a hand down his face. "We've got to step it up. She's won four hands in a row!"

"I warned ya," Conrad called over their heads. He and Gabe were playing pool, and he pointed his cue stick at Alexis's back as she organized her winnings into massive towers of multicolored disks. "The woman's a shark."

"And John sucks at dealing," Skylar said.

John laughed. "Yeah? Let's see you do better." He collected the deck and slapped it onto the table in front of her. She smirked over the rim of her beer bottle before she grabbed the cards and started to shuffle. A few other

Martyrs lingered around the break room, watching the news on the massive TV mounted to the wall near the door or reading quietly in the corner. As Skylar began to deal, Darius glanced at his phone again.

"Everything okay?" Caleb asked.

The question caught the table's attention, and they all turned to Darius.

"Yeah," he said, turning off the screen, but not before Caleb spotted Thorn's name sitting at the top of it. For some reason, Darius felt guilty—of what, he wasn't sure, but he felt guilty all the same. "I was just checking in with Thorn."

Or he'd been hoping *she* would be checking in with *him*. Darius hadn't heard from Thorn at all since he'd texted her the morning after accidentally getting her drunk.

Ah. There it was. The guilt swirled with the memory of Thorn in his arms, her hands tangled up in his shirt, her whiskey breath warm on his face as she leaned so closely against him that he could have counted every lash fluttering around her eyes… if he'd been thinking about her eyes.

Darius swallowed hard and slipped his phone into his pocket.

"How's she doing?" Skylar asked as she finished passing cards around the table.

"Fine," Darius said. As far as he knew. When she'd responded to him, it was all she'd said.

Alexis scoffed across the table. "That's a stretch. The woman's fucking pissed."

"More pissed than when Sloth blew her up?" John asked.

"*Way* more," Caleb said.

"Let's just say I wouldn't want to be Lust right now," Alexis agreed. "Whatever he did, Rose is out for blood."

Darius's hands curled into fists on his lap, and he forced them open to pick up his cards. The two of hearts and queen of spades. He hardly registered them.

"Does anyone know what happened?" John asked. "Half of the details from the report Alan wrote up were redacted. All I gathered was that Amoretto stabbed her *Pec-costium*."

"Then that's all you need to know," Darius said tersely. John's eyes widened while Skylar and Alexis exchanged a dark, uncomfortable look. John opened his mouth like he was going to press further, but Skylar cut him off.

"I still can't believe Lust possessed so quickly," she said.

"Yeah, it's going to cause a lot of problems for us," Alexis agreed with a sigh.

She peeked at her cards and laid them flat on the table again as Skylar dealt the flop. The first two were useless, but on the third, she revealed the two of clubs. Darius glanced at his hand again.

John tossed a dollar chip into the center. "What kind of problems?"

"Well, he won't be as weak as we were expecting," Caleb said as Alexis matched the bet.

John frowned. "I thought they had to rebuild their power reserves after a new possession."

"Yes and no," Caleb said with a shrug as he, Darius, and Skylar threw their chips in, too. "The Sins' power comes from how far their Indirect Influence has spread. That's why the longer-lived hosts, like Autumn Hunt, are so much stronger than the others. That Influence starts to fade when they lose a host, but it doesn't just disappear all at once. It takes time. Since Lust was only non-corporeal for a couple of months, the battery of corruption it built wouldn't have had much time to peter out."

"Oh," John said. "Great. So we killed a Sin, and all we got for it was six months with our guard down."

Skylar flipped the next card. A queen of clubs. Darius's stomach twisted as he looked back at his hand and the two pair he had hidden in it.

"It's worse than just having our guard down," Skylar said. Caleb threw in a chip, and Darius raised him one. Skylar's brows shot high on her head as she and John folded. She leaned forward on the table. "Greed knows we found his apartment, so he's probably abandoned it. All the work we put into planting that tracking device was a total waste."

Alexis and Caleb went stiff in their seats, Alexis pressing her lips firmly shut in a frown. Darius realized she held her cards just as tightly as he did. He laid his flat on the table and stretched his fingers.

"I doubt we're focusing on Greed anymore anyway," he said. Alexis and Caleb both snapped toward him. "We have Lust, and we have Consent. It makes sense to change targets."

Alexis nodded as she matched Darius's bet. Caleb sighed and tossed his cards into the center. "Mulligan is still working on getting a good standing in Greed's circle," she said, "but Rose wants to focus on what Lust is up to, especially with Bently. I'm putting almost all my effort into the mayor now that two Sins have been seen dealing with him."

"You think he could be a pawn?" John asked.

"With Greed *and* Lust on his back?" Skylar asked. "He has to be." She flipped the last card—two of spades. Darius resisted looking at his hand as Skylar laughed. "Hey, if I'd stayed in, I'd have a pair of twos!"

Caleb groaned and grabbed his cards back from the center. "I'd have had a flush," he grumbled.

A sharp smile stretched across Alexis's face as she glanced up to Darius. "Your bet, Jones."

His hand hovered over his stack of chips—a meager collection next to the fortune Alexis had amassed—and he grabbed a couple of white disks from the pile.

"Two," he said as he tossed them in.

Alexis snatched up a red without hesitation and flipped it onto the pot.

"Raise."

Her smile widened, and Darius arched a brow.

"Call."

He matched, and she revealed the five of hearts and ten of diamonds in her hand, which lined up nicely with the five and ten of spades face up on the table.

"Two pair," she said.

Darius smirked and turned his cards over. "Full house."

The victory drained from Alexis's expression. Her jaw tightened into a forced smile as John let out a loud laugh. "About damn time!" He got to his feet, downed the rest of his beer, and dangled the empty bottle above the table while Darius collected the pot and Skylar grabbed the cards. "I'm getting another. Anyone else want one?"

Alexis and Skylar nodded, but Caleb looked at his watch and said, "I'm good. I've got to head back into the city in a half hour."

As John made his way to the minifridge behind the pool table, avoiding Gabe's eye, Skylar started to shuffle. "Now that we know Lust's new identity, are you back on his assignment?" she asked Caleb.

He shook his head. "No, I'm still on the Lamar Verrette case."

Darius's stomach dropped at the name. "What do you mean?"

"Well, we need to keep an eye on him since he decided to stay in New York," Caleb said with a shrug. "Holly is tracking his phone and has cameras on his apartment, but Thorn wants me to hang around the bar when he's on shift as an added security measure."

"Does he know you're a Martyr?" Darius asked. John returned to the table and handed off drinks to the girls. Alexis grabbed her bottle without a thank you.

"If he knew," she said, her tone carrying an impatient point, "it would defeat the whole point of using a Gray agent."

"Thorn doesn't want him to feel like he's being babysat," Caleb offered, "so I'm still undercover."

That didn't sit well with Darius, and he frowned as he glanced at his fresh hand.

"He's got to know we're going to be keeping tabs on him," John said. "Especially since the Sin he's set to go up against is back in the game. How'd he take the news about

Lust?"

"He doesn't know yet," Darius said. "I tried to reach out to him last week, but the earliest he could make time to hop on a call was right before he heads to work tonight."

"What's got him so busy?" Skylar asked.

"People," Caleb said. "He spends almost all his time with friends or family. He's never home."

Skylar whistled. "Maybe it's good that he didn't come to the Underground. He'd go insane down here."

A couple of warm energies approached the room, and Darius glanced over his shoulder as Kit limped through the door. Madison followed right behind him, and her bright eyes swept the Martyrs gathered. When they landed on Darius, she beamed.

"Hey!" she said as she came up behind him. Kit joined Gabe and Conrad at the pool table, nodding in Darius's direction as he walked by. The pair were clearly fresh off a patrol, Kit still wearing his tactical uniform, while Madison had removed her black turtleneck to reveal the white undershirt beneath it. She put a palm on Darius's shoulder. "How's it going?"

The question was directed at the table, and she looked around at the rest of them.

"Oh, you know," John said. "Just adjusting to life in the Underground with a new Sin on the loose. You back on regular duty shifts?"

"Yep," Madison said. Her grip around Darius tightened. "Now that our Virtue missions with this guy have wrapped up. I kinda miss it."

She leaned into Darius, and John threw him a quick look as he got to his feet.

"You should join us." He tapped Skylar's shoulder to get her to scoot her chair over. They all shuffled to make space. "You like beer?"

"Yes, thank you," Madison said. John made his way back to the fridge, and she finally let go of Darius to sit at his left. With six of them, the fit was tight, and Madison's knee pressed up against Darius's beneath the table. "So, what's the game?"

"Texas Hold'em," Skylar said. She dealt the top two cards to Madison as Caleb grabbed the case from the table behind them and started gathering chips for her. "Know how to play?"

"It's been years," Madison said. She pulled a length of dark, wavy hair behind her ear just as John returned with a bottle. He placed it on the table in front of her, and she smiled in appreciation.

"You'll pick it back up in no time," Skylar said. "It's pretty simple."

"But watch out," John said with a laugh as he sat back down. "Alexis is here to take all your money."

His blue eyes rolled in her direction, and Alexis's lip curled into a smirk. "Jones won the last hand."

"I got lucky," Darius said.

"I don't know," Madison said as she gestured to Alexis's chips. Her stacks towered above everyone else's like skyscrapers over Manhattan. "You seem like a natural! It must be in your blood."

Madison giggled, but the humor on Alexis's face dropped. Her icy eyes narrowed as she crossed her arms.

"What the hell's that supposed to mean?"

For a tense moment, the table sat in heavy quiet. Even Kit, Gabe, and Conrad looked their way, and Darius met Gabe's eye over Alexis's shoulder. It dawned on Madison a moment too late. Her face went bright pink as her jaw dropped open.

"Oh, god," she said. "I'm sorry! I was just saying that you're good at poker, that's all!"

Alexis tossed her cards into the middle of the table. "Right. I've got to go. Split my chips evenly. I wouldn't want anyone to be greedy..."

She got to her feet and stomped out of the room. On her way through the door, she ran right into Mackenzie, who swore and gawked as Alexis flew past her. Madison dipped her face into her hands with a groan.

"I'm sorry," Caleb murmured. His cheeks were a healthy shade of magenta, too, as he started quietly piling his sister's chips back into the case. "She's sensitive about the whole Greed thing…"

"I swear, that's *not* what I meant."

"I know," Caleb said. "Don't worry about it. I'll talk to her." He cleared his throat and glanced up as Mackenzie bounced to the pool table in the back. John tracked her, too. When she started talking to Gabe, his shoulders went rigid.

"I'm sure our focus on Greed hasn't been easy for either of you," Darius said.

Caleb clicked the case shut, and his chest opened in a sigh. "This year will be fourteen since he got possessed. I know we need to kill him. I just don't want to be the one to do it."

Skylar laid her cards down and took a sip of her beer. "Alexis doesn't see it that way?"

"She knows he needs to go," Caleb said, "but I think part of her has always hoped that he'd get out the way Mr. Blaine and Thorn did."

Madison frowned. "What about you?"

Caleb let out a sad, defeated laugh. "Let's just say that Alexis and I knew very different versions of our father."

With that, Caleb lifted his cards and hid behind them. Darius and Skylar exchanged a quiet look as they picked up their hands, too. John, however, was still looking over his shoulder at Mackenzie and Gabe.

"Any *big* plans tonight?" the Irishwoman asked as she leaned a hip against the pool table and tilted her head in Gabe's direction. Conrad and Kit stood to the side, watching her like they had front-row seats to a sold-out Broadway show. "You're off, right?"

"I am," Gabe said. He chalked the tip of his cue. "Why? Did you want to grab dinner, McKay?"

Skylar dealt the flop, and the rest of the table focused on their cards, but John's attention was fixated on the conversation behind him.

"No," Mackenzie said, waving the comment away as Gabe grinned at Conrad and Kit. Conrad laughed and spat a wad of chew into a water bottle. "Hate to break it to you, DuPont, but you're not my type."

She winked, and Gabe lined up to take a shot. "You don't go out with TAC guys?"

"Nah," Mackenzie said. "I just like my men *unattached.*"

She playfully bit her tongue, the piercing glinting silver against her teeth. Gabe was as stone-faced as ever as he masterfully landed a ball in the side pocket.

"Generally a good rule," he said as he stood up straight again and cast Mackenzie a coy look with those amber eyes. She crossed her arms and pouted in an amused glare.

"John," Darius said. John glanced back at the table, and Darius dipped his chin toward the cards. "It's your bet."

"Right."

John threw a chip onto the pot without looking at his hand. Mackenzie's voice filtered over their heads again.

"Chris has the night off, too."

"Does she?" Gabe asked as he moved around the table to line up another shot.

"Pretty sure you make the schedules," Mackenzie pressed. "That's part of the assistant director's job, isn't it?" Gabe paused, a frown finally settling over his face, and her smile widened. "Convenient that you two—"

"Jesus, Mackenzie," John suddenly exclaimed. He slammed a fist down on the table, making the pile of chips rattle, as he spun in his chair. "Will you just drop it?"

She gawked at him. The lights in the rec room made her cheekbones stand out, and deep shadows filled the hollow space beneath them all the way to her jaw. Darius frowned. Mackenzie looked thinner, her skinny jeans loose around her hips as she propped her hands upon them.

"What?" she said at last.

"Here." John got to his feet, pulled out his wallet, and drew out a ten. "Take it. You won, okay?"

He waved the money in front of Mackenzie's face, but she shoved it away. Darius stood, and Gabe caught his eye over John's shoulder as he put his cue stick on the table.

"The fuck is wrong with you?" she snapped.

"Your stupid *bet* is what's wrong with me," he said. "I can't believe you're still on this!"

Mackenzie scoffed. "Jesus, get over yourself! This isn't 'my' bet! You were all the fuck in until your ex-girlfriend came into the picture!"

"Oh my god!" John ran his fingers through his hair, pulling the black strands into a mess.

Gabe stepped around the table to stand between him and Mackenzie. "Come on, you two. Let's calm down."

John's eyes snapped toward him, and his shoulders raised in a long, slow breath. "Just tell her."

The whole room was watching now. At first, Gabe stood just as frozen and shocked as everyone else. He looked from John to Mackenzie and back again.

"John…" Gabe began, but John shook his head.

"I know, okay? We *all* know." He waved an arm behind him to indicate the rest of the Martyrs. "Just tell her so she'll leave it the hell alone."

Gabe's jaw set, and he glanced at Mackenzie before considering John again. "This wasn't how we wanted to let you know, man. I'm sorry."

He didn't speak loudly, but his deep voice rumbled through the room with enough power that everyone heard it. Conrad's jaw dropped, and he slapped the back of his hand against Kit's gut as a quiet rustle hushed around the Martyrs. Skylar closed her eyes and wrinkled the bridge of her nose, and Mackenzie's lips threatened to grin—until she turned back to John and saw the broken look on his face. He tossed the ten dollars on the pool table in front of her.

"Congratulations."

Without another word, John walked away, pushing through lingering Martyrs as he headed into the courtyard. As soon as he was gone, all eyes in the room turned on

Mackenzie. Her heart-shaped face lit up bright red beneath her navy hair. She muttered something under her breath, picked up the money, and shoved it into Kit's hands. Then, the two of them disappeared, too.

"I guess this is as good a time as any to call it quits," Caleb murmured as he started sorting his chips and putting them away. He watched the door after Mackenzie, his mouth pulled into a somber curve.

"Yeah," Skylar agreed. Behind her, Gabe put his cue back on the rack. When he hurried out of the room, she shook her head. "It's never going to be easy down here, is it?"

Darius let out a sigh as he tossed his cards to her.

"So, you're saying Chastity never existed?" Lamar asked.

"Right," Darius said as he leaned toward his computer screen. For the last several minutes, Darius had filled Lamar in on everything they knew about Chastity and Consent, from the appearance of the Virtue in Pope Gregory's texts to the Sins' known influence over the Catholic Church and their teachings. Lamar listened with polite attention as Darius spoke. "It's been Consent the whole time. We think the Sins spread the lie about the Virtue's real identity to erase it from history."

Lamar nodded. The high-tech headphones over his ears pressed his locs to his forehead. "That makes sense. The whole idea of purity and virginity is a social construct, anyway. If the Virtue isn't really about sex, does that mean the Sin isn't, either?"

"Yes and no," Darius said. "Lust uses sex as a weapon for power and control. Look at sexual assault. It's not a crime of sex itself… it's a crime of violence."

Images from the security feed outside the restaurant surged through Darius's mind. It was enough to make his chest light up, and he soothed it with a deep breath.

A similar mood settled over Lamar. His expression hardened, and his shoulders drew up. The young Virtue's back was to his bedroom window, and bright light surrounded him in an orange halo. "I can tell you one thing. It will be a *privilege* to take that monster down," he said. "What happens next?"

"We're working on that," Darius said. "We just identified Lust's new host, so now we'll start planning a strike that can get you close enough to destroy him."

"Sounds dangerous."

Darius's mouth lifted into a humorless smile. "It will be."

"I'll trust you to keep me alive, then," Lamar said with a wink. "All I've got to do is touch the mark thing?" He held up his wrist to indicate where Thorn's had manifested.

"The *Peccostium*," Darius said, "and it's a little more complicated than that. There's a mindset element at play, too."

"Mindset?"

"Here." Darius navigated briefly away from the camera feed and opened his server. "I'm sending you the report one of my colleagues wrote on how Virtues eliminate the Sins." After going through a series of complicated security measures Holly put in place to encrypt their data, he pushed the file through and switched back to the video. Bright, white light flashed against Lamar's face as he opened the document. Darius went on. "She was our top researcher. This probably has way more detail than you actually need."

"I don't like how you used the word 'was,'" Lamar murmured. Darius's smile faded, and Lamar's dark eyes flicked right to left for a few quiet minutes as he read. At last, he nodded. "Seems simple enough. So, Lust—you said you found its new host?"

"Yes." Darius made his way to the server again. "His name is Connor Amoretto."

"I'm sorry," Lamar cut in. "Who?"

"Connor Amoretto. I'll send you the file on him, too. We think his possession was completed about three months ago. That means he's still in the early stages, and, theoretically, he'll be easier to take down."

When Darius came back to the call window, Lamar's attention was locked onto his screen, eyes wide like he was staring down the barrel of a gun. Darius frowned.

"Lamar? You good?" he asked.

"Huh?" Lamar looked back at him at last, and he shook his head. "Oh, yeah. What… uh, when do you think you'll be going after him?"

"As soon as possible," Darius said.

Lamar's jaw clenched, and he wrapped his arms around his chest. "I see…"

"Thorn and her team are working on gathering intel right now," Darius said. "I know you're ready to help, but to be honest, it could take months to put a realistic plan in place. Maybe years."

"Sure," Lamar said, but his eyes were focused distantly above his screen.

Darius leaned closer. "Are you sure you're okay?"

"Oh yeah," Lamar said, shaking his head again. His blue fingernails scratched against the marker on his forearm. "Yeah, I just have to get ready for work."

"Right," Darius said, but he wasn't convinced. "Well, if you have any questions, you know how to reach me. Let me know if anything comes up."

"Of course," Lamar said. "I'll talk to you later."

"Talk to you—"

Lamar disconnected the call before Darius was done saying goodbye, and he was left looking at his reflection on a black screen. For a moment, he considered calling back to make sure Lamar was really okay, but he decided against it. Instead, Darius pulled out his phone and typed a message to Thorn.

"Talked to Lamar and got him up to speed. How's everything going?"

He stared at the message. The photograph at the top of her chat made his stomach twist with that old, familiar guilt again. He hit send.

For the next few hours, Darius worked in his office, digging through the latest batch of new Virtue leads that Nicholas's team had put together. The buzz of activity on the upper level of the Underground slowly fizzled as evening crept in. Researchers dwindled to nothing, the hospital cleared out, and soon, Darius was almost alone. The only energy keeping him company belonged to Chris and Gabe, tucked into the office beside his, undoubtedly discussing what had happened in the rec room earlier that afternoon. Part of Darius wanted to check in with them, but he knew this wasn't his place. When they finally left, he tracked their auras as they walked by his door. Then, he checked his phone. Again.

He'd been doing that a lot, turning on his screen just to find it empty. Thorn never responded to him, and by the time 9:00 rolled around, Darius resigned himself to the fact that she didn't want to talk right now. He couldn't blame her.

With a sigh, Darius shut his computer down, made his way out, and locked the room behind him. As he did, the door to the lounge between Alan and Thorn's offices swung open. Darius spun, his heart in his throat.

Alan stepped into the hallway. For an awkward second, they stared at each other. Finally, Alan glanced at his watch.

"You're working late this evening."

"Yeah," Darius replied. They headed down the hallway together. "I had a call with Lamar to fill him in on everything that's been going on."

"Is he managing well?"

"He seemed a little nervous," Darius admitted, "but that's not surprising. It's a lot to handle."

Alan nodded, but it was a short, stiff motion. "I trust you are impressing the importance of joining the Underground? Thorn should not have given him the option to stay behind."

"No, I haven't," Darius said. "And I don't plan to. I

think Thorn made the right call."

"Oh?" Alan's eyes flashed toward him. "How so?"

"Lamar's got a whole community out there," Darius answered. "Friends. Family. People he really cares about."

Alan's jaw tightened. "People he is putting at risk by simply existing alongside them."

"How is that any different than the Underground?" Darius asked as they reached the waiting room. Alan headed toward the elevator, but Darius slowed for a beat as he looked out the glass doors to where Thorn parked her motorcycle. Empty. His stomach filled with disappointment, and he shook his head. "This war puts the people we love at risk every single day, and we hardly have a life outside of it. It consumes everything we do."

When he turned back, Alan was staring at him, spine rigidly straight. "It is *war*," Alan said. "And war is all-consuming."

"But does it have to be?"

"In my experience?" Alan's tone darkened. "Yes."

They reached the elevator, and Alan pressed the button to call the lift. The engine whirred behind the concrete wall.

"I don't know," Darius murmured. "I've spent a lot of time with people who had nothing left but the fight to survive, and do you know what I saw when I looked at them?" He glanced at Alan, who shook his head. "They were… empty. Like ghosts moving through their old routines without realizing they were already dead."

The door opened, but Alan did not immediately get on. A staticky flicker of anger charged the air around him. "Is this what you think the Martyrs have become? Mr. Jones, I have been running this organization for over a century—"

"So?" Darius cut in. He moved past Alan and held an arm out to keep the elevator from closing behind him. Alan did not follow, resigned to glare from where he stood. Darius sighed. "Look, no one can argue that you haven't kept the Martyrs going through some insane shit, but can you really say they've been thriving? That people were *happy*?

There's been a huge shift in this place, and it isn't because we kept doing the same thing you've done for a hundred years. Abraham started organizing meals that pulled everyone together, Chris's tactical classes broke down the divides between departments, and now, Cain has given people passions to explore *outside* of this war. Are you coming or not?"

Darius gestured his head into the elevator. Alan's shoulders drew up, but he did finally step over the threshold. The doors slid silently into place, and as the floor jostled its descent, Darius shrugged. "I'm just saying that things are changing. That's all."

"Change is not always good," Alan countered. "We cannot afford distractions."

"Maybe we can't afford to *not* have distractions," Darius argued. His thoughts drifted to Thorn, somewhere in New York City. She would rather hunt Lust down than talk to him about what had happened the other night. What hadn't happened. *Couldn't* happen. His chest twinged. "Otherwise, we'll get so caught up in fighting that we lose ourselves in the process—lose sight of what makes us human. I think that's worse than dying."

Alan's head snapped around, and he fixed Darius with a cold stare. His black irises contracted, and his lips tightened against his teeth. Before he had the chance to speak, Darius's phone beeped. They watched each other for an awkward moment until Darius drew the device from his pocket. Alan's attention flickered toward the screen, but Darius tilted it so he couldn't see the name at the top. He scanned the message, and his heart plummeted.

The elevator slipped open, revealing a dark, quiet courtyard, but Darius's legs wouldn't move beneath him. He was vaguely aware of Alan lingering at his shoulder.

"What's wrong?" Alan asked.

Darius shook his head. "It's Lamar," he murmured. "He's done."

"Excuse me?"

"He changed his mind," Darius said, passing his phone

to Alan so he could read the text, too. "He doesn't want anything to do with the Martyrs."

CHAPTER TWENTY-TWO

"Talked to Lamar and got him up to speed. How's everything going?"

Thorn stared at her phone, and her heart jolted like it had touched a live wire. Her mind suddenly spun with a flurry of drunken memories. She raised her glass to her mouth, lips brushing it like a tentative first kiss, and *fuck*, the scent of scotch just made the memories stronger. Thorn practically heard Darius's voice, practically felt the delicate tremor of it in her chest. Goosebumps prickled along her arms and up the back of her neck.

Then the tone of that voice changed, and she realized it was coming from in front of her.

"You all right?" the bartender asked. This early in the evening, just after five p.m., there were only a handful of people in the room, and Thorn was the only one sitting at the counter. She glanced up, and the man gestured at her screen with his chin. "Looked like I lost you there for a minute."

"I'm fine." She slipped her phone into her satchel, where she could continue to pretend it—and the messages on it—didn't exist. Then, she cleared her throat, set her scotch down, and leaned in. "What can you tell me about *this* man?"

Thorn slid a printout of Connor Amoretto across the marble. Looking at him again—those bright eyes, deep dimples, and sharp smile—made her stomach fill with fire, which seemed to come all too easily lately. Between the disruption of her powers and dealing with her first hangover in over a hundred years, Thorn was aching for an outlet, and she wanted that outlet to be Amoretto's face. While she was recovering, she and Nicholas had collected everything his team could find out about him: where he lived, who he knew, and what the fuck he did with his time when he wasn't at Crave Media or out assaulting women.

The bartender lifted the photograph. He wasn't the kind of bartender Thorn was used to, but this wasn't the kind of bar she frequented. He'd gelled his hair back and wore a tight-fitting uniform that accented the broadness of his shoulders. Before he answered, he glanced at her with a frown. "Who'd you say you were again?"

"Evelyn Dawson," Thorn said. A twinge of loss made her stomach feel empty. She hadn't called herself Teagan Love for months, but for some stupid reason, she missed the name. More than that—she missed the *life*. Giving up Teagan had meant giving up so much more than just a title. Her old routines. Her old contacts. Her old hangouts.

The name also reminded her of Mackenzie, and fuck, Thorn missed her, too.

"And why do you want to know about this guy?" the bartender asked.

"I'm a private investigator."

"Really?" His eyes went wide as he looked over the picture. "What'd he do?"

"I'm not at liberty to discuss that," Thorn said.

The bartender raised a brow before he shrugged and handed the printout back. "I haven't seen him in a couple of months, but he used to come in every weekend."

Thorn knew that, which was the only goddamned reason she was here in the first place. Nicholas's research had proven that Connor Amoretto lived a pretty lavish lifestyle for a thirty-four-year-old in Lower Manhattan. He'd sublet a luxury loft in Tribeca, worked out three times a week at a boutique gym down the street from his apartment, and regularly visited dozens of high-end establishments in the area. This was one of them.

"What did he do when he came in?" Thorn asked.

The man laughed. "What does any guy like that do when he comes into a bar on a Saturday night?"

Her mouth stretched into a forced smile. "Humor me."

"Let's just say he was a legend around here."

"Legend? What do you mean?"

"I mean, the guy picked up someone new almost every time he walked in that door." The bartender jutted his chin toward the exit behind Thorn's back. "And every one of them was gorgeous. He only nailed straight tens."

Thorn's jaw clenched, and she consciously worked to loosen it. "Did any of the women seem like they weren't into it? Coerced or maybe drugged?"

"Women?" He laughed. "Sweetheart, I saw him bag just as many guys as he did girls. Like I said, he was a legend. We used to make bets on who he'd take home." His eyes wandered down Thorn's body. "If he were here tonight, my money'd be on you."

Thorn's knuckles twitched, and she curled her fingers into a fist around her glass. "You would lose."

The bartender flashed a disgusting grin. "He had a way of getting what he wanted."

And suddenly, Thorn felt Amoretto's hand in her hair and his fingers in her mouth. She raised her scotch and poured the whole damned thing over her tongue to burn the sensation off it. Her throat tightened around the alcohol, and a tickle shivered down her spine. In the mirror behind the bar, she caught a man staring at her from the corner of the room. The second their eyes met, he looked into his pint glass. A ripple of worry made Thorn uneasy. She rose to her feet.

"If he shows up again, call me."

The bartender's smile flickered, but Thorn didn't give him the chance to respond. She tossed a card onto the table, threw her bike jacket around her shoulders, and walked out the door. The man in the corner tracked her movement until she stepped onto the street. The second fresh air hit her face, she closed her eyes and lifted her head toward the sky.

God damn Connor Amoretto and every sleazy bar he'd ever set foot in. She hated the way her heart raced now at any stray glance thrown her way. Her nerves flickered with a vengeful fire.

The next time she saw Lust, she wouldn't be so easy to manipulate.

Thorn started walking north. Early April had been warm and crisp, but as the sun dropped behind buildings and a front of dark clouds rolled in, a chill settled over New York City. She pulled her phone out of her satchel. A list of all Connor Amoretto's favorite hangouts populated the screen.

It had taken Thorn less than eight hours to visit the majority of them, and all she had to show for it was more disdain for the man than she'd started with—which in and of itself was a fucking accomplishment.

On paper, Connor Amoretto looked like a poster child for success, but that "success" was nothing more than gold paint on a rotten legacy. Born into wealth with a mommy and daddy who couldn't say no, he'd developed a history of petty problems as a teenager—bullying, theft, and a couple of cases of inappropriate conduct with other students—which Papa Amoretto swept under the rug with fat donations to his private school and connections to every judge on the circuit.

Those connections also set Amoretto up as an adult. He was involved with dozens of resource groups for up-and-coming young professionals in Manhattan and attended weekly meetings with business incubators in the Financial District. A couple of years ago, he'd even been involved in a Big Brother program at New York University as a mentor for young journalism students looking to get career experience. Even though that had come to an end in 2089, well before he'd been possessed, the thought made Thorn shiver.

She'd called his supervisors, visited his partners, and connected with anyone he'd ever worked with. Everywhere she went, she got the same goddamned answer the bartender had given her: no one had seen the man in months. It seemed that once Lust had taken control, it did what the Sins always did: grown the host's power, collected its assets, and cut it off from the things and people it loved most.

Fuck, she wished they'd looked more into Amoretto when he'd approached her at Bently's event. The signs were right there, and it had taken getting stabbed through the *Peccostium* to see them.

A furious monster rumbled in her stomach, and Thorn scrolled to the next stop on her list. Another bar. God, this fucker clearly had too much time on his hands. The shot of scotch she'd had settled like lead, and the last thing she wanted to do was walk into another room like the one she'd just left. She ached for normalcy. What she wouldn't give for a chance to visit The Cross again, to surround herself with familiar faces and safe spaces, but that door was locked behind her now, and she could never open it again. Thorn drew in a deep breath.

Her phone rang in her palm. Jay Coons's name flashed up from the screen, and Thorn's heart leapt. Speak of the devil.

For a moment, she hesitated. Even though Holly had been tracking him and found no evidence that the Sins were looking for him, part of Thorn was relieved to know he was okay. She was tempted to answer, but dragging the poor guy any further into this mess was selfish and ugly, and Thorn was so damned sick of being that person. Instead, she canceled the call. Seconds later, a voicemail notification blipped at her, followed immediately by a text.

Thorn deleted both without looking at them and blocked Jay's number. Like pulling out a knife. Swift and sharp, but at least it was over.

With a sigh, she silenced her device and shoved it back into her satchel. Sparkie flew in wide circles over her head, and together, they started on the rest of her list.

Four hours, ten stops, and countless disappointments later, Thorn sat on her motorcycle and ran her hands down her face. Nothing, not so much as a fucking *whisper,* about what the hell Connor Amoretto had been up to in the months since his possession.

"Fuck," Thorn breathed into the night.

A sprinkling of rain began to fall. Misty droplets made their way between high-rises and towers, settling onto her shoulders like liquid dust as Thorn tied her hair back and pulled on her helmet. When she engaged the engine, she checked the notifications on the digital dash and paused.

Four missed calls. One from Darius and the rest from Alan. Old panic thickened in her lungs as she tapped the icon. The speakers in her ears began to ring.

"Thorn," Alan answered calmly—too damned calmly for someone who had just tried to contact her three times in a row.

"What's going on?"

A pause. "Mr. Verrette has ended his relationship with the Martyrs."

Thorn froze, so caught off guard by what Alan said that she was convinced she'd misheard him. She shook her head. "He *what?*"

"He wants nothing to do with us," Alan clarified. His tone was short, almost condescending, like he wanted to say, "I told you so," but he knew Thorn would tear him to shreds for even thinking it. "He sent Darius a message saying as much and then promptly blocked his number and has ignored all other attempts to reach him."

The annoyance in Thorn's chest turned to doubt. "The Sins must have found him."

"If they were involved, we would not hear from him at all," Alan said. "He would simply show up dead."

Thorn swore under her breath. "Well, did he say *why?*"

"No. Darius and his team are going to The Eros Project to try to determine that."

"When?"

"Tonight."

Suddenly, Darius's voice came through, quiet and distant, as he spoke to Alan from across the room. "If Thorn can't make it, I'll have Chris assign a different security detail."

Thorn's heart caught in her chest. "I'll be there," she snapped. Before Alan had the chance to respond, she hung up, threw her motorcycle into gear, and zipped off toward Hell's Kitchen.

Darius's stomach was in knots the whole drive to New York City.

More than a block before they pulled up to the corner of 10th and 49th, Lamar's Virtue sprung to life. The force of it tugged on Darius's core, and he stared at the lit-up sign above The Eros Project with a tight jaw. Now that Lamar had accepted Consent, he'd know Darius was coming. There was no going back now.

"Good thing the line is short," Madison said cheerfully as Mackenzie hopped onto the curb and Kit lumbered after her. Up the street, a few people huddled outside the club in a feeble attempt to stay dry in the drizzle falling from above.

"Not short enough," Mackenzie grumbled. She was already shivering beneath a bulky denim jacket that seemed to do little to keep her warm. Her eyes looked restless and glassy as she glanced toward the venue.

"I'll shoot you a message when we're good to go," Kit said as he leaned into the car and tilted his head at Madison. "Should be quick."

"Sounds good. See you in a bit."

Kit shut the door, thumping his hand on the frame twice

to say goodbye before he and Mackenzie hustled off to The Eros Project. Darius peered through the passenger window as they passed by.

"You okay?" Madison asked, her voice soft and concerned. "If you need to talk, I'm here…"

Darius sighed. "I'm just trying to figure out how I'm going to manage this."

Madison drove to the same lot they used every other time they came down and parked along the fence. "I'm not too worried." She shut off the engine, turned to him, and reached out to touch his forearm. "Everything's going to work out. You'll see."

She smiled, and Darius took a deep breath as he tucked his pistol into the holster at the small of his back and got out of the car. Thorn's motorcycle was two spots away, beads of water glistening off its paint like dark pearls on black satin. He looked around, hoping for a glimpse of her, but the lot was empty. Maybe she was already talking to Lamar.

At this point, he didn't know who he was more nervous to see… or who would be more nervous to see *him*.

He and Madison made their way through Hell's Kitchen in silence. The rain fell in a light, steady stream—enough to dampen Darius's hair and shoulders without chilling him to the bone. When they reached 49th, a chill rushed down his spine anyway.

Thorn leaned against the wall halfway between them and The Eros Project. She blended into the shadows beneath a blue awning, her arms crossed, face fixed in their direction as she watched them approach without moving to meet them. There was a nervousness to her, like a smoker gone out for a break only to find her pack of cigarettes empty.

As soon as she was within earshot, Darius swallowed his nerves and said, "I hope we didn't pull you away from anything important."

They hurried under the awning as Thorn pushed off the wall. She shook her head—the smallest of motions.

"Nothing is more important than this."

Thorn's focus lingered on Darius just long enough for his breath to catch. Then, she turned to Madison. "I've secured the neighborhood. What's the status of your team?"

"Mackenzie and Kit are at each exit," Madison said. When she spoke, her spine stiffened, and even though she wore casual clothing, Darius spotted the police training in her stance. "And one of your guys is providing additional security at the bar with eyes on Verrette."

"Caleb Claytor," Thorn confirmed.

"Yes, ma'am."

The corner of Thorn's lip twitched at the title, but she didn't comment on it. "They did their rounds?"

"Kit texted that the coast was clear."

"Good." Thorn spun around and walked toward The Eros Project. A soft layer of water quickly misted the crown of her head, making her sparkle beneath the city lights. "So, what happened?"

Darius laid it all out, from his conversation with Lamar to the text he received hours later. He passed his phone to Thorn, and she read it with a frown as they stopped at the back of the line. It was sparser than Darius had ever seen, in part because fewer people wanted to brave the rain but also because they'd arrived at a quarter past ten on a Wednesday night. Thorn's eyes narrowed.

"This is a huge shift," she said as she handed the device back to Darius. Their fingertips brushed in the exchange, and Thorn quickly drew her arms back to their safe space around her chest. "He was fine when you talked?"

"Seemed like it," Darius said with a shrug, "but when I brought up Lust, he got a little quiet."

Thorn's lips pressed together, and her nails dug into the kevlar jacket on her bicep. Madison pulled a strand of hair behind her ear and glanced between Thorn and Darius before settling on him. "Maybe hearing that it's got a new host made the whole thing too real for him," she offered.

"We won't know until we talk to him," Thorn said. The

line shuffled forward, and they stepped along with it.

"*If* we talk to him," Darius said. Lamar's Virtue was still in the bar below the building, but the sensation of it moved with a jittery energy Darius hadn't felt in the man before. "He might not be willing to see us."

"We'll worry about that later," Thorn said. "Talking to Verrette is the second problem we have to handle tonight."

Madison frowned. "What's the first?"

A slender brow arched on Thorn's head. "They might not let us in. Things didn't exactly go according to plan the last time you were here."

Darius groaned, and Max Douglas's cakey face filled his thoughts. His knuckles ached at the memory of smashing against the man's nose. He flexed his fingers, and Madison's traced up his arm like she was trying to comfort him… or herself.

"What are we supposed to do if they turn us away?" she asked.

"That's up to Jones," Thorn said. "He's the one with the magic touch." Her eyes flashed to where Madison's palm had managed to find itself pressed against Darius's chest. He shoved his hands into his pockets, stepping away from her, but she didn't pull back.

"You want me to Influence us in," he said.

"If that's what it takes." Thorn's voice matched the weather: crisp and cold. She looked up to where the bouncer, Mickey, was letting a group of damp girls into the building. "Think you can handle it?"

Darius frowned. "I've come a long way since Spokane."

Thorn cast him a quick glance, and the hard lines in her jaw softened. "You have," she agreed. "Let's go."

Mickey hid beneath a heavy, black umbrella, and his long, orange hair was pulled behind his head to keep it out of the rain. Darius drew a deep breath, looking the bouncer over for an easy place to touch him. There wasn't one. He wore a raincoat over his uniform, and cotton gloves covered his hands. The only exposed skin was on his face, and even that was protected by a thick beard. Damn it.

But Mickey hardly gave him a passing glance as he held a palm out and took their IDs, starting with Darius's and ending with Thorn's. He lingered on hers, his mouth pinched in a frown as he read the name and carefully considered Thorn's face. The way he looked at her made an uncomfortable sensation coil at the base of Darius's neck, and he couldn't help but remember the security footage from the patio where Lust had looked at Thorn in much the same way right before he'd attacked her. Darius was about to step in and stop Mickey's eyes from wandering when he finally handed her license back to her, took their cover fees, and ushered them into the club.

Madison's face lit up. She nudged Darius's shoulder and threw him a smile. He tried to return it, but the discomfort wouldn't fade.

Music pounded through the basement, pulsing into Darius's feet, up his legs, and settling in his stomach, where it made his nerves dance. Thorn paused over the threshold, her hands on her hips as she surveyed the room through the flashing lights. Mackenzie was nowhere to be seen, but Kit bobbed to the beat by the entrance.

Suddenly, an arm snaked through Darius's.

"All right, handsome," Madison said, tugging him forward, "come buy me a drink!" She smiled back at Thorn. "We'll meet up with you here in a bit."

A static of annoyance hovered around Thorn, and her eyes sharpened. Before she had the chance to speak, Darius gently pulled out of Madison's hold.

"What are you talking about?" he asked.

She blinked. "We're here to go talk to Lamar, aren't we? So we need to do what we normally do… blend in." Madison tilted her head, shrugging her shoulders like she was trying to play dumb, but a flush darkened her cheeks as she threw Thorn another look. Thorn's stature didn't relax.

"Exactly," Darius said, "I need to focus on *Lamar*—"

"And *I'm* your security detail," Madison interrupted. The

words were more confident now.

Darius's jaw dropped. "That's why Thorn's here."

"Right," Madison said, almost snapping. "As an *extra* guard. She can stand at the front." Her annoyance suddenly melted into a saccharine smile. "Oh, c'mon, Darius! If we're going to be stuck here all night, we might as well have a little fun."

She laughed and tried to grab him again, but Darius stepped out of her reach.

"*Stop,*" he said.

Heat rose to his face, red and raging. He had to shout to be heard over the music, which was a good cover for the shouting he wanted to do anyway. "Look, I'm sorry if this wasn't clear, Madison, but I don't want—"

"To drink?" she cut in. "I know that—"

"I don't want *you.*"

She balked, her eyes wide and round as she stared at him. He didn't soften, instead pointing to the back of the room. "And right now, we have a job to do. Go make sure Mackenzie is in position by the other exit, and then come back here to help Kit secure this one."

Madison's cheeks glowed bright, embarrassment flushing over her skin. She nodded before flitting off and disappearing into the crowd. Darius shook his head with a sigh and turned to Thorn. The look on her face was hard to read. He couldn't tell if she was grateful or irritated… or both. His stomach flipped.

"Let's go," he said.

They made their way to the bar. Thorn cut through the tide of crashing bodies with precision focus, as though she'd caught the scent of blood in the water, and Darius trailed in her wake. The counter was emptier than usual, and they found two open stools at the front. Caleb Claytor sat around the bend seven spots down, and he didn't glance their way. Lamar's energy was still fidgeting in the storage room behind the wall of alcohol.

"He's avoiding us," Darius murmured.

"Then we'll have to make ourselves unavoidable." Thorn raised a hand to catch the other bartender's attention.

But it seemed they'd already *had* her attention. Lamar's coworker was speaking into a phone near the register, and she cast Darius an anxious look as she nodded, hung up, and walked their way. The smile was tight on her face as she started to speak. Thorn didn't let her.

"We need to see Lamar."

The bartender froze, and her expression frayed at the edges. She glanced at Darius. "I'm sorry," she said. "He's not here tonight."

"Yes, he is," Thorn instantly replied. The other woman's mouth opened soundlessly, gaping like a shattered window in an old home. Her arms wrapped around her middle, and she took a step back.

Darius sighed. "Lamar asked you to cover for him, didn't he?"

She paused before she nodded. Darius nodded, too.

"I know you're just doing your job," he went on, "but this is important. If he talks to us, we'll leave, and we won't come back. I promise."

The bartender pulled her lower lip between her teeth as she glanced at Thorn and back to Darius. At last, her shoulders heaved in a nervous breath.

"Okay," she said. "But I can't guarantee anything, and he's in the middle of an inventory count right now. It might be a bit."

A band of tension snapped in Darius's chest just to reveal a more painful one beneath it. He forced a smile. "Thank you."

The bartender made to leave, but she hesitated. Her eyes flashed across the room before she looked at Darius again. "Can I get you something in the meantime?"

"Just water."

She glanced at Thorn, who simply said, "Same."

The woman hustled back to the tap. Darius tilted his head in Thorn's direction.

"What?" he teased. "No scotch?"

Thorn let out a short, cold laugh. "I think I've had my fill of scotch for a while."

She didn't look at him. The smooth curves of her cheeks went pink, and her fingers curled into a fist wound tightly enough that Darius wondered if she felt her nails through the palm of her glove. A guilty stone crashed into the sea of nerves swirling in his stomach. Once the bartender had dropped off their water, he sighed.

"Thorn," he began, but she quieted him by raising a hand.

"Don't." Her eyes pressed shut, and she drew a short breath. "Please, Darius. I can't—"

"I'm sorry," he cut in. She turned to him, her expression wide with surprise and sharp with pain. He didn't know what she was going to say. He didn't *want* to know. It wouldn't make this any easier. "That's all. I'm just really, *really* sorry."

Thorn watched him for a moment, and that moment stretched into an eternity—stretched so long that, damn it, Darius wished he'd said something else. Something more.

Then, at last, she nodded.

"Me, too." The words were so laden with disappointment that they instantly sank to the floor and died beneath their feet.

For a couple of minutes, they sat like that, awkward and quiet. The other bartender returned and threw them a noncommittal shrug before speaking to another customer. Lamar did not come out. A gnawing sense of unease grew in Darius's spine, and with every second that passed, that unease rang louder. He peered over his shoulder. Even though the club hummed with the same familiar energy it always had, something felt off. Dancers wearing more skin than clothing melded together, their auras just as blended as their bodies had become. He couldn't see the exit, but he could sense that the hallway above was empty, and the bouncer still stood guard outside.

"What do you think's taking Lamar so long?" Darius asked. He turned back to Thorn as she lowered her water to the counter, the glass now empty.

"He's probably trying to figure out how to tell us to fuck off in the nicest way possible," she said.

"Do you think he's upset enough to call the cops?"

Thorn shook her head. "No, and even if he was, I have Alexis on alert to have her people disrupt any orders to come down here." She glanced at him, and her brows drew together. Suddenly, her back straightened, and she, too, looked toward the exit. Her left hand wandered toward the satchel cinched to her thigh. "Why? What's wrong?"

Darius shook his head. "I don't know, I just—"

Lamar's Virtue finally moved, and the storage closet swung open. Darius tapped Thorn's shoulder, and she spun around as Lamar's focus landed on them. He nodded once and tilted his chin into the room behind him. The nerves in Darius's stomach vaulted to his throat. He exchanged a quick look with Thorn before they made their way over. The second they were inside, Lamar slammed the door shut.

"What the *hell* are you doing here? Can't you take a hint?"

Lamar's voice was high, and beneath the blue shadow adorning his lids, his eyes glistened furiously. The storage room was dark and cold. A single light flickered over boxes of canned beer, baskets of garnishes, and an industrial refrigerator. Black trash bags took over the back corner, and behind them, Darius could just make out shadowy, metal stairs that led to a grate on the sidewalk outside. The three of them were so tight in here that they could have extended their arms and touched one another without moving, which only made Darius's anxiety at this whole damned situation worse. Lamar glared at him, but Thorn was the one who answered.

"You didn't leave us much of a choice," she snapped. "We tried calling—"

"What the hell else is there to say?" Lamar cut in. He

threw a hand into the air. It quivered between them, as unsteady as a seismic monitor before the ground began to shake. "'No' is a complete sentence!"

Darius winced. "Lamar," he tried to say, but the other Virtue cut him off.

"I don't owe you an explanation," he shouted, "and the fact that you think you're entitled to one is *so* violating. *And* you're banned from the club! Mickey wasn't even supposed to let you in here! Now, get the hell out!"

He threw a finger toward the door, and Darius glanced back—not because of where Lamar was pointing, but because something was *wrong* on the other side of the wall. The club's energy had completely shifted, and Darius's sense of dread pitched to the sky.

"Thorn," he murmured. "Do you feel that?"

But she was already ahead of him. She spun on her heels and flew out of the room. Lamar and Darius exchanged a panicked look before they followed after her.

The music still pounded, but almost a quarter of the people dancing had rushed toward the back corner. The drone of their gossip was so loud it was audible over the pulsing, electronic beat. Thorn, Lamar, and Darius forced through the crowd in a straight line toward the bathrooms. As soon as they reached the mouth of the hallway, Kit leapt into Darius's path.

"I don't know what happened, man," he said, shaking his head. "I just found her that way!"

"What?" Darius's throat tightened as he craned his neck over Kit's shoulder to see Thorn and Lamar disappear through one of the doors. "What the hell are you talking about?"

"I thought she just fell down a k-hole," Kit blathered on, "but when I went to check on her, I saw the needle. I don't even know where she got it!"

The pit of Darius's stomach dropped open, and his body flooded with horror as he shoved Kit to the side. People had closed around the door again, and Darius had to push his way between bodies to reach the bathroom. As soon as he broke through, he went numb.

Mackenzie was sprawled on the floor, her skin so pale that she was almost blue. Soundlessly, uselessly, her mouth gaped open in short, empty gulps, and a slick stream of saliva trailed from the corner and down her cheek. While her eyelids were open, her eyes themselves had rolled so far back that all Darius could see was the whites. A spent needle lay on the tile beside her left arm.

While Lamar fumbled with a bright red Narcan box fixed to the wall above the toilet, Thorn dragged Mackenzie to the center of the room. She tilted the Irishwoman's chin up until her dusky lips dropped open. Thorn's hands shook as she pinched Mackenzie's nose and covered her mouth entirely with her own. When she exhaled, Mackenzie's ribcage expanded. Thorn did it again and paused, watching for movement in her chest. There wasn't any.

"C'mon, McKay!" she choked out, terror strangling the words. She dipped her face back to Mackenzie's. One, two breaths. A pause. Nothing. Thorn glanced up. Her black eyes were frantic until they found Darius. "Help me!"

He ran into the room, slammed onto the ground, and wrapped his hands around Mackenzie's palm as Thorn breathed for her again. God, her skin was cold to the touch—like she was a corpse already. Healing energy rushed to his fingertips and poured into her. The heroin was everywhere. Darius felt it pulsing through her veins, her heart, her brain, slow and gnawing and hungry. The effects of it mirrored in Darius's body like a shadow of the high. His head began to spin, and a pinch of nausea tightened his gut. Jesus, he'd never fixed something like *this* before.

Just when the sensation became too much and Darius thought he was going to faint himself, Mackenzie's lungs ripped open. She took a gasping, gurgling breath, and her eyes went wide. Darius stumbled backward as Mackenzie thrashed out in a panicked flail, and suddenly, she jerked to her side and vomited onto the floor by Thorn's knee. Lamar stared at them, the Narcan clutched in his fist.

"*Fuck,*" Mackenzie groaned. Her abdomen buckled, and she retched again before curling into a ball on the tile. Cold sweat saturated her clothing and coated her face, plastering navy hair to her forehead. "What happened?"

"You overdosed!" Thorn's voice crackled with emotion. She snatched the needle off the ground and held it up before furiously throwing it into the corner of the room. "You almost fucking *died!*"

What little color had returned to Mackenzie's face drained as she gawked at Thorn, and Thorn got to her feet to walk away, like she couldn't bear to look at her anymore. Lamar continued to stare, awestruck, as Darius helped Mackenzie sit up. Her body rocked with uncontrolled shivering. He pulled off his jacket and wrapped it around her. She was so small that it swallowed her whole.

Thorn, meanwhile, turned to the crowd hovering in the door. A dozen faces filled the space, taking videos, talking on phones, lingering and watching and *invading* this fucked up moment with cold voyeurism. Her jaw tightened as her attention landed on Kit.

"Get them out of here," she ordered.

Kit didn't move. His pupils were so wide that the color of his irises almost disappeared around them, and Darius realized with a sickening chill that, god *damn* it, he was stoned, too. Thorn's hands curled into dangerous fists. "*GARFIELD,*" she shouted. Kit jolted like she'd struck him. "I said *get them the fuck out of here!*"

She waved a hand, and Kit numbly nodded before he opened his arms and forced the crowd from the room. When the door snapped shut behind him, Thorn turned to Darius.

"Message Lewis," she snarled. "Tell her that Garfield is high as fuck, and she needs to drag his ass back to the car before I kill him."

Darius grabbed his phone. Lamar gawked at the side of his face, then at Thorn, then at Mackenzie.

"She wasn't breathing," he said at last, the unused Narcan spray still clutched in his fingers. "She was practically *dead*, and you…"

"Virtues can heal more than physical wounds," Darius murmured as he finished texting Madison and slipped his phone into his pocket. Even with Mackenzie back from the brink, the sense of anxiety in his spine didn't fade. He couldn't shake it. "Thorn, we need to go."

"The cops," she murmured. "Alexis can block one or two calls, but not this many. God fucking *damn it*." Her hands rolled into fists, and she spun like she was going to punch the mirror, but instead, she closed her eyes and pressed the heels of her palms against them.

"Maybe I can do something," Lamar said as he snapped the Narcan back into its box. His nerves still quaked in his hands, but his young face was set and determined in a way that made him seem older than he was. "I'll call and say it was a false alarm. I don't know if it'll work, but it's worth a shot."

Thorn considered him for a moment.

"I still want to finish this conversation soon," she said at last. "Please."

Lamar gave a tense smile. "Well… needless to say, you know where to find me."

He hurried from the room. As soon as he was gone, Mackenzie shuffled to her knees. Her voice trembled as she said, "Thorn, I'm—"

"Not now, McKay," Thorn snapped, and Mackenzie slumped with the energy of a kicked dog. "Can you walk?" Mackenzie nodded. Thorn did, too. "Let's go."

The hallway outside swarmed with lurkers craning for a look at Mackenzie, like surviving an overdose was some kind of spectator sport. Phones glowed above them, filling the cramped space with disorienting white light, and Mackenzie pulled Darius's jacket over her head to hide from the cameras. Warm bodies packed into the space so tightly that it made sweat blossom across his forehead. They blocked the emergency exit, but even if they hadn't, Darius felt a huddle of hot human auras on the street outside.

"Come on," Thorn said, wrapping a hand around Mackenzie's shoulder and leading her in the opposite direction. Darius's sense of foreboding grew with every step they took, prickling up his spine until he could hardly think around it. For reasons he couldn't quite pinpoint, he focused on the front entrance, too. More people. Mickey stood by the door, but another four or five waited around him. They didn't move. Didn't make their way into the club. It was almost as though they were standing guard…

Darius's heart sank.

"Thorn," he called, but pounding music devoured his voice. He tried to grab her, but Thorn barreled forward. The second she stepped into the main room, someone swung at her.

She anticipated the strike as soon as it came, ducking below the man's fist with a smoothness that felt choreographed. His momentum pulled him forward, and Thorn yanked Mackenzie back as he crashed into another dancer. A couple of them. Four more, all clawing their way toward Thorn with an inhuman synchronization and emotionless eyes.

Mackenzie gasped. "Puppets!"

Thorn thrust her into Darius's arms and dove headfirst into the Puppets. They closed in, focused solely on Thorn, as Darius screamed her name. She threw a wild look back, catching his eye through the crowd.

"Run!"

And then he lost her.

CHAPTER TWENTY-THREE

Thorn disappeared behind a wall of bodies. Darius sprang forward to follow her, but Mackenzie's grip tightened around his wrist, and he snapped back. He lifted her from the ground and sprinted toward the bar.

"Where the fuck are we going?" Mackenzie shouted. "The exit's that way!"

"We've gotta get Lamar!"

Pulsing music pushed against Darius as he weaved between dancers and drunkards, scanning every face for a sign of the Sins or someone under their Influence. The people around him continued to party, reeking of alcohol and ambivalence. He thought he spotted Madison rushing through the crowd, a glimpse of Kit at her heels, but they vanished as soon as they'd appeared. Darius's focus flickered between faces and auras and movement so quickly that he hardly noticed Lamar's Virtuous energy rushing at him until the two of them collided at the edge of the dance floor.

"Lamar!" Darius said, but any fragile sense of relief he could piece together shattered at the young man's expression. Wide, horrified eyes, slick with panic. He grabbed Darius with both hands, trembling like he'd just seen heaven.

Or hell.

Lamar looked over his shoulder. Darius's attention followed.

Connor Amoretto.

Tall and sharp, his blonde hair glistening with rainwater, he tracked Lamar through the crowd like a predator. When he spotted Darius, a smile so sinister spread across the Sin's face that it sent a cold ache of fear into Darius's gut.

Suddenly, the crowd stopped dancing, and a dozen people spun toward them.

Darius tried to drag Lamar and Mackenzie away, but hands grabbed at his arms and face. Nails raked his skin as the Puppets yanked him to the ground. His knee crashed to the tile. Disorienting pain crackled up his nerves, and when he tried to stand, the weight of bodies pressed him back down. Mackenzie screamed, and Lamar flailed beside her. Lust moved in, carving a straight line through the dance floor like a scalpel dividing skin.

BANG!

A bullet crashed into the ceiling, and a distant voice screamed, "Get down!" White drywall dust showered over Lust's shoulders as he jerked toward the sound. He paused, and for half a second, the room paused, too.

Then chaos erupted.

A blanket of Influence coated the club, pulsing at Darius's temples as it filled the basement with blind, frantic terror. People were screaming, sobbing, scrambling for the exits as another gunshot went off. This bullet tore through Lust's shoulder before striking a woman behind him. Her energy flickered out as his control quaked, and the Puppets on top of Darius went unconscious. Lust immediately plucked more from the herd of human souls around him. Men and women stopped running with an alien snap and piled in front of Amoretto—a blood and bone barrier between him and whoever shot him. Darius crawled out from beneath a mountain of sweat and skin, expecting to see Thorn. *Desperate* to see her.

But it was Caleb. He stood at the far end of the bar, his

pistol pointed at Lust's guard, but he didn't pull the trigger. His bright eyes flashed to the woman he'd killed on the floor behind them, and his chest heaved in hard, uneven breaths. The second his focus wasn't on Lust, the Sin charged.

A mass of energy forced its way across the dance floor, and more forced its way toward Darius. He hardly had the chance to duck as another Puppet tried to wrap her long arms around his throat. He kicked her away and fumbled toward Lamar. The young Virtue had pulled himself up and was helping Mackenzie do the same when a man slammed into him. He screamed as he landed hard on the tile floor. The sound gagged deep in his throat when the air was knocked from his lungs. The Puppet lunged for Lamar's neck, but Darius knocked him with an uppercut straight to the chin that sent his head flying backward. He collapsed, unconscious with the others.

Darius pulled Lamar's arm over his shoulder, grabbed Mackenzie's hand, and ran.

The club pulsed with horror. The music had stopped, and the walls echoed with people crying for help, screaming at the top of their lungs as they trampled for the exits. A gunshot went off. Then another—more and more until Darius lost count. He dragged Lamar and Mackenzie behind the bar, where they found the other bartender laid out in a puddle of spilled blood and liquor. Lamar choked out a sob.

"Fuck," Mackenzie breathed. Her whole body shook as terrified tears streamed freely down her face. She couldn't take her eyes off the dead woman beside them. *"Fuck!"*

Darius took a minute to steady himself, ignoring the hot throbbing in his knee as he felt the energy throughout the room. He couldn't make sense of it—there was too much, too close together—but it was obvious that both exits had bottlenecked with people trying to get out. Swearing, Darius looked around. When he spotted the door beside the wall of shattered alcohol bottles, his heart skipped with a brittle flicker of hope.

"This way."

The storage room was cold and dark, but they could still hear the screaming, and Darius's sense of danger was alight like a torch. Dark shadows clouded a set of steep steps, and the metal doors at the top had tarnished to a sickly, rancid green. A padlock held them together.

"I don't have the key," Lamar gasped.

Darius pulled his pistol from the holster at his back. "Cover your ears."

One shot, and the lock burst open. Darius put his weapon away, ignoring the ringing in his head as he climbed the steps. The doors were heavy, and he grunted under the pressure until one finally slammed to the side with a sharp bang. Rain pelted him from above. Now, it was falling so hard that his shoulders and hair were drenched immediately. He turned back to Lamar and Mackenzie.

"Come on!"

He helped them to the sidewalk. The city flashed with movement and light. People running. Police sirens wailing in the distance. A cruiser screeched around the corner, throwing up a fan of water from the gutter. Something overhead let out a cry right before a soft weight landed on Darius's shoulder. The grip around his heart loosened.

"Sparkie," he breathed. Thorn's Familiar ran in a quick circle around his torso before he leapt back into the air and took off down the street. Darius grabbed Lamar and Mackenzie and followed after him. Away from The Eros Project. Away from the Sins. Away from the flood of molten energy pouring out of the club.

But Darius's sense of danger didn't fade—and it *should* have faded. A knot of fear constricted his lungs as his fingers tightened around Lamar and Mackenzie's wrists. A figure up the street walked toward them. No, it didn't walk. It sauntered, unbothered by the rain or the cold or the roaring sirens. Its energy felt familiar, like Darius had met this person before. The hairs on the back of his neck prickled…

A passing SUV swerved onto the sidewalk.

For a moment, the world seemed to slow. Darius was

distantly aware of Lamar screaming and Mackenzie yelling his name as a pair of bright white headlights barreled toward them. Two decades dissolved, and Darius felt ten years old again, walking home from school, his mother's hand warm around his. She turned to him, smiled her last smile, right before a sedan crushed her into the bodega. He'd looked up from where he'd landed in the gutter to see Ayda Jones's blank, lifeless eyes gazing out from her dusky face. Dead on impact.

Reality flooded back. Darius shoved Lamar and Mackenzie behind him and dove to the side. The vehicle crashed into the building between them. Darius rolled to his hands and knees with a wince. Hot energy rushed in from all directions.

He felt them—an army of synchronized people pulling away from the club, from the buildings, from the street. There were so many. More than he could count. Sparkie landed on Darius's shoulder again with a frantic cry just as a shrill, cackling laugh broke over the sound of the storm.

Oh, *fuck*. He knew that voice.

"Darius Jones!" Autumn Hunt called. "It's been a while."

He scrambled to his feet, and he ran. Darius slipped into the alley behind the club, putting as much distance between himself and Mackenzie and Lamar as he could. Wrath didn't seem concerned about them. While the sensation of Lamar's Virtue sprinted in the opposite direction, Wrath's Puppets followed Darius like a pack of hungry hunting dogs. They filed into the alley behind him, ahead of him, on all sides. Closing in…

Darius reached the exit onto the opposite street just as a couple of men rushed through. He ducked beneath their outstretched arms, turned, and sprinted again. Behind him, points of energy abruptly collapsed at the exact same moment that people in his path turned on him. Escaping clubbers. First responders. Civilians. Before Darius knew it, he was surrounded. He swore, his breath rising in foggy clouds through the rain.

The Puppets charged.

All Darius knew was heat and pain. Hot auras piled onto him until he felt like he was burning. Hands pulled at any part of him they could find—his hair, his clothes, his skin. Darius threw punch after punch into anything he could see while Sparkie hissed and snapped, but it wasn't enough. There were so many. Too many. He was going to drown.

Suddenly, a man collapsed. Then another and another. They fell spontaneously, as though their wires were cut, or violently as someone ripped through them like they were made of porcelain. Soon, almost half of Wrath's Puppets crumbled to the ground, the city opened up, and another hand reached him. This one felt different—colder, gentler. Sparkie let out a screaming cry as a Puppet lunged at them. The lizard dove onto the woman's face, and Thorn yanked Darius free.

He gripped her arms, gasping a strangled, relieved sound from deep in his throat. "Lamar," he choked out. "Mackenzie—"

"Caleb has them," Thorn cut in as she dragged him to his feet. "Now *run!*"

They did, and the horde followed.

Somehow, Wrath found more, collecting civilians so quickly it was as though Thorn hadn't cut any off at all. A tidal wave of hot, human energy drenched the street, and it pressed against Darius's spine with treacherous inevitability. Thorn threw a glance over her shoulder, and one of the lead Puppets abruptly slammed into the concrete. The mass bowled over him, slowing but not stopping.

"Shit," she breathed. They reached an intersection, and Thorn grabbed Darius to lead him eastward, barreling through squealing traffic and bewildered pedestrians. Panic constricted Thorn's voice. "She's too fast. We can't outrun her."

He couldn't outrun her. Thorn was holding back. If Darius wasn't here, she could move quicker. Fight harder. He looked back as she pierced Wrath's connection to another Puppet. This time, the tide parted around the body without breaking stride.

"Then what the hell do we do?" Darius asked.

Thorn's jaw tightened, and her eyes flashed up the street. They sprinted another block. Two. All the while, pushing past hurried civilians and around cars. Still, the Puppets closed in. Thorn would cut a couple off and bump the swarm back, but Wrath just picked up more. She started reaching further, extending her control ahead until Thorn was fending off people on all sides. When they made it to the third block, they had just as many Puppets in front of them as they did behind. Thorn slammed to a stop at the corner of 50th and 8th so suddenly that Darius ran into her.

Over forty people rushed toward them. There was nowhere else to go. Thorn pulled her pistol from her satchel, prepared to fight, but the wild spark in her eyes told Darius she knew they couldn't win this time. He frantically looked around, squinting through the rain, and his attention caught on a bright green light outside a building behind them. His heart leapt to his throat as he grabbed Thorn's hand.

"This way!"

He pulled her toward the subway entrance. Thorn shook her head. "Hunt's closing in and you want to go under fucking ground?"

"Do you have any better ideas?"

Thorn groaned and hurried after him. They rushed into the building and down the stairs. Several yards back, the crowd slammed into the glass doors. The narrow opening forced a bottleneck, giving Darius and Thorn even more space to breathe. He glanced back, trying to gauge how long they had before running wasn't an option anymore.

Then Thorn fell.

Her legs suddenly gave out, and her entire body seized like she'd been snared in a trap. She crashed down the last six steps and slammed face-first on the landing with a sickening thud. The gun clattered from her hand, spiraling away to disappear beneath a bench. Thorn gasped out a guttural, pained grunt as she floundered to her hands and knees. Darius dropped to the ground beside her. When he grabbed her shoulders, he found her shaking, the wind knocked out of her.

"What happened?" he asked. "Thorn, what's going on?"

Her eyes darted up the stairs, where the first trickle of Puppets came around the bend in the stairwell. "Sparkie," she gasped, sucking in a sharp, panicked breath. "She has Sparkie!"

Thorn crawled to her feet, but another bolt of pain doubled her over, and she had to hold onto Darius to stay standing. His body went numb, aware of nothing but the hot energy spiraling toward them. He swiped Thorn's legs out from beneath her and carried her to the turnstile, where he gracelessly tossed her over the barrier before leaping through himself. Darius was just lifting her again when a woman slammed into the metal poles, reaching for them with long, grasping fingers.

More followed. Thorn winced as Darius turned a final corner and ran down the platform. Thank god it was empty this late at night. The corridor echoed with his footsteps and the sounds of Wrath's horde pouring after them. Darius made it to the end of the platform before he tucked behind a pillar and set Thorn down. She let out a thick, throaty noise as she pressed her back against the concrete. Darius peered past it, and his mouth ran dry.

Autumn Hunt waltzed around the corner. An entourage buzzed about her—women wearing bright-colored rave outfits alongside late-night joggers in sweatpants, street-clothed men next to police blues. They dawdled, like they'd lost the scent. Puppets looked over the edge of the tracks. In the distance, a train rumbled. The sound growled down the tunnels, moaning through the platform like a great beast's grumbling belly.

"You're slipping, Rose!" Wrath shouted. "You thought you could distract me, but your little pet got too close tonight. I wonder what would happen if I ripped it in half?"

She laughed, her voice sharp as a blade, and her lips peeled apart in a smile as she thrust a fist into the air. Sparkie wriggled between her cinched fingers, his wings flapping wildly as she tightened her grip. He screeched, and Thorn sucked in a breath.

"Darius," she whispered. The subway grew louder, and the ground beneath their feet vibrated. Thorn grabbed his shirt; Darius wasn't sure if it was to keep herself steady or pull him closer. "I need you to listen to me. When the train gets here—"

"No," he said.

"Yes," she hissed. Sparkie cried out, and Thorn's spine arched as she slammed her eyes closed. A desperate, terrified noise filled her throat. "You have to—"

"Shut up, Thorn. I won't leave you, so *don't* ask me to."

She stared at him, her mouth open. Darius swallowed hard as he reached for the gun strapped in the holster behind his back. Puppets were closing in. The nearest point of warm energy was more than halfway to them now. Darius peeked around the pillar again. Fifty yards. All he had were fifty yards between him and Wrath. Rainwater saturated her hair and shoulders, the brown tendrils dark against her tawny skin, and her gray eyes seethed with malice. Darius rolled his shoulders and focused on isolating her aura from the others. Just as the subway squealed onto the platform and the first Puppet rounded the pillar, Darius leapt out.

The second they had something to focus on, Wrath's swarm moved as a unit. Thorn cut the closest ones off from the hive while Darius shot at Hunt. Bodies slammed to the pavement, and more joined the mass. Men and women from the train were sucked into Wrath's web, and they lunged at Darius. Sharp nails dug against the back of his neck. Thorn kicked the guy's knees, sending him to the ground. Halfway down the platform, Wrath began to pull a wall of Puppets in front of her. Darius shot one last time.

The bullet thudded into her stomach.

Autumn Hunt roared as more than half of her Puppets immediately fell. The others stumbled to a stop, and a blue and red blur took to the air with a shrill cry. A hand wrapped around Darius's wrist.

"Go!" Thorn screamed.

She threw him onto the train and jumped in behind him. A half dozen people groped their way through as the doors closed. Most of them piled on Thorn, while a massive Puppet pinned Darius to the ground and wound a thick fist around his throat. He pried at the man's fingers, trying to loosen them as the car jolted. It shot down the tracks, and within seconds, all the energy stilled in a single motion. The Puppets collapsed, and the one on Darius crushed him beneath his weight.

Then the subway was silent. Darius took a moment to reorient himself when the body moved. A wave of panic caught in his chest until he realized Thorn was shoving the guy off him. As soon as Darius crawled free, she knelt at his side and grabbed his head, fingertips firm but gentle against his skin.

"Darius," she gasped. Her eyes searched him—moving from his face to his body and up again. "Are you okay?"

"Yeah," he said. "Yeah. Are you?"

She weakly nodded, and then, she slumped back to sit on the ground. When she pulled her hands away, they trembled. Sparkie leapt to her—Darius hadn't even realized he'd made it on the train—and pressed against her chest. He clawed through her jacket desperately, as though trying to climb back into the safety of her soul. His whole body shuddered, from the tip of his tail to his leathery wings, as he let out a harsh wail that carried the timbre of a crying child. A similar sound escaped Thorn's lips. She closed her eyes and covered her mouth with one hand while the other clutched her Familiar to her heart.

"Hey." Darius touched her knee. She didn't move, so he gently shook her. Still nothing. "Hey, Thorn, look at me."

Her head tilted up, but her gaze passed right through

him. The breath she drew in rattled, short and staccato, like she was on the edge of hyperventilating.

"It's okay," Darius said. He gently brushed a few strands of damp hair away from her cheek. The contact seemed to startle her back. She sucked in a quiet gasp as her eyes focused on him. "That's it. Easy. Take a deep breath."

She did, her chest rising and falling as she inhaled through her nose and released a stream of air quietly from parted lips. After several long seconds, the rocking of the train car a steady rhythm beneath their legs, Thorn's fingers curled against her Familiar's back. At first, Darius thought she had made a fist, but he realized with a flicker of shock that she was tapping her thumb against each of her fingertips, from pointer to pinky. Sparkie settled, and Thorn's trembling leveled off.

Darius attempted a smile. "I thought you said this grounding exercise was stupid."

She choked out a hollow laugh. It stuck in her throat, so she cleared it. "It *is* stupid," she whispered, but still, her hand followed the motions, from finger to finger, to keep her here.

He chuckled as a wave of relief made his legs feel weak. With a sigh, he sat on the floor beside Thorn and gestured his chin at her hand. "What do you see?" he asked. "The broken light? The cracked window? The brown stain under the seat? Ugh, what *is* that?"

He laughed again, but Thorn didn't. She turned toward him, and her black eyes held his with a grip so strong it felt nearly physical. "You," she murmured. Darius's breath caught. "I see you."

CHAPTER TWENTY-FOUR

The Research and Discovery department buzzed with frantic, warm energy.

"God damn it!" Nicholas swore as Darius walked into the room. He pulled his fingers through his hair, furling the yellow strands into disarray as he glared at Daniel Park's computer. "Another video of Darius. Sky, you got this one?"

He glanced over his shoulder, and Skylar threw a thumbs up into the air. "Shutting it down now," she called.

Darius's heart dropped as he rushed to Nicholas's side. "Shit…"

"Shit's right," Nicholas grumbled. Footage of Darius looped back to the beginning. They watched as he dropped to his knees beside Mackenzie and grabbed her by the hand. Seconds later, she lurched awake, and a chorus of shocked gasps filled the speakers. "It's dark, and it's confusing, and it's not like we can *see* you draining the heroin from her system, but it shows your face, and that's bad enough."

Nicholas swore again and ran his hands down his face. The room clattered with keys typing, voices murmuring, and the dull hum of multiple systems playing different videos at low volume.

"I'm sorry," Darius said, shaking his head. The motion made him woozy, and he pressed his fingertips against his eyes. After he and Thorn had made it back to the Underground, he'd hardly slept. While she had gathered her gear and headed back into the city, Darius had been on call in the hospital. Between healing TAC officers as they filtered in and worrying about Thorn, it had been almost impossible to get any rest, and his body felt thin. "God, this whole thing is such a mess."

"If it makes you feel better," Skylar said, the tone of her voice making it clear that what she had to say would make him feel anything but better, "you're probably the least messy thing about it."

She gestured to the laptop on the table she was sitting at, and he pulled out the chair beside her. More video footage—yet another clip from someone at the club—but this time, it showed the shooting.

Darius's mouth ran dry as the scene flickered with light and motion. The tiny computer speakers screamed with frantic cries for help and wails of pain, broken up by the sharp snap of gunshots. Bodies littered the ground, trampled underfoot as people wildly stampeded for the exits. Darius recognized one of them. Kit Garfield, laid out in a pool of blood, there and gone as the camera flashed by. The first of what would end up being three Martyr lives claimed last night. Darius sighed and dipped his face into his palms.

"Videos like this are popping up *everywhere*," Skylar muttered. "And that's not even the worst part. Check out the news."

She tapped a few keys, and her display shifted to a live feed from one of the local New York stations. For several minutes, Darius watched in numb, distant shock as survivors gave detailed accounts of the attack, Commissioner Faust covered the ongoing investigation, and Mayor Bently mourned the dead while simultaneously boasting about the strength of New Yorkers to overcome such tragedies. The "facts," if you could even call them that, flashed by.

Mickey Guthrie, the bouncer, had been "identified" as the assailant—killed on-site by a self-inflicted gunshot wound when the NYPD showed up to save the day. They'd scoured his social media, digging their fingers into his private life to find the most controversial photograph they could track down: a shot from a protest where he held a sign with the words "EAT THE RICH" scrawled in blood-red paint. He was part of the "radical left," they claimed, and he'd finally snapped, taking out years of frustration with the one percent by shooting up the bottom ninety-nine. Darius's jaw clenched furiously.

Then real facts. Real figures. These were worse. The cold casualty numbers cut into Darius like a blade. Thirteen dead, and more were expected to follow. Over twenty wounded men and women had been brought into local hospitals, several of them in critical condition. Many others had disappeared entirely, and crying family members pleaded for answers. At the bottom of the broadcast, other headlines revealed more events around the city, including a potential mass suicide at the 50th Street subway station.

Suddenly, a familiar face filled the screen, and Darius felt the blood drain from his cheeks.

"Our sources indicate there may have been a second shooter," the newscaster was saying. "Lamar Verrette, a bartender at The Eros Project, was seen leaving the club shortly after the incident began. When police arrived at Verrette's apartment this morning, they found one of his roommates killed by an apparent gunshot wound to the head. Anyone with information about Verrette is encouraged to come forward but exercise extreme caution. He may be armed and dangerous."

"His roommate?" Darius spun to Skylar.

"The Sins must have gone to Lamar's apartment as soon as they figured out who he was," she murmured.

"Is this the first time they've mentioned him?" Darius asked, indicating the screen.

"Yes," Skylar groaned through a sigh as she swiped back

her laptop. "They're trying to smoke him out."

"Not just him," Parker Boseman said. She sat at the station just behind Skylar, and Darius turned to her. Her screen was divided into two sections: one a map of Manhattan pocked with dozens of pinned markers and the other a photograph. "His family is going to freak out when they see this."

Darius got to his feet and leaned over Parker's computer. The picture was from last Christmas, showing all five Verrettes posing in matching pajamas. Lamar's mother and father had their arms around him and his two little sisters, their eyes bright and smiles wide. The girls had to be at least ten years younger than Lamar—maybe more—and his parents hardly seemed old enough to have a twenty-four-year-old son themselves. A swell of anxious nausea rumbled in Darius's stomach.

"Where are they?" he asked.

Parker shook her head, throwing him a dark look from beneath her mop of ringlets. "I don't know. The girls are probably in school. Their parents—Matthew and Loretta?—run a little flower shop down the street from their apartment, but they weren't there when our TAC team went by. A bunch of weirdos are, though. Probably Puppets, or at least Sentries, looking for them like we are."

Darius swore as Nicholas came up beside him.

"The Sins will use anyone Verrette cares about to get to him," Nicholas said. An alert buzzed to his phone, and he drew it from his pocket without looking at the screen. "Colleagues. Friends. We have to—"

He froze as he finally glanced at his device. Darius and Parker stared at him as his eyes darted left to right. His nose curled indignantly.

"Fuck!" Nicholas snarled, and the whole room froze.

"What happened?" Skylar asked.

"That damned newscast is already working." Nicholas shoved the phone away, and instead of speaking to Skylar directly, he considered his entire research team. "The other roommate called the police hotline and painted a god-damned target on her back! We need to track her *and* the family down—*now.*"

A chorus of harrowed agreement and panicked clicking followed as everyone turned their heads back to work. Nicholas strode to his desk at the far end of the room, Darius at his heels.

"Do we know which roommate was killed?" he asked.

"If the girl is the one who called," Nicholas said, throwing himself into his chair and turning on his screen. His eyes scanned the intel report they'd collected on Lamar when they first discovered him. "The kid's name was Jace Larsen. Jesus, he was only twenty-two."

"What did the other roommate say when she talked to the cops?"

"Not much," Nicholas said. "They want her to come in for questioning. I'd bet the last half of my soul that they plan on using her as leverage to get to Verrette. *Fuck*, what a shit show."

He groaned and pressed his fingertips against closed eyes. Darius stood awkwardly above him.

"Does Lamar know?" he asked.

"I don't see how he could," Nicholas grumbled. "No one's talked to him yet. Who usually breaks this kind of news?"

He glanced up at Darius, and Darius swallowed hard. "Abraham."

Nicholas's jaw clenched. "Well, that doesn't do us a damn bit of good now."

Darius sighed. "I'll handle it. Call me if you find anything else out, yeah?"

"You got it," Nicholas said, without hope or heart. He turned back to his computer, and Darius made his exit, thinking through how exactly to have this conversation. Every step toward the elevator felt heavy, and the ride to the lower level dragged on with a slow, dull haze. By the time he reached the room they'd assigned to Lamar, he had no idea what he was going to say. As he raised a fist to knock, Lamar's energy leapt up, and the door flung open.

The two Virtues stared at one another for a few long seconds, and Darius's chest squeezed around his heart.

Lamar clearly hadn't slept. A topography of bright vessels mapped the whites of his eyes like cursed tributaries to a blood-red Nile. The black liner along his lash line had smudged, leaking down his brown cheeks in wet, black streaks. He wiped away a fresh trail with the back of his hand.

"What do you want?"

"I, ah…" Darius cleared his throat. "I have some updates on what's going on if you want to hear them…"

Lamar's lips pressed together, and he nodded through a wave of unshed tears. He gestured Darius inside without a word. Darius stood awkwardly in the middle of the room as he extended an arm toward the single queen bed along the back wall.

"You might want to sit down," he said.

"No." Lamar crossed his arms. He'd changed out of last night's work clothes, now wearing an ill-fitting white t-shirt and a pair of gray sweatpants provided by the Martyrs. They hung wrinkled from his body. "No, whatever it is, just… just spit it out."

Darius drew a slow breath. "Sit down, Lamar."

Those three words seemed to suck whatever strength Lamar had left straight from his body. He made his way to the bed, and the second his thighs hit the mattress, his whole spine curved inward. He clasped his hands between his knees. They were shaking.

God, Darius wished there was a better way to do this.

"The Sins found your apartment," he said. "Jace… didn't make it."

Lamar's lips slipped open, and a quaking breath pulled through them. He cleared his throat, but it didn't stop his voice from trembling as he said, "And Naomi?"

"She's alive," Darius said, and Lamar instantly choked

out a strangled sound that blended relief and horror. "But she did call the police hotline, and if she meets up with them, it won't be good. We have people out looking for her now. We're also trying to find your family. When I hear anything, I'll let you know. Immediately. I promise."

Lamar looked down at the beige carpet between his feet. "The club…" he began. "How bad was it?"

When he met Darius's eye again, Darius sighed.

"Really bad."

For the next few minutes, Darius recounted everything he'd just learned in the R&D headquarters. All the while, Lamar simply stared. A numb dissociation washed over his expression, like he was hearing Darius without truly listening—until Darius brought up the bouncer.

"They're blaming *Mickey?*" Lamar cut in. Darius nodded, and Lamar threw a hand out. "Mickey wouldn't do this!"

"I know—"

"No, you don't understand," Lamar interrupted again, getting to his feet and pacing a few steps away. "He'd finally caught his big break. His agent was setting him up with this huge audition for some show they're shooting in Midtown. He'd never throw it all away like this!"

"This is what the Sins do," Darius began, but Lamar groaned and dipped his face into his hands.

"Why did you come back?" he asked. He spun toward Darius, his eyes full of furious tears, and his voice poured out in a sob. "Why couldn't you just leave it alone? If you hadn't shown up last night, none of this would have happened!"

Darius's mouth fell open, and for a moment, he and Lamar watched one another. Lamar's whole chest rocked in hard, heavy breaths, and a tear escaped the cage of his lashes to wind down the path carved by others on his skin. At last, Darius sighed.

"You're probably right," he admitted quietly. Another tear joined the first, and Lamar rubbed them away. "I am *so* sorry. I didn't know what else to do. You're a *Virtue*, Lamar.

One of only *four* left. When you cut all communication, I had to rule out that something else wasn't going on."

More silence followed, and this time, Lamar swallowed hard. He sucked his lower lip in as though he was considering giving Darius an answer, but he never got the chance. Darius's phone rang. They both jumped at the sound. Darius drew the device from his pocket; Nicholas's face stared up at him. His heart leapt into his throat as he answered.

"What's up?"

"We found them," Nicholas said. Darius's eyes widened, and he glanced at Lamar to find him staring. "His family. They're alive."

———

"Lamar!"

The moment Darius opened the door to Alan's office, Loretta Verrette started to sob. She scrambled up from a chair in front of the desk, nearly tripping over herself as she pulled Lamar into a fierce hug.

"Mama," he managed to choke out, but the fragile grip he'd held on his emotion fractured before he could say more. He dipped his face into the crook of her neck and quietly cried. His father joined them, wrapping his arms around their shoulders.

"It's okay," Matthew Verrette murmured, the gravelly bass of his voice grinding. He planted a soft kiss on the crown of Lamar's locs. "We've got you. Everything is okay."

Lamar nodded into his mother's long, silky braids as she clung to him. Darius closed the door and glanced at Alan, who was sitting behind his desk. The two shared a solemn look before Alan got to his feet.

"Mr. and Mrs. Verrette," he began, holding a hand, palm up, in Darius's direction. "This is Darius Jones."

Loretta didn't move, but Matthew looked up. He pulled one arm away, offering a broad hand for Darius to shake.

"Mr. Jones," Matthew said, clearing the tension from his

throat. His grip tightened around Darius's palm as tears swelled in his eyes. "I was told you saved our son. Thank you."

Lamar's shoulders went rigid, and a guilty knot caught up in Darius's chest. At first, he could only nod, but even that felt dishonest. "I'm sorry your family got dragged into this. I wish—"

"Where are Jordan and Bianca?" Lamar cut in. He pulled away from his mother and glanced around the room with mounting panic. "Are they okay?"

"They're fine," Loretta reassured him. "Mr. Blaine asked one of his nurses to take them downstairs to play some games while we talked. After they heard about the club, I thought they'd never stop crying. How are *you?*" She grabbed Lamar's hand, drawing closer, but he shook his head.

"How did you get out of New York?" he asked instead of answering her question, looking both his parents up and down. "Did they find you? Are you hurt?"

Matthew frowned. "Did who find us?" he asked. "We were chaperoning the twins' field trip to the Met when your friends here picked us all up and told us what happened." His frown deepened, and he turned to Alan. "Or… is something else going on? Is someone trying to hurt my family— to hurt my *son?*"

Alan stepped around to the front of his desk. The awkward movement of an unfamiliar aura hobbling down the hallway outside caught Darius's attention. He and Lamar both turned as Alan said, "Yes—"

The door to his office swung open. Thorn stood on the other side, a slick of dried blood across her throat and collar, as she supported a wounded woman at her side. Matthew stared at them while Loretta covered her mouth with her hands, but Lamar yelped.

"Naomi!"

He ran to her before Darius could even think to intervene. Blood clumped her vibrant, red hair in swatches around her face, and a deep cut on her scalp dribbled onto her eye, tinting it like gory shadow.

"Lamar," Naomi said, gripping him by the shoulders with shaking fingers while he and Thorn guided her into one of the chairs. Lamar grabbed her face in his palms. "What the *fuck* is happening! I saw the—"

She gasped, thoughts stolen from her head as Virtuous magic poured into her body. Over Lamar's shoulders, his parents watched in awe as the cut on Naomi's face stitched together so securely it left nothing more than a trail of blood behind. When he drew back, she touched her own flesh, hands trembling even harder now as they gently dabbed at the spot on her hairline that was an open wound only seconds before. Her dark eyes widened as Lamar threw his arms around her in a tight embrace.

"D-did I…" Loretta stammered, quietly moving her hands away from her mouth. "Did he…? Lamar, honey, what did you *do?*"

Alan cleared his throat, pulling everyone's attention back to him.

"Mr. and Mrs. Verrette," he began, "I am afraid this is much larger than you know. Please, have a seat."

The moments that followed washed by in a blur. Thorn excused herself only to return moments later with a couple of metal chairs from the conference room. They managed to squeeze the seven of them into Alan's office, the Verrettes and Naomi sitting before the desk while Alan positioned himself behind it again.

Darius and Thorn stood back by the door. Listening. Waiting. Alan explained the war they were fighting and Lamar's place within it all, answering the onslaught of questions with a rehearsed patience Darius knew came from a century of having this exact conversation with thousands of others. Meanwhile, Thorn dabbed at a knife wound beneath her collarbone, her expression set into a curious frown. When Alan mentioned the phenomenon of *Oblitus Peccatum*, heads spun in her direction, and Darius was sure Loretta's umber skin lost its luster at the sight of Thorn's healing injury.

"These… these Sins, you said?" she began slowly, turning back to Alan. "They're after my baby?"

She reached across her lap and grabbed Lamar's fingers.

"They are," Alan said.

"Because he's a Virtue?" Matthew added.

"That's right." Alan held a gracious hand toward Lamar. "We may be able to kill the host bodies the Sins inhabit, but only the Virtues can destroy their very essence. Your son has the power to eliminate one of these Sins from the world, and they will do whatever they can to stop him… including coming after *you*."

Matthew's shoulders went rigid, and Loretta's grip on Lamar tightened.

"Now that they have identified Lamar, they will hunt down anyone important in his life," Alan went on. His chin tilted ever so slightly toward Naomi. "We have already seen their attempts at work, and they will not rest until one of two things happens."

"What things?" Naomi asked.

"Either they kill *him*," Thorn said, her voice cutting through the room like a bullet, making them jump. "Or *he* kills Lust. Until then, none of you are safe in New York City."

A dense quiet fell around them.

"For how long?" Matthew finally asked.

Alan drew a slow breath. "It's impossible to know, but there is a very real chance you will never be able to go back."

Loretta swallowed hard. "What about our friends? Our family?"

Alan shook his head. Tears pooled in Loretta's eyes, but she nodded.

Lamar, however, scoffed.

"We can't just leave—"

"Lamar," Matthew cut in, leaning behind Loretta to land a broad palm on his son's shoulder. "It's okay." Then he looked back to Alan. "Where do we go?"

Alan opened his mouth to speak, but Lamar interrupted him.

"It's *not* okay, Dad!" he said. "What about Gigi? And that private school you worked so hard to get the girls into? Your flower shop?"

Matthew forced a tense smile. "It's just a store, son."

"It's your *life!*"

"No." Matthew's fingers held tighter. "*You* are my life. You, your mother, Jordan, and Bianca. That's *all* that matters, and I'll do whatever I have to do to keep you all safe." His jaw clenched together, and he cleared his throat before turning back to Alan again. "Where do we go?"

"There are a couple of options," Alan began. "You are more than welcome to join our cause and live here, in the Underground, but that life does come with a substantial risk—"

"Does Lamar have to stay?" Naomi interrupted.

"No," Alan said, "and he has already expressed a desire *not* to. In that case, I can establish you somewhere safe with new names and identities." He laced his fingers on his desk. "Think of it like a witness protection program. It will take time to get your paperwork and accounts set up. A former colleague of ours has property in Missouri, where she specializes in trauma therapy and spiritual healing. I am positive she would happily house you all until we have the details sorted out."

"No!" Lamar leapt to his feet, pulling his hand out of his mother's to drag his fingers through his locs. "New York is our home! Everything we have is *here*."

Loretta shook her head. "Lamar, please—"

"Mama," he cut in, his voice tight around the word, as he looked down at her, "you've already given up so much because of me. You can't give up on this, too! You just can't."

Alan sighed. "I'm afraid you do not have much choice," he said. "The Sins will Program everyone who ever knew you. They have already begun. The minute any of you show your faces in the city again, they will find you."

No one spoke for a long moment. Lamar glared at Alan, his narrow chest rising and falling in hard breaths as Naomi, Loretta, and Matthew watched him. At last, he twisted toward Thorn. "What if I destroy Lust?" he asked. "You said we could come back then?"

One slender brow arched high on her head, and she crossed her arms. "Or if he kills you."

"Either way," he said, "my family can go home?"

This time, Thorn nodded. Loretta jumped up.

"Absolutely not!" She grabbed Lamar's hands again, holding so tight that the tendons in her fingers pressed against her skin. "If we go, we *all* go."

Lamar sighed, and he spoke more softly. "Mama…"

"I won't hear it, Lamar," Loretta said. Her voice shook with emotion, and the sound made a lump catch in Darius's throat. "I won't let my baby boy—"

"I'm not your baby boy anymore, Mama," Lamar said. He drew their closed fists up to his chest and held them against his sternum. "I have to do this. For you and Dad and the girls."

Loretta's mouth dropped open as though she planned to argue with him more, but instead, a strangled sob escaped her throat. She glanced at her husband, like she was hoping he would back her up, but his jaw was set, and he shook his head. A fresh wave of emotion pooled behind her lashes as she threw her arms around Lamar's shoulders in a desperate embrace.

"Keep that foolishness out of your mouth," she murmured. "You will *always* be my baby boy, no matter how grown you get. You better take care of yourself first, you hear me? Always take care of yourself first."

Lamar nodded, a line of tears falling down his cheeks to match those on his mother's. Matthew returned to them, wrapping them both in a tight hug, and he glanced over Lamar's head to invite Naomi to join them. The four stood in silence for a moment longer, like they knew this might be the last time they were together like this, and they wanted to savor every painful second of it. Darius's eyes stung, and he glanced at Thorn.

She was staring, her black irises glistening like a mirror.

CHAPTER TWENTY-FIVE

Waves of cool water danced along her skin in a familiar song of hurt and healing.

Over the decades, Thorn had found only a few things that helped soothe her. Most of them, like fighting and fucking and filling her body with toxins she couldn't feel, were temporary at most—a distraction to cover up the shit she didn't want to deal with.

Swimming, though, was different. Meditative. Her steadily beating heart, her arms breaking the water's surface, her breath on every seventh stroke drawing deep into her lungs—all of it slowed her mind and made this hellscape a little easier to cope with.

Usually.

A whisper interrupted her rhythm. Loretta Verrette, the words thick with tears.

"You will always be my baby boy."

Thorn's thoughts wandered away from the water, landing on Lamar instead. His face filled her mind, and then that face morphed, lengthening, lightening, until it wasn't Lamar Verrette at all anymore.

It was Donovan Rose.

His sallow skin. His sunken eyes. His dark hair, matted

and dirty and sticky with blood. He'd cried for her in the end. Sobbed her name from the far side of the Huddlestone Arch. His voice had echoed against the stonework, and then, it echoed in her mind for years. Decades. It was *still* there, screaming forever inside her skull.

Thorn's heart plunged into the empty cage in her chest. She reached the far end of the pool, misjudged the distance for her flip turn, and spun early. Her feet were too far from the edge, so instead of shooting back into the lane, she fumbled beneath the water. With a groan, she stopped, stood, and swiped her hands down her face.

"God damn it."

The room swallowed the sound of her voice, gently lapping water devouring it before it had the chance to bounce off the concrete walls. Thorn swam to the side, where Sparkie sat on a folded towel next to the pool. When she lifted herself out of the water, her Familiar followed her movement. His beady eyes focused on her face as she climbed to her feet, wrapped the towel around her waist, and pulled her swim cap off with a snap. When she was done, he leapt to her shoulder. His leathery wings clung to her wet skin like plastic wrap.

It was late, so the locker room and the gym on the other side of it were empty. Thorn preferred to swim at times like this, when she was least likely to be interrupted and the distracting bustle of cold human energy settled down. As she walked to the showers, she could feel most of the Martyrs stretched out to the right and left, tucked quietly into their beds. A few lingered in the alcoves around the courtyard, and even fewer above her head, where a handful of researchers were still working. Thorn turned on the hot water, stripped from her suit, and draped her towel on a hook beside the door. Then she froze, staring at her raised hand.

A new scar, fine and white and barely noticeable, stood out on her forearm—exactly opposite of where the *Peccostium* sat inside her left wrist—from where a blade had pierced through her. Furious, nauseous bubbles twisted in her stomach, and Sparkie wrapped more tightly around her throat as she stepped into the water. It was so hot it nearly scalded them, but Thorn didn't care. Maybe it would burn off the tainted parts of her, revealing a whole, fresh person beneath.

She sighed into the steam.

She'd relived so much, *too much*, in the last couple of weeks. No matter how many laps she committed to, she couldn't outswim the horrors. Lust invading her body. Wrath invading her soul. She could still feel the phantom sensation of Connor Amoretto's fingers in her hair and Autumn Hunt's around Sparkie's ribcage. The lizard shuddered as a cold shock of the terror she'd felt last night burrowed into her bones.

She didn't want to imagine what would have happened if Wrath had won. If that bitch had managed to keep Sparkie to herself, to drag Thorn into a worse hell than the one she'd spent twenty years of her life fighting to escape, to ruin not just the soul inside of Thorn's body but the innocent part of it trapped out here.

She didn't want to imagine what would have happened if Darius hadn't been there.

Thorn's heart skipped again, but this time for a completely *different,* just as treacherous reason. She pressed a hand against her naked chest, tilted her head back, and tried to focus on the hot water running in clean streams through her hair, between her shoulder blades, and down the valley of her spine. Thorn closed her eyes and tapped her fingertips against her skin, one at a time. The second she did, Darius's face filled her mind. The memory of his touch upon her cheek, his thumb caressing her lower lip, was almost enough to make her forget why he'd been trying to heal her in the first place. Sparkie let out a restless groan.

Swearing to herself, Thorn turned the heat down and scrubbed the chlorine residue from her skin before washing her hair. Sparkie leapt from her shoulder and peered down from the top of the door. His tail twitched against the frosted glass, carving tiny, delicate patterns into the fog coating its surface. When Thorn was done, she wrapped the towel around her torso and made her way to her locker. Sparkie glided behind her and perched on her shoulder as she pulled her gym bag out and started to get dressed. An aura walking across the courtyard made her pause. Thorn's throat went tight, and Sparkie ruffled his wings before he climbed into her bag.

Mackenzie.

She was unmistakable. Her ice-cold aura was brighter than anyone else in this place, nearly impossible to miss no matter where she was in the Underground—and in the last twenty-four hours, she hadn't been allowed anywhere outside the hospital ward. Even after Darius had dissolved the heroin in her system, Harris wanted to keep an eye on her. He hadn't called it an intervention, but Thorn could read between the lines of his bullshit.

He was worried about her. Fuck, they all were. Thorn was more than just worried. She was pissed.

And she was terrified.

The tightness moved into her chest. Thorn pulled on her leggings, socks, and shoes. Mackenzie's aura entered the gymnasium and, seconds later, the women's room. Thorn got to her feet, slung her gym bag over her shoulder, and shut her locker with a snap.

"Thorn?"

Mackenzie's voice reverberated through the corridor. Thorn didn't respond. She didn't think she could. Her vocal cords felt strangled. Sneakers squeaked on the tile, and that glacial aura walked down the hall.

It wasn't until Thorn sensed Mackenzie's presence just behind her back that she finally turned around.

The Irishwoman paused outside of the locker alcove. Somehow, she looked smaller than Thorn remembered— smaller, even, than she'd been when they'd found her doped and delirious on the floor of the shit-hole apartment Sloth had been using as a home base. Jeremiah had insisted they leave her behind, but Thorn couldn't do it. Mackenzie had only been seventeen at the time—just a fucking kid caught in a war she'd never been given the chance to understand or the choice to be a part of.

Now, standing here almost two decades later, Thorn felt like she was looking at that kid again. Her navy hair lay limp to her head, and her cheekbones pressed against her skin. She picked at chipped nail polish with shaky hands.

"Hey. Chris, uh… Chris told me I'd find you here."

"I thought you were confined to the hospital ward," Thorn said.

The words came out more biting than she meant them to, and she clenched her jaw together to stop herself from saying anything more. Mackenzie's cheeks flushed. She swallowed hard.

"Not confined," she said. "Not really. And anyway, I just have to… well, no. I *want* to…"

Her voice tapered off, drifting into the silence around them. Mackenzie glanced down at her feet and took a deep breath, as though steeling herself. When she looked back up, Thorn's breath caught.

Mackenzie's bright, blue eyes glistened with tears.

"Jesus, Thorn," she muttered. "I am *so sorry.*"

A weight of surprise crashed into Thorn's lungs.

"It's been so hard," Mackenzie went on, rumbling, rambling, like she had to get it all out before she just couldn't fucking do it anymore. She wiped her eyes with her knuckles. "Losing Lina and Abraham and everything that's happened… I was just trying to take the edge off, that's all, but once I started, I couldn't stop."

Thorn opened her mouth, wanting to speak, wishing she knew what to say, but her skull closed around her thoughts and Mackenzie barreled on.

"I fucked up," she said. "I fucked up *so badly.* I ruined our mission, I put everyone in danger, but worst of all, I let *you* down."

The pit in Thorn's chest ached deeper. "Mackenzie—"

"I wouldn't be here without you," she cut in. "You *saved* me. You could have let me die, but you didn't. You brought me here. You helped me get clean. You gave me something worth living for… and I threw it away. Fuck, Thorn, I threw it *all* away!"

She choked out a strangled sound. Inside Thorn's gym bag, Sparkie whined.

"I don't expect you to forgive me," Mackenzie said. "I don't deserve it. I just had to—"

Thorn dropped the bag, strode across the room, and threw her arms around Mackenzie. The Irishwoman sucked in a shocked gasp, and her whole body froze in Thorn's embrace. Thorn held tighter.

"I'm sorry, too," she said. "I wasn't here for you. I didn't notice. I didn't see how much you were hurting, and I fucking *should have.*"

All at once, Mackenzie's strength gave out. She melted against Thorn, sobbing into her collar as she gripped her shoulders desperately. Thorn kept her upright, running her fingers through Mackenzie's hair as she drew her in as close as she could.

"But I'm here now," Thorn went on. Emotion welled in her throat, and she swallowed it down. "We'll get through this, okay? Together."

Mackenzie nodded. Thorn suspected it was all she *could* do. She just nodded, over and over again, grasping Thorn more fervently, crying more freely. Thorn pressed her cheek into the side of Mackenzie's head. When she closed her eyes, tears fell down her cheeks, too. At first, it was a trickle, but soon, the trickle was a stream, and that stream carried away weeks of tension, of anger, of sadness, until all she felt was relief.

Thorn set a mug in front of Mackenzie. The ceramic landed on the wrought iron tabletop with a dull clang.

"I don't know how you can even call this coffee," Thorn murmured. Her voice carried across the vacant courtyard, disappearing in the stagnant air between empty alcoves and vine-filled planters. "It's ninety percent sugar."

Mackenzie chuckled as she lifted the mug. "Some people like their coffee black, and the rest of us don't hate ourselves."

She brandished her drink in a toast, winking one puffy, bloodshot eye at Thorn over the rim. Thorn smirked and shook her head. She took the chair across the table, raised her own coffee to her lips, and breathed the steam in deep. Sparkie laid against her back, his wings tucked beneath her damp hair while his head crested the crook of her neck. His beady eyes trained on Mackenzie.

After several minutes of crying and holding on to one another, making up for all the missed moments in the last few weeks, the two of them moved into the courtyard for a late-night cup of coffee. Now that they were sitting, a silence sank around them—not the calm, quiet kind, but one full of untold stories and open wounds.

Mackenzie stared into her mug between sips. Thorn couldn't stop watching her. She'd spent so much time avoiding Mackenzie that she had missed so many obvious signs. Her face was gaunt, her arms stuck out from her sleeves like skeletal remains, and her painted nails were bitten down to tender nubs. Even her eyes, usually bright and carefree, looked heavy beneath the dark circles.

"Are you okay?" Thorn asked, the sound of her voice sudden and loud in the quiet of the courtyard.

"I've had better days," Mackenzie said with a scoff. "I've been on an apology tour all evening, making up for all the dumb, thoughtless, and downright shitty things I've done and said and… been."

The muscles along her neck tightened, which made Thorn's lungs feel heavy.

"Oh yeah?"

"Yeah." Mackenzie exhaled a sigh as she propped her

chin on the heel of her palm and absently swirled her coffee. "It's *super* fun. Darius made me cry by being obnoxiously understanding."

Thorn chuckled, glancing at the mug in her hands. "Sounds like Darius."

"Stupid Kindness," Mackenzie grumbled, but when Thorn looked back to her, she seemed lighter. A smile teased at her mouth. "Chris and Gabe were good about it, too, and Caleb said he's just happy I'm okay. Nicholas was too busy to really give a shit… John shut the door in my face before I said anything. Can't say I blame him."

The smile disappeared, and Mackenzie inhaled a slow, deep breath. For a moment, neither of them spoke. Thorn's eyes flicked to Mackenzie's left arm, where the memory of a needle in her vein still lingered like an afterimage. At last, she shook her head. "How long has this been going on?"

Mackenzie hesitated before exhaling a sigh and sitting up straight. Her focus fixed on her coffee. "The heroin was just the one time," she murmured. "Some guy was selling it by the bathrooms, and I thought one hit wouldn't…" She drifted off, her gaze glassy and distant. After a moment, she seemed to realize it and cleared her throat. "Turns out I don't have the tolerance I used to have. Guess I'm out of practice."

She forced a laugh, but Thorn's jaw clenched.

"That's not funny."

Mackenzie's humor snuffed in her mouth. "You're right. I'm sorry. Fuck, I've been saying that a lot lately." She let go of her mug and pressed her fingers against her eyes. "Ugh. Anyway, no… it actually started with Kit."

Thorn frowned. "Garfield?"

"Yeah," Mackenzie said. "When we started bringing in all the recruits from the NYPD, Chris made a big deal about making sure they felt welcome. So, I was welcoming, talking to people, getting to know them…"

She paused, leaned back in her chair, and looked out at the courtyard, like she was searching for the exact memory, the exact moment, when it had all gone to hell.

"It was really tough," she continued quietly. "These people had a lot of messed up shit going on, and Abraham wasn't there to hear it. Any of it. Mine, either." She looked back to Thorn. "D'you know how hard it is to deal with someone *else's* fucked up life when it feels like yours is falling apart?"

Thorn scoffed and raised her brows. Before she could answer, Mackenzie groaned again.

"Fuck. Of course you do. That makes what I was going to say *so* much worse."

"Just say it."

Mackenzie shrugged. "Well, it was different with Kit. He was easier to talk to 'cause the shit he was dealing with was shit I knew all about."

"What shit was that?" Thorn pressed.

"Addiction," Mackenzie said. "Ever since he got hurt, he'd been hooked on opioids."

Sparkie's head tilted as Thorn shook hers. "How the hell did he get past our screening? Chris's recruitment protocol looks for that kind of problem."

"It was never formally reported," Mackenzie said with a shrug. "The precinct handled it under the table and didn't put it in his file. Otherwise, he wouldn't have been able to work."

A spark of anger unfurled in Thorn's gut. She crossed her arms. "He wouldn't have been able to join the Martyrs, either," she snapped.

Mackenzie's eyes narrowed, and she pursed her lips. Behind them, her tongue piercing rattled against her teeth.

"Which is exactly why he couldn't talk about it with anyone," she shot back. "He didn't even admit it to *me* until I picked up on the signs. No one else understands what it's like. People are quick to label us as fucked up and throw us away." Her voice tightened, and she took a moment to steady herself. "I know you've been through some awful shit, Thorn, but you can't even *get* addicted, so I don't want to hear it right now."

Guilt stuck in Thorn's throat like a dry-swallowed pill, choking her anger, and her Familiar shrank behind her back. "You're right," she said. "I'm sorry."

She gestured for Mackenzie to continue. Mackenzie nodded, the motion stiff, before she went on.

"At first, that's all it was. Talking. About why we were sober, what made it hard… how much we missed using. Until, one day, Kit came back from patrol with a bottle of oxy. I told him no, that we couldn't do it, and that I'd have to talk to someone if he did. He promised to throw it away."

She paused again, and Thorn leaned forward on the table.

"But he didn't?"

"No," Mackenzie murmured.

"So, what happened?"

"October happened," Mackenzie said. "October twelfth. Lina's birthday. And all we fucking did was have some stupid moment of silence at dinner. Half the Underground wasn't even there. It's like she didn't matter. None of it mattered!"

Her voice shattered, cracking like glass in her mouth until it fell out in a jagged sob. Sparkie exhaled a whimper from beneath Thorn's hair as Mackenzie went on.

"And I got so hungry for the high. So fucking hungry for something to take those feelings away. And normally, I'd talk to Lina about it, or Abraham, or *you*, but they were gone, and you had so much other shit on your plate… So I went to Kit instead."

Mackenzie stopped then, looking at her hands. They quaked on the table. Thorn frowned, but she didn't speak, and after a few long seconds, Mackenzie shook her head.

"After that, he would try to get more whenever he was on duty. He didn't always land some. It depended on if he could sneak away from Madison and get the right timing to do a pick-up. We had some pretty long dry spells in between hits. Until we started looking for the new Virtue. Once I was setting the schedules and running the patrols, we could get more. We wanted to build a stockpile."

Thorn's mouth slipped open. "A *stockpile?*"

"I already told Alan," Mackenzie said, flicking her wrist. "I'm sure they've gotten it out of Kit's room by now… Anyway, when we started going to the club, we could snag more stuff. We started taking Valium, too, and we'd even sneak back and do ketamine in the bathroom on slower nights."

"Jesus, Mackenzie…" Thorn murmured as she pinched the bridge of her nose.

"I know, okay?" Mackenzie wrung her hands and pulled at her knuckles until they popped. Then, she kept pulling and pulling until Thorn wondered if she was hoping to pry her fingers off. "I know it's bad. It's *so* bad. I have felt so fucking guilty, and now Caleb lost his job, John's probably never going to talk to me again, and Kit—"

His name snagged on her teeth, and she dipped her face into her hands. Thorn drew a slow breath to ease the ache pinching between her lungs.

"Claytor will be fine," she said. "He's moving into TAC."

Mackenzie shook her head without lifting it. "But finding a replacement for the Gray Unit—"

"And Waters will get over it," Thorn interrupted. "Give him time. As for Garfield…" She paused, choosing her next words carefully. "You can't shoulder all the blame. You didn't dig this hole alone."

"No…" Mackenzie sighed into her palms. "But he's the one who ended up buried in it." She started crying again, quietly, and her shoulders slumped toward the table. "Thorn, I'm so sorry."

Thorn grabbed Mackenzie's hands and pulled them away so she could look her in the eyes. At first, Mackenzie clamped them closed, but Thorn tightened her grip around her fingers and waited until Mackenzie finally glanced up.

"It happened," Thorn said. "We can't change it, so let's

focus on what happens *next*. We got through this once. We can do it again."

Mackenzie sniffed and shook her head. "We can't."

"Yes, we can," Thorn insisted, but Mackenzie continued to shake her head. A fresh wave of tears built up behind her lashes.

"I already talked to Alan," she said, "and he agreed that I shouldn't be in the Underground—"

"*What?*" Thorn cut in. Cold fury settled over her, and Sparkie's wings flared. "No. No! That's *insane*. This is your home."

"Thorn—"

She shot to her feet. "I'm going to talk to him," she snarled. "You aren't going *anywhere.*"

Thorn stormed toward the eastern block of rooms, and Sparkie leapt from her shoulder to arc in the air above them. Mackenzie rushed up behind her and grabbed her by the wrist.

"Jesus, Thorn, I'm not *leaving,*" she said. Thorn spun around. "At least, not... forever. I'm going to rehab."

For a moment, Thorn didn't know what to say. Her eyes narrowed as Sparkie landed on her shoulder again. "Rehab? You don't need rehab. Last time—"

"Last time, the Underground *was* my rehab," Mackenzie interrupted. "It got me out of my fucked up patterns, but where are my patterns *now?*"

She opened her arms wide in a gesture around the court-yard. Thorn didn't follow the movement. Her gaze locked onto Mackenzie, and her teeth clenched.

"I have to go," Mackenzie murmured. "I deserve this."

"No," Thorn said. "You don't."

Mackenzie chuckled, and a soft smile turned up her lips. "Yes, I do. I deserve to get help, to heal, to be *happy*. I want to be at my best here, and I haven't been for a while. You don't have to like it, but it's not about you. I'm doing this for *me.*"

Thorn's throat tightened, and she tried to swallow

through it. Mackenzie watched her, waited for her, and finally, Thorn let out a sigh.

"When do you leave?"

"Next week."

"How long will you be gone?"

"The program I joined lasts six months."

Thorn's jaw dropped. *"Six months?"*

Mackenzie laughed. "You're almost a century and a half old!" she said. "I'm shit at math, but six months has gotta be a fraction of a percent of your life. You'll hardly even notice I'm gone."

She winked like this was all a joke, but Thorn couldn't bring herself to laugh. The idea of walking through these halls and knowing Mackenzie was not within them left a deeper pit in Thorn's chest than she had expected. Six months, six years, six *lifetimes*—it didn't matter. It hurt. It hurt *so* much.

Fuck, why did it hurt so much?

"Thorn? Are you okay?"

Mackenzie frowned, and Thorn realized she'd been staring at her—staring through her. She took a breath and shook her head.

"No," she admitted. The corners of her eyes stung, and Sparkie let out a soft cry. "I'm going to fucking miss you."

Thorn had lost count of how many tears Mackenzie had shed that evening, and as her irises glittered with more, Thorn felt herself tumbling over that edge, too. Without warning, Mackenzie flung her arms around her. Thorn closed her eyes as the ice-cold chill of Mackenzie's aura settled against her skin, already counting down the days until she would feel it again.

CHAPTER TWENTY-SIX

Darius didn't recognize this mockery of a city. The streets, the structures, the sensations gave the distinct impression that this place was pieced together from dozens of sources and stitched at the seams to create a patchwork that abstractly resembled New York. Massive concrete walls rose up as far as Darius's visor display could see, gray, sharp, and insurmountable. A labyrinth of artificial steel.

Rattling gunfire sounded dull and distant in his helmet. He paused at the edge of one of those walls and turned his back toward it, drawing in a low breath. Martyr energy hummed in a wide radius from where he stood.

"Get ready," Chris commanded, her voice crisp in Darius's ears. "They're coming!"

The pit of his stomach dropped out as he spun around. A swarm of aura-less puppets, smooth, cold, and featureless, materialized in the distance.

They started to run.

Darius turned and sprinted. Though he couldn't sense them, he could hear the simulated sound of feet against the ground and see digital shadows stretching longer as they closed in on his heels. Adrenaline spiked in his bloodstream, and sweat bloomed beneath the full tactical gear bogging him down. He made it ten yards, turned a corner, and kept moving. The mannequins tumbled behind him, a stampede of gray flesh and moaning voices.

Then a string of nonsense words overwhelmed his brain—TAC officers announcing their locations, asking for clearance, swearing, and finally, Seth Graves called a warning that the weapon was live.

"Moment of truth!" he screamed.

A piercing sound shot instantly through the room, so loud and abrupt that it rattled Darius's nerves and made him stumble. But it didn't matter. The writhing mass of creatures clawing at his back collapsed. He stopped running, breathing so hard that the armor around his chest rose and fell in heavy motions. A few seconds of silence stretched around him.

"I'm down," Gabe called.

"Yeah," Charlotte Davis said. "Me, too."

"God *damn* it," Holly swore into her mic.

The environment flickered. All around Darius, the buildings, the streets, and even the sky shimmered with an electric gleam before they deconstructed themselves and left him and the others standing on the shooting range's wide, open floor. The digital puppets at Darius's feet vanished like unraveling lines of code as Chris tapped into the coms.

"Let's regroup," she said. "Head on in. Darius, Lamar, I need you for healing."

The TAC team made their way to the front of the firing lanes, walking in from wherever they'd ended up in the room. Darius was at the furthest end by the bullet trap. He searched the Martyrs as he headed in. Even without an aura and dressed in the same full combat gear as everyone else, Darius could always find Thorn. The way she carried herself was unmistakable: spine straight, shoulders strong, head high. He spotted her walking through the center of the room, and when she pulled her helmet off, a dark scowl marred her pale and perfect complexion.

He jogged to reach her.

"What's wrong?" he asked, removing his helmet, too.

Thorn glanced at him, frazzled strands of black hair clinging to her forehead and cheek. "This *has* to work."

"It will," Darius said. "It's already a ton better than the first few tests."

"Better isn't good enough," Thorn growled. "If we're going to eliminate Amoretto, we can't *afford* better."

A knot twisted in Darius's chest. It had been just over a week since Lamar's parents and sisters had gone to stay with Samira, and since then, destroying Lust had been the Martyrs' number one priority.

"It's not like we're going after him tomorrow," Darius said in an attempt at reassurance he knew sounded feeble. She threw him an annoyed glare. "Let Holly do what Holly does best. She'd never let us out there with technology she didn't believe in."

He touched a palm to the back of Thorn's arm, half-expecting her to pull away, but instead, she drew a deep breath. Her shoulders, however, held their rigid shape.

"Speaking of that," she said, more evenly now, but her voice carried a dark, doubting tone. "How's Lamar?"

The two of them glanced up to the front of the room, where Chris was walking down from the control booth. Lamar followed on her heels. Even from way the hell back here, the kid seemed worn.

"Not great," Darius said with a sigh.

"Forget the weapon," Thorn murmured. "Will *he* be ready to take on Lust?"

She cast Darius a look, and he shook his head. "I don't know."

They merged into the crowd, moving through Martyrs to Chris. More than fifty men and women surrounded them. Most were TAC agents, though a few TAC-approved volunteers from other departments peppered the room. Darius spotted Alexis, who had joined her brother on his first official duty as a fully-fledged TAC officer, and she passed Thorn an anxious frown as they pushed through. Just behind Caleb, Madison glanced up, brunette beach waves curling around her throat. She caught Darius's eye and immediately looked down at her feet.

When they reached the front, Lamar was already healing Charlotte Davis. She'd pulled her long locs around her shoulder so he could press his fingertips against her temple. Gabe stood to her right, and he removed his helmet.

"Fuck," he said with a wince. A line of blood dribbled down the side of his face, where it got caught in the shadow of stubble on his neck. He worked his jaw and massaged the joint beneath his ear. "That hurt like hell."

Chris offered a tender smirk as she dabbed at the blood with a gauze pad, but Conrad snorted.

"Quit yer bitchin'," he grumbled. He'd taken a seat at the bottom of the stairs and stretched a thick leg out in front of him with a groan. "I think I pulled a muscle."

"I'm pretty sure a ruptured eardrum hurts worse than a pulled muscle, Carter," Deidra Cummins jabbed. "Stop being such a baby."

Conrad thrust a middle finger at her as she laughed. Thorn pushed past them, walking around Conrad to head up the stairs to the control booth.

"How the hell did you pull a muscle?" Darius asked, glancing after Thorn as he touched Gabe's temple. A subtle mirror of Gabe's pain echoed in Darius's ears for an instant before washing away on a wave of healing power. He focused back on Conrad. "This was a simulation."

"He tried to lean on one of the fake walls," Amelia Chan said with a snicker. "Fell right on his ass!"

Conrad brandished the same gesture to her as Darius chuckled and squatted at his side. He'd rolled his pant leg up to his knee, which was already starting to swell. It took seconds for Darius to mend the muscle beneath. Conrad grumbled a thank you.

"Next time, stick to the paths," Darius said with a grin, offering a hand. Conrad took it, nearly pulled Darius down as he hauled himself to his feet, and slapped a meaty palm against the armor on his back so firmly it sent Darius staggering to the side. Chris rolled her eyes and stifled a smirk.

"All right," she said to the room, her voice booming with authority. The murmuring snapped silent. "Take ten, then we'll get back at it."

"Same drill?" Seth asked.

Gabe nodded. "Yep. We're really pushing to stress the system. These devices reliably delay when there are only a couple of us, but now that they're trying to manage signals from multiple sources, we need to force them to adapt. The more chaotic it is, the better."

"Maybe Conrad falling through the wall was a good thing," Amelia joked. A chorus of laughter followed her, and Conrad joined in this time. Chris grabbed the sonic weapon from Seth and took the stairs back to the control booth. Lamar moved to follow her, and Darius came up beside him.

"Thanks for your help," he said, attempting a smile.

Lamar didn't even look at him. "No problem."

Then he climbed the steps a little faster, leaving Darius behind, and Darius's smile dissolved. When they reached the control booth, the door opened to arguing.

"...it *is* working," Holly insisted. "Like I have told you a thousand times, the AI program in the helmets is collecting data every time we run these tests and learning how to compensate."

She and Thorn stood at odds across the metal table at the center of the room, arms crossed and brows furrowed. Taylor Simmons sat near the gear locker, busily prepping another sonic disruptor. Beside her, Naomi Mori leaned against the wall. She smiled as Lamar walked in. That smile turned into a scowl when her eyes landed on Darius.

While the Verrettes had left the Underground, Naomi decided to stay by Lamar's side, but she made no effort to hide her distaste for this place. No. Not the Underground. If Darius were completely honest with himself, he knew it was him and Thorn she really had a problem with. He nodded in her direction. Her glare sharpened.

"You've been running tests for weeks," Thorn said. "How the hell is it *not* ready?"

Holly pushed her thick-rimmed glasses up the bridge of her nose. Her nostrils flared. "Every round of testing focuses on a different variable," she said. "We've tested it with stationary objects, moving ones, through obstructions like glass or concrete, through *multiple* obstructions, different altitudes, around corners, at temperature extremes—"

"We've run this thing through the wringer," Taylor chimed in without looking up from what she was doing. Holly threw a hand out to her in emphasis.

"And *this* is the final hoop," she continued. "As many moving targets as possible, guaranteeing the device can sync up with all of our headsets every single time it's activated, and you can see that it's learning!" Holly pointed at her screen, which displayed a graph that looked like pure nonsense to Darius. "So, and I mean this in the kindest way possible, can you please get the hell off my back and trust me to do my damned job?"

Thorn's mouth pressed together, her fingers tight around her bicep as Holly held her glare with one just as unyielding. Darius glanced at Chris, who shrugged, before he cleared his throat.

"This new simulation program helped," he said, tilting the helmet in his hands. Thorn glanced at him, and Holly finally followed suit.

"Good," she said. "The whole idea was to force our people to move the same way they might in an actual combat situation."

"It's phenomenal," Chris agreed. "I'd love to integrate it into some of our TAC training procedures, if that's possible."

"Of course it is."

"Did you build it?" Darius asked, peering at the visor. He could hardly believe the thing functioned as an augmented reality screen.

Holly shook her head. "Nope. Believe it or not, Simmons got it from her contact at the Pentagon. Turns out, she *is* handy to have around."

"I'm *right here*," Taylor said.

"Yeah," Holly said dismissively, "I know."

Taylor rolled her eyes and stood up, walking to the table.

"All right," she said. "This one's ready to go." She handed the fresh sonic disruptor to Chris, who traded it for the spent one. The items looked like nondescript soda cans, silver and unassuming, except for an activation button on the top.

Thorn propped her hands on her hips. "How long do they take to recharge?"

Taylor shrugged as she returned to her corner, where ten devices sat in a grid-like pattern on a power station. She clicked the eleventh one into an open slot, leaving a single space open for the one in Chris's palm.

"A couple of hours," Taylor said. "We shouldn't have any lag in testing since the first will be fully juiced up by the time we get to the last. Theoretically."

"Wait," Naomi said. Everyone spun to where she and Lamar had tucked out of the way at the opposite side of the room. She crossed her arms. "You can only get *one* blast per charge?"

"It takes a lot of power to produce a sound wave this loud," Taylor said. "The batteries are drained near to nothing."

"How is that even useful?" Naomi argued. "I've seen the sonic cannons that cops bring out at riots or whatever. They run them *constantly.*"

Thorn's brows twitched together as Holly's raised into her bangs. Taylor, however, simply shrugged.

"The LRAD devices the NYPD uses are designed for crowd *control*, not disabling Puppets," she answered. "They take time to get together and they have to be hooked up to massive power sources in the back of a tank—not exactly feasible in a Sin situation. Ours are louder, faster, and the sound waves from one blast are enough to disable anyone within a twenty-meter radius. We shouldn't *need* more than one per charge to take out a whole street full of Puppets."

Naomi's annoyance didn't soften.

"And we won't be able to use these devices at all if we don't get back to testing," Holly said. "So unless you have any other *important* questions…"

"I do, actually," Naomi said. A muscle in Holly's cheek twitched. Naomi's glare flashed at Darius again. "If he's your *healer*, why the hell is he out there running combat tests?"

Darius's lips parted in surprise. As he watched Naomi, her black eyes unforgiving as she stood, just barely, in front of Lamar, he realized something. She wasn't just angry…

She was scared.

"Because healers see combat," Thorn said. "He has to be ready for it."

A cold chill settled around the room. Naomi's throat flexed as she swallowed, and the gleam of fear in her expression was clearer now.

"Let's get back to it," Chris said. She handed the sonic device to Thorn. "We've got a lot of testing left before we're done here."

She turned to the door and held it open. As Thorn and Darius headed out, he glanced over his shoulder to see Naomi's hand around Lamar's forearm. Darius sighed and shook his head.

"She's not trying to be mean," he said.

"Yes, she is," Thorn responded, "but it's not about us. It's about Lamar. She's fucking terrified for him."

Darius frowned. "If you knew that, why did you make her worry? It won't help."

"Neither will coddling her," Thorn argued. "Lamar stayed because he wants to destroy Amoretto. The only way he's going to do that is by walking right into the fire. He has to understand that, and so does she."

They reached the bottom of the stairs, and Thorn turned

to Darius, looking at him in a way that made him suspect she wasn't thinking about the upcoming fight against Lust but a future one with a different Sin and Virtue at the center. His cheeks flushed.

"If this weapon works," Thorn went on, tearing her gaze away as she put her helmet on, "he stands a better chance of walking out of it alive."

Then she moved away, meeting Gabe halfway across the shooting range. Darius watched after her for a moment before he pulled his helmet over his head, too, and got into position. Minutes later, Chris called for the room to get ready, and the augmented city sprung to life around him. When the digital puppets swarmed, Darius imagined they were real men and women pulled by Envy's corrupted strings, trying to end *him* before he had the chance to eliminate the Sin for good.

Three days later, the sonic disruptor was officially approved for combat use. By the end of the first, all problems had been resolved, but Holly forced two more full rounds to be completely confident. Now, TAC was training on how and when to deploy their new weapon.

And Darius was working with Lamar.

"Wait…" Lamar shook his head. "You *failed* to destroy Sloth?"

Nicholas laughed. He and Lamar sat on the beige couch in Darius's office while Darius took the armchair on the other side of the glass coffee table.

"*Miserably,*" Nicholas confirmed. "I was a mess, not that I'd ever think it at the time." He threw Darius a wry smile, and Darius raised his hands with a chuckle.

"Your words, not mine."

"Because it's true," Nicholas said. "I was a cocky asshole with a chip on my shoulder, which meant…"

He drifted off with a shrug. Lamar leaned forward,

clasping his hands between his knees.

"You didn't have the right mindset to get rid of the Sin."

"Exactly."

Darius's smile tightened. What Thorn said at the shooting range had lodged in his brain like a barb. It didn't matter that the new weapon was ready if Lamar wasn't, so he'd brought in an expert—the only person in the Underground who actually knew what it was like to destroy a Sin firsthand.

"I had to learn some hard lessons before I could take on Sloth," Nicholas admitted. "We could've had the guy locked in a vault somewhere, and it wouldn't matter. I couldn't destroy him, no matter how much I wanted to, until I figured that part out."

Lamar frowned. "How did you know when you had?"

Nicholas paused, throwing an arm along the back of the couch as he considered the question.

"You never really *know*," he said after a moment. "It's not like when you accept your Virtue and suddenly the world is on fire and you've got a new name inside your skull. Instead… I guess you just start moving toward your Sin on instinct."

"Instinct?" Darius asked. He leaned forward, too. In the nearly two years since Sloth had been destroyed, he'd never heard Nicholas talk much about it. The old Diligence glanced at him.

"Yeah," he said. "The Virtue *wants* to rejoin the Sin. That's the easiest way I can explain it. Some instinctual pull."

"Like those turtles that lay eggs on the same beach they were born?" Lamar offered.

Nicholas laughed loud and hard, which made a smile break over Lamar's face for the first time since he'd come to the Underground. Darius smirked.

"Yeah, I guess it is kind of like that," Nicholas said, "That was the first sign that something was different. I was drawn to where Sloth was hiding out." He tilted his chin toward Darius. "You know how you found *me* because you read an article about my event and knew it was important?" Darius nodded. Nicholas did, too. "When I looked at the locations I'd narrowed down, one of them suddenly stood out. I knew it was where I had to go. The same thing happened when we had him pinned. I just *knew* what I had to do, like the instructions had been unlocked at exactly that moment."

It was as though a switch went off in Nicholas's brain, dimming the light behind his eyes. He went distant, no doubt trapped in darker times. Darius glanced at Lamar, but the young Virtue had latched onto Nicholas like a hungry child desperate for scraps of food. After a few seconds, Lamar spoke again, his voice a murmur.

"What was it like, destroying Sloth?"

Nicholas's focus landed on him before sliding to Darius. He shook his head like he'd woken from a disorienting sleep.

"Well," he said, clearing his throat, "at first, it was like anything else Virtues do. Healing, Influence, all of it boils down to pouring our energy into someone else. This felt deeper, though. It wasn't just energy that I was pouring out. It was my soul. And it… hurt."

The last word ground out of his mouth like crumbling stone. He pressed a hand against his sternum, and his bright irises constricted, again dissolving into memory as a frown tightened his face.

"The pain started in my chest," he continued, "and the colder and weaker I got, the more it radiated until my whole body just fucking ached, like thousands of needles were pushing out from my bones. I thought I was dying. I *expected* to die. But instead, I opened my eyes and found myself curled up on the ground. It felt like my heart was collapsing."

A quiet second stretched between them. Lamar's full lips dropped open as he stared at Nicholas. Darius hadn't realized how shallow his breathing had become until he took a fresh one, and his lungs begged for more.

"Does it get easier?" he asked.

Nicholas shrugged. "You get better at managing it."

The three of them sat in silence, all eyes diverted away from one another as they stewed in what Nicholas had gone through—what they would *all* go through. A phantom shadow of painful emptiness bloomed between Darius's lungs, and he raised a hand to it.

Lamar cleared his throat. "What happens if I'm never ready to face him?"

Darius looked up. Lamar, like him, had flattened a palm against his chest, and he lowered it only to wrap his arms around himself instead. He looked between Darius and Nicholas anxiously. His dark eyes glistened with fear.

"Don't worry," Nicholas said, shaking his head. "You will be. If an asshole like *me* can get over myself long enough to wipe out a Sin, you'll have no problem."

He attempted a smile, but Lamar only shrank further.

"No, like… what if I *can't?*"

Darius frowned. He glanced at Nicholas to see him watching Lamar with the same confused concern. Darius leaned closer. "What do you mean?"

"I mean, what if I can't do it?" The young Virtue got to his feet and walked toward the door, wringing his hands. "What if I can't beat Connor?"

The name fell out of Lamar's mouth with a note of choked familiarity—like it was *more* than a name. Darius's concern deepened, and his gut churned with a sudden understanding. He stood up, too.

"Lamar," Darius began, "did you know Connor Amoretto before his possession?"

Lamar nodded without looking at him. Nicholas eyed Darius cautiously as he shifted in his seat. When Darius spoke again, he kept his tone even, not sure what to expect. "Did something happen?"

Lamar turned back, his eyes full of tears, and he choked out three words:

"He *raped* me."

The room froze for a breath, Darius's mouth agape and eyes wide. Then, Nicholas exploded up from the couch like a pipe bomb had detonated beneath the cushions.

"He *what?*"

Lamar sucked in a shaky breath. "My third year at NYU. I was part of this program that hooked us up with alumni mentors for career experience. Connor was one of them, and god, I thought he was amazing. Older, charming, hot as all hell… Everyone wanted to work with him, but he picked *me*. I felt like I'd won the damn lottery. Can you believe it?"

He let out a strangled, frantic laugh that lacked any joy as his arms wound around his center again. "Everyone treated Connor like a prince. He took me to all his favorite spots and introduced me to his friends… I'd be a liar if I said I wasn't into it. I knew we were skirting the line for what was appropriate, but I didn't care."

Then Lamar paused, breathing in a sigh. Nicholas edged closer to Darius, the rage pouring off of him so palpable that he may as well have been another of Wrath's discarded vessels. Neither of them said anything as Lamar quietly went on.

"One night, he invited me back to his place, and we started *really* crossing lines," he muttered. "Nothing sexual, but god, the want was there. When he tried to go further, I told him I wasn't ready, so he backed off, and we settled in to watch a movie with some wine and popcorn. Ten minutes later, I felt fuzzy."

A cold darkness opened in Darius's gut, and he absently imagined he'd been possessed by Wrath, too.

"There was something in my drink," Lamar hissed, the tears in his eyes pooling fervently. "I couldn't move. I couldn't *think*. I just sat there, trapped in my body, while he did whatever he wanted with it. For hours."

"Jesus fucking Christ," Nicholas snarled.

"When it wore off," Lamar went on, voice constricted, "I gathered all my clothes and got out of there. Connor was just sitting on the couch. He didn't even look at me as I left.

The next time I saw him at the university, I tried to talk to him about it, but he acted like *I* was the one with a problem. Like… like I'd had too much wine and *regretted* what happened. Then he smiled at me and told me the whole campus knew this was what I did. Got drunk and fucked around."

"Lamar," Darius began softly, but the young Virtue talked over him.

"And you know the worst part? He got away with it! Nobody took me seriously!" Lamar threw his hands up and started pacing by the bookshelves as the words poured out. "I took all the right steps. I reported him to the school, but they sided with him. Connor told the same lies he tried to sell me, and they *bought it*. Everyone I met through the stupid program wouldn't talk to me anymore. Even the police refused to file the report. They laughed me out of the damn building! Told me they didn't handle 'lovers quarrels' and wouldn't 'ruin a young man's life' over false claims. But what about *my* life?"

He stopped abruptly, his focus darting to the scars buried beneath an array of crisp ink doodles on his arm. They spun a whole new story now, the words Lamar couldn't say slashed clear as day into his skin. Darius's fists clenched until his nails pressed against his palms.

"It took me *years* to feel anything again," Lamar said. He didn't meet Nicholas's or Darius's gaze as he coiled around himself. "My parents gave up *everything* to keep me here. They supported me when I dropped out and spent their whole life savings to break my lease, take on my debts, and get me into a therapist who specialized in sexual assault, and now they can't even come home until I take down the guy who did this to me in the first place?" His eyes snapped up to Darius, catching his desperately, and the tears finally began to fall. "I wasn't strong enough to stop him when he was just a man! How the hell am I supposed to stop him *now?*"

Lamar dipped his face into shaking hands and sobbed. Darius hesitated for a moment, unsure what to do, knowing damn well that nothing he said or did could fix this. He stepped forward, gently touching a hand to Lamar's shoulder, just to make sure he knew he wasn't alone.

And Lamar collapsed against him. His arms wound around Darius as he cried. Darius held him close, and they stood like that for several aching seconds until Nicholas scoffed.

"Strong," he said. The strange, bitter cadence pulled their attention to him. "'*What doesn't kill you makes you stronger*,' right? What a load of horse shit."

Lamar and Darius pulled away from one another, Lamar wiping tears away with the back of his hand as Darius frowned. Nicholas shook his head.

"I hate that stupid platitude. The truth is, trauma doesn't make you stronger. Trauma rips you to pieces, and it doesn't give a shit if you never get back to your feet."

A spark of familiar frustration lit in Darius's chest, and he was about to intervene to shut Nicholas up. Before he did, the former Diligence grabbed Lamar by the shoulders, leaned forward until they were linked eye-to-eye, and said, "Trauma doesn't make you stronger. *You* do. The asshole who did this doesn't deserve *any* credit for the incredible person you've become. You did the work. Now, keep doing it—for *you*. For your family. For the people you love. Not for him. Never for him. He's *nothing* compared to you."

A new wave of emotion spilled down Lamar's face, but this felt different. Grateful and relieved. The young Virtue nodded, and Nicholas's grip tightened, holding fiercely, as though he could fortify Lamar's strength with his own two hands.

It seemed to be working.

CHAPTER TWENTY-SEVEN

The morning chill had barely begun to fade, whisked away as sunlight reflected onto the streets below. A late-night rainfall sprinkled the city with condensation. Remnants of it patterned the sidewalk and streets with dewy blotches and humid shadows, and the very air blended a strange mix of fresh spring and city filth. Thorn breathed deep, her motorcycle helmet providing little in the way of filtering for the sounds, the smells, and the sights around her. Steam lifted from street grates. Sirens blared in the distance. Advertisements flashed by on the backs of buses or pinned to trash bins on the side of the road. One of those advertisements drew her eye, and her heart lodged in her throat.

A poster of Lamar Verrette for the whole city to see on a virtual billboard attached to a bus shelter.

His face shone out from the backlit display—an AI-generated mugshot that looked so real that Thorn knew no one would question its authenticity—while a marquee of text spun around the bottom.

Wanted. Armed and dangerous. $100,000 cash reward.

Furious heat rippled through Thorn's body, tightening her muscles until her hands ached and her teeth crunched together. Her gaze followed the image as she zipped past it, and Thorn's mind swam with a complicated mix of emotions and thoughts. Ahead of her, a haze of cold energy moved closer.

A car slammed on its horn. Two cars. More.

Thorn turned around just in time to see a swarm of people crossing the road at Reade and Church. She screeched to a halt, nearly laying her bike on its side, and stopped just in time to avoid smashing into a frazzled man in the intersection. He spat foul names at her as he kept walking. She flung up an apologetic wave and straightened her bike. The rest of the pedestrians leered at her, and Thorn adjusted her gloves, swearing under her breath. Sparkie, who was following high in the sky above, flew in an angry, anxious circle.

God damn it, this whole situation had her so worked up that she was getting sloppy.

A spark of fury uncoiled deep in Thorn's belly. She stretched her spine, each vertebra sliding into place as she lifted her head. The sounds of New York City hummed around her like the inner workings of a giant machine— grinding along, running without care or concern about who was caught and crushed between the gears. Thorn's gaze darted around the high-rises on every side, wondering if Lust was hiding within one.

Though Connor Amoretto had disappeared from Holly's cameras and all of his old hangouts, he was still plainly visible if you knew where to look. The wanted poster was only the beginning. Every major media conglomerate had doubled down on their attempts to weed Lamar out of hiding. It hadn't gone without notice that the rest of the Verrettes had disappeared, so naturally, they were presumed to be on the run together. Dozens of Lamar's old friends had begun showing up in interviews, giving detailed reports about who he was and what he was capable of that didn't align at all with the young man Thorn had gotten to know.

Remarkable, she thought, how quickly people turned on those they loved when the Sins' corruption and Influence were at play.

But none of that mattered. Not really. Knowing that Lust was still using his Influence to mess with the city didn't make it any easier for Thorn to find him. With the new weapon ready and Consent safely in the Underground, Amoretto was the last piece. They couldn't very well destroy Lust if they didn't know where the hell he was.

The light turned green, and Thorn pulled forward, unsure of what the fuck to do now. As she turned the corner, heading further north, an alert chimed in her ear, and Nicholas Wolfe's name scrolled at the top of her visor screen. About damn time. She answered the call.

"Did you find the information I asked for?"

Nicholas scoffed on the other end of the line.

"Would it kill you to say 'hi' every once in a while?" he asked. "Good morning, by the way. I hope you're having a productive day hunting Connor Amoretto."

Thorn rolled her eyes. "No, I'm not. That's why I need that information that I—"

"Of course I found it," Nicholas interrupted. "Why do you think I'm even calling? And you were right. She's been busy as fuck."

A brief burst of excitement immediately soured in Thorn's mouth. "When it comes to Wrath," she said bitterly, "I usually am."

"Check out the server," Nicholas said. "I put it in your inbox. The new folder should be at the top."

Thorn glanced around the street, looking for an easy place to pull over, and popped her motorcycle onto the sidewalk to park between a graffiti-ridden mailbox and an a-frame sign advertising the "best pierogies in New York City." She grabbed her phone from the pocket on her thigh and navigated to the Martyr server. A smile turned up the corners of her mouth.

"'Wrath bullshit?'" she read.

"That's it."

A laugh rumbled in her chest as she opened the folder.

Instantly, the levity died. Nicholas had compiled dozens of notes, reports, and articles. She scanned them as Sparkie landed on a rooftop high over her head, the heat from the morning sun barely reaching him through their cold mood.

"A copycat killer?" she said at last. The word felt heavy on her tongue.

"Mmmm," Nicholas grunted in confirmation. "Five days ago. All the big papers are too busy trying to convince the rest of the city that Lamar is some kind of psychopath to cover it, but it's all the smaller presses can talk about. A club in Manhattan Valley. Sixteen dead."

"Manhattan Valley…" Thorn murmured. "That's where Lamar was living."

"Yep."

Thorn swore. That was a hard coincidence to ignore, and this kind of senseless violence was exactly what Wrath loved to instigate. She kept scrolling, kept reading. Another headline stood out. It didn't match the rest.

"A missing school bus…" Thorn said. "Did this get sorted into the wrong folder?"

"Nope," Nicholas responded. "It was from Lamar's sisters' school—their class, actually. Twenty-four fourth graders just disappeared when their bus didn't show up for a field trip to city hall yesterday."

Thorn's stomach dropped. Fuck. That couldn't be a coincidence, either.

"She's trying to punish him for getting away," she mused aloud.

"And kill him if he tries to come back," Nicholas agreed. "Did you see Alexis Claytor's reports?"

Thorn hadn't, and she kept digging through the files until she found them. This document was huge—a collection of dispatch calls and reported incidents that Alexis and her network of sympathizers in the NYPD had collected over the weeks since The Eros Project had gone up in a storm of bullets. The pattern laid out was clear as fucking day: there was a marked increase in violence against young Black men—men like Lamar. So far, there hadn't been any fatalities, but plenty of hospitalizations and even more arrests. Thorn wasn't surprised that *this* hadn't found its way to the media yet, either.

"Fuck," she growled.

"You think they're working together on this?" Nicholas pressed. "Wrath and Lust?"

"Yeah," Thorn said. "I do. Wrath might be a lone wolf, but Lust is the one other Sin she collaborates with this much. They know Lamar's a Virtue, and they want him dead."

"Right," Nicholas agreed. "But how does that help us?"

Thorn's spine went rigid as her mind filtered through a dozen decades-old memories she'd spent the last hundred years trying to forget—memories of plans and schemes and vendettas that Wrath and Lust had carried out together.

"If I can find Hunt," she said at last, "maybe I'll find Amoretto, too."

"Any idea where *she* might be?"

Thorn chewed on the corner of her mouth and considered where she'd felt Wrath's Influence. It was a long shot, but…

"Can you do me a favor?" she asked. "Dig through any triggered facial recognition sightings of Wrath on Andrews's cameras in The Bronx—anything that's even a thirty percent match. Most of them are probably false positives, but it's worth a shot."

Nicholas paused. "The Bronx? Really? What the fuck would she be doing up there?"

"I don't know," Thorn admitted, "but it's all I've got to go on."

"Hmm…" Nicholas thought for a moment, and in the space behind his silence, Thorn heard the rustling sounds of the R&D headquarters. "All right. I'll have Dan start right away. I hope you're right about this, too. I want to tear this guy to fucking shreds."

A darkness settled over the words, and Thorn's grip

tightened around her phone. She knew the feeling. Ever since Darius's report of Lamar's history with Connor Amoretto had passed her desk, Thorn's stomach had been full of a vengeful fire she just couldn't put out. It was the only shred of a silver lining she could find in this whole damned thing: it made her want to kill the man that much more.

She sighed, tapping her fingertips against her thumb as she considered the city.

"How's Lamar doing?" she asked.

"I don't know," Nicholas murmured. "Not great, but he seems better since we talked. Darius is teaching him all that Virtue self-care shit he tried to make me do. I have a feeling the kid's going to be a better student than I ever was." He let out a humorless laugh.

Thorn's brows pulled together. "You're not helping?"

An awkward breath huffed through her speaker. "Nah. I never made a good Virtue. I figure Darius can handle that, and I'll put my energy into tracking this fucker down so we can send him to hell where he belongs."

A somber smile lifted Thorn's lips, more bitter and understanding than anything else. "I'm going to head up to The Bronx and get a feel for the area. Let me know what you find on those videos."

"You got it."

They said goodbye, Thorn making an actual effort in sincerity for it, before she made her way north. It took nearly thirty minutes in morning commute traffic to get through Manhattan, and by the time she crossed the Willis Avenue Bridge, Nicholas had texted to confirm her suspicions.

Three weeks ago, barely visible in a traffic camera off Bruckner and Leggett, Autumn Hunt had been in The Bronx.

Thorn parked her bike in a paid lot near St. Mary's Park, and she analyzed the photograph. Her core spun, full of a monstrous fire, as she looked into Wrath's face. The mirror obscured the upper half, but her chin and mouth were visible, and Thorn would recognize that scowl anywhere. There was no denying it. Hunt had been here. The question now was if she still was.

And who was with her. Wrath had been the passenger in a navy blue sedan, and the person behind the wheel was more difficult to see. It was clearly a man, his forearms visible through the rolled-up sleeves of his button-up shirt, but the sun visor shielded his head, and his left arm was turned in just the right way to where Thorn couldn't tell if he had the *Peccostium* beneath his wrist. She had a sneaking suspicion it might be Connor Amoretto, but she had no way to fucking prove it.

But it was a start, and that was more than she'd had in months.

Thorn began combing the neighborhood on foot. Her motorcycle may have made things faster, but speed also meant she was more likely to miss smaller details. Instead, she stopped by a local java cart, grabbed a cup of hot, black coffee, and headed toward Bruckner.

The Bronx… God, she hated being here again.

Her heart clenched with a stale pang of loss, and she took a sip to still it. The drink was so bitter that Thorn half-worried it would turn her Forgotten Sin gut. She winced and tossed the whole damn thing in a bin, undrunk.

Nothing like a cup of sludge to make you miss old, familiar comforts. These cold streets reminded her of all the things Teagan Love had built that Thorn had abandoned: her coffee shop, her bar, her community. Strange and fractured and broken as they all were, they'd been *hers*, and now, Thorn had to start over from scratch. Again.

With a sigh, she zipped her bike jacket to her throat, shoved her hands in her pockets, and started walking.

The next couple of hours passed with the same level of momentum that her search in Manhattan had. She had shit to show for it.

Unlike the Financial District, where massive towers clawed so high into the sky that they ripped through the blue expanse with sharp fingers of glass and steel, The Bronx had no such sign of strength and status. Buildings here were little nubs, jutting from unkempt streets like weeds that refused to die. That was one of the things that had drawn Thorn here when she was crafting her Teagan Love persona in the first place: somehow, these neighborhoods felt less confining.

She'd combed much of the southern streets, avoiding the ones that plucked at the sensitive spots in her soul. Instead of heading west toward Mott Haven, Thorn had moved through Port Morris before following Bruckner to the east and weaving her way up and down the boroughs beside it. She wasn't sure exactly what she was looking for, but she made a point to show her face everywhere she went, catching the eye of every commuter, transient, and passerby she could.

If nothing else, Thorn knew Wrath would have Sentries around, and those Sentries would be looking for her. So far, though, no one had behaved in a way that indicated they'd been Programmed, and she was beginning to think this was another waste of goddamned time.

The light at Leggett Avenue turned red right as she reached it. The overpass above rumbled with traffic, and she paused at the corner. Thorn frowned, considering the eight-lane road, the decrepit traffic lights hanging above them, and the concrete pillars covered in urban street tags. This was where the photo had come from… Thorn wondered if she could figure out which way Wrath had gone.

She pulled out her phone and opened the image of Wrath's latest appearance again, comparing it with the intersection. This angle was wrong. When the light turned green, she jogged across the road to get a view from the other side. A beady, black camera lens sat on top of one of the far traffic control boxes, and Thorn positioned herself as near to it as she could. She looked down at the photograph again.

Wrath had turned right onto Leggett, heading into Hunts Point.

Maybe she was searching the wrong part of The Bronx.

Thorn slipped her phone back into her pocket. A massive, blue bridge crossed a river of train cars in the Oak Point Yard. Directly on the opposite side, Thorn came out between a row of warehouses and an old gas station. If she were hiding out nearby, the first person she'd Program would be someone right at the entrance to the neighborhood—someone who saw everything and everyone.

Like a clerk.

Thorn walked into the gas station convenience store. A chime rang through the building, announcing her presence, and an older, balding man behind the counter glanced up. The moment his beady eyes landed on her, he pulled a phone out of his pocket. Thorn's stomach flipped.

"Good morning," he said, maintaining eye contact and smiling at her. All the while, his thumbs tapped on the screen as though following some implicit muscle memory. "How can I help you?"

Then he put his device away again, and still, he hadn't looked down at it.

"What was on your phone?" Thorn asked.

The man's smile disappeared, replaced with a confused frown. He patted his pockets, shaking his head.

"I'm sorry. Do you need to make a call?"

A tickling anticipation crawled up Thorn's spine, and she turned to leave without another word. That had to be Programming.

Part of Thorn knew she should leave—mark this area as a point of interest, set Holly and her team to monitor it, and come back with a full TAC escort to sweep the neighborhood. She also knew that leaving now meant she might never discover who created this Sentry and what they were meant to do. So, instead of heading back to the Underground, Thorn looked around. She needed somewhere to hide while she kept an eye on the gas station, but this industrial neighborhood was more open than Manhattan and severely lacking in public buildings she could hide inside. Her attention caught on a warehouse across the street. It didn't offer much for cover, but it *did* provide vantage.

This would have to do.

Thorn tucked around the structure and leapt over a wrought-iron fence that enclosed a tiny, concrete courtyard. A small nook created a corner between the taller portion of the warehouse and a shorter wall—the perfect place to scale to the top.

She paused, sensing the energy of the streets around her, and waited for it to disperse before she rushed at the corner and vaulted upward until her fingertips barely snagged on the rooftop ledge. Then, she hoisted herself over and hopped behind the brick parapet. For a few seconds, she sat there, still and quiet, as she waited to see if any of the nearby auras moved this way.

None did, and Thorn breathed a sigh. She crouched low as she looked over the edge, but the station was still not as clear as she wanted it to be, and she didn't feel quite high enough off the ground to avoid detection. Even if the Sins couldn't sense her aura, any movement she made might draw their eye. The rooftop came in three levels, the one Thorn was on being the lowest. She quickly climbed onto the second and then the third, where she was easily thirty feet off the ground. This rooftop did not have a ledge to hide behind, so Thorn flattened onto her stomach, the black rubber warm through her clothing. From here, she could see the whole gas station and most of the streets around it. Over her head, Sparkie flew in wide, consistent circles, his sharp eyes keen and alert as he kept watch on the more distant parts of the neighborhood Thorn couldn't see from here.

Then, they waited.

For several minutes, nothing of interest happened. The roads hummed with traffic, which contained significantly more eighteen-wheelers than Thorn ever saw in Manhattan.

Fewer pedestrians, too. The station served a modest number of customers coming through its doors, but nothing like what Thorn experienced in busier parts of the city and nothing that sparked her interest.

After sitting there for almost half an hour, she started to think she'd been wrong. Maybe the clerk *hadn't* been Programmed.

But that didn't sit right with her, either. Something kept her here, a hunch or maybe just a wild hope. Thorn propped up on her elbows and looked further around the gas station. In the distance, two blocks north on Barry Street, a sleek, black SUV pulled up on the corner. It reminded her of the old cars the Martyrs had used to move their TAC agents through the city. She frowned, and Sparkie arced overhead before flying in that direction. The SUV opened, and a man climbed out. Thorn's eyes went wide.

His shirt bulged around his chest, clearly indicating a protective vest underneath, and he had a handgun strapped to the small of his back.

Thorn's focus moved up, sweeping more of the neighborhood. Similar vehicles parked beyond the range of her Sin senses, where she couldn't detect the auras of the people inside, and more men piled out. Sparkie circled wider and wider, finding one, two, three more SUVs and eight people. Thorn froze where she was, certain they hadn't seen her. Confident that she was safe.

Until Sparkie flew over a distribution center a half mile away. A central brick tower extended above everything else, and on top of that tower, a single man sat waiting just as quietly and calmly as she did. Sparkie swooped a little closer, and Thorn's blood ran cold.

A sniper. And his rifle was pointed right at her.

"Fuck."

Thorn scrambled away from the edge of the roof and leapt to her feet. She heard the gunshot—loud in Sparkie's ears—just as searing pain blasted through her thigh. She cried out and slammed back down.

Gritting her teeth, Thorn forced herself to stand. Her left leg quaked, hot blood soaking into her leggings so quickly that she worried the bullet might have nicked her femoral artery, but she couldn't do a damned thing about it with that sniper's scope still trained on her. She rushed across the warehouse, her wounded leg weighing her down like an anchor, but she managed to dive onto the next roof down just as another bullet crashed into the rubber at her feet.

Thorn winced and pressed her back against the wall, heart pounding wildly in her chest. She touched her wound and realized with a jolt of horror that the shot hadn't just gone through her leg—it had destroyed her phone. The device shattered against her skin, pieces of glass and metal digging through the fabric of her leggings and into her flesh. Her handgun was still in place inside the holster strapped beneath her jacket, but it wouldn't do a damn bit of good against a fucking sniper rifle.

Frantically, she looked around the edge of the building as Sparkie circled above her. The men from the SUVs headed her way. Thorn swore and peered down to the parking lot below.

A twenty-foot drop was better than a bullet in the brain. She leapt.

The second she landed, her wounded leg gave out beneath her, and Thorn's knees crashed painfully onto the concrete. Again, she forced herself up, and again, she ran. The only goddamned blessing of her location was that the rail yard to the west had prevented her from being surrounded. Thorn made it back to Leggett Avenue, and a swarm of cold energy turned the corner behind her. The man in the lead shouted something she couldn't hear.

Thorn sprinted.

Searing pain shot through her leg from ankle to hip, but Thorn ignored it as she dove right into traffic. Cars and trucks laid on their horns. Thorn weaved in and out of them, using the sensation of the drivers' auras and Sparkie's aerial view to guide her through the river of steel and glass. Her pursuers slowed, and Thorn pulled ahead.

But she wasn't fast enough. With her leg wounded, Thorn barely managed to keep the distance between them, and the moment she reached Bruckner, they were catching up again. Thorn kept running until she hit Southern Boulevard, and then, she sprinted west toward more familiar streets.

All the while, she was aware of a cluster of cold energy following her, trained on her scent like bloodhounds on the hunt.

Her stomach twisted. Something wasn't right. These men were too precise to be Puppets, too intentional to be Sentries, and not a single one of them had tried to open fire on her, like they gave a damn about drawing attention or hurting civilians. There was no Influence here… So what the fuck was happening?

Thorn kept sprinting, and the people on her back trickled off. She lost one, then another, and before long, only the man in the lead was left. No matter how often she turned, darted through traffic, or backtracked, he was fast behind her. She was running out of ideas—and worse, options. Her leg throbbed, and she'd lost so much blood that she was starting to shake. She needed help.

Another block. Two. Three until Thorn turned a corner, immediately took to an alley, and popped out on the other side. Then, she slipped into a building she knew.

Grind House Coffee.

She shut the door behind her and ducked beneath a standing table by the glass facade. A minute later, the man's aura sprinted past. Thorn breathed a sigh, wincing as she pressed her palm against the open wound in her leg.

Across the empty room, the barista stared at her, his mouth open, brows arched so high that his thinning hairline seemed less receded.

Painful nostalgia tugged at Thorn's chest. Years of history and bitterness unraveled in a fragile thread between them, and he gaped like he was looking at a ghost. Thorn couldn't blame the guy. The last time she'd seen him, she'd made it clear she never would again.

Now, here she was, wounded and covered in blood.

Thorn stood up with a groan and limped toward the counter. The hole in her leg screamed, and her muscles felt weak. Damn it, this was bad.

The barista swallowed hard. "Jesus, what happened to you?" he breathed at last. He held a cell in his hands and quickly tucked it into his back pocket. Thorn's gaze followed the motion.

"I need to borrow your phone," she said. "Please."

She opened her palm, expecting him to pull the device back out, but he stared at her. A glint of fear flashed in his eyes, and they darted to the door behind her back.

"W-why don't you sit down?" he asked instead, and Thorn's stomach dropped as realization sunk in. "Let me get you some water or something."

Fuck. It was too late.

"Give me your phone," she growled, her lip curling. This time, she poured Influence into the words, giving him the idea that she would hurt him if he didn't comply, and he instantly did as she asked. The device plopped into her open fingers. It was locked, but a message preview from an M. Jimenez looked up at her from the screen.

"Keep her there."

Fury unlocked in Thorn's gut. She looked at the barista again, and a chain of dread snaked down her spine. This wasn't Influence. It wasn't Programming.

This was *him.*

"P-please," the barista stammered. "They just want to talk."

Thorn dropped the phone and rushed from the building. She hadn't made it more than twenty feet before an energy turned the corner behind her, and the man who'd been chasing her sprinted down the sidewalk. He drew his gun, and finally, he shot.

The bullet thudded into the armor on her back, cracking her scapula beneath it. Thorn howled and threw caution and care into the gutter beneath her feet as she forced her Influence out in a vengeful wave. Pedestrians screamed and ran, but the man with the gun didn't. As the rest of the street emptied, he pushed through her power, his brows knitted, teeth gnashed. Thorn's chest flared with dangerous heat. She pulled her weapon with her one good arm, raised it, and shot him in the throat.

His energy blinked, and he collapsed, a heap of warm flesh on the concrete. Thorn glared through the windows of Grind House Coffee, where the barista's face pressed against the glass, harrowed and terrified. A painful ache of betrayal doused her rage.

She turned and ran.

***

Thorn never expected to end up in The Cross again… especially not like *this*.

She rested her back against a stack of boxes in the storage room, a torn strip from her ruined leggings clenched between her teeth as she addressed the wound on her thigh. The bar was still closed, so no one was there to hear her scream as she plunged her fingers deep into the muscle. The sound welled in her throat, guttural and growling, as she tenderly pulled another shard of glass from her flesh. Sparkie writhed on her shoulder, his cries less muted.

"Fuck," Thorn hissed, taking the shred of cloth from her mouth as she considered the glass. She dropped it onto the floor beside the rest of her phone, reduced to chunks of bloody shrapnel on the wood. Her hands shook, and she rested her head against the box.

She *hurt*. Her right shoulder blade swelled beneath her jacket, making that arm weak and heavy at her side while the bone slowly fused back together. That was nothing compared to her leg. If the bullet *hadn't* nicked her femoral artery, it had hit something else big enough to cause massive blood loss. She'd torn the bottom of her pant leg off and fashioned a makeshift tourniquet to slow the bleeding. It seemed to be working, but her face and fingers still felt clammy, and every muscle in her body was weary and tired.

But she was safe.

Thorn closed her eyes and took a deep breath, willing her power toward the parts of her that needed healing. She lost track of time then, or maybe the blood loss had been more serious than she thought, and she'd been drifting in and out of consciousness. Either way, it didn't matter because she hadn't felt Jay's aura approaching until it was too late.

He opened the back door—the one Thorn had broken in through—and his voice jolted her nerves.

"What the hell?"

Thorn sat up straight, panic wound around her throat like a fist. Jay's cold energy entered the hallway. Fuck, was it time for The Cross to open already? She clumsily crawled to her feet, Sparkie hiding behind her back as Jay's footsteps moved closer. They thudded on the wood, slow and careful. Thorn held her breath, praying to god he'd keep walking.

But he stopped outside the storage room door, reached for the handle, and pulled it open.

For the second time that day, Thorn stared at a phantom from her past.

Jay's jaw plummeted, his blue eyes just as wide. Thorn swallowed hard.

"Jay—"

"That's it!" Jay threw his hands in the air. "I'm calling the cops this time, Teagan! Jesus *fucking* Christ!"

"Jay, wait!"

He turned to leave, but Sparkie leapt across the room. Thorn's Familiar wound around Jay's hand, wrapping his wings in a tight grip as Jay went for his phone. Poor Jay yelped and jumped backward until his back slammed into the opposite wall. Thorn limped through the door after him.

"What the *fuck!*"

"Wait," Thorn said again, grabbing Jay. She grimaced as the movement sent pain rippling from her shoulder. "Please. I need your help."

Jay stood, too stunned to move, and he took her in. The panic in his expression softened to an affectionate concern that made Thorn's empty chest feel even more hollow. At last, he shook his head.

"Teagan, what the hell is going on?"

She let out a rough laugh. "It's a long story."

He frowned. "Are you actually going to tell me this time?"

Thorn's teeth ground together.

"I don't think I have any other choice."

They moved into the main bar, Jay watching aghast as Thorn cleaned her bloodied bits and pieces off the storage room floor. When they were settled, Thorn began to talk. She wasn't sure where to start or what to say, so she tried it the Darius way:

She told Jay everything.

She told him about the Sins and the Virtues. She told him about the Martyrs and the war they were fighting. She told him who she really was, *what* she really was, and she'd proven it with a blade to the palm.

Around this time, Jay poured himself a drink.

Then she explained every weird fucking thing she'd never been able to explain before: the alley where he'd first seen her covered in blood, the time she tried to kill Sloth in the middle of The Cross, the private moments ruined by sudden alarms and vanishing acts, how she'd found herself here today.

And Jay listened without saying a word, sipping his whiskey and nodding like she was an accountant bitching about line items on a spreadsheet he didn't understand. Every so often, his eyes flicked to where Sparkie lay across Thorn's shoulders, but he kept his mouth firmly shut.

When Thorn finally stopped talking, it *stayed* shut.

They sat in silence for a few minutes—Thorn at her regular stool, Jay standing on the other side of the counter. If this weren't such a bad fucking situation, Thorn would have relished being here again. The light pouring through stained glass windows, the musty smell of old church oak, the glittering altar of spirits behind the bar. It was all so familiar. So comfortable. She missed the ritual.

Suddenly, Jay turned away from her and walked to the wall of liquor. Thorn straightened in her seat as he pulled the whiskey bottle down again.

"You okay?" she asked.

"Absolutely the fuck not," he answered. His voice shook. So did his hand. He poured himself another drink, paused, and grabbed a second glass. As he filled that one, too, he sighed. "But everything is starting to make sense."

He returned to the bar, setting the fresh whiskey in front of Thorn before shooting his down his throat. Thorn's fingers wrapped around the rim.

"I'm sorry," she murmured. "I didn't want to pull you into this mess."

Jay nodded, but the motion was choppy. "Yeah, I appreciate that, but Teagan—" he abruptly stopped, pinching the bridge of his nose "—fuck, *Thorn*. You're in danger. People are after you."

Thorn scoffed. "I know," she said, lifting her glass to her lips with a wince, but Jay's face darkened.

"No." He placed his palms flat on the counter to lean toward her. "I mean *other* people. Regular people. Didn't you get my messages?"

A guilty knot twisted in Thorn's chest, and she shook her head. Jay sighed, exasperated with her as always, but at least now he understood why.

"After that guy—that Sin? Ugh, this is fucking crazy." He groaned and ran his hands down his face. "After you got stabbed through that fucking mark on your arm, the lead singer from my old band called me. Some woman from his agent's office has all their clients looking for *you*."

Thorn's mouth slipped open, and her spine went rigid. "What woman?"

"I don't know," Jay said, "but she works at Gibson Artist Agency. They're the biggest talent scout in the *country.*"

A cold chill shivered through Thorn's body. "Why do they want me?"

"I *don't* know," Jay repeated, "but she told her clients that anyone who can get her information about you will be bumped to the front of the list for any audition they want. A mutual friend told Trey he thought I knew you, and he was furious when I wouldn't give him your number. He said it would've been his 'big break.'"

A grateful wave tightened Thorn's throat. She was reminded of what had drawn her to Jay in the first place. He was a good man. She'd always hated lying to him. Using him.

But she might have to use him again. One last time.

"Could you get me Trey's information?" she asked.

Jay frowned. "What? Why? These people are bad news, Tea—Thorn—fuck!" He raked a hand through his auburn hair. "You shouldn't go anywhere *near* them!"

"I know," she said, "but the *only* people who would put this much effort into finding me are the Sins… and I need to find them, too."

Jay considered her for a long moment before he crossed his arms around his navy button-up. "You want to set a trap for them?" Thorn nodded, and he sighed. "Okay, fine. But after this, I want to go back to worrying about normal shit, like paying bills and not getting fired again."

"Again?" Thorn asked.

"Yeah," he said. "Mercourier canned me on the spot when I ruined my uniform and abandoned my route." His eyes flashed to meet hers, and Thorn grimaced.

"I'm sorry," she said.

"It's fine," Jay responded. "I'd do it again."

Gratitude warmed her chest, and Thorn couldn't help but give Jay a somber smile. He returned it, but it was just as sad. She drew a deep breath.

"When this is over," she began slowly, "I can make you forget. I have the ability to…" She paused, choosing her next words carefully. "…hide memories. This can all go away."

He stared at her, his features curved in dark curiosity.

"Would it hide *you?*"

The question surprised her, and Thorn blinked.

"It could," she said. "If that's what you want."

Jay thought for a moment before he shook his head. "No," he said with a sigh. "No, leave the memories alone… and then leave me alone, too." Jay's throat tightened, like the words were hard to say. "I hope you win. Really, I do, but you were right. I don't want to be dragged into this."

Thorn nodded and looked into her glass, where her shadow loomed, a ghost floating in the whiskey. She wasn't sure what she'd been expecting, but somehow, she felt more torn apart than she had two months ago when Jay had cut off their relationship.

This time, he wasn't saying goodbye to Teagan Love. He was saying goodbye to *Thorn.*

CHAPTER TWENTY-EIGHT

Thorn's thigh groaned in protest as she shifted in her chair. Hours had passed since the sniper's round had blown through her leg, and while the goriest parts of the wound had healed by now, the tissues by the bone were still fusing themselves back together. Thorn massaged her knuckles against the muscle, which made the ache pulse deeper, and Sparkie winced on her shoulder. To her right, Darius watched her. His concern was so apparent she could almost taste it in the air.

"Whelp," Holly Andrews said as she clicked a key on her laptop. The paper-thin, retractable screen descended along the conference room's far wall with a hum. "This has been going on for *months.*"

The tech lead sat across from Thorn, Nicholas on one side, Chris on the other, while Alan took the head of the table. Thorn had called Holly to have her investigate what had happened as soon as her TAC backup arrived at The Cross. After seeing Dr. Harris and cleaning up, she'd debriefed the rest of the Martyr directors on what had happened before Holly joined them to talk about what *she'd* uncovered. It wasn't looking good.

"How many months exactly?" Nicholas asked.

"From what I can tell," Holly said as she rattled her keyboard with rapid taps, "they've had people looking for Thorn since September."

Alan frowned. That's all he'd done since walking into this room: frown, his face frustratingly hard to read. He worked his jaw to loosen it, but the expression stubbornly stuck.

"How can you be certain?" he asked.

"We hacked into the Gibson Artist Agency's servers," Holly responded. "One of their administrative assistants started sending these emails on September 21, 2092."

Holly struck a key, and the giant display filled with text. The headline read, "WE NEED YOUR HELP." Thorn scanned the message, the rage in her core bubbling more with every word:

Dear GAA Talent,

We are reaching out to alert you to a very serious situation at the Gibson Artist Agency, which has put us and all of our artists, active and otherwise, at risk.

A disgruntled former client hacked into our systems and gained access to classified information for our entire agency, including personal memos, contact details, home addresses, and the terms of our contracts with all major studios. Unfortunately, you may be impacted.

GAA has alerted the proper authorities, and we are cooperating with their ongoing investigation. However, to further help law enforcement, we ask anyone within the Gibson Artist Agency to please alert us if they become aware of Teagan Love's whereabouts (photo attached below).

As a show of gratitude, any artist who provides information that can help the police locate Ms. Love will be moved to the top of our audition list for any upcoming projects in which they are interested.

The Gibson Artist Agency has been helping creatives like you make their dreams come true for over sixty years.

With your help in locating this person and bringing her to justice, we can carry on this important work for another sixty. We are more than a business—we are a family, and we will do whatever it takes to keep our family together.

Best wishes,
Marlena Jimenez
Senior Executive Assistant
Gibson Artist Agency

An attachment link stood out at the base of the email. Holly opened it to show a low-quality photograph of Thorn that had been snagged from some security feed. If she had to guess, it was from outside the Pfizer building a few years back. Her hood was up, a cigarette held to her mouth, hand obscuring the bottom half of her face, but it was still enough to identify her if you looked closely. Sparkie's wings ruffled uncomfortably as Darius sighed on Thorn's right.

"Jesus Christ," Nicholas said. "This is a convincing scam, but it's *clearly* a scam. Did no one think to challenge this?"

"Scams work best when they scare the hell out of you. This went out to *thousands* of people across New York, and no one filed any complaints," Holly said. Then, she glanced at Thorn above the edge of her laptop screen. "After you discovered Lust's new host, they put out another blast with an updated photo, a warning that you might be using a different name, *and* they added a cash reward for information that led them to you. The Gibson Artist Agency also has clear connections to Crave Media."

Holly tapped around some more, and the display filled with a mosaic of images, screenshots, and details that rivaled the organized chaos of Thorn's office walls. Holly circled one of the screenshots with her cursor. "Pre-possession, Connor Amoretto worked with this Jimenez woman to book actors for commercials, ads… whatever they needed."

Thorn's jaw clenched at the sound of Lust's name. "Are

there ties to the other Sins?"

Holly shook her head. "Not that I could find, but I did take the liberty of digging a little deeper into their client list just to confirm what your friend told you about his old bandmate."

She highlighted one of the documents, which displayed a massive sheet of names.

"You thought he might be lying?" Nicholas asked.

"I don't trust anybody, Wolfe," Holly said with a smirk. "Not even you. But he was right. Trey Gamble was on the list, along with Mickey Guthrie, the bouncer from The Eros Project, and an actor-turned-barista named Howard Poole…"

Holly's brown eyes shifted back to Thorn, and Thorn's heart dipped. The barista at Grind House Coffee had sold her out. She'd already known it, but the confirmation stung. A numb wash flowed down Thorn's spine until Darius spoke. His voice pulled her back to the table.

"Mickey…" He groaned and ran his hands down his face. "That must be how they found us at the club."

Holly nodded. "Yup. I figure he didn't turn you guys in earlier because Thorn's license didn't say 'Teagan Love,' but once he heard she might be using a different name, he went all in."

Alan passed Thorn a grim look. "And he paid a hefty price."

"But why are they gunning so hard for Thorn *now?*" Darius asked. "What's changed?"

His voice was tighter than Thorn was accustomed to. Unlike Alan, who kept his emotions tucked so far up his sleeve that she wondered if even he knew what they were half the time, Darius wore his bloodied and bared open for the room to see. Right now, he was worried. Really fucking worried.

About her.

Darius glanced at Thorn, his teeth clenched, green eyes deep and tender. Her heart somersaulted behind her ribs.

"Everything has changed," Chris said, forcing Darius to tear his gaze away from Thorn. "We've been taking them out left and right. At this point, *three* Sins have been completely eradicated. They're panicking."

"Understandably so," Alan said. "Until a few years ago, we were nothing but a nuisance—a nest of ants swarming for crumbs. Now, we are more than simply a threat. We are *the* threat."

Darius shook his head. "But then why are they coming for *her?*" he pressed desperately—almost *angrily*. "Why not *me?* I'm the Virtue, aren't I? *I'm* the threat."

He looked at Thorn again, and her lips slowly parted. He was trying to change the situation—to plant a target on his own fucking back to save her from the one branded onto hers. Around the table, all eyes shifted in her direction, like they were wondering the same thing. Holly, Nicholas, and Chris stared at Thorn, too, and Sparkie quickly tucked behind her hair.

Alan, however, looked beyond her—beyond all of them—with his steepled fingers firm against his lips.

"Because without Thorn," he murmured, "we are crippled, and they know it."

The room settled, dense and heavy, like sediment drifting to the seabed after a storm. Thorn watched Alan, if only so she didn't have to see the look on Darius's face. Even her Familiar staunchly refused to turn his way, burying his head beneath red webbing and black hair.

But it was Darius who broke the silence.

"So," he started slowly, and Thorn's attention landed on him at last. His mouth settled into a frown. "The Sins are hunting you down. They have been for *months…* and you want to set a trap for Amoretto with *you* as the bait."

He didn't ask but stated it because he knew Thorn well enough by now to guess at her motives with startling accuracy. She would have been flattered, but she could tell he hated every word he'd just said.

"Yes," she answered. Her mind flashed back to the knife

driven through her *Peccostium*—to the taste of Connor Amoretto's filthy hand in her mouth. Her fury swelled. "I want that son of a bitch dead."

Darius's frown didn't budge, but Alan's did. For the first time since he'd sat down, his expression flashed with something new. Wide eyes, parted lips, an instant of surprise immediately drowned by worry.

Nicholas scoffed and crossed his arms. "If you were *anyone* else, I'd think you were joking."

"I'm not," Thorn said.

"I know. You're fucking *insane.*"

A bite of annoyance soured Thorn's tongue, and she ran it along the bottom of her teeth as she glared at Nicholas. He didn't falter, didn't budge, those icy eyes resolute as always.

"Look," Thorn said, working to keep her tone even. She leaned forward onto the table. "For the first time since I joined the Martyrs, we have the advantage."

She slowly looked around the room, her focus landing on each and every face. They all watched her, quiet, curious, and unconvinced.

"We know what they want," Thorn went on, "we know how they're searching for it, and we have the manpower, opportunity, and skill not just to win but to *obliterate* Lust. We have to take it."

"It's not that simple, though," Chris argued. Thorn's attention snapped to her, and her jaw clenched. "They're not just using Puppets this time."

"That's right," Darius agreed, quickly latching onto the criticism. "You said the guys that chased you from Hunts Point didn't seem to be under any Influence at all."

"Mercenaries, most likely," Alan said. "They are much harder to disable."

His chin slowly tilted toward Thorn, watching her down his sharp nose with stern condemnation, like she hadn't considered this before. Her lip began to twist in a sneer.

"Not with Andrews's new weapon."

"Which will do *very little* against a sniper standing five hundred yards from your position," Alan challenged.

Thorn sat up straight and crossed her arms again. Her healing leg ached with the movement, like it wanted to remind her that she'd been shot, too. She ignored it, just like she ignored the concerned look Darius threw her way.

"It's a good thing we have a sniper of our own, then," she snapped. "One that *won't* miss."

A muscle ticked in Alan's jaw, and his hollow eyes flashed furiously. Thorn didn't shy away from him, even as the rest of the room shuffled uncomfortably around her. Her chest roiled with anger, buzzing like a swarm of threatened insects.

"Right now," Thorn went on, "there are over one hundred TAC agents in the Underground trained and ready to go—the largest force I have ever seen. Our new weapon can disable Puppets *and* normal men on a mass scale, and Alexis's team of sympathizers can slow the NYPD response, maybe even stop it entirely."

The swarm rallied again, and Thorn paused to breathe into it, trying to hold it all in. Her fingertips absently tapped against her bicep, pointer to pinky, as she looked around the table, from Alan to Nicholas, Holly to Chris, Darius… His green eyes sloped with doubt, and her heart skipped. She shook her head.

"I am sick and fucking *tired* of the Sins controlling this goddamned battle," Thorn said at last.

"But they *don't*," Nicholas argued. "They're down by three—"

"And it could be *four!*" Thorn cut in. "We have a shot at luring Lust to the table on *our* terms, and we'd be out of our goddamned minds not to try!"

Silence followed. Darius continued to watch Thorn as if she were standing at the edge of the Brooklyn Bridge, poised to jump. Alan mirrored the sentiment, teeth clenched so hard together that his mouth was tight behind his goatee. Even Chris and Nicholas seemed unmoved, his arms crossed like Thorn's while Chris breathed a sigh. Thorn wanted to fucking scream.

How could no one else see what she saw?

Holly cleared her throat and raised a hand.

"I know I don't have any voting power," she said, "but Thorn's right."

Pressure loosened around Thorn's lungs.

"We've never had the resources and manpower to put into this kind of mission," Holly continued, "and I don't know if we'll ever get another opening like this again."

Chris glanced at Thorn, hair pouring like silky, yellow falls around her shoulder. Her bright eyes narrowed, then closed, and she sighed. "Okay. Hypothetically, what would an operation like this even look like?"

The grip of anger released Thorn, and her shoulders relaxed at last.

"We would send an anonymous tip to Jay's friend on where I'm going to be," she said. "With a short lead. I'm thinking thirty minutes. That way, the Sins wouldn't have time to mobilize. They'd just have to act."

Alan shook his head. "But would they?"

Thorn's eyes flicked in his direction. "Yes. They did with The Eros Project."

"But this time, we'd be prepared for them," Holly said. Her energy matched the way Thorn felt—excited, maybe even eager, as the pieces of a plan clicked together. "Our guys would be on the scene hours before Thorn even shows up. I'll also get camera feeds running around the neighborhood to give us a better visual."

Holly started typing. Nicholas frowned and tilted over her shoulder to read the screen while Alan drew a deep breath, making him taller and more rigid. Darius looked at Thorn again. She saw the motion in the corner of her eye, and again, she ignored him.

"Since we'd control the location," Chris added, "we can choose somewhere that gives us an even greater advantage." She leaned back, more at ease now. Fuck, Thorn could hug her. "Better access for our TAC units to get in, maybe even fewer civilians for Lust to Puppet…"

"Exactly," Thorn agreed.

"What if Lust doesn't show up?" Darius cut in. "What if it's Greed? Or even *Wrath?*"

What if Wrath showed up? Thorn reveled in the idea of eliminating Connor Amoretto *and* killing Autumn Hunt. She *hoped* Wrath showed up.

But she shook her head. "Amoretto is the clear link to this talent agency," she said. "I don't expect him to come alone, but he *will* come."

A vengeful spark lit up in Thorn's chest. Nicholas breathed a heavy sigh.

"I have to admit," he said, "the idea of destroying that fucker is tempting as hell, but that brings up another question… Is Lamar ready to do it?"

Holly stopped typing, and the quiet that followed hung as thick and heavy as smoke. They all considered Darius. For a moment, he looked around at them, like he didn't want to tell the truth. Doubt rolled down Thorn's spine.

But at last, he said, "He's excelling in all the exercises I have him doing, but we won't know if any of it worked until he's close enough to test it."

"This is the perfect opportunity to get him that close," Thorn said. "And if he's not, we can still destroy the host."

Darius scoffed. "So you're telling me that you'd rather risk Lamar not being ready and kill Amoretto, which could make this take *years* longer? Why not just wait until we *know* Lamar can do it?"

Thorn shook her head. "Because a different host might be easier for him to confront," she said. "A host *without* history."

Again, the room was silent, and this time, Darius didn't look at her. His eyes cast down at the table while Nicholas scratched the back of his head and Alan maintained his perpetual frown. Thorn held her breath.

Chris spoke first. "Thorn and Holly are right. We should

do it."

"I agree," Nicholas said.

Thorn's lips tightened, threatening to smile, but she held back because Alan and Darius both shifted. Her uncle's expression didn't change—still carved from a slab of alabaster and just as soft—but Darius…

She wished she hadn't looked at him. The worry mixed into his face was almost enough to make her want to call the whole thing off. His olive complexion washed out, making the striking green in his eyes pool deeper.

"What do *you* think, Darius?" Chris asked.

He didn't answer right away, and he didn't look at Chris. He was caught on Thorn, his focus snagged like she was a sharp point unraveling his nerves.

"You already know what I think," he said at last. "It's too much of a risk." His eyes seemed to pierce through Thorn as he addressed her directly—her alone. "We *can't* lose you."

The air around them stung as though an arctic current had pushed through the room, and Thorn's stomach swam with it. Sparkie rustled behind her hair. Darius kept watching her, and Thorn watched back, acutely aware that everyone else was fixed on them, too, but Alan and Nicholas, Chris and Holly felt far away. Darius was all she saw.

Thorn ached to touch him. To press her forehead against his, to run her nails through the stubble on his cheeks, to taste his breath on the air between them as she told him this would be okay.

But empty promises never helped. If anything, they carved deeper wounds.

"Before we rush into this," Alan said, "we must know if Mr. Verrette is even interested in exploring this avenue. If he is not, we will reassess the situation." Alan tilted his head in Darius's direction, and Darius nodded. "In the meantime, however, let's presume to move forward. Mr. Wolfe, work with Miss Andrews on choosing a location that will give us the greatest advantage. Miss Silver, start organizing your

TAC units and determining the best way to camouflage them. Thorn, can I speak with you in private?"

Thorn nodded, her body ringing with a wide-open net of excitement, apprehension, and possibility. She and Alan got to their feet. As they led the way from the room with the rest of the Martyr directors following, Thorn glanced over her shoulder. The nervous look on Darius's face made her hesitate.

"Thorn," Alan called.

Her fingers tightened on the wood, and she swept into the hallway. Darius's final expression haunted her the entire walk to Alan's office. He opened it for her, guided her into the room, and quietly shut them inside. Rae sat in front of his desk, and her sharp eyes made Thorn frown. The fur on her hackles hovered like she was charged full of static. Thorn turned to Alan.

He stood by the door, eyes closed, fingertips pressed to his lips while his other arm wrapped around his chest. That hand curled into a fist so tight the tendons strained against his skin.

"I need to know," he murmured after a moment. He opened his eyes. "I *need* to know that this driving desire to eliminate Connor Amoretto is not some wild shot at revenge."

Sparkie jolted on Thorn's back, vaulting to her shoulder so he could stare at Alan the same way she did. Her mouth fell open.

"Of course it's not."

Alan's glare deepened. His brows were so tight that they cast heavy shadows and made his eyes hard to see. "You 'want that son of a bitch dead.' *That* is what you said."

Thorn scoffed. "Jesus, Alan, we *all* want him dead."

"You are not the only one who remembers how close Lust and Wrath have been throughout the centuries," Alan snapped. Thorn's eyes widened. Alan rarely spoke of his time as the Sin. He looked her over, his focus wandering to her left wrist. "After what Amoretto did to you—"

"That has nothing to do with this," Thorn interrupted, furious at the implication and even *more* furious at the lie coming out of her own goddamned mouth. She shook her head. "I can't believe you would even insinuate—"

"This is *suicide*, Thorn!" Alan shouted. "You are practically walking into the Sins' jaws, open-armed, begging to be swallowed!"

Thorn propped her hands on her hips. Sparkie's wings flared beside her head.

"I have fought these bastards for decades," she said, her voice rattling with forced calm. "I have led *hundreds* of missions against them, but you still act like I'm some half-cocked gun waiting for any excuse to go off!"

He opened his mouth to argue, but Thorn steamrolled over him.

"What will it take, Alan?" she exclaimed, throwing her arms out. "What do I have to do to get you to treat me as a goddamned equal?"

His nostrils flared. "I want to see that you're driven by motives other than—"

Alan abruptly stopped, jerking his head away like he couldn't stand the sight of her. The monster in her stomach howled with pain.

"Other than *what?*" she hissed.

"Other than anger!" Alan answered, spinning toward her again. "Than vengeance! Than the exact same things that motivate Wrath!"

He gestured a palm toward her chest, and Thorn sucked in a quick, affronted breath. She suddenly heard him screaming at her again—an old memory dragged from the depths of her psyche where she'd tried to hide it along with all the bodies she'd buried.

"You are no better than Wrath!"

In the present, Alan continued. Here, his voice was softer, but only just.

"You must not lose sight of what raises you above her," he implored. "What makes you *more.*"

Thorn scoffed. "I can't believe this."

She turned away from him, refusing to let him see the pain mixed with the anger on her face. Rae had stood, and she took a step forward. Thorn looked away from her, too.

"We must be careful," Alan said. His voice was closer at her back. "Since our possession, we are—"

"Damn it, Alan," Thorn snarled, pressing the heels of her hands against her forehead. She twisted around and glared up at him. "Why can't you just *trust* me?"

He gaped, his eyes wide, and all he did was blink.

"This is *not* what happened after Donovan died," Thorn asserted, "and you know it! I'm doing the damned job *you* wanted me to do!"

Alan still didn't speak. Not for several long, heavy seconds. His black eyes trained on hers, clung to them, and a flash of something flickered through the irises.

"I do trust you," Alan began quietly now. "I also… worry about you."

Thorn's lips slipped open, and Sparkie's frazzled wings froze behind him.

"You are willing to take so many risks, to put yourself in harm's way, to lay it all on the line for a chance to destroy the Sins… but you take precious few for *yourself*."

Thorn's chest tightened. She shook her head. "That's not true."

"Name one," Alan challenged.

She stared at him, mouth still open, eyes still narrow, but she had nothing to say. Her brain scrambled for an answer, but all she found were decades of this same fucking pattern. Alan nodded.

"This war has been your life for a long time," he murmured, "but it should not be all you live for."

Thorn tried to swallow, but her throat ran so dry that her tongue stuck. "It's safer this way," she defended. "We know where this road ends… and it's *not* happy."

"The ending rarely is," Alan agreed solemnly, "but the journey itself is full of wonderful moments… moments you deserve, Thorn. Moments you have deserved for a long time."

They stood there for a second longer. The fury in Thorn's core sizzled and died, swept away by a colder, darker feeling.

"I know how terrifying it is," Alan went on, as though he could sense more than anger through their mutual link to Wrath, "opening ourselves up to the inevitable tragedy, the frailty, of mortal life… But being alone is no way to live."

Thorn's brows drew together. "You're alone."

At this, Alan cracked a smile. A sad, somber smile.

"I never had the fortune to build a family of my own like your mother and father did," he said. He walked around Thorn, passing near enough to her that his long, black coat brushed her arm. She tracked his movement, stunned. While Alan rarely spoke of his time as the Sin, he spoke of his life before that even less. When he reached his desk, he shifted items around its surface, straightening each pencil, each report, absently. "I was much too… flawed… once Wrath had its hooks in me to have that for myself. I imagined I would be without one forever, and I was at peace with that… until I found you again."

He glanced over his shoulder. Rae let out a long, vocal sigh beside him. Thorn's breath caught.

"I have set standards, expectations, and rules for myself," Alan went on, "because *I* have been reluctant to take risks. I know those standards have bled into the rest of this place. They've bled into you."

He paused again, turned back toward her, and his mouth shaped into a thin, concerned arc.

"You deserve more than this warrior's life, Thorn," he said, "with whatever… and *whoever*… makes you happy."

The room went quiet, a heavy quiet. Alan watched Thorn, and her chest tightened—with fear, with grief, but mostly, with affection. It overwhelmed her.

Alan cleared his throat and looked toward the ground.

"Well," he began, "we will see how Mr. Verrette feels about your plan. Until then—"

Thorn strode across Alan's office and hugged him. Alan hesitated for only a moment, a second of shock, before he wound his arms around her. His hold was exactly as Thorn would have expected: firm and steady, just like him. He pressed his lips against the crown of her head, the way a father might, and Thorn closed her eyes. She couldn't remember the last time they'd done this—the last time she and Alan had embraced as a family rather than opposed one another as peers. Maybe they never had.

After several long seconds, Alan's grip finally loosened, and Thorn stepped away. Her heart skipped when she looked up at his face.

His dark eyes glistened, a single tear leaving a trail down his cheek.

CHAPTER TWENTY-NINE

Darius had been certain that Lamar wouldn't be ready to face Connor Amoretto, and Thorn's insane plan to lock herself in a cage with a starving pride of lions would fall apart before it even came together.

But two weeks later, he stood in the tactical room, helping Chris put the young Consent into his armor. As she cinched a protective vest around Lamar's torso, nerves rattled Darius's chest, and he wrapped his arms across it.

"There we go…" Chris pulled the last strap tight. "Perfect fit."

She stood back, and Lamar ran his hands down his sides, shaky fingertips exploring the kevlar. His eyes were as round and glassy as marbles.

"How's it feel?" Darius asked.

"Good," Lamar answered quietly. "It's lighter than I thought it would be. Is it going to work?" He pressed his palms flat over his heart as though to add another level of protection because this one didn't feel secure enough. Chris offered a patient smile.

"High-velocity weapons can pierce through it," she said, "but this will protect you from most handgun rounds, which is what we usually see in close combat situations like this."

Lamar's cheeks washed out, and he swallowed hard. Chris grabbed his arm reassuringly. "It's also a precaution. You'll stay in a fortified vehicle until we get Lust disabled."

Lamar nodded, but there was no confidence in the gesture. "How will I know when that happens?"

"Your helmet's tapped into the TAC frequency," Darius answered, "and your security team will keep tabs on the line. They'll escort you right to him."

Darius tried to smile, too, but he knew his own anxiety leaked into the expression. The younger Virtue chewed on his lower lip as he searched Darius's face.

"Who's my security team?"

"Gabe and Amelia," Chris said. "Two of my best. You're in good hands."

Lamar nodded again. This time, he seemed more sated.

"They're with Naomi in the waiting room," Chris continued. We're done here, so if you want to sit with them while Darius and I finish up, you're free to go. We'll head out shortly."

Darius hadn't thought it possible, but Lamar's complexion lost even more color. He mumbled some kind of agreement before he ambled out. Darius tracked him until he made it to the hallway.

"Is he okay?" Chris asked. When Darius turned back around, her eyes trained on him, brows sloped in concern.

Darius breathed a tense sigh. "It's a little too late to worry about that, isn't it?"

Chris nodded. Slowly. "Are *you* okay?"

His teeth clenched as he grabbed his bulletproof vest off the bench. The Underground felt uncomfortably empty, the locker alcoves, the garage, and even the lower level eerily vacant. With nearly half of their TAC agents already in the city, hardly anyone was left. This place was a ghost town.

Darius shook his head and threw the vest around his shoulders, acutely aware that Chris's focus hadn't moved from him since Lamar had walked out of the room.

"I will be," he grumbled. "When this is over. Who's in

the healing van?"

He asked without looking at her, pulling his armor straps tight around his black turtleneck as meticulously as he could, like maybe if he took his time, he could slow this scene down long enough to make it stop entirely.

"Conrad and Charlotte," Chris responded. "Madison was given the opportunity, but she specifically requested a separate assignment..." Chris's voice drifted off as she nudged him with her elbow and smiled. Darius tried to return the gesture, but the muscles in his face staunchly refused to listen.

"Great," he said, but thoughts about Madison quickly morphed into worries about a different woman entirely. He finished his vest before grabbing a holstered handgun and fixing it to his belt. Chris's warm aura pressed close beside him, and a hand landed on his shoulder. He glanced up, expecting the same comforting look she'd given Lamar, but he was surprised to see a reflection of his fear in her eyes.

"This plan is solid," Chris murmured. Darius got the feeling she was trying to convince herself just as much as she was trying to convince him. "She'll be fine."

Just the idea of speaking made his throat close up, so Darius simply nodded. Then Chris gathered the rest of her gear, too. His TAC boots felt particularly heavy this morning as they headed down the hallway. The conference room door stood ajar, and Thorn's voice floated through it. Darius's heart jolted at the sound.

"The bell tower attached to the chapel is the tallest building on the premises," she said. She stood across the room, Sparkie perched upon her shoulder. When Chris and Darius walked in, her eyes flashed up to meet them. They lingered on Darius, wandering from his face to the tactical uniform to the gun at his waist. Her jaw tightened at the sight of him, and she forced it apart as she focused on Alan again. "You'll be able to see most of the cemetery from there."

"That does not guarantee safety," Alan said. His focus fixed on the table, where a map of Queens had been spread out. A massive gun case sat beside it. Darius assumed it housed Alan's rifle. "A skilled sniper with a powerful weapon will have a range well beyond fifteen hundred meters. Any building in the area may give him the vantage he needs."

"The Mount St. Mary Cemetery is covered in trees," Thorn countered, pointing at a green rectangle on the map. "Chris and Nicholas selected this location *specifically* to minimize the risk of mercenary snipers. Even *you* won't have a great visual range, and you'll only be one hundred meters away."

Alan frowned, wrapping his arms around the bulletproof vest on his chest as he considered the map, too. His black eyes darted around it with military precision, and his expression betrayed nothing of how he felt. Neither he nor Thorn were in TAC colors. Alan dressed in all black, while Thorn wore her kevlar bike jacket over her typical clothing. As the bait, she had to present herself as naturally as possible, but the sight of her so vulnerable and unprotected made Darius's stomach uneasy.

"I do wish it were further from Hunts Point," Alan said quietly, like he was voicing thoughts aloud, "but I understand the logic. Anything too far from the main boroughs in the city will raise alarms. Quite frankly, being off Manhattan might be suspicious enough."

"Manhattan is too heavily populated," Chris said. She approached the table, and Darius joined her. "The Sins will have fewer civilians around to Puppet here."

"True enough," Alan agreed, "but their mercenaries might still make an appearance."

"We'll handle them if they do," Chris said. "My units are already in position, and they're on the lookout for any unusual activity."

"Nicholas, too," Darius added. "He and Holly both have their teams monitoring the cameras in the area, and they've set up more to give us an even broader view of what's going on down there."

Thorn nodded. "And Alexis has her network of NYPD officers and dispatchers ready to disrupt any calls," she said. "The Sins won't even realize they've been cut off until it's too late."

Alan drew a long breath and exhaled it in a short sigh. "I suppose there is little left to discuss," he said. Darius realized Alan was doing exactly what *he* wanted to do: biding time, avoiding the inevitable. "If that is all—"

A knock on the doorframe behind Darius made them all startle, and he whipped around to see Cain's head peering through the crack.

"Actually," the old Forgotten Envy said, easing fully into the room. A tight, anxious smile warped his face. "There is *one* more matter. I would like to join you."

Darius's jaw dropped. As did Thorn's. Alan's eyes, however, sharpened, and his spine went rigid.

"After our last mission," he said, "you made it clear that you would not be part of another one."

Cain bowed his head. "Very right," he agreed, "and I'm sure I will regret this decision well before we even step foot outside of this room, but the fact still stands: *that* mission put me directly into the line of fire, and Thorn was there, ready to pull me out of it. Now that the tables have turned, the least I can do is return the favor."

His gaze landed on her, and his smile filled out, but Thorn settled into a soft frown.

"Cain," she said, shaking her head, "you don't have to do this."

"Of course I don't," he agreed, "but what happens if you get yourself stabbed, shot, or otherwise torn to shreds while I sit comfortably back in the Underground? I could *never* forgive myself."

Thorn blinked, her eyes wide. Sparkie quietly darted behind her hair.

"Now," Cain went on, "before I lose my nerve, where will I be of the most use?"

Chris glanced from him to Thorn to Alan, as if she were

waiting for someone to tell her what to do. Thorn didn't respond, but Alan dipped his head in confirmation, and Chris looked down at the map.

"Most of our TAC units are already in place," she said, indicating several locations around the cemetery. "Seth and I will be dropping off Alan and his security detail in front of the mortuary before we get into position here." She pointed to a corner near the entrance. "You're welcome to ride with us, or you can join Darius in the medical van. They'll be stationed in the golf course to the north."

Cain curled his nose and shook his head. "I would rather be more central to the action. God, I can't believe what I'm saying." He heaved a sigh. "But I am of little use shoved away in back alleys."

For a moment, Chris thought about it, her lips pursed. Then she glanced at Thorn. "What about the hearse?"

"A hearse?" Cain let out a garbled laugh. When no one laughed with him, the sound floundered on his tongue. "Surely you're joking."

"Verrette and his guard will be hiding out here," Thorn said. She dragged her finger along a road winding inside the Mount St. Mary Cemetery. "A hearse will go virtually unnoticed, but we've equipped it with armored doors, bulletproof glass, and everything else we need to make it safe."

Cain's face went white. "That's… very close to where you will be meeting Lust, isn't it?"

"It must be close," Alan snapped. "The plan is to hide Mr. Verrette in plain sight. Once Amoretto has been disabled, we will have just minutes to destroy him before the Sins regroup. We can waste *no* time."

Cain's throat shifted in a deep, hard swallow. "I do hate to admit when you're right… Unfortunately, I find myself with few other options."

A smirk tugged on Thorn's lip. "You said you wanted to be more central to the action."

"I did, indeed," Cain murmured. Then, he stood straight. "Very well. I will accompany our young Virtue in this *pale horse* of Death. If this mission were a theater production, I'd say the symbolism is far too on the nose. Absolutely no subtlety—"

"Cain," Alan cut in, and Cain's rambling died. "If you are joining us, go get your equipment. Miss Silver?"

Alan turned to her, and Chris nodded. She led Cain from the room. As they made their way to the tactical lockers, Alan drew in a breath and held it deep within his lungs before he turned to Thorn and Darius again. They were the only three left—he and his niece on the far side of the table while Darius stood with his back to the door. At last, Alan settled on Thorn.

"When will we contact Mr. Trey Guthrie?"

"As soon as we hit the city," Thorn answered.

"Very good," Alan said with a nod. "Then we should be on our way."

He lifted his rifle case from the table, but when he looked at Thorn, he paused. For a few seconds, they watched one another, mirrors of black and white, but Alan's concern contrasted with Thorn's confidence. He reached out for her, placing a palm on her shoulder.

"Be careful," he murmured, the emotion in his voice deeper and more ardent than Darius had ever heard before. Then, his eyes flashed toward Darius, and he quietly pulled away, striding from the room. The door clicked shut in his wake.

Seconds passed in silence—long seconds, saturated in tension and feeling—until Thorn finally let out a cold laugh.

"He tries to hide it," she said, "but he's such a worrier."

Darius smirked. It felt lifeless on his face. "He's not the only one."

Thorn's brows drew softly together. "Yeah," she said as she started moving around the conference table. "I've been walking on eggshells around everyone these last couple of weeks. Chris. Cain. You…"

She reached him, stood right in front of him, and watched him with a frown. Silky, black hair framed her face, and she pulled it behind an ear. Darius's eyes followed the motion, alighting on her cheekbone, where his memory caught on an old scrape he hadn't been able to heal. He could almost feel her skin at his fingertips again, her lower lip soft and inviting beneath his thumb. His chest ached at the thought, at what might have been.

"You know," he said, "every time you go out there, I wonder if this is it. If this is the time the Sins win. If *this* is the time you don't come back."

A surprised glint sparked in Thorn's expression, parting her mouth just long enough to draw Darius's attention to it before she closed it again.

"I will come back," she said.

"You can't know that, Thorn," Darius argued. He tried to stay calm, but now that the words were coming out, anxiety gripped them, strangling them, and he couldn't stop them from pouring over his tongue in a nervous rush. "This isn't a normal strike. They're after *you*, and they're going to do whatever it takes to—"

"Darius."

Suddenly, Thorn's hands found his face, her nails gently running through the stubble on his cheeks and sending a shiver down his spine that made his panic stumble to a stop.

"I *will* come back," she said again, lower, deeper. "I will *always* come back."

"Thorn," he started, but she quieted him by touching her fingertips to his mouth. His heart caught, stuttering in his chest as Thorn stepped forward. They were so close that he could feel her breath against his chin, warm and welcoming, as she murmured:

"All seven Sins couldn't keep me from you."

Her voice filled with a longing that made Darius hungry to close the gap completely—to hold Thorn so tight against his body that not even a ray of sunlight could come between them. A cold, smooth sensation snaked around his throat as Sparkie leapt to him, pressing his face to the underside of Darius's jaw.

Thorn, still, watched him. She drew her hand away, leaving his lips starving for the taste of her. Her eyes pooled with so much heat, so much passion, that Darius was sure he could drown in those black depths.

God, he wanted to drown.

Darius took Thorn by the waist. The curve between her hip bones and ribs perfectly matched his palms, like they were always meant to find their way together. A smile danced onto Thorn's face as Darius tilted toward her, and her mouth parted, daring him to finish what she'd started…

Chris's warm aura moved up the hallway. They both froze, inches apart. Thorn's focus tore from him, darting over his shoulder. Her smile disappeared, disappointment and doubt clouding her expression as she considered him one last time.

Then she stepped back. Darius's grip on her relented as quickly as it had come to life, leaving his hands painfully empty. Sparkie unraveled from around his neck and dove back to Thorn, hiding behind her hair with a soft whine.

Chris opened the door.

"Cain's geared up," she started, but when she spotted them both there, still standing *so* close, she paused, and her cheeks flushed. "I'm sorry, I didn't mean to interrupt."

"You're fine," Thorn answered. She swept past Darius, her arm brushing his as she walked into the hallway. "Is everyone else ready?"

"Uhh…" Chris glanced from Thorn to Darius before shaking her head and following behind her. Darius joined them, walking as though the ground beneath him was as insubstantial as a cloud. "Yes. Conrad and Charlotte are waiting in the medical van, and Gabe is loading the hearse now. Cain's not pleased about it…"

Thorn laughed. "He'll get over it."

They reached the waiting area. On the other side of the doors, Alan spoke with Seth Graves outside of a dark SUV disguised to look like a city water vehicle. Behind it, a white hearse stood with its rear door open. Lamar sat in the back,

Cain and Rae beside him, and gazed toward them. His eyes landed on Darius through the glass as Gabe shut the hatch and walked to the front.

Inside, Skylar and Nicholas talked by the exit. Naomi stood beside them, the fury in her eyes a mask to hide the terror she clearly felt at watching Lamar drive away. As Darius, Thorn, and Chris entered the room, Nicholas glanced at them. He stepped forward and held out a hand.

"Good luck out there today," he said as Thorn grabbed his palm. "Don't die."

Her lips pulled into a smirk. "You can't get rid of me that easily, Wolfe."

"You'd better be right," Nicholas said. "Do you know how much of a nightmare training your replacement would be?"

He smiled, but all the same, his grip tightened around Thorn's hand. Like everyone else in her life right now, he was worried. Thorn's expression faltered.

"Don't worry," she answered. "I'm coming back."

And while she didn't look at Darius, Sparkie's eyes trained on him, and Darius's stomach flipped. As the hearse spiraled up the steep drive, the rest of them headed into the garage. Chris joined Seth and Alan while Darius and Skylar made their way to the medical van. Thorn's motorcycle was parked behind it, and she threw her leg over the bike while Darius climbed into the vehicle. She zipped her kevlar to her throat, pulled her helmet over her head, and engaged the engine.

But before she rode away, she lifted her visor. Those dark, sharp eyes pierced through Darius's window and landed right on him. Then she raised a hand and tapped her thumb against her fingertips, from pointer to pinky, until she landed on the pointer again. Darius's heart jumped to his throat, and he mimicked the gesture. Her voice echoed in his head.

"I see you."

He saw her, too. He only saw her.

CHAPTER THIRTY

Afternoon sun shone through the branches above Thorn's head, casting a mosaic of dappled light across her face. She leaned against the tree, its trunk sinking into the groove of her spine. It was sixty degrees, perfectly comfortable, and on any other day, Thorn would have removed her jacket to enjoy the feeling of spring on her skin.

Today, though, she kept it securely zipped up to her throat, ready to keep out everything from a passing May breeze to a sudden barrage of bullets.

Sparkie swooped overhead, surveying the cemetery. Holly had sent a message to Jay's friend over thirty minutes ago, just as Thorn was parking her motorcycle in the neighborhoods above the Kissena Park Golf Course to the north. The entire walk down, she'd played out the plan in her head. Fifteen TAC units disguised as work trucks, moving vans, or other inconspicuous vehicles dotted the area in a quarter-mile radius, more heavily located on the northern and western edges where the Sins were most likely to enter. From where Thorn stood, she could see the bell tower above the cathedral and Alan's dark figure inside of it. A modest network of paved roads wound through the Mount St. Mary Cemetery, and a white hearse parked just around a bend south of Thorn's position. She felt Gabe DuPont and Amelia Chan waiting inside, and though she couldn't see them through the tinted windows, Thorn knew Lamar, Rae, and Cain were with them.

Everyone was in position. The trap was set. Now, all they had to do was wait.

Thorn hated waiting.

She breathed a sigh, checking the time on her phone before she slipped it into her satchel next to her handgun. The cool metal brushed against her knuckles, and Thorn grabbed the grip to get a sense of comfort. She'd never felt so *exposed* on a mission before. What she wouldn't give for full body armor and a real weapon. Instead, she had nothing but a thin layer of kevlar, a single sonic disruptor, and the motorcycle helmet pinned between her arm and hip. Thorn drew a shaky breath.

Fuck, were those *nerves?*

She'd never felt like *that* before, either. It wasn't that Thorn didn't get nervous before a fight. Adrenaline was one hell of a drug. No, it was that this time, she felt like she had more to lose… and more people to let down.

Darius's face filled her mind. His voice. His smell. His touch. She closed her eyes as she tapped her fingertips against the weapon in her bag—pointer, middle, ring, and pinky—and let herself sink into the memory of him.

Thorn had made some heavy promises today. Promises she couldn't afford to break.

A lump grew in her throat. She dug through her satchel again, craving a cigarette for the first time in… god, she couldn't even remember. Weeks. Maybe months. So, it wasn't a surprise that she didn't have any on her. She swore under her breath.

"Are you all right?"

Alan's words droned in the covert com unit tucked inside her ear. His candor told Thorn he'd tapped into a private line. She touched the device and made sure she was still muted on all other channels before responding.

"I'm not sure how I feel about being in your scope," she said with a wry smile, glancing up to the bell tower. Alan chuckled on the other end of the line.

"My finger is off the trigger," he reassured her. "You didn't answer the question."

Thorn took a deep breath and pulled her phone out again, glancing at the map, where she could see all her units' positions. Including Darius's. She lingered on the blinking green dot that belonged to the medical van, safely tucked deep into the golf course. At last, her eyes darted up to the time.

"They're late," she finally said.

"It's only a quarter after two," Alan countered. "It takes time to commute from Manhattan. Be patient."

Thorn scoffed as she considered the landscape again. A sea of green grass and granite gravestones washed around her, centuries of life and death laid out as far as she could see. She was in an older part of the grounds—not the oldest here, but old enough to where there wasn't a single death date less than fifty years old. One snagged her eye, and she paused.

Mary Palmer. Born in 1946, the year Thorn had entered the world, and died in 2024… the year Donovan left it.

Her immortality rolled over her like a train, crashing her thoughts and feelings into a pulp of pain in her mouth. Thorn swallowed it down, vaguely aware of her body buzzing and distant around her.

Amelia Chan drew her in with softly spoken words.

"Hey," she said. "Lamar says things 'feel different.' That mean anything to anyone?"

"Yeah," Darius responded. That single syllable was enough to fill Thorn's empty chest with heat. "It means Lust is coming."

Fire flooded Thorn's veins, bringing her back to life and forcing her to focus on the things she knew how to deal with. She tapped her earpiece and unmuted her mic.

"Eyes sharp," she commanded. "Don't let him catch us

off guard."

Several more minutes passed, but whatever calm they'd had before evaporated into silent tension—like a muscle pulled so taut it was ready to tear free from the tendon. Thorn closed her eyes, relying on Sparkie's sight as he circled the skies above while she used her Sin senses to track movement down here. Nothing, not even the rustling of leaves in the wind, drew her attention…

"I see something," Caleb Claytor said.

Thorn swiped her phone up again to find Caleb on the map. He and Madison Lewis were positioned less than half a mile up Booth Memorial Avenue, where Kissena Boulevard intersected the park. Sparkie's wings spread wide and caught a draft, pulling him up and to the west.

"What's happening, Claytor?" Chris's voice rang over the coms.

"People have started heading in Thorn's direction," he responded. "A guy just dropped his basketball and walked away from the courts, and a woman across the street stopped halfway through trimming her bushes."

"And the dog walker," Lewis added. "She let all the animals loose…"

"They are being Puppetted," Alan said.

"Remember your training," Chris commanded. "The Sins will pick low-resistance targets—targets easy to immediately and completely control. Fortify your mind, stay focused, and they'll move right past you. All units, keep an eye out for strange behavior."

Reports began trickling in from their teams along Booth Memorial Avenue. More movement, more people, more Influence. Though Thorn couldn't sense Lust's power, she didn't need to. Supernatural bullshit was clearly at play—mothers abandoning children, city workers leaving their posts. Sparkie spotted a navy sedan slowly driving down the street that looked remarkably like the one Autumn Hunt had been spotted in. She relayed the information to Alan.

"I see it," he said. "I cannot confirm that Amoretto is

the driver, but whomever it is, they are alone."

A knot twisted around Thorn's throat. Wrath wasn't here. Not yet, anyway. She couldn't tell if she was relieved or disappointed.

Within minutes, TAC counted nearly thirty individuals walking toward the cemetery. Sparkie swooped high in the sky above their heads, watching as a drawling, zombie-like horde ambled Thorn's way. The navy sedan pulled up along the side of the road near the cemetery's western entrance and parked in a red zone. Thorn's muscles tightened.

Before the Puppets had even reached the property, they dispersed. A handful divided from the rest, going south down 164th Street or slipping through open gates in the wrought iron fence to the graveyard. The others held back, biding time, spacing out, before they moved, too.

Soon, Thorn felt them. Pinpricks of cold energy entered her awareness, distant and deliberate. A few to the north. Some behind her. More walking along the southern edge. Thorn had to admit, she was impressed. The Sin's control was impeccable. Its Puppets came in with such an unpredictable pattern that, if she weren't looking for it, she never would have noticed she was being surrounded.

But she *was* surrounded. Thorn drew a slow breath.

"Get ready," she murmured.

She shifted where she stood, adjusting her helmet beneath an arm as she looked around the cemetery. Some of the Puppets were near enough to see but still too distant to tell, simply by looking at them, that they were under a Sin's control. The others hovered back, trying to act as naturally as possible. All the while, Sparkie circled the blue sedan until its front door finally opened.

Connor Amoretto stepped out.

The fire in Thorn's blood chilled, frigid and deadly, as her fingers tightened on the helmet's chinstrap. He was still too distant to sense, and he seemed to know it. He slowly walked along the sidewalk, entering the Mount St. Mary Cemetery on the furthest edge from where Thorn stood.

Then he hovered by the gate, and his Puppets began to approach.

"He's here," Thorn said. "I have confirmation of Amoretto on scene. Alan?"

"I see him," her uncle responded, "but I do not have a clear shot through the trees, and he is not close enough to risk trying. He could too easily escape."

"Not to add to an already stressful situation," Holly suddenly chimed in, "but we just spotted a guy who looks like Anton Claytor on a traffic camera exiting the Queens-Midtown Tunnel. We might be dealing with another Sin here in fifteen minutes. Probably less."

Thorn's teeth clenched. "Great," she murmured. "Then let's speed this along…"

She stood where she was for a few moments longer, feeling the sensation of ten, twenty, thirty men and women wandering toward her through the trees. She waited until it was undeniable—until no one could have believed she wouldn't have noticed the strange sensations—before she moved. Thorn pushed herself away from the tree and pulled her helmet over her head.

The Puppets sprinted.

Nearly three dozen auras rushed at her in a cold typhoon. A circle of people tightened around her, visible now through trees, around tombstones, along the road. Adrenaline surged through Thorn's body, and she spun, counting them, calculating what best to do next.

Ultimately, she decided on… nothing.

They slammed into her. Dozens of fists and feet and figures crowded in, cutting off Thorn's awareness of anything outside of them. A mixed spread of faces filled her view. Tall, short, young, old, healthy, spent—they all attacked with the same brutality. Nails swiped at her skin, legs lashed out to trip her, fingers tried to wrap around the ponytail sticking out from the base of her helmet.

There may have been more of them, but Thorn was stronger. Faster. She slammed her elbow into a man's throat, which sent him sprawling to the ground, unconscious before he hit the grass. Another woman lunged in, and Thorn wound her fist around her neck, lifting her six inches and throwing her into the wall of Puppets at her back. Whenever a body went down, another joined it. Thorn was vaguely aware of more energy coming in to replace the fallen. All the while, Martyr voices buzzed in her ears as Chris gave orders, as units moved into position, as Alan called what he could see so they could more easily charge in when Amoretto was vulnerable.

But the swarm never relented, and Lust never moved closer. Sparkie still circled, tracking the Puppets around Thorn and the Sin himself, who hadn't budged from where he stood along the far fence line. Thorn ducked, dodged, deflected, darting through gravestones and using the environment to slow the mob. A hand finally managed to wrap around her jacket sleeve, yanking her around. Thorn rolled backward over a granite monument to dislodge the man and give herself more space.

"You're moving away," DuPont shouted into his mic. "You've got to get closer to the hearse!"

"I'm *trying!*" Thorn snapped.

She spun back, dove beneath the outreached arms of yet another Puppet flying at her from the right, and rolled back onto the road. A man jumped on top of her, nearly pinning her, and for the first time in minutes, Thorn felt Amoretto's energy move at the edge of her range.

But the second Thorn broke free and vaulted to her feet again, he froze. A sudden realization struck her just as Chris's voice broke through.

"We have reports from Wolfe's team of several black SUVs headed this way on the Clearview Expressway," she said. "Could be mercs. Get ready to pull out!"

"No," Thorn hissed, anger and panic tightening around her throat. She shook her head, jerked around, and slammed another Puppet to the asphalt. The woman's head cracked against it, and streams of blood poured from beneath her blonde hair. "I know how to get Lust! I've got to let them catch me!"

"*What?*" Alan growled.

"He won't move if I'm not disabled," Thorn snarled as she sprinted back toward the cathedral, an army of Puppets on her heels. The hearse was visible again, just barely, between bodies and gravestones and trees. "Chan, DuPont, just be ready to—"

"Wait!" DuPont shouted. Suddenly, Thorn's ears filled with a flurry of noise, and Chan's voice called after DuPont. Thorn was surrounded again, Puppets closing in. She drew a breath, ready to surrender, when a familiar face pushed into the crowd, and Gabe DuPont attacked her.

Thorn's eyes widened as he threw a punch at her head, but he aimed so wide that it never stood a chance of landing. He wore his suit, the jacket bulging with a bulletproof vest hidden beneath it, but his TAC helmet was nowhere to be found. Thorn shook her head.

"What the fuck are you *doing?*" she screamed as she avoided more Puppets. A man managed to get his arm around Thorn's throat, and DuPont came in like he was prepared to help the guy take her down, but instead, he pried his fingers away and shoved him to the side.

"Helping," DuPont breathed. He grabbed Thorn's left hand, his cognac eyes darting to her wrist, and understanding cracked like a crowbar against Thorn's skull. "Let him *think* you're disabled. Then, when he's close enough—"

"Your helmet," Thorn cut in. "Your ears!"

"He'll notice a helmet a mile away," DuPont insisted. He yanked Thorn into him, twisted her around until her back was against his chest and her arm was pinned between their bodies, and wrapped a hand just above where the *Peccostium* sat beneath her wrist. "We've got to sell it. So scream!"

Then DuPont dropped to his knees, dragging her down with him. A grateful surge paralyzed Thorn for a moment, catching her breath in her chest, but then her mouth ripped open and roared rage into the sky. Without hesitation, every single one of Lust's Puppets piled on top of them. Gabe braced himself, curling around her as much as he could to shoulder the brunt of the attack, but hands still found her, wound around her, tugged at her hair and her clothes and her flesh wherever they could. Thorn slammed her eyes shut and maneuvered her way into her satchel, hunting for the sonic weapon in the dark.

"Amoretto is moving in," Alan said.

"All units," Chris shouted, "get ready!"

Lust's aura rushed toward them. Sparkie watched from the sky as Connor Amoretto wove through gravestones and across the grass, sprinting straight toward where Thorn and Gabe were buried under a mountain of Puppets. Thorn's heart lodged in her throat as her fingers finally wrapped around the sonic device. She pulled it free, held it tightly between her knees, and hovered a thumb over the button.

"I need some range," Thorn said to Gabe. "Somewhere to throw it."

"I've got you," he said.

Amoretto was halfway to them now. Closing in. A hundred meters. Eighty. Fifty. When he was close enough to see the writhing mound of bodies, he slowed, and a hungry grin warped his face. The fire in Thorn's belly threatened to explode, and it took all of her self-control to keep Sparkie from screaming in the sky above them.

"Rose!" Lust shouted as he walked closer, stepping over the fallen forms of Puppets she had disabled in the fight. He casually slipped his hands into his pockets, his cockiness ringing off of him like a warning bell. "What a *coincidence*, running into you here."

He laughed, and the sound of his voice echoed through Thorn's mind, attempting to drag her back to that little fucking restaurant where he'd plunged a blade through her wrist. Thorn's teeth gnashed, and her grip tightened around Gabe's weapon, but she didn't activate it. Not yet. She needed him closer…

And he came closer. Slowly now. Deliberately. Like he

was *certain* she was powerless to do anything to stop it. His Puppets began to relent at last, all but those closest to Thorn pulling back to give him the space to see her. One tried to tear Thorn's helmet from her head, but she shook it so aggressively that the woman's fingers couldn't find purchase on the polyethylene shell. Lust laughed again.

"Mmm, still a lot of fight in you," he said. A ravenous spark made his voice deep. Now that Thorn could see him through her visor, fighting the urge to detonate the weapon and rip him to shreds was almost impossible. Amoretto kept walking forward. "God, I can't wait to sink my—"

Then he stopped abruptly less than twenty feet from where she knelt, and his blue eyes darted to the man behind her back. Dawning realization wiped the smirk right off his face. Thorn's heart sank.

Oh, fuck. This close, he'd be able to tell that Gabe DuPont was *not* linked to his cerebral net—that he wasn't a Puppet.

They'd been caught.

Lust's mouth twisted into a snarl as Thorn shouted, "*NOW!*"

Gabe released her and leapt to the side, tackling the two nearest Puppets to the ground at the exact moment Thorn slammed the button and threw the sonic disruptor into the air. It landed with a thud on the grass ten feet away. Lust's horde dove onto her again—

Sound exploded through the cemetery. The wave was so powerful that it pushed against Thorn's chest and made her heart skip a beat. Gabe fell to his knees at the exact moment that every single Puppet attached to Lust collapsed in a heap. The Sin howled and stumbled away, hands clamped around his head. Blood dribbled at the heels of his palms.

Thorn tore back to her feet and drove her shoulder into him, knocking him over a gravestone to sprawl on the grass behind it. Then she was on top of him, straddling his chest as she grabbed both of his wrists and dug her fingernails into the *Peccostium* beneath his left.

He screamed.

The sound tore from his throat as he convulsed beneath her. A rush of venomous joy made Thorn's body buzz. She made sure her grip was secure around the mark of the Sins before she pulled her pocket knife free. She flipped it open, stretched up, and stabbed the blade into his hand, right at the base of the two fingers the fucker had shoved down her throat. He screamed again and kept screaming as Thorn wrenched her knife left and right until those fingers were severed entirely and rolled into the grass. She looked Amoretto dead in the eye as she came back, flashed the knife in front of his face, and buried it to the hilt in his side, relishing the feeling of it piercing through skin, fat tissue, and muscle.

"Not a lot of fight left in *you*, now, is there?" she taunted.

TAC leapt into action. Gabe crawled back toward the hearse while Amelia Chan jumped out, helmet on and rifle in her hands. The back door swung open, revealing Lamar, Cain, and Rae. They all climbed down, but just as the wolf's padded feet hit the asphalt, a rush of cold energy approached from the east.

"Mercenaries!" Chris shouted, her voice ringing in Thorn's ears. "Intercept them!"

Suddenly, the cemetery swarmed in chaos. Thirty Martyrs darted in from all sides of the property, donning full riot gear as they sprinted in Thorn's direction. Before they got halfway across the cemetery, more men in black armor came around the cathedral and met them head-on. Rae rushed off to join them.

Below Thorn, Cain and Chan guided Lamar up the road. She kept Amoretto pinned, one hand still tight around his *Peccostium* and the other holding firm to the blade in his side. Sparkie circled overhead, crying out as Consent drew closer, and a smile split Thorn's face. She released her knife and opened her visor, her heart pounding fervently at the furious, terrified glint in Amoretto's expression.

"It's *over*," she growled.

But Chan's energy stopped moving. Thorn looked over her shoulder to see Lamar frozen in place, his feet inches from the grass, eyes wide and panicked as he stared at Connor Amoretto bleeding in Thorn's hands. Beneath his tactical helmet, the young Virtue's face lost its color. His lips fell open, and his chest rose and fell in short, choppy breaths. Thorn's vindication fractured, and panic leaked through the cracks.

"Lamar!" she shouted.

He didn't move, like he couldn't hear her, couldn't see her. Chan wrapped a hand around his arm, trying to tug him forward, but Cain slapped her fingers away before putting himself directly in front of Lamar. He completely obscured the boy as he leaned forward, palms at Lamar's cheeks, his head bobbing as he spoke words Thorn couldn't make out above the noise.

Then, a sudden, cold flare lit in her chest, and Thorn's heart stopped beating.

"Wrath is here!" Alan shouted. "Defend our Virtue team!"

Autumn Hunt's power gorged, immediately consuming more souls than Thorn could fucking count as she amassed a Puppet army on the opposite side of the cemetery from where their entire TAC force was holding off the mercenary line. Another sonic disruptor went off, scrambling the enemy so some of their people could sprint this way, but Thorn knew they wouldn't be fast enough. Cain's head snapped up. He turned to Thorn, catching her eye with a terrified stare. She looked to the south, and his gaze followed.

A mass of men and women stampeded toward them, crawling over the wrought iron fence like a raving colony of fire ants. Sparkie hovered above them until he found Autumn Hunt, spitting and furious, at the front of the horde. Thorn hardly recognized her. For the first time in as far as she could remember, the Sin wasn't wearing plainclothes, instead donning a ballistics vest, like she knew how much more she was risking by facing the Martyrs now than she had even a year ago. Her brown hair was pulled back, her gray eyes sharp, and the anger radiating off her was enough to stir up a storm in Thorn's gut. A pistol glistened in the Sin's right hand. She raised it.

The first bullet thudded against Thorn's chest, digging into the kevlar and bruising her collarbone beneath it. Thorn stumbled just enough for her grip on Amoretto's wrist to loosen, and her hold on his *Peccostium* slipped.

He rolled away, shoved Thorn to the grass, and scrambled to his feet. She lunged for him again, but Wrath pulled the trigger a second, third, fourth time, on and on until she emptied the clip...

Into Cain.

The battle screeched to a stop. Thorn watched in horror as Cain threw Lamar behind him and used his own body as a goddamned shield to absorb the full brunt of Hunt's attack. Most of the rounds rocked against the armor on his torso, but others hit his legs, his stomach, his neck. Thorn was hardly aware of his name pouring from her mouth in a haggard scream as Cain Guttuso collapsed to his knees and then his face on the pavement.

Rage blinded her. Her ears rang with a drone so loud that nothing else registered. A sonic disruptor flew into the sky above her head and discharged a blast that knocked Autumn Hunt's Puppets out in a single shot. Thorn climbed to her feet just as Rae sprinted past her and Alan called a command she didn't care enough to hear. Wrath glared at her from down the road, and Sparkie cried out a sharp, harrowed screech.

Then, a shot from the cathedral bell tower pierced through Hunt's shoulder, blasting her armor apart and sending her spiraling.

Thorn charged. As Chris announced more mercenaries entering the graveyard, as Holly warned of Greed and his Puppets approaching from the west, as Alan called to abort the mission and get Lamar to safety, Thorn set her sights on

Autumn Hunt's retreating back. A deep hunger, a desire, a fucking *need* to tear the Sin apart ripped Thorn's chest open. The image of Cain on the ground stoked the fire, creating a vortex of pain and hatred that was too much for Thorn to shut down.

And she didn't want to.

Up ahead, Wrath sprinted back the way she'd come, clumsily reloading her firearm as she threw a look over her shoulder. Rae was on her heels, closer to her than Thorn was, close enough that she'd overtake the bitch well before she had the chance to vault over the wrought iron fence and disappear beyond it. Another shot from Alan's rifle zipped through the trees, thudding into a branch by Wrath's skull. The Sin snarled, her eyes darting from Thorn to the wolf to the tower in the distance.

Then her clip snapped into place, and she started shooting again.

This time, her attack was wild and unfocused. Bullets clattered into turf, into gravestones, and into thin air in a messy spray. Rae came closer, and Thorn began to close the gap. The animal howled—

One of Hunt's shots slammed into Rae's open mouth.

Alan's Familiar let out a horrible cry, and he roared in pain on the other side of the radio line. Thorn's stomach twisted as Rae tripped into the grass and writhed. The foggy tendrils of her head started pulling themselves back together in a squirming, ghastly display.

Beyond her, Wrath reached the fence, and she vaulted over it without looking back. The fury in Thorn's gut snarled as she hurried after her, ready to jump, too. All the while, orders berated her. Chris, Alan, Holly, more, all telling her to let Wrath go. Thorn ignored them.

Darius's voice cut through the clutter in her brain.

"Thorn!" He shouted her name, strangled and terrified. "Come back!"

For a second, she hesitated. Just a second. Her heart ached to find him, begged her to turn around. But then, at the far end of the alley, through corroded iron bars, Autumn Hunt stopped running. She glared back with so much loathing and venom that Thorn could feel it dancing in the link between them.

And all she could see was Donovan dying in her arms, his life pouring out in a rushing, red river from a knife in his back and a bullet in his heart.

Thorn tore her helmet off, discarded it on the grass, and followed Wrath.

The Sin sprinted again, her aura pulling away so quickly that Thorn struggled to track her movement. She leapt over another fence and darted into the mid-day traffic on the Long Island Expressway, her Influence flying out in a wall and forcing cars to a stop in both directions. Vehicles slammed into one another, horns blaring, voices screaming, as Wrath ran to the other side. Thorn kept close behind her.

Then, they were in the neighborhoods, and Hunt pulled further ahead—so far that, fuck, Thorn could barely make sense of her anymore, and even Sparkie couldn't spot her as she darted between cars or beneath tree branches. She turned right, left, left again, until Thorn got twisted around. Hunt was barely a blip, a ghost of energy surrounded by the sensations of the city. Thorn stopped, breathing hard, and looked around, a tangled knot of fury hot in her throat.

Wrath's Influence flared.

Thorn's heart pounded as she followed the draw. She was closer than Thorn expected, but something about this felt different. A wide net, like Hunt had collected a new swarm of Puppets, but it lacked the substance of human souls. Thorn tore around a final corner to a dead-end parking lot in a small business park. Wrath was pinned on the far side, crouching behind a massive, red delivery van. The fragile threads of her Influence spread from her aura like spindly spider legs, thin and wispy. Thorn dipped her hand into her satchel, grabbed her pistol, and rushed forward.

She hadn't made it halfway before a child stepped out in front of her.

Thorn slid to a stop, and the raging hurricane of anger stuttered in her core. The girl was young enough that she didn't have an aura Thorn could detect—nine, maybe ten, barely younger than Thorn had been when Wrath had first dug its talons into her soul all those decades ago. She looked unkempt. Her fluffy, brown hair was matted and filthy, her eyes sunken, and the school uniform on her back had clearly been worn for multiple days on end.

Suddenly, more children appeared, dozens more, walking out from behind dumpsters, inside stairwells, or around vehicles. They all had that same haunted look, like they hadn't eaten, hadn't slept, and they encircled Thorn shoulder to shoulder three layers deep, watching her with a familiar, dead-eyed stare. A piercing laugh cut through her stomach, and she felt sick with the realization….

They were Puppets.

"What's wrong?" Autumn Hunt called from across the lot. A new wave of Influence rolled off of her body, the pressure of it a dull sensation in Thorn's head. Nearby energy slowly meandered away, leaving them alone. Wrath strode around the van, just enough to be seen, as she applied pressure to the gunshot wound on her shoulder. "This should be *easy* for you."

Wrath cackled again as her Puppets took a step forward. God, there were so fucking many of them. Sparkie dove to Thorn, keeping an eye at her back while she focused on the children between her and Wrath. They all held some kind of rudimentary weapon—kitchen knives, sharpened steel pipes, screwdrivers—and Thorn realized with a jolt of nausea that their uniforms matched the first girls'. Her mind flashed back to a newspaper article Nicholas had shared with her two weeks ago: the Verrette twins' missing school bus.

Fuck. This was a trap. And Thorn had run right into it.

"You're *sick,*" she breathed.

"Awe, don't be like that," Hunt said. "You and I both know you're not the *average Jane* who faints at the thought of violence." Thorn's eyes sharpened, and she threw a venomous glare across the lot. Wrath's lips twisted into a sinister grin. "Are you really going to let a couple of sniveling brats stand in your way? You used to be *so* much more than this. A queen. A fucking *god*. How disappointing."

Wrath's smile widened, and Thorn's teeth clenched. She looked beyond the girl to where the Sin was still half-concealed behind the van twenty yards away. If she caused enough chaos, she could clear the space between them before a single child got near enough to touch her. Thorn just needed a break in the line.

She felt for the strings connecting the children to Wrath and sliced through one. The first girl's eyes rolled back in her head as she slumped to the ground. Thorn reached for another—

A boy plunged a pair of scissors into his own throat.

Thorn gasped, her heart seizing as he collapsed at her feet, his eyes wide and mouth open. A gurgling slurry of saliva and blood bubbled from his lips and nostrils, coating his chapped lips in pink foam. Sparkie screamed as the other children moved in to close the hole. Their heels landed on their classmate like he was trash on the street.

"Try that again," Wrath hissed, all the joy in her voice cold and deadly. "*Please*. I'll kill them all."

The kids came forward further, more tightly. They held their weapons up, not toward Thorn but at themselves. The points of blades pressed against young necks. Thorn's instinct was to step back, but she had nowhere to go.

"What the fuck do you want?" she shouted.

"You know what I want."

Her eyes darted up to Wrath again, finding the Sin watching her with a carnal hunger that wasn't all that unlike Lust's. Her smile had disappeared, leaving her face gaunt and insatiable. Thorn's blood ran cold.

"Drop your gun," Wrath whispered, "or this is on *your* hands."

Thorn hesitated a breath too long, digging for another

solution—*any* other solution.

A second child drove her weapon upward. The jagged end of the pipe pierced into the soft flesh beneath her chin. She hardly had the time to yelp before the pain cut her off from Wrath, and her blue eyes rolled backward. The girl crumbled in a bloody mess on the ground, her blonde pigtails soaking in a gush of red. Thorn stared at her, helpless. Horrified.

"Drop. Your. Gun."

A numb wave overwhelmed Thorn, her mind drifting back to Darius Jones and the promises she'd made and immediately broken. Her fingers felt weak and worthless, the grip of her firearm tumbling free. Before it even hit the ground, the children were upon her.

Sparkie flew into the sky, avoiding tiny hands and rough rope. Wrath lashed a length around Thorn's throat and yanked her forward, forcing her to her hands and knees before she jerked Thorn's arms behind her back and tied her wrists together. Then, she stepped in front of her as one of the Puppetted children approached with a fabric sack, his expression a dead void. Hunt's face distorted in a victorious smile.

"This is why I was always going to win," she murmured against Thorn's cheek. "Because *you* will do the *right thing…* even if it means believing a lie."

The numbness melted with a fresh coat of anger, but it was too late. The sack came over her head, shrouding her in darkness, and Wrath fastened it so tight around her neck that Thorn struggled to breathe. No. She *couldn't* breathe. Her mind began to go foggy just as she heard the tell-tale *snick!* of a pocket knife flicking open.

A familiar aura sprinted up the lot behind her.

"Thorn!" Caleb Claytor shouted.

She wanted to turn, to tell him to run, but the rope pressed against her screams, suffocating them. Thorn's face went cold, and her mouth gasped open in empty gulps as her entire world dissolved.

CHAPTER THIRTY-ONE

She reminded him of Sophie.

Long, blonde hair. Pale skin. Blue eyes barely visible through half-closed lids. She was around the right age, too. Or, she would have been if Sophie hadn't been murdered by Envy nearly three years ago. Darius's heart hurt at the memory and at the sight of this new child laid out on the asphalt. Blood from a gnarled wound beneath the girl's chin dribbled down her throat, painting the yellow pigtails splayed out on either side of her neck ruddy and red. He gently touched her jaw. Her skin was warm under his fingertips.

Energy surged from them, winding its way into her body and pulling the torn edges of her flesh back together. When the healing was done, she still didn't wake up. That was probably for the best.

No one should wake up to *this*.

He got to his feet in a daze and wiped the tears from his cheeks. His senses were muted, the colors duller, sounds softer. Even the sensation of the sun on his face felt like a phantom—a false warmth in this nightmare.

Children lay around him. Two dozen dirty, hungry, haunted children spread out between parked cars and garbage bins. The Martyrs had collected them together, creating a line of boys and girls two layers deep so Darius could walk between them to heal their wounds. Sliced necks. Broken bones. Bruised bodies. Only one had been dead before they got here, thank *god*, but one was still too many. Darius couldn't erase the image of the boy from his mind— couldn't unsee the scissor shanks sticking out from his neck, the crimson lake pooled around his shoulders, and the empty look in his eyes as Seth Graves had draped a sheet over him.

It was as though Darius had traveled back to another time, another place, where a completely different group of kids had been cut down by the Sins. His stomach swirled, nausea climbing up from it. A massive, warm hand landed on his shoulder.

"You doin' okay?" Conrad asked.

Darius shook his head. With the lump in his throat, it was all he could do.

Twenty minutes had dissolved in a blood-red blur. The chaos in the cemetery exploded and died with the same intensity as their sonic disruptors. Once Lust weaseled his way out of Thorn's grip, the mercenaries disengaged and disappeared, and Greed abandoned his advancement before he'd really gotten underway. When his first wave of Puppets had been so easily disabled, he turned and ran back the way he'd come, leaving the Martyrs alone, scattered and seething.

No one had seen Thorn.

Focusing on healing had been nearly impossible. Darius made his way through their wounded, addressing injuries absently while all his mental energy was swept up in listening to reports on the search for her. Nothing else got through to him. Not Gabe, freshly mended, dragging the few dead Martyrs away for transport. Not Amelia, attempting to stabilize Cain right there in the middle of the road. Not even Lamar, tear-streaked and traumatized in the back of the hearse, watching the others work with a wide-eyed stare.

Then Darius had been called *here*, and things had only

gotten worse.

Chris's energy rounded the corner, leading Seth and Madison into the parking lot. Darius's attention instantly snapped up to her. Alan's, too. He stood in the center of this space, his rifle slung across his back while one arm wrapped around his chest armor and the other pressed a fist to his lips. Rae paced behind him.

"We've combed every street from 65th to 71st," Chris said. "There's no sign of her anywhere."

Darius's chest cored out, the very essence of him ground up and sucked dry. To his side, Alan stiffened, and his fist curled tighter. The slender bones in the back of his hand stretched against his skin, clawing for escape.

"What about Mr. Claytor?" he asked.

Chris shook her head, flattening wisps of blonde hair that had fallen loose from a frayed and frazzled ponytail. She and the rest of their search parties had removed their helmets and armor to avoid standing out as they swept the area. While Alexis had her team keeping the police delayed, the Martyrs on the ground didn't need to make a bad situation worse.

"No sign of him, either," Chris responded. "Skylar tried getting a location off their phones and found both of them destroyed along Utopia Parkway with Caleb's helmet. It was covered in blood…"

Alan's eyes sharpened. A growl rumbled in his Familiar's throat.

"She has them," he murmured, spinning away from the Martyrs. He walked to the back of the lot, where a blood-red van was parked behind a restaurant. He stared at it, his lip curling, heavy breaths rocking his shoulders. The part of Wrath tainting his soul seeped into the air like an electric charge. Suddenly, he raised his hands above his head and slammed them onto the van's hood. Metal cratered beneath his fists, bucking up as the car alarm wailed to life.

"Wrath has them!" he roared. Rae howled at his heels, her fangs bared and hackles raised. Alan twisted back around as

Gabe hurried to shut off the alarm. His face contorted with so much rage it made the hairs on the nape of Darius's neck hum. For a breath, the parking lot went deadly quiet.

Until Chris, her voice shaky, eyes full of tears and terror, whispered, "What do we do?"

Alan looked at her, then at Darius, then at the Martyrs around them.

"We find her."

He tapped his earpiece as Chris and Darius exchanged a look. "Miss Andrews," he said, "I need you and Mr. Wolfe to put all your energy into locating Autumn Hunt. Start your search in Flushing and move out in a circle from there." He paused then, and he met Darius's gaze. "Call me the instant you know anything."

Alan disconnected the call, took a steadying breath, and turned to the gathered Martyrs.

"We take our search wider," he announced. "While Miss Andrews looks for Wrath on the cameras, we will look for her on the streets. She was last seen in Hunts Point, so we begin there, but I will scour this whole *damned* city if I have to."

He threw the back of the SUV open and whipped his rifle around, dismantling it with quick, precise movements. He tucked the pieces into the foam in the case and snapped it shut. Then, he reached for a smaller box, which held a handgun.

"How many TAC units do we currently have?" he asked as he threaded a holster through his belt and slipped the pistol into it.

"Nine, sir," Chris said. She and Darius followed behind him, standing just outside his reach. "We lost four Martyrs, and another two were too badly injured for Darius to completely heal without depleting his power, so six of our Units are incomplete. I have an additional five on patrol in Manhattan."

Alan nodded. "Call them in. I want one team to remain here to watch over these children until we can pass them to the proper authorities. Agents who have lost their partners can escort the wounded and dead, as well as Mr. Verrette and Mr. Jones, to the Underground."

He reached for the back hatch and slammed the door shut. The sound rocked Darius's chest, rattling his heart.

"Escort *me* back?" he asked. Alan threw a hot look over his shoulder. "No. No way! I'm coming."

An angry hush whispered down Alan's spine, drawing him taller as he turned around. "Darius…"

"I can heal." Darius pressed, and he propped his hands defiantly on his hips just as he'd seen Thorn do a hundred times before. "I can fight, and I can sense when things are getting dangerous. I can also track energy *just* as well as you can, so I might pick up something the others won't." He paused and inhaled deep to steady himself. It didn't help, and the next words he spoke came out with a shudder. "Please, Alan. I can help find her. I *need* to help find her."

Chris's face darted in his direction, and he felt her eyes trained on him, but Darius didn't look away from Alan. The Martyr leader's expression didn't soften, but an understanding furrow pulled at his brows. After a moment, Chris cleared her throat.

"We need to move…" she murmured.

Alan sighed. "All right, Mr. Jones. We will alert our medic van that you will not—"

"Cain! Cain, wait!"

Chris, Darius, and Alan spun to see Amelia Chan frantically trying to get in front of Cain as he limped up the sidewalk. The look of him was enough to make Darius's stomach fill with lead. His left leg was wound in blood-stained bandages, and a brace around his neck was so saturated in crimson that it nearly looked like it was meant to be that color. His right arm was pinned tight against his torso in a sling, and every step made a shock of pain flash over his face. But he kept coming, and his bright eyes zeroed in on Alan. Alan's lips pressed together as Rae uttered a growl.

"I'm so sorry, sir," Amelia said. "I told him to get into

the hearse and return to the Underground, but he refused."

Cain ignored her. "Alan," he started, but Alan waved a hand.

"Not now, Cain. We are getting ready to leave."

"Alan," Cain pressed. "Please—"

Alan's rage flared. Rae's midnight fur stood like a ridge of mountains along her spine.

"I said *not now!*"

He made to walk away, but Cain's left hand darted out. With a wince, he grabbed Alan around the bicep and pulled him back.

"ALAN! STOP!"

When Alan turned again, Darius was convinced he planned to strike Cain. He stepped forward, ready to intervene, but before he'd moved three inches, Cain pulled his wounded arm away from his chest. Darius's heart careened to a stop in his ribcage, and Alan's jaw dropped.

Sparkie curled in the hollow between Cain's wrist and stomach, his wings and tail wrapped so tight to his body that he was no larger than a child's shoe. At first, Darius thought he was dead, and a wave of shock, sudden and daunting, threatened to pull him to the ground.

But then he remembered that Familiars couldn't die. Sparkie's tiny body seized with a painful jolt, and he let out a high-pitched cry. God, that was worse. Darius felt so sick with dread that he hardly felt Chris's hand wind around his wrist.

"Where did you find him?" she breathed.

"I didn't," Cain answered. "He found me. While I was waiting for the medical vehicle to arrive, I spotted him crawling through the grass."

Darius's throat constricted. He forced a single word through it. "Crawling?"

Cain looked at him, and Darius's stomach fell. Fuck, he'd never seen Cain this scared. "He seemed to be coming in and out of consciousness..." he whispered.

Sparkie let out another sound, this one deeper, a grunt,

as though he'd just taken a punch to the stomach that knocked the wind out of him. Rae's maw split in a rough bark while Alan stared at the piece of his niece's soul, laid bare and broken in Cain's arms. He raised a hand to the reptile's face. His fingers trembled.

"Alan…" Cain began. Alan's eyes flicked up to meet his. "My old friend… Bring her home."

Alan's jaw set. "I intend to."

He walked away, hesitating for just a second longer as Sparkie writhed again. Chris followed immediately after him. She didn't bother to hide the tears streaming down her cheeks. Darius paused.

"Cain, I—"

"Stop," he said, raising his good hand with a wince. "There will be time enough for this later. Here." He tenderly adjusted, rolling Sparkie into his palm before holding him out. Darius's eyes widened as he opened his hands. Cain placed Sparkie into them like he was handling a delicate piece of freshly-fired porcelain.

"He may be of some use," Cain murmured. Terror clenched around his voice. "To help you… or her. Now, go."

Darius nodded, turning back to join Alan in the SUV. Chris had disappeared, as had almost all the TAC agents in the lot. Before Darius opened the passenger door, he raised Sparkie to his face. The lizard lifted his chin and looked Darius dead in the eye; a fragile flicker of hope flashed between them.

"Thorn," Darius whispered. "I'm coming for you."

"I'm coming for you."

Thorn tapped her thumb against each of her fingers. Her wrists were bound behind her, shoulders pulled so tight against the back of a chair that she could hardly move, but she could do *this*. She kept her eyes closed and focused on

Sparkie's senses. For a few precious seconds, she wasn't here...

She was with Darius.

Thumb to pointer, and she could see his face, watching from above, those bright eyes narrowed in a pain she hadn't meant to cause, but fuck, she knew she had. To middle, and she heard his voice, deep and terrified as he talked with Alan. To ring, and she smelled the sting of panicked perspiration soaking his clothes. And to pinky, where she felt him, *she felt him*, his hands on her skin, warm around her, like a shield—

A blow slammed into Thorn's jaw. It didn't matter that the metal was cold; the pipe struck her flesh with hot white intensity. A jagged end tore a gash open on Thorn's chin while the force of it crashed her teeth together. A rush of blood filled her mouth. Something else, too. A canine loosened in her gums before dislodging entirely and swimming in the fluids spilling under her tongue. With a groan, she twisted her head and spat the whole damned thing to the floor. Wrath *tsked* impatiently.

"Oh, no," she said. "We can't have that. Bently, get the tooth."

Thorn's eyes cracked open. Her memories of arriving here were shaky. Wrath had kept her unconscious the entire drive. Thorn would wake up, her lungs gasping and gaping for air, only for the rope to pull tight again and drag her back into the dark. It went like that for... god, Thorn didn't even know. When the bitch had finally let her come to, she'd been tied to this chair in the middle of a warehouse, surrounded by people. Some of them, she recognized.

Mayor Bently grimaced as Hunt threw him a joyous look. Thorn wanted to be surprised at seeing him here, but somehow it made fucking sense that he'd be working with the Sins. He brushed his hands against his suit jacket, the fabric sprayed with a fine mist of Thorn's blood. His uneven gaze darted around the room as though he was the one who needed to be saved, but no one came to the rescue. He shuffled forward, walking like the ground was covered in shit, and he didn't want to get any on the soles of his expensive shoes. When he reached the splatter Thorn had hawked onto the concrete, his face went green.

"Surely, you can't expect me to—"

"Get the fucking tooth," Wrath snarled.

Bently leapt like she'd touched him with an electric rod before crouching down and snatching Thorn's canine between pinched fingers. He held it at arm's length, delivering it to Wrath with his nose curled.

"Good boy," the Sin purred. An angry flush powdered his cheeks, but Bently said nothing as she turned back around.

The mayor wasn't the only familiar face. Both Anton Claytor and Connor Amoretto stood behind Hunt. Greed seemed as uncomfortable as ever, and for once, that smug smile had been wiped clean off Lust's fucking face. That gave Thorn just enough strength to raise her head. His suit jacket had been discarded, and the navy button-up beneath it was saturated with deep red at his side from where Thorn had driven her blade into him. He held that knife now, wrapped in his right hand while his left dangled by his side. His two middle fingers were reduced to raw, red nubs, and he glared at Thorn in a way that let her know he couldn't wait to cut something of hers off in return. A young Latina woman flanked him like a disciple walking on water in the footsteps of her savior.

Around them, more people filled the space. Thorn could hardly make sense of them all. A handful were Puppets— whose Thorn didn't know because they sure as fuck didn't belong to Wrath—standing close enough that their auras created a ring around her. Worse, though, were the men in black. Mercenaries. There were dozens of them armed with tactical vests, short-range rifles, and pistols. Thorn's heart plummeted.

Fuck, this wasn't good.

Wrath considered the tooth in her hand, holding it up to

the light with the delicacy of a jeweler admiring a diamond.

"You're too pretty to have a fucked-up smile, Rose," she murmured. Her eyes slowly wandered over, ensnaring Thorn's face. She grinned, passed the steel pipe off to Greed, and took a step forward. "Say 'ahh.'"

Hunt reached for Thorn's mouth, but Thorn clamped her jaw shut, and when the Sin tried to pry it open, her fingers slipped against the blood on Thorn's chin. The joy in Wrath's expression melted into malice. She pulled back a fist and punched Thorn in the throat. Thorn choked, coughed, gasping for air, and a hand instantly wrapped up in her hair. Wrath forced her head back, twisted the tooth in her fingers one last time, and jammed the thing into Thorn's skull.

Her breath came back in a howl. It echoed off distant brick walls and wood pallets as Thorn arched against her bonds. She gasped in to scream again and inhaled a river of bloody saliva that made her feel like she was being held underwater. All the while, Wrath held on, her hand twisted in clumps of black hair while she pressed the tooth into Thorn's gums until her healing took effect and attached the root back to the bone. When Thorn stopped thrashing, Wrath let go, thrusting her head away so violently that she knocked the whole chair over. It crashed to its side on the concrete. Pain exploded through Thorn's shoulder, through her skull.

The room quieted for a moment, just long enough for Thorn to suck in a breath, all eyes on her. Most were calm and professional, but Mayor Bently's face was so pale he looked like a man made of marble. Wrath threw a wild gesture in Thorn's direction, and two mercenaries rushed over. They grabbed her by the arms, lifting her and the chair back to its legs. It wobbled beneath her weight like the fall had loosened the joists, and when Thorn jerked her body around to break out of the men's hands, she felt the wood creak at her calves. She pulled against the ropes again, testing their strength.

"That's not a good idea," Wrath said. A smug smile

pulled on her expression. "Even if you somehow broke free, even if you got out of this *building*, we own the neighborhood… There are people out there waiting to take another *shot* at you…"

Hunt tilted her head backward, and Thorn's focus followed the motion. In the distance, so far she could hardly make sense of it, an aura floated well above the horizon—high enough for a sniper to get a good vantage point of the whole block. Thorn's mouth gushed blood. She spoke around it.

"You never used to hire outside help." Her eyes flashed back to Wrath. "You're slip—"

Another blow smashed against her cheek, whipping Thorn's face to the side. Blood spilled from a new cut on her lip in a warm runnel down her chin. She choked out a harsh sound and flicked her head around. Fury coiled around her throat as she glared at Autumn Hunt from beneath mangled strands of black hair.

"What's wrong?" Thorn grunted. Her tongue darted out to press against the wound at the corner of her mouth, feeling the flesh mold itself back together as quickly as all the others had. "You seem angry."

Wrath's nostrils flared, and she struck her again. Thorn crushed her jaw together, trying to hold onto the yelp in her throat, but it leaked out as a moan between clenched teeth.

"I'd hit you harder," Hunt hissed, "but that uncle of yours shot me through the shoulder." She rolled her arm around the joint. The motion was stiff, but Wrath didn't wince. "It's just like the first time I met him. He hadn't been smart enough to shoot me in the head back then, either. Some people never learn…"

The corners of her eyes pinched in, and at last, she smiled. It warped her face, made her look more demon than human, as she leaned down. Her hands landed on the tops of Thorn's thighs, fingernails digging into the muscle so deep that a numb shiver rolled to Thorn's toes.

"But I *do* learn, Rose," she whispered, her face inches

away, her breath a fog of foul air. "I have learned a *lot* since I've been rid of the two of you, and you know what's the most *interesting* thing I've learned?"

Thorn's nose curled. She tilted her head away. "I assume it has nothing to do with brushing your teeth…"

Wrath hit her a third time. She shoved Thorn, both hands on her chest, and the chair toppled backward. Thorn's skull cracked onto the pavement, sending a sunburst of pale stars across her vision. She closed her eyes, and as she breathed in deep, she breathed in Darius again.

He was still in Alan's car, searching for her—a single, broken soul in a city of ten million. His palms cradled her Familiar in his lap. If she focused enough, Thorn could feel the roughness of his skin, the callouses at his fingertips, as they stroked Sparkie's wings.

Her heart was torn between hoping to be saved and praying for damnation. There were so many people here. Too many fucking people. The Martyrs couldn't take them all down, and Thorn couldn't stand the idea of more of them getting hurt because of her.

Hands wrapped around her biceps again, and the same two men lifted her back off the ground. Wrath glowered down at her.

"No," she hissed. "What I've learned is that you're like a *cockroach*. You just don't fucking *break*. No matter how hard, how *much* I hit you or kick you or *crush you*, you keep crawling back…"

Hunt delivered an uppercut to Thorn's jaw, followed by another and another. She assailed Thorn's head, blow after blow landing on her cheekbone, her orbital socket, her temple, until all she could see was the color red and all she could smell was the metallic stink of blood. Thorn gritted her teeth, baring through it, until the attack slowed and then stopped entirely. Wrath's energy drew back, and Thorn's chin tilted toward her. Through swollen eyes, she could see the bitch's ribcage expand and contract in harsh, heavy breathing. Thorn inhaled deep through her stinging nose, jutted her head forward, and spat a mouthful of blood against Hunt's chest. She'd been aiming for her face, but fuck, it was close enough.

Wrath looked like she was going to attack again. The corner of her nose twisted and pulled her lip into a snarl. She stepped forward. Thorn braced for more.

But instead, the Sin leaned in, and she said, "You're strong, Rose." A pointer finger pressed against her sternum hard enough to hurt. "*You* are strong, with that immortal body and all the power I shoved into it. It's fixing itself up right now. I *created* you. You can take anything I can throw at you. But the rest of those meat sacks out there… They're not so lucky. Are they?"

A frown crinkled Thorn's brow as Wrath drew back again and snapped her fingers. One of the mercenaries pulled another chair in front of her while a shuffle of cold energy approached from the back of the warehouse. For the first time since waking up in this hell, Thorn focused on it. What she sensed made her stomach cave in.

Two men dragged Caleb Claytor into the circle. Old blood caked the side of his head, dyeing his platinum hair crimson from the crown of his skull to just behind his ear. A bruise beneath the eye on that same side of his face made the blue iris stand out, sharp and scared. He frantically looked around, hesitating on Greed with a jolt of horror before he spotted Thorn in the center of the room. A strangled sob broke from his throat.

"T-Thorn!" He shook his head. "Thorn, I'm sorry! I—"

One of the men shoved Caleb into the chair. He gasped as they fastened ropes around him, too, but instead of binding his hands behind his back, they fixed them to the wooden arms. Caleb's breathing hitched, and he threw Thorn a desperate look.

"This little boy sang like a bird," Wrath said. She grabbed him by the chin and forced him to look at her. His bright eyes opened into frigid disks. "None of it was very helpful, though. Not with Blaine's damned Programming in my way… but he can still be of use…"

Wrath backhanded Caleb. He yelped as her knuckles collided with his cheekbone and snapped his head around—snapped it so fast that, fuck, Thorn was worried she broke his neck. A garbled cry distorted his voice. Fury ignited in Thorn's core.

"Leave him alone!"

The room stilled for a moment. Thorn and Caleb sat less than five feet apart—so close that Thorn would have been able to reach him in a single leap if she weren't tied to this goddamned chair. Wrath stood between them while Connor Amoretto and Anton Claytor waited off to the side. The woman with Amoretto seemed to revel in this torture, but Bently's jaw clenched hard, as though he was trying to hold back a wave of nausea building in his gut.

Wrath considered Thorn for a moment, a smile twisting her lips. "You mutilated one of my friends' hands," the Sin murmured as she casually walked behind Caleb's back, trailing her nails along the edge of the chair. "I think it's only fair that I return the favor." She stopped on his right side. Thorn's teeth gnashed together as Hunt grabbed Caleb's pinky.

She broke it.

Caleb's finger snapped as easily as if she'd pinched a wafer and watched it crumble in her palm. He screamed a high, throaty cry that rang in Thorn's ears like a gunshot through the Huddlestone Arch. She pulled against her ropes and lunged forward, moving the chair two inches on the pavement. When she spoke, the words came out in a roar.

"I said leave him alone!"

Anton Claytor shifted uncomfortably. He looked from Amoretto to Thorn to Wrath, his pale face more colorless than usual, as he gingerly fingered the jagged end of the pipe in his hands. Thorn's blood speckled the steel.

"Hunt," he began, and again, he looked at Thorn. Her eyes snapped to his, and he nearly recoiled at the venom in them. "Are you sure this is a good idea?"

"Yes," Bently chimed in. He held his shoulders back like he was scraping at threads to try to gain control of a room he'd never had any control over in the first place. "This was *not* in our arrangement! I never said—"

Wrath cut him off by shattering another one of Caleb's fingers. He screamed again, and Thorn's breath caught, stealing oxygen from her brain to fuel the fire burning in her chest. Hunt's expression gleamed.

"I can't break you by hurting *you…*" she went on as though they were the only three in the room, her voice so quiet that Thorn struggled to hear her. "But what happens when I hurt the people *around* you?"

Another snap, another scream, another swell of heat, stoking the blaze boiling in Thorn's core.

"What if I hurt this poor, pathetic lamb?"

Snap!

Caleb cried, begging for help, for god, for his father, who stood not three meters away without an ounce of recognition in his cold eyes.

"What if I carved him up, bit by bit, while you watched? How would *that* make you feel, Rose?"

Autumn Hunt moved onto Caleb's thumb, dislocating it with a disorienting pop. At this point, Thorn could hardly hear him anymore. His voice weaved into the static in her head. At first, the pain had made him buck against his ropes, but now that Wrath was moving to his left, he slumped into them, melting on the chair until his head drooped down.

Thorn pried her teeth apart. Instead of yelling this time, she hissed. "If you lay one more hand on him—"

"You'll what?" Wrath cut in with a smile as she crouched on Caleb's other side. He didn't move to acknowledge her. "You'll *stop* me? Okay. *Stop me.*"

Hunt took Caleb's other pinky and crushed that, too. His screams were drowned out by Thorn's own. She roared until her throat hurt and pulled against her restraints again, jerking forward another couple of inches. The ropes cut into her wrists. Even through her gloves, she felt bruises casting roots to the bone.

"Autumn," Greed tried again, louder this time. "Are you sure you know what you're—"

"I won't end here," Wrath went on as though Anton Claytor was a gnat in the air. Her focus homed in on Thorn like the scope of a sniper. "After I kill *this* one, I'll track them all down. Every single one of your little Martyrs, all your *sheep*, and I'll gut them right in front of you. And I'm going to start with *Alan Blaine.*"

Wrath's smile exploded into a grin so wide, so delighted, that it pinched at the corners of her eyes and wrinkled the bridge of her nose. Every muscle in Thorn's body froze, holding her tight as a vise. She swam outside of it.

"How long could your flock stay together without their shepherd, Rose?" Wrath whispered.

Thorn shook her head. "You'll never get to Alan," she tried to assert, but her voice felt like smoke in her mouth— weak and wafting.

Wrath laughed. "Get to him?" she taunted. "I don't need to *get* to him. He's going to walk right into my arms, and do you know why? Because I have *you*. You are the key. You are the only thing in this entire fucking world that man cares about. He'd burn it *all* to the ground if he had to. He'd sacrifice *everything* for you…"

A veil dropped around Thorn, stealing the color, the sound, the sensations of the room in a flickering, gray curtain. Fuck, she'd been so *stupid*. The realization ran down her spine like blood from a head wound. Torturing Thorn would never be enough for Wrath… Not if Alan were alive.

She hadn't just walked into a trap. She *was* the trap.

Thorn's entire body went numb. The pain, the panic, the pull of ropes around her wrists and ankles and chest dissolved. Spots speckled her vision, circling tighter and tighter until she wasn't looking into the warehouse anymore but instead through Sparkie's eyes. He was frantic, spinning around Darius's lap like a wild thing. She had to warn them to stop. To turn around. To leave her behind and get as far from this place as they fucking could. Darius grabbed her Familiar, and the phantom feeling of those strong hands was warm and secure around her body. A heartbroken gasp surged into Thorn's lungs, and tears stung her eyes.

"It's okay," his voice echoed in her mind. *"We're coming."*

"No," Thorn whispered.

A scream cracked her walls, and the room swam into focus. Caleb's head tilted back, sobs rocking his entire chest. Wait. Not Caleb. A different man squirmed under Wrath's touch now. Taller. Thinner. With pale skin and black hair and sunken eyes. He jerked around to look at her, and her heart shattered into a million sharp, deadly shards.

Donovan.

He sobbed her name.

"Mom!"

Thorn's jaw dropped, her mouth dry. Wrath wrapped her fist around yet another finger. He howled as her gaze landed on Thorn.

"And when I'm done with Alan," she murmured, "who's to stop me from cutting your favorite Virtue into tiny, little pieces?"

Thorn's resolve ruptured. Waves of panic and nausea and terror poured out of her. Her eyes went wide, a pearl of water falling from one to trail a line down her bloodied face. She breathed in hard gasps because if she didn't, she wouldn't be able to breathe at all. Thorn's entire body felt fuzzy, like it wasn't real, like *she* wasn't real.

Hunt paused, a frown tightening her expression for a fraction of a second before that expression opened up in awe, followed by abhorrent glee. She stood, walked away from Donovan—no, from *Caleb*—and knelt in front of Thorn instead. Wrath wiped the tear from her cheek.

"Oh, no…" she murmured, but a predatory grin sliced her face in two. "You poor thing. You don't learn, either, do you? How many times have I told you that I will kill *everyone* you love?"

Thorn sucked air in rapid bursts, and her fury began to

erupt. She fought to stop it. Behind her back, thumbs tapped to fingertips, but it didn't work. Everything led back to Darius. How his laughter unlocked a warmth in her chest she'd forgotten existed. The way his eyes drank her in like she was a virgin cherry mojito on the hot dance floor. His hands gently grasping hers as they danced, brushing hair from her temple, wrapping around her waist with the desperate hold of a man who knew he'd sink to the ocean floor without this lifeline.

Fuck. She couldn't breathe. She couldn't see. She could hardly *think*.

"I won't just kill this one," Wrath whispered against her ear. "Just for you, I'm going to make Darius *suffer*. Whatever you're feeling right now, Rose, I'll make him feel *more*..."

Thorn looked over Wrath's shoulder to where Donovan slumped in the chair, a bullet wound opening on his chest like a red rose blooming. He was wasted, a shell of the young man he'd been. Wrath had sliced his spirit into pieces, shredding his soul without ever laying a hand on it directly. Breaking him the way she hoped to break Thorn... the way she *planned* to break Darius.

Someone was screaming, and the part of Thorn's mind that knew it was her began to turn off. Wrath cackled and stepped back again. When she spoke to Amoretto, giving him the order to kill the man in the chair and make it last, Thorn's vision spiraled. When Lust stepped forward, flipping *her* pocket knife in his hand, Thorn's hearing dissolved. When he plunged the knife into her son's side, all the pain in her body vanished like a slate wiped clean.

A primal side of her psyche that Thorn hadn't seen in seventy years came to life with a howl. Her rage mingled with the terror in her chest until it created a new monster. It felt familiar, like Thorn had met it before, but that thought melted with all the others.

The ropes around her wrists tore, the wood splintered behind her back, and a pulse of horror doused the room like a flash flood. More screaming filled her ears, but this time, it didn't belong to her. Thorn rose to her feet as everything faded into a cloud of red static.

CHAPTER THIRTY-TWO

Darius sat in the front seat of the SUV, his heel tapping as a stretch of water glistened outside his window. The Throgs Neck Bridge carried them high over where the East River connected with the Long Island Sound. For a moment, the energy of the city disappeared. Only Alan Blaine, the other drivers on the I-295, and a dense weight of dread rolling in his stomach kept him company.

Sparkie cried out—just like he had more than a dozen times already. His tiny body went rigid in Darius's lap, jerking as though he were being struck, and Darius's chest constricted. He laid his palms over Sparkie's wings. They trembled—the wings, the hands, or both. Darius didn't know, and it didn't matter at this point. Rae whined in the back of the car as Sparkie finally stopped writhing. His ribcage expanded and contracted in rapid, gasping breaths.

A thick silence swam around the SUV for a moment.

"That was the longest episode yet…" Alan murmured. His fists were so tight around the wheel that the bones in his knuckles pressed white.

Darius shook his head to force his thoughts back in order. "How long until we reach Hunts Point?"

"Ten minutes. Perhaps fifteen. It depends on traffic."

Traffic. Darius wanted to scream. He couldn't believe they were worried about *traffic* right now.

Back in his lap, Sparkie shuffled. Between bouts of pain, he did this—spinning in circles, wings frazzled and mouth open. When Darius cupped his palms around him, the Familiar quieted, but his beady eyes darted about the SUV. Darius resisted the temptation to scoop him up and press him to his chest. Instead, he stroked two fingers down the animal's spine. Sparkie nudged his forehead against the heel of Darius's hand. His heart ached.

"What do we do when we find her?" Darius asked quietly.

Alan drew a breath. "Whatever we must."

A couple more minutes passed in silence. They reached the far side of the water, and Alan merged onto I-278, an armored motorcade of Martyrs following at their back. Sparkie suddenly froze. His legs and tail went rigid, and an umbrella of red, leathery wings vibrated over his back. Darius glanced down at him. The reptile's eyes went distant, like he was trapped with Thorn wherever the hell she was instead of sitting in this car with them. He frowned.

"Alan—"

Sparkie screeched. Alan's hands jerked on the wheel, jolting the vehicle to the left as Sparkie ran in frantic circles on Darius's lap. The animal cried again, his voice grating on Darius's brain and sending a chill through his nervous system. Sparkie tried to leap to Alan, but Darius caught him before he crossed the center console. Claws scratched at Darius's palm, and wings flapped against his bare forearms, stinging his skin. The lizard screamed again, and Darius pulled him close.

"It's okay," he murmured. Sparkie thrashed, so Darius tightened his grip. "We're coming."

It didn't help. If anything, Darius's voice just made Sparkie more frenzied. He twisted and turned in Darius's hands so furiously that Darius was worried he was going to hurt himself. The vehicle wavered as Alan's focus pulled away from the road. Darius was absently aware of Chris's voice coming over their car radio, asking if everything was okay. Neither of them answered her.

And after a couple of minutes, Sparkie froze again. All at once, the movement stopped, his body cold and still as stone, eyes glassy. Darius glanced at Alan. The Forgotten Sin wore a look of such thick dread that it made the feeling in Darius's nerves burrow deeper.

Sparkie collapsed. He went from rigid to limp in an instant, falling like a leaf into Darius's palms. His heart plummeted.

"Alan! Thorn is—"

The words crashed to a stop against his teeth as Darius spun to Alan to find him staring out the windshield. His eyes trained on a point in the distance Darius couldn't see. Terror tightened every muscle in his face. Rae let out a deep, rumbling whine.

"Oh, no…" he murmured.

"What?" Darius asked.

Alan tapped on the radio, connecting their microphone to the master TAC channel. "All units," he said. The forced calm to his voice crackled like static. "I have a lead. Southwest of our position, just over a mile. It looks like we were right. Follow me, and as we approach Hunts Point, watch out for Influence."

A buzz of confirmations rolled over the speakers, and Alan muted their mic again. As the voices petered off, Darius held Sparkie closer. He drew the Familiar to his pounding heart. "Wrath is using her Influence?" he managed to ask.

Alan swallowed hard. "I hope it's Wrath."

Darius's lips parted in numb shock. "Are… you saying it could be *Thorn?*"

To this, Alan simply nodded. His foot pressed the gas pedal and propelled them forward. Vehicles started moving out of their way as though being pulled on an invisible string. Darius wondered if Alan was using his Influence, too.

"But how?" he asked after a moment. His focus shifted back to the lizard in his hands. "Sparkie's unconscious! Doesn't that mean Thorn is, too?"

Alan's jaw clenched. "Not necessarily."

The implications rattled Darius's nerves, shaking down his whole body until his fingers quaked. "Alan, what the *hell* is going on?"

The other man cast a glance his way as though weighing Darius—deciding if he was worthy of this new information—and a flicker of anger battled with the nerves in Darius's stomach. At last, Alan said, "I have seen this happen only once before, when Thorn was conscious but her Familiar was not. It was nearly seven decades ago—"

Darius gasped, his mind triggering on an old conversation with Thorn. "When Donovan died," he breathed. Alan's eyes widened, and Darius shook his head. "She told me she had a psychotic break, went after the Sins, and her scars…"

Darius glanced at his arm before turning back to Alan. The surprise on his face was almost enough to mask his worry. "Yes," he confirmed, like he couldn't believe Darius knew any of this. "Yes, it was as though Thorn's dissociation forced her Familiar into a sedative state. In those final hours, she was completely detached from reality. Her body was moving, but her mind… she was not there anymore. She had no idea where she was, who *I* was…"

He let the sentence escape him as his focus shifted back to the road, drawn again in the direction of Influence.

"You have to understand, Darius, Forgotten Sins are *human*," Alan continued, speaking quickly. "We are susceptible to the same faults and failings. The difference is that, when we fail, the consequences can be *much* more devastating. If *you* were to have a violent psychosis episode, you would be relatively easy to control. Thorn, on the other hand…"

The last word barely squeezed out of his mouth, high and painful. Alan cleared his throat as Darius leaned closer.

"When this happened before," Alan went on, "she was

completely out of control. I tried to speak with her, but it was useless. She was so badly wounded that she could do little more than scream insults, but still, every time I tried to approach her, she attacked. In the end, the only thing that stopped her was—"

He abruptly cut off, his eyes flashing with hurt at the memory, but Darius already knew what had happened next. Gluttony had shown up and…

"Are you saying that the only way we can snap Thorn out of this is to *shoot her?*" Darius asked.

"No," Alan hissed. "Absolutely not—"

"Then what the hell *are* you saying?" Darius challenged, louder now, as panic settled in. "That we *can't* stop this? That Thorn is—"

"I'm saying that she cares about you!" Alan shouted.

Darius's heart vaulted into his ribs.

"I have no idea what we're about to walk into," Alan continued, his voice straining against his throat. Rae growled in the back, a deep, somber sound. "But I *do* know that your opinion *matters* to her, that she would not want you to see her this way, and that if something were to happen to you, if you were to get *hurt* or even *killed*, it would ruin her *completely.*"

The pain in Alan's eyes glittered with fury, with *fear*, and Darius could only stare at him. His own rage simmered as what Alan said sank in. He turned away, considering Sparkie, still limp and listless against his chest.

Damn it. Alan was right. He clutched Sparkie closer, his eyes stinging.

They made their way through Soundview, across the Bronx River, and turned southbound. The Martyrs followed. Once they officially crossed into Hunts Point, a nagging itch pulled at the back of Darius's neck. He straightened in his seat.

Moments later, their vehicle slammed through a force of Influence so intense it nearly pulled the breath from his lungs. Darius gasped, drawing a palm away from Sparkie to grip the handle above his head for support. His Virtue power made him immune to Influence, or so he thought, but even he felt the swirling of something swimming in his head that didn't fully belong to him—and the realization of what it was made his stomach drop.

Terror. Pure, unfiltered terror. An errant tear escaped his lashes and trailed a wet line down his cheek. Darius wiped it off as their radio blared to life.

"Alan…" Chris stammered. "Alan, we're having a… hard time back here."

Her voice broke through in choppy pieces. At first, Darius thought the radio must be malfunctioning, but as she kept talking, it became clear that *she* was the source of the interference.

"We can't… we can't get through," she went on. It sounded as though she were trying to speak through tears. "People are freaking out. Amelia's having a panic attack. Deidre nearly lost control of her car. Seth can't breathe. Conrad—"

She broke off, catching on a sob. The weight of Thorn's fear sat heavy on Darius's chest. He pressed a hand against it.

"Hold back," Alan commanded.

"What?" Darius gasped.

"No, we can…" Chris started to argue, and again, words escaped her. In the background of her mic, Darius heard someone wail.

"Retreat behind Spofford," Alan went on. He didn't slow, their car plowing through Hunts Point as he spoke. "That seems to be as far as the Influence has reached. I won't repeat myself, Christine."

"Yes, sir," Chris responded. Darius turned around, and he and Rae watched the line of Martyr vehicles fall back.

"When you are more collected, try again, but tread carefully," Alan continued. "Losing our heads will only make this situation worse."

Chris confirmed again, and the radios went silent.

Darius's heart pounded.

"What the hell are we going to do without backup?" he asked.

"Feel around you," Alan answered, and Darius frowned. "We will not need backup."

Darius did, and his eyes went wide. He couldn't believe he hadn't immediately noticed it. The neighborhood was almost completely free of any human sensation, and whatever was left behind lay static and still, like they were unconscious or simply too terrified to move. As Alan drove south on Tiffany Street, it became even clearer—empty within a one-hundred-meter radius of any sign of life at all.

Except for one single point of energy above them, on the second floor of an old, brick warehouse. Just before Alan parked, that point of energy blinked out. Alan's face paled as he turned off the engine. Darius gazed up at the building. Foggy windows overlooked the streets, several of the panes cracked and broken in their iron frames. No movement flickered through them.

"There's no one here…" Darius murmured.

Alan drew a deep breath and unbuckled his belt. His eyes were still trained on the second floor. A worried knit pulled his brows together.

"Yes," he said, "there is."

Darius's stomach swirled with nausea, but he unbuckled, too. Alan laid a hand on his shoulder.

"Stay here," he said.

"But—"

"Darius," Alan interrupted. "I will bring her back. I promise."

His grip tightened, compassion and concern filling his expression. A painful knot wrapped around Darius's windpipe. He nodded, and Alan mimicked the gesture before opening the car. Rae dove between the seats to follow him onto the street. The door snapped shut, and Alan was gone. He whispered around the building like a specter.

Darius watched the spot where his back disappeared

with numb focus, Sparkie held against his chest, a heavy pounding in his ears drowning the rest of the world out. He felt himself fading—his consciousness detaching from this suit he called a body—so he started tapping his thumb against his fingertips the same way he'd taught Thorn. Seconds ticked by, turning into minutes. Several minutes. A shiver ran up Darius's spine, and he looked at the windows again.

Something wasn't right.

Darius adjusted Sparkie against his chest, unlocked the car, and got out. Voices slipped through the broken glass above—a deep drone Darius took to be Alan's alongside something more feral. The shiver pulsed into a growl, making goose bumps rise along Darius's shoulders and down his arms. His jaw set, and he made his way around the building. A door on the western wall had been left ajar. Darius slipped into it.

He almost stepped right back out.

The room was massive, extending the length and width of the warehouse, full of pallets stocked with merchandise, metal shelving, and bodies. Dozens of bodies. Maybe more. Darius couldn't count them. The distinct scent of dust and death assaulted his senses as he walked further in, and he covered his mouth with one hand while the other clutched Sparkie. Almost all of the cargo had been moved to the walls or tucked beneath an iron staircase at the far wall, which opened up the space in the center.

Corpses littered this area in a wide arc around a bloodied swatch on the concrete floor. Nearly all of them were civilians with smashed skulls or broken necks, but Darius noticed a handful of mercenaries dressed in black armor and a man who might have looked like Mayor Bently if his jaw hadn't been separated from his head. Between the bodies, lying in thick, crimson pools, were weapons. Too many weapons, like their owners had dropped them and run while the others were bludgeoned to death.

Most horrifying of all, though, wasn't the bodies on the

floor… it was the one in the chair. Darius stepped toward it. The man was propped up, his wrists tied to the arms while ropes lashed around his torso kept him from collapsing to the ground. Bent and broken fingers curled onto his palms, and the side of his head nearest to Darius was crushed so badly that he couldn't make out his face, but he didn't need to. The Tactical colors told him all he needed to know. Darius's heart sputtered as he walked around and looked into Caleb Claytor's dead, open eyes. Bile burned up his throat and threatened to spill into his mouth. He clamped it shut and turned away.

A sound up the stairs carried down to him. Thick, like a bat striking a bag of sand.

Thorn let out a shrill, terrified scream.

Another thud, and this time, Alan grunted. Darius ran across the ground floor and paused at the base of the stairs. Golden beams of dull light drifted down from above, illuminating dust as it floated through the air. When Darius placed his foot onto the bottom step, he paused, waiting for it to squeak beneath his weight. It didn't.

"Thorn!" Alan's voice was deep, grinding with pain. "Thorn, it's me!"

Thorn screamed again, and something smashed against the wood floor. Darius took another step and another, measuring each one to be as quiet as possible until his eyes crested the landing. A single body lay here—one of the mercenaries, his head twisted around so that his face pointed in the wrong direction. Darius swallowed hard, looked up, and peered into the room. The second story came to life, bright and barren… His jaw dropped.

Alan and Thorn stood opposite of one another. No. *Alan* stood, his feet planted, arms raised in a defensive position as Thorn attacked. She was relentless, wielding a metal pipe, coming in again and again as Alan did what he could to keep her from landing a blow without raising a finger to strike back. Rae tag-teamed with him, barking and intercepting whenever Thorn got too close. Darius gawked.

Suddenly, Thorn sprinted forward and swung for Alan's face. He deflected it, guiding the weapon and the woman to the left as he spun to keep her in sight. Rae stalked a wide circle around them, hackles raised.

"Thorn, *please,*" Alan implored. The words were dense, like he was speaking around a broken jaw. Darius had no idea what the hell had happened before he got up here, but it was clear Alan had taken more than a couple of hits. Blood congealed into the hair on his upper lip, painting his mouth cherry red, and one of his eyes was so swollen that, even as it healed, there was nothing but a slit for him to see through. He took an awkward side-step that made Darius wonder if his leg had been wounded, too.

Thorn lunged for him again.

Somehow, she looked worse than Alan. She had no apparent damage, no swelling, no signs of injury, but her black hair tangled around her head, and a slick of dried blood coated her chin and throat all the way down to her chest. Her protective kevlar had been removed, exposing her bare shoulders to the room. They were speckled in crimson droplets. So was the pipe in her hands. It was practically painted, its jagged end red and dripping.

But the scariest thing—the thing that made Darius's heart feel like it was going to explode inside his ribcage— was the look in her eyes. Terror. Tears streamed down her cheeks, cutting through the red plains in clean rivers. Thorn stared at Alan like he was an alien, a monster, a nightmare she couldn't escape. She attacked again. This time, he blocked it with an arm. From across the room, Darius heard the crunch as Alan cried out.

"Thorn—"

She screamed again. Swung again. Alan grabbed the pipe in his other hand and yanked it to the side. Thorn held on, ripped it free. The sharp edge cut against Alan's palm. As she held it up to try again, Rae swept in and nipped at the back of Thorn's thighs. Instead, she turned and aimed for the wolf. Alan dove forward and tried to get the weapon a second time. As his fingers wrapped around it, Thorn spun back to him, wild and frenzied.

"Listen to me!" He had both hands on the metal now, yelling inches from her face. She pressed back against it, her teeth gritted, muscles rigid, heels digging into the wood at her feet. Alan held his ground. "I am not here to hurt you! I'm here to—"

Thorn cried out and jerked her entire torso to the side. Alan's wounded leg faltered beneath him, just long enough for Thorn to knock him off balance and loosen his hold on the pipe. She tore it out of his hands, pulled it behind her shoulder, and swung.

The pipe crashed into Alan's temple with a crack, and he went down hard. Darius gaped as Alan's entire body flew to the side and rolled across the dusty floor. Rae howled, shaking her head, while Thorn kicked him in the ribs. He groaned as her boot thudded against his armor, and she held the weapon over her head. Before she drove it down, Rae was upon her. The wolf sank her fangs into Thorn's calf and dragged her backward, thrashing side to side. Thorn roared again and stabbed the sharp end of the pipe into the Familiar's face, over and over until Alan was screaming and Rae released her with a yelp. Then she turned back to Alan, knelt on his chest, and pressed the pipe against his throat.

"Thorn!" He choked on her name. "Thorn, stop—"

But then he couldn't speak. He couldn't breathe. Rae came at Thorn, crying and growling and biting at her arms and legs and hands, but even the Familiar was weak now. One massive paw swiped toward Thorn's left wrist but missed, and Rae stumbled.

Darius could only watch. His body screamed at him—told him that he was in danger, that he needed to get as far away as he could—but the light weight of Sparkie's unconscious form in his hands kept him grounded. Without thinking, without knowing what the fuck he was going to do but knowing he couldn't do *nothing*, Darius vaulted up the last few steps, leapt over the body on the landing, and jumped into the room.

"Thorn!" he called out.

Her head swiveled toward him with a violent jerk, and those dangerous, black eyes connected with his. A shiver rushed down his spine and froze Darius where he stood as Thorn stared at him without seeing him. The pistol clipped to his belt felt heavy at his hip. His hand hovered toward it.

But then he stopped. Alan had warned him that this wasn't Thorn, but now that he stood before her, he realized just how wrong that was. Darius had stared the Sins in the face, had seen firsthand how empty they were. Thorn was anything *but* empty. She was full—*so full*—of the things she always tried to hide. Her fear. Her pain. It had buried her alive.

Instead of grabbing the weapon, Darius raised his hand. He watched Thorn as he touched his thumb to each fingertip in slow, deliberate motions. She didn't look at it—glaring past it as she focused on Darius's face. Alan weakly reached for her as Rae collapsed.

"What do you see?" Darius asked.

Thorn's heavy breathing slowed, but the panic in her eyes shone just as deadly. Darius's other hand wrapped more tightly around Sparkie. He stroked the crest of the lizard's skull.

"What do you hear?" he went on, voice constricted, eyes pouring. "Smell? Feel? Ground yourself."

Sparkie's tail twitched. Darius's lungs opened to exhale a desperate breath, but he didn't dare look away from Thorn. Her gaze softened, her mouth slowly shifting from a scowl to a gape, and her fingers tapped on the weapon still pressed against Alan's windpipe. Pointer to pinky. Darius swallowed hard.

"Come back, Thorn," he murmured. *"Come back.* I'm here. You're safe."

At last, she blinked. Then, her breathing picked up in a gasp. Sparkie's eyes snapped open, and Thorn leapt to her feet.

"Oh my god…" she whispered.

She looked from Alan to the pipe and froze there, staring at it as though seeing it for the first time. Her whole body trembled as she drew the weapon toward herself… Darius, struck with the sudden image of her slicing the sharp edge against her own throat, cried out.

"Alan! Get the weapon!"

Thorn dropped it. Took a step back. And another. Her boots left a trail of bloody footprints until a full body length of space stood between her and Alan. He choked out a harsh cough as he rolled to his hands and knees. Rae rushed to his side to support him, and he wound his fist deep in her black fur. When he spoke, his voice ground like gravel in a tin bucket.

"Thorn—"

"What happened?" she cut in. A grateful surge pushed Darius toward her, but the stricken look she threw him cemented him to the spot. Sparkie cried out, soft and scared, as Thorn's chest heaved in shallow gulps. She opened her hands, finding her gloves saturated in blood, her shaking fingers stained with it. Her attention snapped up to her uncle. A fresh wave of tears flashed behind her lashes. When she spoke again, it came out sobbing. "Alan! *What happened?*"

"It's okay," Alan said as he stood. His focus trained on her like there was nothing else—no one else—in the world. A rush of relief glistened in his black eyes. He smiled and held out his hands, reaching for her. "Everything is okay, Thorn. You're—"

Glass shattered. Alan's chin snapped up. A fan of red spray burst from the back of his skull as Rae crumbled into dust.

CHAPTER THIRTY-THREE

Darius stared in horror as Alan's body fell in an arc and thudded to the floor. Thorn screamed his name, collapsing to her knees at his side, while Sparkie ripped out of Darius's grip and took to the air with a cry. Darius stared, and he stood, until a weight of dread told him to get down.

He hit the ground as a second bullet clattered into the brick wall behind his back. All his senses came careening into focus again. He looked up as Sparkie torpedoed out one of the broken windows, and Thorn draped across Alan's chest like she meant to protect him from another attack.

An attack… Darius's heart clenched. Fuck, they were under attack.

He crouched as low as he could get, made his way to Thorn, and wrapped a hand around her shoulder.

"Come on!" he shouted.

Thorn didn't move. She stared at Alan, and his empty eyes stared back, unseeing. A clean hole cut into his skull just off-center of his forehead. As another bullet ripped through the brick wall well above their heads, her expression began to disconnect again—to slip back into that dangerous place. A warning tingled down Darius's spine. He grabbed her face. "Thorn!"

She finally looked at him, finally *saw* him, and a strangled sound shuddered through her open mouth. Darius stroked his thumbs across her cheeks.

"We need to go!"

Thorn turned to Alan, blinked back a rush of pain, and lifted him from the ground. Darius helped ease her to her feet—not that she needed him. She bore Alan's dead weight as though he weren't there at all.

Darius led the way to the main floor. Thorn looked around, her face colorless as she took in the bodies and the blood. She nearly stumbled when she saw Caleb, and she let out a gasp. Darius squeezed her arm and pulled her through, trying not to think about the lives lost here.

They reached the door, but Thorn paused. Her focus moved to the southwest, where, nearly at the edge of Darius's range, he could barely sense an indistinguishable dot of human warmth hovering above the horizon. Thorn's fingers tightened around Alan before she started forward. The street was just as empty now as it had been when Darius and Alan had first arrived, but the pressure of Thorn's Influence had lifted. Energy barreled around the corner, and a Martyr vehicle slammed to a stop behind their SUV. Then another. And another. Thorn watched in horror as they filed in.

Chris jumped out from the first, fully armed. The instant her green eyes landed on Darius, on Thorn, and on Alan draped in her arms, she froze, and her mouth dropped open. Before she could even speak, Thorn shouted.

"Get out of here!"

Chris's eyes never left Alan's face. "Is he—"

"Wrath is sitting on a storage tank up Oak Point Avenue," Thorn cut in. "She has a sniper rifle. Sparkie's distracting her, but we need to get our people out! *Now!*"

Chris gawked for a moment longer, glancing from Thorn to Darius to Alan and finally up the road beyond them.

"What are you waiting for?" Thorn cried. "We've got to *move* before this place is swarming with Puppets!"

At last, Chris nodded. She tapped into her earpiece and gave the commands. Thorn ran to the SUV Darius and Alan had driven. He opened the back, and she laid her uncle's body into it.

"What about Caleb?" Darius asked.

Thorn didn't look at him. "I can't go back in there," she murmured, emotion gripping her throat. "And I don't want anyone else to… to see…"

Her eyes pressed closed, and she shook her head, like it was all she could do to stop the swell from dragging her into the depths. Darius's jaw set.

"Start the car," he said. "I'll be right back."

Thorn's eyes shot open. "Darius, wait!"

But he was already gone, sprinting back around the building as the tactical team pulled away. Just as he opened the door, chunks of brick blasted off the wall beside him, and he ducked inside. Then, he put on mental blinders, avoiding looking at anything but the chair in the middle of the room and the man tied to it.

Caleb Claytor's pale face had lost even more color. Without a beating heart to pump blood through his body, he was left gray and ashen. His mangled fingers clawed forward, barely attached to hands that would never again type a report, hold a camera, or play a game of poker. Darius's chest hollowed out as he scrambled to untie the ropes, but they were too tight, and pulling on them didn't do a damn bit of good. He spotted a knife lying on the floor by Caleb's feet and snatched it up, ignoring the blood on the blade—blood Darius was sure belonged to Caleb.

It took minutes to carve through the bonds to get Caleb free. Once he was, Darius threw the knife to the side and heaved Caleb's cold body over his shoulders. His hands shook so badly that he could hardly hold on.

When he reached the street again, Thorn was waiting by the door. She walked between him and some unseen point in the distance like a human shield until they got to the SUV and laid Caleb beside Alan in the back. Darius jumped behind the wheel before Thorn could argue with him about it. The engine was already running, so as soon as Thorn shut the passenger door, he tore them away from the side of the road so quickly that the tires burned on the asphalt. As they howled around the corner, another bullet ricocheted off the reinforced hood, gouging the metal.

Then, they were gone, far away from that warehouse of death, from those empty streets, and from Hunts Point.

Quiet stretched between them. Thorn opened her window, and Sparkie flew inside. He thudded against her chest, pressing his belly as close to her sternum as he could. She laid a hand over him as she stared ahead. Thorn never spoke, but when Darius stole a look at her from the corner of his eye, he saw quiet tears running down her face.

An hour floated by like a bloated body in the water: sullen, silent, and sinking. For a while, the radio had crackled with questions—from Chris, from Holly, from Nicholas. Every time Alan's name was mentioned, Sparkie flinched like he'd been struck. Neither Thorn nor Darius responded to these calls. After the fifth, he turned their unit off. Then, those same messages started assaulting his phone. Notifications lit up his watch screen, all asking the same thing:

Was Alan Blaine dead?

Darius's numb mind could hardly process the answer.

They reached the Underground with the surreal normalcy of any other day. The building looked the same. The car wash entrance opened just as it always had. Even the descent into the earth mirrored every other descent before it. Martyr energy swelled below, but the warmth from it seemed hollow. Fake, almost. Like Darius was imagining it.

People filled the garage before they reached the loading area outside the hospital's triage doors—more people than Darius had ever seen crammed into this small entry space. Chris stood at the front, her armor discarded, her blonde hair falling from her ponytail in a frazzled mess. Over her shoulder, others stared up the drive. Dr. Harris. Nicholas. Cain. Alexis Claytor. Her bright eyes were bloodshot.

Darius could see the pink ring around them as he parked. He opened the door.

The room was deafeningly quiet.

"Chris," Darius started, then stopped to clear his throat, hoping it made his voice sound more natural. It didn't. "Get everyone out of here."

Her green eyes glistened like she'd heard what he meant rather than the words that had actually come out of his mouth. She nodded, and Gabe drew a deep breath behind her.

"All right," he said, turning to the crowd of TAC agents, researchers, and security staff hovering by the doors. "Everyone, inside and downstairs. Let's go."

People stretched upward, standing on their toes and craning their necks as they tried to peer through the tinted glass to the back of the SUV. Gabe extended his arms and guided them out. Cain and Nicholas lingered at the edge, and Darius nodded at them to indicate they could stay with Chris and the doctor. Alexis was the last to leave.

"But, Caleb," she stammered. By now, her cheeks were slick, and she pressed against Gabe's chest just inside the door, trying so hard to stay. "Where's Caleb?"

"Alexis," Gabe murmured. "Come on."

"Where is he?" She was crying now, and she looked desperately at Darius. "I need to see him!"

A hard lump caught in Darius's throat. "You don't want to see him, Alexis…"

She stopped fighting, then. Alexis stood still for a moment, her mouth an open sliver against her face, as her eyes darted away from Darius to the tinted windows into the back of the car and, at last, to the closed passenger door. The bridge of her nose wrinkled.

"You did this!" Alexis suddenly shouted, not at Darius or Gabe or anyone standing in the garage. She raised a hand and pointed at Thorn's silhouette, still sitting in the car. "This is *your* fault! If you hadn't run! If you hadn't left—"

The rest of her words drowned in harrowing, heart-crushing howls. Alexis's knees gave way beneath her, and Gabe caught her before she hit the ground. He carried her away. Even when the doors shut, her sobbing echoed in Darius's chest.

Then, the garage went silent. Thorn still hadn't moved, staring out the front windshield the same way she had the entire drive. By the time they reached the Underground, she had run out of tears, but the trails they'd left behind cut through the blood on her face and down her throat.

Elijah pressed a closed fist to his lips as he watched her through the glass. "So it's true," he said.

His steely eyes shifted to Darius, who simply nodded. Nicholas's jaw clenched as Cain's dropped open. Chris gasped and covered her mouth.

"We need to let the Martyrs know," Darius said. "They already suspect it, and rumors will only make this worse. Nicholas, can you handle that?"

Nicholas frowned. "People will have questions."

"And you'll say you don't have answers yet," Darius responded. Nicholas's brows raised, but he didn't argue as he turned to the Underground and disappeared inside. Darius looked back to the rest of them.

"Alan and Caleb," Darius went on. His throat clenched as the image of them lying in the back of the SUV derailed his train of thought, and he wasn't sure how to continue. Elijah raised a hand to save him the trouble of trying.

"My staff will take care of it," he said.

Darius dipped his chin in a thank you as Elijah rushed through the triage room doors. Then, Darius turned to Chris. He didn't even have to speak; she nodded without a word and made her way to the vehicle. Darius's chest ached as she opened it, put one foot on the step, and reached a hand inside to lay on Thorn's knee.

The triage room opened again, and Elijah returned. Colette, Raquel, and a couple of other nurses wheeled stretchers out behind him. When Elijah reached for the hatch, Darius's face went cold. Gray spots blurred his vision, stealing the color from the room, and he took a stumbling step back-ward.

A hand gripped around his bicep.

"Let's get you inside," Cain murmured, his voice like a whisper from a faraway rooftop.

Darius hardly knew how he got from the garage to his office, or how he found himself sitting upon the couch, his hands shaking on the brown suede. He laid his face into his palms as Cain turned on the lights and took the chair beside him. Though his wounds from the battle hadn't fully re-solved, they'd been cleaned and tended to, hiding behind small patches of gauze instead of massive bandages. His arm was no longer in a sling, and he crossed it with the other around his chest as he waited.

And he waited a long time. Minutes passed in silence un-til Darius could finally make sense of the rushing inside his skull, and the room sorted itself out.

At last, he looked up. Cain was watching him, and Darius was stunned to see tears in his eyes.

"Was it her?" the old Forgotten Envy asked. His voice clenched around the question. "Did Thorn kill Alan?"

A stone formed in Darius's throat. He swallowed past it and shook his head. Relief shuddered down Cain's spine. He dipped his chin with a sigh that practically fell out of his mouth.

Then, Darius murmured, "But she tried to."

Cain froze, eyes open, face downward, fingers dangling between his knees. They were the first part of him to move. He wound them together, clutching his hands as he sucked in a breath and muttered one word.

"*Fuck.*"

Darius blinked. He'd never heard Cain swear so openly before. The Forgotten Sin got to his feet and stepped away, pressing his fingertips to his lips as he thought.

"What happened?" Cain asked at last, spinning back to face Darius. "What *exactly* happened?"

Darius's focus went hazy as he remembered that

room—every cracked skull, every broken neck, and a bloody pipe clenched in Thorn's hands. The memory of a soul shattering flitted across his brain like a carrion moth.

"I don't know," he murmured. "When we got there, Alan told me to stay inside the car—"

"Why?" Cain interrupted.

Darius floundered for a minute, rubbing his temples. "Why the hell does it matter, Cain?"

"Did he speak with her?" Cain asked, coming to sit again. This time, he didn't take the chair but instead joined Darius on the couch. "Did he have the chance to *speak* with Thorn?"

Cain was frantic, nearly manic. His bright eyes attached themselves to Darius's face with a desperation he hadn't seen in the man since he moved back to the Underground.

"I don't think so," Darius said at last. "Thorn… wasn't in a place for talking."

Cain nodded. Slowly at first, before the pace picked up, and he was nearly shaking instead.

"God *damn it*, Alan," he said. "If I did not have a strict rule against speaking ill of the dead, I—"

And all at once, as though saying the word aloud had pierced his armor like a bullet, Cain broke down. He dropped his face into one hand, covering his eyes while he openly wept. His narrow shoulders curled toward the ground and shook in gentle, quiet sobs. Darius stared at him, stunned.

"We were *family*," Cain said through tears, echoing words he'd spoken to Darius months ago. "We *argued*, and we bickered, but still, Alan was like a brother. I loved him. That stupid, *stupid* man."

Cain cried again, harder now, and empathy pinched around Darius's heart. He grabbed Cain's free hand, squeezing it tight, as the weight of what they had lost came crashing down against his skull.

The eighteen hours since Alan Blaine had taken his last breath felt like eighteen years, all of them restless. Darius clasped his hands on the table as he, Chris, and Nicholas sat in the conference room in silence. They were the only three, Darius and Chris on one side, Nicholas on the other, with the head chair decidedly empty. Darius watched it, numb and distant, until finally, Chris cleared her throat.

"I realize this isn't a good time to talk about what happened," she began quietly.

"No shit," Nicholas scoffed without looking at her—at either of them.

Chris sighed. "But we need to. For the Martyrs…"

Nicholas shook his head. "What is there to say?" he asked, but there was no venom in the words. If anything, Darius caught a cold chill of fear seeping from his mouth. "This was a fucking *disaster.*"

Chris nodded. She looked like she hadn't slept at all. Her blonde hair frayed around her shoulders, and dark circles made her green eyes somber. She closed them, pressing her fingertips against the lids. "Yeah," she agreed. "Yeah, it was. We lost a lot of friends yesterday. Four at the cemetery, then Caleb and Alan—"

Her voice pinched up an octave. Darius grabbed her shoulder, and she laid a hand over his. Nicholas's mouth sloped compassionately before he wound his arms around himself and focused on Darius.

"How's Lamar?" he asked.

"I don't know," Darius said. "I talked with Dr. Harris this morning. He thinks Lamar had a panic attack, and Cain agrees. He froze the instant he saw Amoretto."

And Darius couldn't blame him. He hated himself for that. If he'd listened to his gut and insisted that Lamar wasn't ready, they wouldn't be having this conversation right now.

Nicholas's jaw hardened until a muscle in his cheek ticked. "This whole situation is *fucked,*" he said. "We've got to get our people back here *now.* With Alan gone, all of the protective Programming he installed in the Martyrs will start to wear off."

"I've already recalled all TAC units and grounded them until further notice," Chris said, "and Gabe got in touch with all our Recon teams. Most of them were already heading home. News spread fast…"

"Good," Nicholas said, but he looked more troubled than settled. He took a deep breath and held it for a moment. "Has anyone called Mackenzie?"

Darius's stomach churned as images of the Irishwoman rushed his brain—and his body. He felt the sensation of healing her, of pulling heroin out of her system until she could finally breathe again. It was enough to make his lungs contract.

"Maybe we shouldn't call her," he murmured.

Both Chris and Nicholas spun toward him, eyes wide. Chris shook her head. "Darius, we can't just *leave* her…"

"I think we have to," he said. "She picked a no-contact rehab program to avoid distractions—"

"This isn't a *distraction*," Nicholas cut in. A deep frown furrowed his brow. "Alan Blaine is *dead.*"

"And Mackenzie is sick," Darius argued. "She *needs* to get better. One of the things that triggered this relapse was Lina's death. What do you think Alan's would do to her? What if she starts using again?" His breath caught, and he tried to swallow past the lump wedged between his lungs. "I can't lose Mackenzie, too."

Nicholas didn't challenge him on that, instead falling silent and thoughtful while Chris chewed on her lower lip, her eyes glistening. At last, Nicholas relented with a sigh. "Fine, but I'm not going to be the one who explains it to her."

"I'll handle it," Darius said.

They wafted into a tense quiet again. It felt foreign, being in this room with half their number missing. Darius's eyes wandered again to the empty chair at the head of the table. After a moment, Nicholas cleared his throat.

"So…" he began. "Have either of you heard from

Thorn?"

Darius glanced up to find Nicholas watching him intently, as if the question hadn't been meant for Chris at all, but both she and Darius shook their heads. Nicholas did, too, and then, he swore under his breath. His eyes, however, never left Darius.

"What really happened in that warehouse?" he asked.

His tone caught on Darius's nerves, making him more alert, and he sat up straight. It wasn't just bleak or curious… it was prying. Nicholas's blue eyes narrowed as he waited for a response. Darius finally shrugged.

"I don't know," he said. Chris's attention was on him now, too. He could feel her gaze zeroed in on the side of his face. "By the time we got there, Thorn was the only one left, and she didn't seem like she remembered anything."

Nicholas's frown deepened. "That's what I mean, though." He leaned forward on the table, hands clasped in front of him. "The place was *full* of bodies, Darius. That's what you said, right? The mayor, a ton of Puppets and mercs… But the Sins weren't there. It was *just* Thorn?"

A cold current settled over Darius's already-numb body, dragging it further under the ice. He nodded. Nicholas's eyes darkened.

"So, what the hell happened to Alan?" he pressed. "I talked to Harris. He wasn't just shot. The man was beaten to *hell*. If the Sins were gone, if *everyone else* was already dead… Who hurt Alan?"

Darius didn't say anything. There was nothing he *could* say. Images of the attack bounced around the inside of his skull like a spray of ricocheting bullets—Thorn screaming and crying as she came for Alan again and again, her expression so wild and terrified it was clear she couldn't tell him apart from Autumn Hunt herself. Darius's account was damning. He *knew* it was.

Nicholas knew, too. It was clear in the understanding on his face. Darius's silence was confirmation enough of everything Nicholas suspected. Soon, the pieces fell into place in Chris's head. She let out a short, quiet gasp, and her fingers moved to cover her mouth. Echoes of Nicholas's voice from an old conversation nearly two years ago intruded upon Darius's thoughts:

"That bitch will snap, and she'll take you down with her."

A biting, protective instinct wound around Darius's chest. His lip curled, and his fingers wrapped into fists. "Nicholas, don't," he began, but Nicholas raised a hand.

"I hope she *never* remembers," he said. Shock drowned Darius's impulse to fight as Nicholas's expression softened, the hard surfaces melting away until all that remained was weary compassion. "The Sins are insidious… Whatever they put Thorn through in that warehouse is better left buried."

Darius's heart stung, and his chest felt empty, but a flicker of gratitude lit up inside of it. He wasn't sure what it would take to get through this, but he knew they could figure it out together.

CHAPTER THIRTY-FOUR

It was a week of funerals.

Six lives lost. Six families mourning. Six services with stories and sorrows that doused the Underground in a melancholy sea.

Darius attended every single one. He was one of only three who did. He sat to Chris's left in the front, wearing the same suit he'd worn to Skylar and Raquel's wedding, while Cain spoke beautifully of the glory of life and tragedy of death. Some of them whispered by, while others roared with so many people, so much warmth, that Darius could almost forget what a cold affair it all was.

Alan's service didn't just fill the memorial hall. It overflowed beyond it. Rows of Martyrs spilled into the courtyard. The retractable glass panels at the exterior wall had been opened up as wide as they could to accommodate more seating, and two columns of chairs stretched nearly forty feet back. Cain had extended a red carpet down the central aisle and decorated the entire space with black and white paper flowers. They accented the crystal and obsidian chandeliers, the backlit alabaster walls, and the black marble statues of lost founder Familiars on the dais behind the podium.

Darius watched the crowd gather from a distance. Chris and Nicholas smiled and spoke with people as they walked up. Like everyone else, they'd dressed in the appropriate formalwear for the bleak occasion: dark shirts, slacks, and dresses. Darius was back in his suit from the wedding, but he'd swapped the emerald button-up for a black one. He anxiously smoothed it down his stomach.

He was supposed to be up there, too, welcoming the Martyrs as they laid their leader to rest, but he'd had a hard time working up the strength to come down here today. Of all the funerals Darius had attended, this was the one he'd been dreading most.

The walk across the courtyard felt longer than usual, every step heavier than the one before it. The final stragglers were starting to settle, but a pair standing off to the side caught Darius's attention. Lamar and Naomi tucked away from the others, hovering at the edge as though they were intruding on a grief that wasn't theirs to share. They spoke quietly, Lamar small and subdued, while Naomi made assertive micro-gestures with her hands that betrayed an anger she was trying to hold back. Darius frowned and made his way toward them. The instant he felt Darius approaching, Lamar's head snapped up, and Naomi stopped talking with a scowl.

"Hey," Darius said, holding out a hand. Lamar took it, but Naomi watched him with the same vitriol she always had. "How are you doing?"

"Fine," Lamar muttered. He anxiously adjusted the cuffs on his navy dress shirt, and his jaw clenched, making the smile he tried to force look even less natural on his face. "Just here to pay our respects."

Naomi's eyes flashed to him, and Darius glanced between them, wondering where the secret was hiding. "Thank you," he said. "That means a lot to us."

Naomi scoffed. "It means a lot to *you*," she snapped. "No one else wants us here."

She glared over Darius's shoulder, and he followed her

gaze. Conrad and a handful of other TAC agents glowered at them from the back row. The second Darius spotted them, they busied themselves with quiet conversation.

"What's going on?" he asked, turning to Lamar again. The young man seemed smaller now and wouldn't meet Darius's eye.

"It's nothing," he started to say, but Naomi cut him off.

"Lamar, tell him," she insisted.

"It's *fine*, Mimi."

"It's *not* fine," she hissed. The fresh look she sent in Conrad's direction was dangerous enough to rival one of Thorn's, and Darius's heart twinged. "This is *not* your fault, no matter what they think… *or* what you think."

A frown darkened Darius's expression as Naomi's head swiveled back around, scarlet hair swinging. Her eyes softened when they landed on Lamar, and his filled with tears. He quietly dabbed them away with the pads of his fingers to avoid smudging his eyeliner.

"If I hadn't frozen," he began, emotion tightening his throat, "if I'd just done my *job*, this wouldn't have happened." He looked at Darius and shook his head. "I'm *so* sorry—"

"Lamar," Darius cut in, placing a hand on Lamar's shoulder. "No. If *I'd* done *my* job, this wouldn't have happened."

Naomi's eyes widened as Lamar's mouth slipped open in surprise.

"You weren't ready," Darius continued, "and we never should have rushed you into pretending that you were. If anyone needs to apologize here, it's me… I was in the room where these decisions were made. I could have fought harder to stop it. I'm sorry. I should have been better."

Lamar's face twisted in a frown as he held back a rush of emotion. Darius squeezed him once more before pulling his arm back.

"When I first came to the Underground," he went on, "Alan offered to set me up with a life outside of it, and I know he would have offered the same to you. You should *never* be trapped somewhere you feel unwelcome or unsupported. I can talk with… god, I don't know, but if you want to go, I can figure it out."

At first, Lamar seemed stunned. Naomi watched him and Darius in silence until Lamar finally shook his head.

"Thank you," he said, "but I need to stay. I *want* to stay. I might not be ready to face Connor yet, but I'll *never* be ready if I run away from this problem now. I'm all in."

He held out a hand, and this time, when he smiled, it lit his face up like the joyful young man Darius had met all those weeks ago.

"I'm glad to hear it," Darius said. "And next time, we'll get it right. *I'll* get it right."

Lamar nodded, and then he and Naomi said goodbye and walked down the center aisle to find their seats. As they passed by the back row, Conrad glared after them. A steely weight filled Darius's gut as he strode up behind the man and grabbed him roughly by the shoulder. When Conrad spun around to see him, Darius leaned in close.

"If I hear that you're giving Lamar a hard time *ever* again," he hissed, "you'll be stuck in maintenance for so long that we might as well move your bed to the basement."

Conrad's body stiffened under Darius's touch, and the entourage of TAC officers surrounding him gawked. Darius's focus shifted around their faces, too.

"That goes for all of you," he went on. "We should be better than this. I'm disappointed that I even have to point that out."

Eyes darted to the ground, all but Conrad's, who had the decency to meet Darius's gaze and mutter some apology.

"Thanks, Conrad," Darius said, "but I'm not the one you should be apologizing to."

Darius straightened up, adjusted his suit jacket, and walked to where Chris and Nicholas were still welcoming people at the entrance to the hall. As he approached, Chris frowned and tilted her head in Conrad's direction.

"What was *that* about?" she asked.

"It's nothing," Darius said. The look Chris gave him begged for more, but he ignored her as he scanned the crowd. His hopes weren't high to begin with, but they shattered when Nicholas sighed beside him.

"No sign of her," he said.

Darius's soul ached. Chris drew a breath.

"Give her time," she murmured. "It's only been a week."

"Yeah," Nicholas said, "but this is her *uncle's* funeral…"

Seven days ago, Thorn had retreated to her room and hadn't been seen since. While the rest of the Underground functioned at a level barely above autopilot, Thorn spiraled alone. Darius had tried to reach out to her. Chris, too. Even Nicholas. She'd ignored all the messages, the phone calls, the knocked doors. More than once, Darius found himself missing Mackenzie. He doubted she'd have been able to get to Thorn, but he would have sold his soul for one of her ten-buck-bets just for a break in the tension.

"She'll show," Darius said at last. Even though Mackenzie wasn't here to take his money, he was putting it on the table anyway.

Right now, he needed something to believe in.

The last Martyrs wandered through and shuffled to their seats. Darius didn't bother counting. Every director had called their units back to the Underground, and not a single drop of human energy moved anywhere else in the entire structure. Everyone was here.

Well, almost everyone.

"Time to go," Nicholas whispered, knocking Darius with his elbow as he nodded to the reserved section at the front of the room. Four spots sat open: one for each of the three of them and one for Thorn. As Chris led them in that direction, a cold hand without an aura grabbed Darius's shoulder. His heart leapt as he twisted around.

Cain smiled; Darius tried to hide the disappointment on his face.

"Darius," Cain said. After his breakdown days ago, he'd

instantly transitioned into a mode of getting shit done, probably as a way to avoid the darkness. He tilted his head to the side. "May I have a word?"

They quietly excused themselves, slipping behind one of the black curtains framing the ingress. Once they were out of earshot, Cain reached inside his suit jacket and pulled a folded sheet of paper from the inner pocket. He handed it to Darius.

"What's this?" Darius asked as he started to open it.

"Your speech," Cain said.

Darius's mouth fell open. "*My* speech?" he repeated. When Cain nodded, Darius shook his head. "I can't give a speech."

He tried to give the paper back, but Cain acted as though he couldn't see it. "You can," he insisted, "and you will."

"Cain—"

"These people have lost more than another Martyr, Darius," Cain interrupted. "More than a leader. They have lost *hope*. I am not the man who can bring that back to them." He pushed the speech toward Darius's chest, that clever smile brightening his face again. "Don't let us down."

Cain walked away without giving Darius a chance to argue further and sat on Chris's right. She glanced over her shoulder with a frown while Gabe whispered something to him from her other side. Darius sighed and opened the sheet, scanning it without absorbing a single word on the page. His heart thrummed as he looked back out at the gathered Martyrs. All of them, all but one, murmuring and mourning. He took a deep breath.

The front of the memorial bay had been decorated in black and white. An iron arch stretched above the dais, where sheets of pearly satin draped behind the black marble statues of the peacock, the fox, the macaque, and the bat. Darius wondered when a wolf would join them.

He floated along the side of the room, past granite slabs filled with the names of the dead, and made his way to the podium. With every step toward it, the room quieted, murmurs fading to whispers, then to nothing at all. By the time he stood before them, the Martyrs were silent and staring. Darius unfolded the speech Cain had prepared.

"Good evening," he read. The mic squealed with feedback, making him wince, and he adjusted it before clearing his throat and starting again. "I wanted to thank you all for coming here tonight as we celebrate the life of a great man, Alan Blaine. Losing someone is never easy, but—"

His voice caught, and Darius clenched his teeth as his eyes darted to the crowd. He wasn't sure what he was looking for—strength or maybe just a sense of what these people needed him to say, who they needed him to be. Cain watched from the front row, hands folded neatly in his lap. His lips twitched into a warm smirk. Darius swallowed hard and looked beyond him.

An ocean of agony looked back. Darius read more than grief in the tide of faces. He read confusion, uncertainty, and fear. So much fear.

Chris sat beside Gabe, stony and still, but their interlaced fingers were clasped so hard that the skin pressed cold. Four rows back, Holly watched him with silent tears pouring down her face. God, Darius had never seen Holly cry, could have never even imagined it until it was displayed right in front of him. She dabbed her eyes from beneath thick glasses as Taylor Simmons wrapped an arm around her.

Beyond them, even more. Raquel and Skylar comforted one another while John sat with a glassy-eyed Madison. Elijah, Colette, and their two teen sons, who had been born and raised in the Underground and never known a world without Alan Blaine. Alexis Claytor, her eyes stained scarlet and cheeks caved out from days of sobbing that only seemed to let up because her exhausted body just couldn't keep going anymore. Darius sighed, about ready to read again, when his gaze flicked up. That sigh stuck in his mouth.

Thorn stood behind the back row.

He'd almost missed her. The courtyard lights were

dimmed, and Cain had adorned the planter trellises with black satin drapes. Thorn practically disappeared within them, camouflaged entirely by her curtain of dark hair and a sleek, floor-length dress that extended down her arms and up her throat. The only prominent part of her at all was her face—an oval of white in the darkness, hollow and haunted. His chest seared, all at once reveling and distraught at the sight of her.

She looked more lost than all the others combined.

Darius tore his eyes away at last to consider Cain's speech again, but this time, the words felt wrong. He frowned, folded the sheet up, and slipped it into his pocket before looking back out at the crowd. They shuffled anxiously as they waited for him to speak.

"When I think about the Martyrs," Darius said, "I think of Alan Blaine."

A murmur of consensus sighed through the room. Darius nodded. "I'm sure that's true for every single one of us," he continued. "Alan has been there since the very start, taking us in, explaining this war, and offering sympathy for whatever tragedy brought us into it to begin with. Then, he made sure we knew we had a place here. A *home.*"

His attention wandered to Lamar. The young Virtue smiled.

"Alan felt untouchable," Darius went on, and then he sighed. "In some ways, he still does. He was so consistent. So reliable. Wrath put him through hell and back, but even with a part of that Sin still tainting his soul, he always fought to be the opposite... to be calm and collected. He taught us that leadership didn't have to come at the cost of compassion, and when he made mistakes, he owned them. Alan challenged us all to be bigger than ourselves... to be better than we were the day before. He might not have known how to show it or how to say it, but he was so proud of what we've accomplished here."

Darius paused as a bittersweet surge rose through his vocal cords. He breathed through it. The crowd breathed with him, gazing numbly… so numb that Darius couldn't tell if he was having any effect at all. He kept going.

"It's impossible to measure the impact Alan Blaine has had on us. He didn't just lead the Martyrs. He *created* the Martyrs, and he kept us going through things that would have brought anyone else to their knees. Without him, I wouldn't be here. *None* of us would be here. He was our foundation. Now, we're all wondering… What the hell are we going to do without that foundation?"

A chilly cloud settled over the service, drifting down the central aisle until the crowd was still and silent. Cain squared his shoulders as he watched Darius, and in the far back, Thorn shrank. Her arms wound around her center, like her own gravity was too much to bear, and she was on the verge of collapsing into a black hole. Darius drew a deep breath, imagining Alan, tapping into a strength he wasn't sure he had as he held himself tall.

Then, he said:

"We build a new one."

The stillness rustled. People shifted, spoke, shushed. Nicholas frowned as he crossed his arms, but a curious glint in his eye gave Darius the confidence to keep talking.

"Look," he said, "I'm not going to pretend that we haven't suffered an extraordinary loss. We have. It's going to hurt for a long time, and we'll have the scars to remind us of what we've survived." He paused, shaking his head. "But the Martyrs are not strong *because* of Alan. The Martyrs are strong, *period.* The cracks left behind from Alan's absence won't feel overwhelming forever. In time, we'll fill those cracks in with our own strengths, our own passions, our own tenacity, and the foundation he laid for us will be *indestructible.*"

Now, the shift was obvious. People nodded again, but this time, more earnestly—almost *desperately.* The tears trapped behind Chris's lashes threatened to spill free as she watched Darius with a tight smile and rigid jaw. Cain all but beamed beside her.

"Alan once told me that the Martyrs will endure," Darius said. "I don't think that's true. We'll do *more* than endure. We'll heal, we'll grow, we'll thrive, and we'll do it together."

More nodding. More sighing. More voices in the distance, whispering in agreement. The pit in Darius's chest felt warm, and bit by bit, his doubt shrank into something he could hold—something he could manage.

"This organization, this war, this *purpose* was Alan's entire life," he said, "and the best way to honor that life is to see it through to the very end."

Then, Darius looked up, right at Thorn, and held onto her gaze like she was the only goddamned thing in the room. She hadn't moved, hadn't spoken, but even from here, he could see a fresh glean shining behind her lashes. He swallowed hard.

"Alan Blaine may be gone," he told her, projecting it across the room, "but we're not."

A starved, breathless silence fell. Darius didn't look away from Thorn, and she stared back. He wanted to go to her, and he considered abandoning the podium just to wrap his arms around her, but a quiet noise snapped him back to the present. Someone was weeping. Darius glanced to the front row, where Chris cried openly. She touched an open palm to her heart and mouthed the words, "Thank you." He smiled and then looked around at the other faces, other Martyrs. The veil of hopelessness began to lift, slowly at first, but soon, a tidal wave of human warmth grew in front of him. He hadn't even realized a brush of tears had filled his eyes until he felt one trickle into the stubble on his jaw. He choked out a laugh that felt more like a sob as he looked up to the back again. His heart sank.

Thorn retreated, a lonely silhouette in the darkness, as she disappeared into the Underground without looking back.

ABOUT THE AUTHOR

MC Hunton is a bright personality with a shockingly dark taste in the stories she writes. She graduated with her bachelor's degree in Creative Writing in 2010 and has been working on her debut series, The Martyr Series, since 2005. The first book, Resurrection, won first place in the fantasy category of Writer's Digest's Best Self-Published E-Book Awards in 2022 and took home the win in the paranormal category in the Indie Reader Discovery Awards in 2023. She has a penchant for fast-paced action, deeply-rooted sociopolitical and spiritual themes, and emotionally driven plot and character development.

Check out what she's up to by visiting her website:
www.MCHunton.com

www.ingramcontent.com/pod-product-compliance
Lightning Source LLC
Chambersburg PA
CBHW070228200726
48293CB00005B/1516